CANDLE IN THE
DARKNESS

Books by Lynn Austin

All She Ever Wanted

All Things New

Eve's Daughters

Hidden Places

Pilgrimage

A Proper Pursuit

Though Waters Roar

Until We Reach Home

While We're Far Apart

Wings of Refuge

A Woman's Place

Wonderland Creek

REFINER'S FIRE

Candle in the Darkness

Fire by Night

A Light to My Path

CHRONICLES OF THE KINGS

Gods & Kings

Song of Redemption

The Strength of His Hand

Faith of My Fathers

Among the Gods

THE RESTORATION CHRONICLES

Return to Me

Keepers of the Covenant

CANDLE *in the* DARKNESS

LYNN AUSTIN

BETHANYHOUSE
a division of Baker Publishing Group
Minneapolis, Minnesota

© 2002 by Lynn Austin

Published by Bethany House Publishers
11400 Hampshire Avenue South
Bloomington, Minnesota 55438
www.bethanyhouse.com

Bethany House Publishers is a division of
Baker Publishing Group, Grand Rapids, Michigan

This edition published 2014
ISBN 978-0-7642-1190-4

Printed in the United States of America

The Library of Congress has cataloged the original edition as follows:

Austin, Lynn N.
    Candle in the darkness / by Lynn Austin.
        p. cm.—(Refiner's fire ; bk. 1)
    ISBN 1–55661–436–5
    1. Virginia—History—Civil War, 1861–1865—Fiction. 2. Antislavery movements—Fiction. 3. Women abolitionists—Fiction. I. Title.
    PS3551.U839 C36 2002
    813'.54—dc21   2002010129

Cover design by Kirk DouPonce, DogEared Design

15 16 17 18 19 20 21   8 7 6 5 4 3 2

For Ken, always

and for
Joshua, Benjamin, and Maya

Prologue

RICHMOND, VIRGINIA 1864

Silvery moonlight slanted through the closed shutters, faintly illuminating Caroline Fletcher's bedroom. A pattern formed on the hardwood floor, a pattern that reminded her of prison bars, and she shivered at the thought of what she might soon face.

It was useless to remain in bed waiting for sleep. It refused to come. Caroline's mind and heart were much too full. She tossed aside the tangled bedcovers and crossed the room to light a tallow candle. Downstairs, the chimes of the hall clock announced the hour. She paused, counting each stroke—ten . . . eleven . . . twelve. Midnight.

Caroline had lain in bed for more than two hours, whispering urgent, tearful prayers for all the people she loved. But she felt no relief after bringing her concerns to the Lord. She'd pleaded especially for Charles, for Jonathan and Josiah, and for her father and Robert, begging God to keep them alive and safe throughout this long, dark night. And she'd prayed that her foolish mistakes and failures would not bring them harm. She hadn't prayed for her own rescue.

The water she was now treading was much too deep, the currents too swift for her own safe return to shore.

If she could begin again and not become so entangled in this long, horrible war, would she watch from the sidelines as a spectator this time? Would she choose differently, take fewer risks? Caroline had asked herself these questions countless times and had reached the same conclusion each time. She would do everything the same, walk the same path. But how could she explain her reasons to the people she loved? How could she hope to make them understand?

Her thoughts spun in useless circles as she quietly paced the room. If only she had some paper, then she could write a chronicle of her actions, explaining exactly why she had placed herself and her loved ones in such danger. But finding paper in besieged Richmond was as impossible as finding meat—and nearly as costly. Some newspaper editors had resorted to printing their latest editions on sheets of wallpaper.

Caroline halted mid-step. The walls of her front foyer were decorated with imitation marble wallpaper. Her father had purchased it on one of his trading ventures, and although it reminded Caroline of him and of the gentle life they'd once led, perhaps it could now serve a more important function. It was paper, after all—sheets and sheets of paper. And what earthly good was wallpaper in a house that Union troops might burn to the ground any day?

She remembered seeing a loose corner of wallpaper that had come unglued beside the library door. Caroline carried the smoky, homemade candle downstairs and set it on the floor near that spot, then knelt to gently peel the paper away from the wall. To carefully strip the entire entrance hall would require more patience than she possessed in her distressed and sleepless state, but before the clock chimed the next hour, she managed to tear away a ragged piece nearly a foot and a half long. It was enough to begin. She would make her script as small as she possibly could.

Praying for the right words and mindful of the urgency of her task, Caroline sat down in the library behind her father's mahogany desk and began to write.

As I write this by candlelight, Union troops have my beloved city of Richmond under siege. The hall clock tells me that it is well past midnight, but I am unable to sleep. I no longer know what tomorrow will bring, nor do I know when my arrest will come—but I'm now quite certain that it will come. Lying awake on nights like tonight, I listen in the darkness for the knock on my door. I think about Castle Thunder and wonder if I will soon join the gloomy prisoners who peer out from behind the barred windows.

I don't fear for myself but rather for all the people I love. I need to explain why I've done what I have done, to tell my story in my own words before it's told by those who won't understand. They will surely call me a traitor and a murderer, and I suppose I am both of those things. I have betrayed people who trusted me. Men have died because of me. My involvement with certain events in Libby Prison has led to accusations of moral improprieties, but as God is my witness, I am innocent of those charges. Even so, people will believe what they choose to believe. And when a host of vicious rumors is added to the list of my misdeeds, I'm not sure anyone will ever understand why I've acted the way I have. I can only pray that they will try.

I don't fear prison, nor do I regret a single decision I've made. As the Bible says, "No man, having put his hand to the plow, and looking back, is fit for the kingdom of God." I only regret that I've hurt innocent people. I've tried so hard never to lie, but I realize as I'm writing this that falsehoods can consist of more than words—and I have been living a lie. For that, I beg God's forgiveness.

These long, sleepless nights have afforded me plenty of time to think things through. In my mind I've traveled all the way back to where my journey first began, to the morning I awoke to the sound of Tessie weeping for her son. I need to see if I could have done things differently, made different choices, and perhaps have ended in a different place than I am today. I've decided to write down my story, telling it from the very beginning. I pray that you will read all of it before deciding if what I've done was a sin.

Here, then, is my tale.

Part One

Whoever loves his brother lives in the light, and there is nothing in him to make him stumble. But whoever hates his brother is in the darkness and walks around in the darkness; he does not know where he is going, because the darkness has blinded him.

1 John 2:10–11 NIV

1

RICHMOND, VIRGINIA 1853

The first scream jolted me awake. The second one chilled my soul.

I sat up in bed, searching for Tessie in the darkened room, but the pallet where my Negro mammy usually slept was empty.

"Tessie?" My voice trembled with fear. "Tessie, where are you?"

Rain drummed against the windowpane, keeping time with my heart. Beyond the shuttered windows, the day had dawned dark and dismal. Thunder rumbled in the distance. Then the heartrending cries broke the silence once again.

"No . . . *please!*"

The tumult came from outside, just below my room.

"Please don't take him, please don't take my boy from me, *please!*"

The voice, barely recognizable in its anguish, was Tessie's.

I couldn't believe it. For all of my twelve years, as far back as I could recall, Tessie had been a happy, carefree presence in my life, always humming or singing as her elegant brown hands dressed me and brushed my hair; cheering me when I was lonely, chasing away my sadness with her laughter, her smile lighting up her dark face. Mother was the one who had "spells" that caused her to weep and pine away in her room for days on end, but I'd never once heard Tessie weep before. And these were such horrible, anguished cries.

"*Please* don't send my boy away, I beg you, Massa! *Please!*"

Then Tessie's son started screaming as well. Grady was nine—just three years younger than me—and I hadn't heard him cry since he was a baby, sleeping in the wicker basket in the kitchen beside the fireplace. Tessie had let me play with him as if he were a living baby doll, with plump brown cheeks and a giggle that made me laugh out loud. I remember being fascinated by his little hands, with their tiny brown fingers and soft pink palms.

Outside, the begging and weeping grew more distant. I climbed from my bed and hurried to the window that overlooked our rear garden. It took me a moment to open the shutters because I'd never done it. That was Tessie's job every morning.

Two strangers tramped down the brick walkway and through the wrought-iron gate, dragging Grady, screaming, out of the safety of our backyard. They were rough-looking fellows, dressed like laborers, and I watched as they lifted Grady into a wagon waiting at the curb. The wagon was packed with Negroes of all ages and sizes, some in chains and leg-irons. The men prodded the slaves with whips, shouting at them until they shifted themselves around on the wagon bed to make room for Grady.

Daddy stood watching near the back gate, his arms folded across his chest. He was already dressed for work, and rain darkened the shoulders of his overcoat and the brim of his hat. Big Eli, our stable hand, stood in the middle of the walk, struggling to hold on to Tessie as she screamed for her son.

"No! Don't take my boy! He all I got! Please! No!"

I turned away from the window and ran downstairs in my chemise, not bothering with slippers or a dressing gown. As I raced outside into the rain, Esther, our cook, spotted me from the kitchen, which was a separate outbuilding behind our house. She ran outside and grabbed me before I could reach Tessie, then pulled me into the kitchen's smoky warmth.

"Whoa now, Missy . . . where you going in you nightclothes?"

"I want Tessie," I said, squirming to free myself. I tried to dodge around Esther and make a dash for the door, but she moved surprisingly fast for a woman her size, blocking my path with her broad body.

"No you don't, Little Missy. You not be going outside in the rain dressed like that."

"But . . . but Tessie's crying. And Grady is, too. Where are those men taking him in that wagon?"

"Massa Fletcher not be telling me his business. Hear, now! Stop you fussing, Missy!"

Esther held me as I struggled to break free, but she cast a worried eye on the ham she'd left frying in the pan for our breakfast. I could hear Tessie's pitiful screams above the sound of the ham sizzling in the pan, the fire crackling in the hearth, and the rain drumming on the roof of the kitchen. Then I heard the clatter of hooves and wheels as the wagon finally drove away.

A few minutes later, the kitchen door opened and Big Eli trudged inside, carrying Tessie in his arms like a child. She no longer fought against him but lay limp in his arms, her hands covering her face. Rain soaked both of them, streaming from their curly hair and running down their faces like tears. Tessie sobbed as if her heart would break, and I saw that it wasn't just rain that coursed down Eli's face. He was crying, too.

"God knows all about it, Tessie," he soothed as he sat her down in a chair near the fire. "God know how you suffering. They took His son away, too, remember? He know how it feel to lose His boy."

Esther finally released me and hurried back to her cooking. She flipped over the ham slice with a smooth flick of the frying pan, then shoved the pan back into the fireplace. I was free to run to Tessie, but I didn't. I backed away from her instead, overwhelmed by her despair. Rarely had her attention been focused on anything or anyone but me. Even when Grady was a baby, she would leave him crying in his basket to tend to me if I demanded it. For the first time in my life, Tessie seemed completely unaware of me, as unaware as my mother was during one of her spells.

"Shh, don't cry," Eli murmured. He lifted Esther's shawl from the nail by the door and draped it around Tessie's shoulders. "Don't cry...."

"No sir!" Esther suddenly shouted. She slammed the frying pan down on the table with a *clang* that made my skin prickle. "You let that girl cry," she told her husband. "I know how she feel and so do you. Isn't our son sold and gone, too? That pain don't never leave a mother. Never! I feel it to this day."

Tessie lifted her head to face Esther, her features twisted in anguish. "Your boy only over to Hilltop. You know where he at. My boy's gone to auction and I ain't never seeing him again!"

"Only for this lifetime, Tessie," Eli soothed. "Then you be with Grady all eternity."

Tessie wiped her eyes with the heels of her hands and pulled the shawl tightly around her shoulders to stop her shivering. Her gaze fell on me for the first time. She looked me straight in the eye, something she'd never done in my entire life. No servant dared to look a white person in the eye. Tessie's eyes were cold with hatred.

"This here your mama's doing," she said, her voice hushed with rage. "Your mama behind this."

"Tessie!" Eli said in horror. "Hush your mouth!"

I turned from them and fled, crying as I ran across the yard, into the house, and upstairs to my room.

I didn't see Tessie again for the rest of the day. Luella came up with my breakfast tray a little while later and helped me get dressed and brush my hair. But Luella didn't hum or sing like Tessie always did, and she brushed too hard, snagging my hair in the bristles and bringing tears to my eyes.

"Where's Tessie?" I asked her as she made my bed. "Why did those men take Grady away?"

16

Luella shrugged her bony shoulders. "Don't know, Missy. Don't know nothing about all that."

I sat alone in my room all morning, gazing through the windows, watching the rain gather in puddles in the street below. Our house on Church Hill stood on the corner of Grace and Twenty-sixth Streets, and from my bedroom in a rear corner I could look down on our backyard and the street. The gate stood open, swinging a little in the wind. I stared at the spot where the wagon had stood, willing it to return, willing the men to bring Grady home so our lives could all return to normal. But the carriages and wagons that splashed past our house never even slowed, much less stopped. Grady didn't come back.

Around noon, my mother's maidservant came to fetch me. "You mama asking for you," Ruby said. "She's wanting you to eat lunch with her today. In her room."

It was the first time I'd seen Mother since her latest crying spell had begun, several weeks ago, and I had no idea what to expect. I was very nervous as I approached her suite down the hall from my room—especially since Tessie wasn't with me to prod me along and give me courage. As soon as I entered the room, I saw that Mother was in one of her cheerful moods. Ruby had drawn her curtains back and thrown her shutters open, and even though it was still rainy and gloomy outside, her room was not the dismal, depressing place it usually was during her sad spells.

"Hello, Sugar," she said, smiling faintly from her chair near the window. "Come on over here and give your mama a kiss."

I crossed the floor and brushed my lips on Mother's cheek. She looked painfully thin, her bones sharply defined beneath her pale skin. But my mother was still a very beautiful woman, one who stood out among her peers. I'd inherited my wavy brown hair from her, but not my dark eyes. They came from my father. Mother's eyes were a soft, faded gray, like spring storm clouds. I wondered if the many tears she had shed had washed the color right out of them.

Mother motioned for me to sit across from her at the little table by the window. She had a frenzied intensity about her, as if a relentless, pulsing current raced through her veins. While Ruby laid out all the food, Mother chatted excitedly, hopping from one topic to the next like a little bird flitting from branch to branch. I barely listened. Instead, I studied my mother's perfect, moon-shaped face, her graceful movements, watching the sweep of her small, round hands as she spread her napkin across her lap.

Her breathless voice and rapid words made her sound as though she were running up flight after flight of stairs to the very top floor of a building, where a thrilling view awaited her. Once she reached that place, where all the world lay spread at her feet, I knew that her days would be filled with laughter and happy conversation. She would make glorious plans for all the things she would see and do: shopping in Richmond's finest stores, ordering fancy silk dresses and bonnets imported from England and France, attending balls and parties and elegant dinners. I'd been to the top with her before, and I knew what would come next. Inevitably, she would begin to descend the stairs once again. The pleasant conversation and laughter would gradually die away as she trudged downward, until one day she would finally reach the cold, dark basement, where she lived with sorrow and tears.

I remembered Tessie's bitter tears earlier that morning and summoned all my courage. "Did you send Grady away?" I asked when Mother paused for breath.

"Hmm? Did I do what, Sugar?" she asked absently.

"Did you send Grady away . . . my mammy Tessie's boy?"

"Now, Caroline, you know I don't have anything whatsoever to do with those servants—except for Ruby, of course. She has belonged to me ever since I was just a little girl like you. Did I ever tell you that? Ruby has been my own dearest mammy for just as long as I can recall. My daddy gave her to me for a wedding present when I got married because he knew I wouldn't be able to get along for a

18

single day without her. Just like you and your mammy. But Tessie and all the rest of them are your daddy's property, not mine. It's his job to see to them, and—"

Suddenly she stopped. Mother frowned at me, and for a horrible moment I was afraid she was angry with me. Maybe I shouldn't have asked her about Grady. What if she decided to send me away, too? But a moment later she said, "Who made that awful mess of your hair, Caroline? Why, your part is as crooked as a country lane—and it's nowhere near the middle of your head. And the rest of your hair is sticking out of your net like . . . like an old bird's nest."

Mother set down her teacup as if she couldn't possibly take another sip with my hair in such a state. "Ruby!" she called. "Ruby, come see if you can do something with this child's hair. What in the world has gotten into your mammy that she would make such a mess of it like that?"

"Tessie didn't do my hair. Luella did."

"Luella! But she's only an old scrub maid. Whoever heard of such a thing—a common scrub maid brushing my daughter's hair? Why, it's disgraceful."

"Luella had to help me today because they took Grady away and Tessie was crying, and—"

She put her hands over her ears. "I told you, Caroline, I don't want to talk about those people. Proper young ladies don't concern themselves with such unpleasant subjects as slaves. I've warned and warned your father that you were becoming much too familiar with them, and see here? I was right. This is exactly what I was talking about. It isn't good for you at all. Ruby, don't just stand there gawking; fix the child's hair."

"Yes, ma'am."

Ruby guided me out of my chair and seated me at my mother's mirrored dressing table. I watched as she took off the net that Luella had clumsily pinned on and began brushing my hair with my mother's silver hairbrush. The soft bristles caressed my head the way Tessie's gentle fingers did when she stroked my temples to soothe me to sleep.

"She have your hair, ma'am," Ruby said. "So thick and nice. She look like you when she grow up . . . see?" Ruby deftly twisted my hair into a little bun and held it up on the back of my head like a grown-up lady's. Somehow she had made it puff out on the sides, too, so that my face looked fashionably moon-shaped, like my mother's.

"Can Ruby pin it up like that, Mother?" I begged. "So it looks like yours?"

"Heavens, no. You're much too young."

"Please, just for fun?" I don't know what made me so brave. I was usually too timid to say a word to anyone, especially to my mother, who was a virtual stranger to me. But I missed Tessie, and I took courage from the fact that Mother seemed to be climbing her way up from her sad spell again. As I watched her face, reflected in the mirror, she finally smiled.

"Oh, all right. Pin it up for her, Ruby. Then Caroline and I can sip our tea like two Richmond belles."

Ruby expertly parted and pulled and twisted my hair, sticking hairpins in the back and tucking a pair of Mother's beautiful ivory combs on the sides. My head felt strange and wobbly. I stared at myself in the mirror and barely recognized the grown-up girl who stared back.

"Missy Caroline gonna be beautiful, just like you, ma'am," Ruby said as she worked. "And she have your skin, too. Just as white as milk."

"If only we can keep her from running all around in the backyard from now on, it just might stay white, too," Mother said. "I told her father she's twelve years old now, and it simply won't do to have her pretty white skin all freckled from the sun. Or worse still, to have her looking as brown as a Negro. Honestly, it's disgraceful enough that she plays with one of them all day without her looking like one of them, too."

Grady.

I suddenly recalled the feeling of warm sunshine on my hair and my face, of cool grass beneath my bare feet, and the sound of Grady's rippling laughter as we chased each other around the backyard. High above us, I remembered my mother standing behind her curtained window like a shadow, watching.

Tears filled my eyes. Grady was gone—my playmate, my friend. They'd thrown him into the back of a wagon full of Negro slaves wearing chains.

Mother didn't seem to notice my tears as she rattled on and on. "Goodness, you do look all grown up, Caroline. Why, before long you'll be too old to wear short-sleeved dresses. We'll be sewing hoops to your petticoat instead of those girlish cords you're wearing. But I really must remember to tell that worthless cook of ours to give you more to eat. Honestly, you're thin as a willow."

I was fine-boned and very small for a twelve-year-old, but it wasn't Esther's fault. She did her best to try to fatten me up, complaining that I didn't eat enough to keep a sparrow alive. She swore that a good, strong wind would pick me up and blow me clear to Washington, D.C.

"Now, come back over here and sit down, Caroline. We have some very important changes to discuss."

Mother's words sent a shiver through me. I slipped into my place at the tea table, but I was suddenly too nervous to eat. I hated change of any kind. Other girls my age went on afternoon social calls with their mothers, visiting the homes of their friends, learning the art of polite conversation. But my mother, once the belle of Richmond, hardly ever left our house. I'd pieced together the reason why by listening to the servants whispering and by watching the family doctor come and go from my mother's room. Her spells of deep sadness, which made her weep for days on end, were caused by the fact that she hadn't been able to give my daddy a son.

I once heard Ruby say that Mother had "lost" her baby, and I worried for the longest time that Mother would lose me, too. For months, whenever I ventured outside with my mother on those rare occasions when she went visiting or attended church with Daddy and me, I clung to her skirts for fear of becoming lost. I later learned that the "lost" babies had died before they were born.

When I was eight, Mother did give birth to a son. She and my daddy were overjoyed. But their happiness quickly turned to grief when the baby died just a few hours later. My brother had been a "blue" baby, according to Ruby, and was simply too weak to live. Mother's grief lasted a very long time. I didn't see her for months, but it didn't really matter. I had Tessie to take care of me. Tessie's slender brown arms hugged me close; her long, graceful fingers wiped my tears. And I had Grady to play with.

My mother's spells followed a cycle after that. She was joyously happy when she was expecting, and in deepest despair when the baby was lost. Over the years, she gradually withdrew from the glittering Richmond society she had once presided over, unable to leave her bed when she was in a family way, unwilling to leave it after her hopes were cruelly dashed once again.

I became as much of a recluse as my mother, more at home in the kitchen with the Negro servants than visiting with the few relatives and acquaintances who still called on my mother from time to time. I had no idea how to talk to grown-ups—and no desire to talk to any of them, either. Shy and awkward, I became as jumpy and high-strung as a hummingbird. When I was nine, Daddy hired a governess to teach me reading, writing, needlework, and how to play the piano. She lived with us for three years, then quit a few months ago to marry a clerk from one of Daddy's warehouses.

Now I fidgeted on the scratchy horsehair chair in my mother's room, waiting to hear what these new, important changes in my life were all about.

"Listen, Caroline," she began, "I've decided that it's high time you attended a real school every day, with other girls your age."

Cold fear froze me to the chair. I wanted to shout, *"No!"* but I couldn't get a single word out of my mouth.

"Your father and I are sending you to the Richmond Female Institute. It's where I went to school when I was a girl. All the arrangements have been made."

Her words sent a shudder of fear through me. I always became ill at the slightest deviation from my usual routine and would even get sick to my stomach when church services varied at Christmas and Easter. The idea of entering an unknown school, facing a stern headmistress and a horde of strange girls, filled me with terror. My hands flew to my mouth as my stomach began to seethe.

"Now, don't you give me that look, Caroline, like you want to run and hide under the bed. I won't stand for any more of that nonsense. I don't know what your Negro mammy has done to you to make you so skittish, but it's high time you grew into the proper young lady you're meant to be. And that means learning how to get on in society, learning what's expected of you. I'm sorry that my poor health has prevented me from teaching you properly, but it can't be helped."

"But you're well now, Mother," I said hoarsely. "Can't you teach me here at home?"

"Don't be silly. It's much better for you to be out among other girls your age. By the way, classes begin at the school in two weeks."

I covered my face and sobbed.

"Caroline Ruth Fletcher, you stop crying this instant! You are no longer a baby, and you are going to that school, so you had better get used to the idea, you hear? Look at me."

I lifted my head and nodded, but the tears kept falling.

"I'll have to see about hiring a seamstress to stitch you a new dress," she continued. "I believe girls at the school still wear outfits of forest green broadcloth with white collars. That's been the tradition since I attended as a girl. It's such a lovely color of green, and it will look very pretty on you. I'll order some matching ribbons for your hair, too. And under no circumstances is Luella ever to touch your hair again, you hear? Your mammy will either have to pull herself together immediately or face a whipping. Why aren't you eating, Caroline? Finish your tea and sandwiches."

I felt so sick I didn't know if I could eat. I dutifully picked up one of the finger sandwiches Esther had made and nibbled half-heartedly around the edges as my mother rambled on and on about her memories of the Richmond Female Institute. It would take much longer than two weeks to get used to the idea.

By the time lunch was finally over, Mother was ready for her laudanum pill and an afternoon nap. She dismissed me at last, and I was secretly pleased when she forgot to tell Ruby to take my hair down again. I floated carefully out of the room with my head held high so my hair wouldn't escape from the combs.

Talking with my mother had made me feel all mixed up inside, as though I was being pulled in two directions at the same time. I liked the grown-up way I looked with my hair done up fancy, but I didn't want to be grown-up enough to attend school. I liked eating sandwiches and drinking tea with my mother, but I missed having Tessie fussing over me and babying me. Tears filled my eyes every time I thought about Grady or recalled the hateful way my mammy had looked at me. I still hadn't seen Tessie since morning.

I decided to go searching for her and eventually ended up running outside through the rain to the kitchen. Esther bustled around the steamy room, barking orders at poor Luella. "Move faster, girl, or this here sauce gonna burn to a crisp!"

"Where's Tessie?" I asked above the din of rattling pots and dishes.

"She sick in bed," Esther replied. "Luella, I said bring me the *jar* of salt, not that puny little old saltshaker. You hearing me?"

"But I just looked in my bedroom," I said, "and Tessie wasn't in her bed."

"She up where us folks sleep." Esther motioned with a tilt of her head to the ladder that led to the slaves' quarters above the kitchen. I started toward it, but Esther stopped me again. "Oh, no you don't. You get on out of here, Missy. You leave Tessie be."

"But why can't I see her? Is she mad at me?"

"Land sakes, child. Why she be mad at you? She you mammy. You her precious girl-child. She grieving over her boy, that's all. And you has to give her time to do that."

I slumped down on a kitchen chair, hoping Esther or Luella would talk to me, but they were busy cooking a huge, fancy dinner and had no time for conversation. I finally wandered back to the house and upstairs to my room again, disappointed that neither of them had noticed my hair.

Rain raced steadily down my windowpanes all afternoon. I couldn't remember a day without Tessie by my side, and I felt terribly alone. She didn't even come upstairs to tell me to take a nap, so I decided I would rebel and not take one. I sat in a chair and read a book instead, careful not to mess up my hair.

When it was nearly time for my daddy to come home, I tiptoed to the upstairs hall window and knelt on the bench to watch for him. Maybe if I begged Daddy to bring Grady back, Tessie wouldn't be sad anymore. And maybe if I told Daddy how scared I was to go to school, he would tell me I didn't have to go after all.

At last his carriage pulled up to the front of the house. I ran down the stairs to the entrance hall and pulled the heavy front door open for him all by myself—something Tessie would have had a fit over if she had seen me. Gilbert, Daddy's manservant, held an umbrella over Daddy's head as he hurried up the walk to the door. My father looked tired; the deep lines in his handsome, square face made him look old. I knew by the silvery threads in his hair and in his mustache that he was several years older than my beautiful mother, but just how old I didn't know. I also had no idea what kind of work my daddy did all day—only that he owned warehouses near the James River, that he sometimes traveled far away for months at a time, and that he constantly worried about his ships, which sailed back and forth to South America. But in spite of the rain and his fatigue, Daddy looked pleased to see me. He smiled the familiar, cockeyed smile that I loved so much, making one arched eyebrow and one side of his mustache lift in amusement.

"Well, now! Nobody told me that we had company! Who is this lovely young lady who has come calling at my house?" He bowed like a gentleman and kissed my fingers.

I covered my mouth with my other hand and giggled. "It's me, Daddy!"

"No! This can't be my little Caroline. Why, you look just like a Richmond belle."

I danced from foot to foot, waiting for Gilbert to take Daddy's coat, my stomach writhing in an agony of nerves. When I finally found my voice, it sounded very small. "Can I ask you something, Daddy?"

"Why, certainly. Right this way, young lady, if you please." He offered me his arm and led me into his library. Daddy sank into his usual armchair behind his desk, but I was too fidgety to sit. I stood in front of him, squirming with anxiety.

Suddenly I didn't want to be a fine lady anymore. I longed for Daddy to open his arms wide and invite me to crawl up onto his lap and hug his neck the way I hugged Big Eli. I loved my daddy because he was so handsome with his neatly trimmed mustache and wavy brown hair, his finely tailored clothes and crisp, white shirts. Daddy was kind to me and brought me all sorts of treats whenever he returned from one of his long trips. But I could never recall sitting on his lap. If I needed a man's strong arms to hold me close and comfort me when I was upset, I ran to Eli.

"Now, tell me why you are all dolled up today," Daddy said as Gilbert handed him his evening drink. "Did you have a gentleman caller, Sugar?"

"Daddy!" I blushed at the thought, then drew a deep breath as I remembered my mission. "Mother says I have to go to the Richmond Female Institute."

"You'll be the prettiest girl there," he said after taking a swallow.

26

"But do I have to go? Can't you hire another governess to come and teach me at home?"

"Now, Caroline. It isn't good for you to stay shut up inside the house all the time."

"But Mother does."

His crooked smile faded. "I know. But that's different. Your mother is . . . delicate. You're a strong, healthy girl."

I waited for him to take another sip of his drink, then I blurted the truth. "But I'm scared to go."

"All the more reason why you should go. You need to make friends with girls your own age, Sugar. Get over your shyness."

I hung my head in disappointment, fighting tears. Daddy set his drink on the desk and leaned forward to lift my chin.

"Look at me, Caroline. I happen to agree with your mother this time. You've been spending far too much time with Tessie and Eli and all the other Negro servants. You're a young lady now, and it's high time you made some proper friends."

"But they *are* my friends—my very best friends."

"No, Sugar. I don't want to hear any more arguments, understand?"

I nodded, choking back tears and protests. Daddy appeared satisfied as he settled in his chair again. But at the mention of Tessie, I remembered the awful scene I had awakened to that morning and the other question I needed to ask.

"Daddy, where did those men take Grady?"

He selected a cigar from the box that Gilbert held out to him. "You don't need to worry about all that, Caroline."

"Tessie said we'll never see him again. Is that true?"

"Yes," he said with a sigh. "Yes, I suppose it is true."

"But why? What did Grady do wrong to make you send him away?"

"Why, not a thing, Sugar. What made you think that he had?"

"Some of the men in that wagon had chains on their legs, like they were going to prison."

He shook his head. "They're not going to prison. Only slaves who have tried to run away wear chains. I'm sure Tessie's boy has better sense than that."

"Tessie said it was all Mother's fault. That sending Grady away was *her* doing."

Daddy's expression changed. He looked very uncomfortable all of a sudden, and he stirred in his armchair as if the springs had poked him. For an awful moment I was afraid that I'd made him angry, that he would glare at me in the same hateful way that Tessie had. But Daddy looked down at the cigar he was fingering, not at me.

"Listen, Caroline. Grady is a grown boy now. It's time for him to go out into the world, just like it's time for you to go to school. You need to make new friends, and he needs to start earning his keep."

"But Grady does earn his keep. He helps Eli with the horses, and he carries water and wood for Esther, and—"

"A bright, healthy boy like Grady can be trained for something useful—how to be a blacksmith or a carpenter or some other trade that will benefit his new owner. Besides, we have enough help around here without him."

"But Grady—"

"Hush." Papa placed his fingers over my lips to silence me. "We no longer own Grady. I sold him. And that's the last I ever want to hear about the boy. Understand? Forget about him."

Daddy finished his drink in one gulp and laid aside the unlit cigar. "You'll have to excuse me now, Caroline. Your mother and I are expecting company for dinner and I need to get ready."

Esther fed me all by myself upstairs in my bedroom that evening. She looked worn out from cooking all day. "Missy," she said, wiping the sweat from her face with her apron, "I so tired I could fall asleep standing up, just like the horses do."

"Will Tessie come up to tuck me in bed?" I asked.

"No, child," she said gently. "Let Tessie finish grieving in peace. She be herself tomorrow. You see."

"But who will help me get undressed? I can't reach the fasteners in back by myself . . . or undo my corset laces . . ."

"It have to be Luella or Ruby. I clean wore out." She turned to leave the bedroom, then paused. "And listen, Missy. Don't you be talking about Grady and asking Tessie bunch of questions tomorrow. Best thing is to forget him, and she can't do that if you talking about him all time."

It was what my father had told me, too. Forget him. Forget Grady.

"But may I ask her—"

"No, Miss Caroline. You can't be asking her nothing about that poor boy."

The day ended as strangely as it had begun. Luella came upstairs to help me undress, but her hands were so rough and callused from all her scrubbing and polishing that I only allowed her to unfasten my bodice and loosen the corset laces. I took off my petticoats by myself. Luella didn't know how to pull back the bedcovers like Tessie always did, either. Or how to tuck me in properly.

It seemed strange to see my mammy's empty mat across the room. I had never gone to sleep all by myself before. I begged Luella to leave a candle burning.

"Just don't be setting the house afire," she warned before hurrying back to the kitchen to finish scrubbing the dishes.

As I lay in bed watching the candle's wavering flame, I couldn't help thinking about Grady even though Daddy and Esther had told me not to. I'd watched Grady nurse at Tessie's breast and helped him take his first toddling steps. I'd seen him grow from a plump, contented baby to a carefree little boy who'd played with me as if we were brother and sister. We'd romped in the garden together, climbed the magnolia tree, and pestered Big Eli while he worked, barraging him with our endless questions. Soon Grady had grown big enough to be put to work, and while I'd learned to read and write, he had learned how to take care of the horses and grease the carriage wheels. But every afternoon when our work was finished, we had played together.

Grady was as happy and good-natured as his mother, and the chores he did every day—hauling wood and toting water—molded him into a sturdy, muscular youth. By the age of nine, he'd grown as tall as me and twice as strong. But he had looked so small and helpless this morning as those men had dragged him down the sidewalk, so lost and despairing as they'd thrown him into that slave wagon. Daddy said I had to forget him. He said I would never see Grady again.

I rolled over onto my stomach, buried my face in the pillow, and sobbed.

2

SEPTEMBER 1853

On my first day of school at the Richmond Female Institute, I was so terrified I refused to get out of bed. Tessie had to yank the covers off my head, pry my fingers from the sheets, and drag me out of it. She kept up a steady stream of chatter as she wrestled me into my new uniform, telling me how much I would like the new school, how many new friends I was going to make, and a lot of other foolish things like that.

"But I'm scared!" I wept. "Don't make me go, Tessie. I'm scared!"

She finally stopped coaxing, and a frown creased her smooth brow. Even when she was angry, Tessie was one of the most beautiful women I've ever seen. Her figure didn't need a corset to give it a perfect hourglass shape, and she wore her faded, homespun dresses with the grace and elegance of a fine lady in silks. Tessie's face was perfectly proportioned, too, with a delicately flattened nose, thick, full lips, and slanted, almond-shaped eyes. Daddy had purchased her as my mammy a month before I was born, when Tessie was just fourteen.

She gave my shoulders a gentle shake. "Stop you fussing, Missy.

Why you want to be shaming you daddy thisa way? Don't you know he one of the richest men in this city? How you think he feel if his only child scared to leave her own house? You want people laugh behind his back?"

I stuck out my lower lip, defiant. "Mother never leaves the house."

"Humph!" Tessie grunted. "And don't all of Richmond know that, too? You be strong, now, like you daddy. Else you be growing up all strange-acting, like you mama—lying around in bed all day, crying all the time, swallowing them pills."

I stared at Tessie, too shocked to speak. Never in my life had I heard any of the servants speak so disrespectfully about my mother. I wanted to slap Tessie for saying such things—even if they were true. My daddy would probably whip her good if I ever told him what she'd said. But I knew it was because Tessie still blamed my mother for selling Grady to another owner.

The day after they'd taken Grady away, I had awakened to find Tessie throwing open my window shutters, just like she always did, and saying, "Time to get up, sleepyhead." I'd waited until she sat down on my bed, then I'd wrapped my arms around her and hugged her for a long, long time. I could tell by the way she hugged me back that she had missed me, too. I remembered what Esther said and didn't ask Tessie any questions about Grady. Tessie never once mentioned her son, either. Everything seemed the same—except Grady was gone, and Tessie no longer sang or hummed to herself.

Now Tessie took advantage of my shock after her bitter words about my mother to finish buttoning me into my uniform bodice. Her words had hit their mark, though. I did want my daddy to be proud of me. And I didn't want to stay in my room most of the time like my mother did.

Tessie brushed my hair, then steered me over to the bedroom table where a plate of ham and biscuits with redeye gravy awaited me. My stomach rolled sickeningly at the smell, even though I usually loved Esther's ham and biscuits.

"I can't eat. . . ."

"Yes, you can, baby," Tessie said gently. "Come on, now." She crouched down beside me and began spoon-feeding me small bites, as if I were two years old instead of twelve. When she saw that I'd reached my limit, she helped me to my feet again. "You daddy wants to see you before he leave for work. He in the library."

I descended the gracefully curved stairs with dragging feet. Daddy sat behind his desk reading the *Richmond Enquirer* while he ate his breakfast. He folded the paper and laid it aside when he saw me.

"Well, now. Aren't you quite the young lady in your new uniform?" I wanted to beg him not to make me go, but my mouth was so dry I couldn't talk. "You'll be the prettiest girl in school—and the smartest one, too. You mark my words."

Before I could reply, Esther shuffled into the room. "You wanting more coffee, Massa Fletcher?"

"No, I'll be on my way shortly. I was just waiting to see Caroline off on her first day of school."

"That gal looking mighty sickly, if you ask me," Esther mumbled as she turned to leave. "Strong wind blow her clear to Washington, D.C."

Daddy stood. "I know you're nervous on your first day, Sugar. It's only natural. But I want you to be a brave girl for me, all right? Make me proud of you."

I remembered Tessie's words and mumbled, "I-I'll try."

I followed him into the front hallway where Gilbert waited with Daddy's hat. Outside, our carriage stood at the curb.

"Can Eli drive me to school?" I begged. I had always been a little afraid of Gilbert with his slightly pompous ways, but I loved gentle Eli. I spent more time with him than with any other person except Tessie.

"Well . . . all right."

This was the first good news I'd heard all morning. With Eli beside me I wouldn't feel so alone. "Can he walk all the way inside the school with me, too? Please, Daddy?"

He hesitated a moment, then nodded. "All right, but tell him he has to wear livery, not his dirty old stable clothes." He said this loudly enough for Tessie to hear as she waited in the hallway behind us.

"Yes, sir," she replied. "I tell him."

I was sick to my stomach before leaving, losing the small amount of food I'd eaten for breakfast. Tessie hugged me good-bye and hustled me into the carriage, heedless of my tears and pallid face. Eli snapped the reins, and we quickly drove off. But as soon as we'd rounded the corner, out of sight of the house, we stopped again. Eli hopped down from the driver's seat and, to my utter amazement, climbed into the back of the carriage and sat down beside me. I quickly scrambled into the safety of his arms, burying my face in his broad chest.

"I'm scared, Eli! I don't want to go." It felt different to hug him in his scratchy uniform, and he didn't smell like the same old Eli I loved. At least his deep, gentle voice was the same.

"I know, Missy. I know you scared."

"Please, take me back home . . . or . . . or let's just drive around all day."

"Now, you know I can't do that. Massa Fletcher have my hide if I don't do exactly what he say. But why all this fussing? You forget all them stories I tell you and Grady? You forget how Massa Jesus always with you, taking good care you?"

"Tell me again," I begged.

I loved listening to Eli talk about Massa Jesus. It seemed like ages since I'd sat with Eli in the carriage house, Grady on one of his knees and me on the other, listening as he told us what the Good Book said. I was pretty sure that Eli's Jesus was the same person who the minister preached about every Sunday in church, but the stories sounded better when Eli told them. They sounded as though they might have really happened.

"It ain't doing no good to tell you again," he warned, "if you not hiding them words in you heart."

He tapped his chest with his forefinger, and I remembered how Grady, solemn-eyed, would tap his own chest in imitation and say, *"They in there, Eli. They all hiding right down in there."*

I pointed to my heart. "I'll remember. I promise."

"All right, then." Eli settled back against the carriage seat and I leaned against him, gripping his burly arm. "In olden times," he began, "there a great big giant man name Goliath. Everybody scared of him. Grown men run and hide when he come out, waving his shiny sword all around in the air. 'Who gonna fight me?' Goliath ask every day. And I shamed to tell you that all them soldiers in God's army so scared they turn tail and run.

"Then one day little David come along. He bringing some ham and sweet potatoes to his brothers in the army. Now, David hardly believing the way them grown men running scared. So little David say, 'I fight him! I fight Goliath 'cause I ain't afraid! I got God on my side.'

"Then David tell the king how one time he and God kill theirselves a lion, and how they kill a bear another time. And David, he just as sure as can be that he and God can lick old Goliath, too. So the king say, 'All right, son. You go ahead, now. You go kill that giant.'

"Goliath like to laugh hisself silly when he see little David stepping out to fight him. Goliath say, 'What you think I am? A dog? Why you send a boy out here to fight a giant man?'

"But David say, 'No sir! You fight with a big old sword and a fancy spear, but I fight in the name of the Lord God Almighty! And He gonna help me lick you!'

"Goliath got all riled up when David say that. But David still not scared. He drop a stone in his slingshot, and he twirl it round and round, and when he let go, the Lord sent that stone a-flying straight into Goliath's head. Knock him right to the ground, dead as a doorknob."

I felt the same thrill I'd always felt at the end of Eli's stories. He spoke so confidently about God, convinced of His strength and power.

"Now then," Eli said, giving my shoulder a gentle squeeze, "what you gonna hide away in you heart?"

"That . . . um . . . that if God is with me . . . I don't have to be afraid of giants?"

He grinned. "Not giants or anything else what stands in you way. And you know why that is?"

"Because God will help me fight them?"

"That's not a question, Little Missy, that's the truth! The Lord always by you side if you ask Him to be. He fight all you battles. He gonna walk beside you into that old school today and you don't have to be scared of nothing."

I gulped, trying to feel brave. "Will . . . will you come inside with me?"

"What you need me for, Missy? Massa Jesus is with you!"

"I-I know, but . . . will you come inside anyway?"

He shook his head as if he was disappointed in me, but I saw a glint of laughter in his dark eyes. He broke into a gentle grin. "Sure thing, Missy Caroline. I go with you just as far as they let me go."

The carriage rocked as he jumped down from his place beside me, then swayed again as he climbed into the driver's seat. The motion made my stomach roll. I closed my eyes and tried to imagine the Lord sitting on one side of me and the boy David on the other side, slingshot in hand. In my mind, David looked a lot like Grady.

Eli whistled and snapped the reins. The carriage lurched forward. We turned onto Franklin Street, and a few minutes later we were hurtling down Church Hill. I could see the city and the capitol building up ahead, perched on the next hill we would have to climb. Traffic slowed when we reached the bottom, then came to a halt near Fourteenth Street to allow a gang of Negroes to cross in front of us. Some wore chains on their legs. I watched them enter a fortress-like building where black faces peered from behind barred windows.

I scrambled over to the opposite seat to kneel behind Eli, hanging on to his broad shoulders to keep from falling. "Is this where they brought Grady?" I asked in a hushed voice.

"I reckon so. This where they hold the slave auction."

"Wait!" I cried as the carriage began slowly moving forward again. "Can't we go look for him? Maybe we can find him and bring him back home." I began scanning the dark, somber faces, but when I glanced at Eli he was staring at the reins in his hands, shaking his head.

"Ain't no use, Missy. Nice boy like our Grady be long gone by now."

"But where? Where did he go?"

"Only the Good Lord know that."

I knew from the globe in my daddy's library that the world was a very huge place. The thought of my friend Grady all alone out there gave me a lost, helpless feeling. I glanced over my shoulder at all the harsh white faces in the crowd, then at the dark, bent heads, and I knew that wherever Grady was, he must be terrified. I suddenly felt guilty for being frightened just to go to school. I settled back on the carriage seat again and drew a deep breath, determined to be brave.

We arrived at the Richmond Female Institute, a three-story brick row house with white pillars by the front steps and neat black shutters on the windows. Eli gave my hand a reassuring squeeze as he helped me down from the carriage.

"You all right, Miss Caroline?" he asked. I nodded, knowing somehow that I would be. But I couldn't help wondering, as I walked through the open front door for the first time, why God hadn't helped Grady defeat his enemies the same way He'd helped David.

I was still sick every morning for several weeks, even with Eli and Massa Jesus by my side. Sometimes I had nosebleeds, which the doctor said were caused by fright. I once overheard my teachers whispering about my mother's "condition," but they seemed to take pity on me, declaring me a "sensitive" child. They never made me read or recite aloud.

While I can't say I enjoyed school, I did learn to tolerate it. The best part was the long carriage ride with Eli twice a day. He drove a different route to school after that first day—one that wouldn't take us past the slave market again. And at the end of each day I'd find him waiting for me outside the school, smiling as though he hadn't seen me in a hundred years. He sat high on the driver's seat as we rode up and down the hills, looking stiff in his fancy topcoat and hat, and mumbling under his breath all the way to the school each morning and all the way home again in the afternoon.

"Who are you talking to, Eli?" I finally asked him one morning.

"Sometime I talking to Massa Jesus, but today I talking to these here horses."

"To the horses? Can they understand what you say?"

"Sure can, Missy."

"And do the horses talk back to you, too?"

"Sure do."

"What do they say?"

"Well, for one thing they say, 'We sure glad our Missy a little thing. We glad we not toting that big old Missus Greeley up these hills all day long.'"

I giggled. Mrs. Greeley, my very stout headmistress, was even bigger around than Esther.

"What else do the horses say?"

It became a game for us after that. Every day I would ask Eli what the horses were talking about, and every day he would tell me something different. "Today they say 'I wonder when this rain ever gonna stop? We be up to our hocks in mud.'"

Or, "Today them horses say 'Why you cracking that whip over our head, Mr. Eli? Don't you know Little Missy ain't in no hurry to get to that old school?'"

I laughed with delight at all his horse conversations. Before long, my nosebleeds stopped. Gradually my fear subsided, too.

One Saturday morning, when I didn't have to go to school, I heard Eli mumbling to himself as he raked the leaves outside in our yard. "Who are you talking to now?" I asked. "The horses can't hear you—they're in the carriage house."

"I know, Little Missy. I talking to Massa Jesus."

I was dying to ask the question that had been bothering me for some time. "Is He the same Jesus the minister talks to when we pray in church?"

"He the same. There only one Jesus I know about."

I couldn't imagine how Eli could talk to Him while raking leaves in the backyard. "Don't you have to be in church or kneeling down to talk to Jesus?"

"Nope. If He your friend, you can talk to Him anytime, anywhere." He piled the leaves beside the curb and bent to light a match to them. I inhaled the wonderful fragrance of burning leaves, even though the smoke burned my eyes when the wind shifted my way.

"What do you talk to Jesus about?" I asked, swinging back and forth on the open gate while I watched him work.

He stood, leaning against the rake for a moment. "Well . . . I tell Him all the things I worried about."

His answer perplexed me. Why would Eli have any worries? He certainly didn't have ships to fret about, like Daddy did. "What kind of things?" I finally asked.

"Oh, like whether Little Missy be getting along all right in that school of hers, and whether Grady feeling homesick wherever he at. Whether he scared or missing his mama."

I knew how badly I missed Grady, but it had never occurred to me that Grady might be missing all of us, too.

"And sometimes I talk to Jesus about my own son," Eli continued. "I ask Him take good care him for me."

I recalled what Esther had said that terrible morning, how their son had been sold to Hilltop, my grandfather's plantation. "Do you miss your son, Eli?"

"Sure do, Missy. He born right here in this house, grew up here. Then he had to leave us and go on out to Hilltop."

"What's his name?"

"Josiah." I heard the love in his voice as he spoke his son's name. "Sometimes I recollect how he use to curl up on my lap like you and Grady, and my heart about breaks for missing him. That's when I start praying to Jesus and asking Him take good care my boy. Make sure Josiah minds his massa so the overseer not beating him, and such like."

"Does Jesus answer you, too . . . like the horses do?"

"I ain't hearing Him in my ears, Missy, but I know He listening. And I know He gonna do something about what I asking."

"How do you know that?"

Eli paused, poking at the fire with his rake. "Because after I finish talking to Massa Jesus, my heart empty of worry . . . and I feel better. It's just like when I get to worrying about one of the horses that may be limping a little bit, or worry about something else belonging to Massa. If I take my worry to Massa Fletcher and tell him all I thinking about, he say, 'Okay, I take care of it.' And Massa Fletcher good as his word. He find out what ails that horse and see it gets taken care of. Now, if I just worry and don't say nothing, horse still be limping. But if I turn everything over to the massa—all the things too big for me—I know he take care of them. They his horses, you see. He care about them even more than I do."

I was confused, failing to see the connection. "What does that have to do with Jesus?"

"That's what I about to tell you. Massa Jesus same way. This is His world. You and Josiah and Grady be His children. Anything I can't fix, I take to Jesus. Then I don't have to worry no more. Massa Jesus take care of it in His own time, His own way."

I hopped down from the gate and kicked at the leaves with my toe. I longed to talk to him about Grady but I was afraid to. Then I remembered that Eli had mentioned Grady first, and I finally summoned my courage.

"Can I tell you something?"

40

"Sure, Missy Caroline."

"Daddy said I need to forget about Grady. Esther said so, too. But I can't forget him, Eli. I miss him so much."

"Me too. He like a son to me."

I looked up at Eli in surprise. "But . . . but Grady *is* your son, isn't he?"

"No, I'm married to Esther, not Tessie."

"Then who's Grady's daddy? Is it Gilbert?"

Eli's thick gray brows met in the middle as he frowned. "This not a fit subject for Little Missy to be asking. That's Tessie's business, not you and mine."

"But . . . but Grady has to have a father, doesn't he? Everyone has to have a mother and a father."

Eli turned away and resumed his raking. He looked more distressed than I'd ever seen him. I couldn't understand why he was so afraid to answer a simple question. Grady and I had asked him much harder ones than this. "Why won't you answer me, Eli?"

He stopped raking, his head bowed as he stared down at his feet. "Little Missy, you and me we talk about a lot of things. I always do my best by you, try and answer all your questions. But this here . . . this time . . . I ain't having this conversation."

"But why not?"

He looked frightened, desperate, glancing around in all directions as if someone might overhear us. "*Never* ask a slave who fathered her children," he said in a harsh whisper. "They kill a gal if she tell."

I didn't believe him. It seemed preposterous. "Kill her? Why would they do that?" But Eli had turned away. He continued raking, as if he hadn't heard my question.

A moment later Gilbert came outside through the rear door. I watched him walk toward us in his light, gliding step—like an empty ship sailing upriver. I wondered how old he was. Younger than Eli, certainly, but at least ten years older than Tessie. He saw me watching him and quickly looked down at the ground.

"Afternoon, Missy." He tipped his hat in greeting, his eyes carefully averted. I wished he would smile so I could see if his grin resembled Grady's—Grady almost always had a smile on his face. But I realized as Gilbert disappeared into the carriage house that I had never seen Daddy's servant smile.

"You go on in the house now," Eli said. "Before your hair and clothes be smelling like smoke and Tessie chews me out."

"But—"

"Go on! Get!" It was the only time in my life that Eli had ever spoken harshly to me. He turned his back and moved away, raking in the opposite direction as if his life depended on it.

CHAPTER

3

JULY 1854

By the time I grew accustomed to going to the Richmond Female Institute every day, the school year ended for the summer. I'd celebrated my thirteenth birthday by then, and I was sometimes allowed to eat dinner in the formal dining room with Daddy and his guests—and with Mother when she was well enough to join us. The three of us were seated at the dinner table one warm July evening when we heard an urgent pounding on our front door. Gilbert stopped serving and sailed out to answer it, returning a few minutes later to speak to my father.

"Excuse me, sir. Young gentleman at the door say he your nephew, Jonathan Fletcher. He don't have a calling card."

"Jonathan?" Daddy's face registered surprise. "Show him in, Gilbert."

He wasn't a "young gentleman" at all but a boy not much older than me, looking hot and tired and dusty, as if he'd traveled a long distance. But even in his disheveled state, the resemblance between him and my father was uncanny. They had the same handsome square face and aristocratic nose, the same wavy brown hair and dark eyes.

A pale shadow on Jonathan's upper lip foretold a mustache just like Daddy's in a year or so.

"Good evening, Uncle George . . . Aunt Mary." He bowed politely in greeting.

Daddy didn't rise from his chair. "Jonathan. What brings you to Richmond at this hour?"

The words rushed from Jonathan's mouth as if he'd been holding them back for a long time. "Father says you'd better come to Hilltop right away, sir. Grandfather is ill."

Daddy resumed eating, cutting his meat without looking up. "Is he dying?"

I watched Jonathan's face twist with emotion. He gazed up at the ceiling, as if to keep the tears that had sprung to his eyes from overflowing. "I . . . um . . . I believe so, sir." He cleared his throat but his voice still sounded hoarse. "He had a dizzy spell, and now he . . . he can't move . . . or speak."

Daddy's eyes met my mother's. She shook her head slightly, then looked away. "You know how I hate it out in the country, George. The smell, the flies, all those Negroes . . ." She seemed oblivious to the fact that three Negroes, Tessie, Gilbert, and Ruby, were in the room serving us dinner.

"Would you like something to eat, Jonathan?" Daddy asked.

"Yes, thank you, sir. But I'd like to wash up first, if I may."

Daddy returned to his meal while Gilbert showed Jonathan where to freshen up. Ruby hurried to set a place for him at the table. When Jonathan returned I saw that he had won the battle with his emotions.

"Sit down, son," Daddy said, motioning to the empty chair across the table from me. Then, almost as an afterthought, he said, "Caroline Ruth, this is your cousin Jonathan."

"How do you do," I said. Jonathan looked up at me in surprise.

"Very well, thank you." His words sounded stiff and formal. I wondered if he was making fun of me. But then he flashed a friendly grin, and I saw a glint of humor and mischief in his eye. He reminded

44

me so much of Grady it astonished me. I usually wasn't comfortable around strangers, but I liked Jonathan from that very first night. He bowed his head in prayer for a moment, then began to eat, displaying the finest of table manners.

"We'll leave for Hilltop first thing in the morning," Daddy said after a moment. "I have a few things to take care of downtown first."

Jonathan appeared surprised. "But . . . Father said you should . . . I mean, he thought that you might want to come right away . . . tonight."

"You may return home tonight if you wish," Daddy said, "although I would recommend you spend the night and rest yourself and your horses. Either way, I'll follow you in my own carriage tomorrow. That way I won't be dependent on anyone to drive me back to Richmond . . . afterward."

Mother rested her hand on Daddy's arm. "George, I'd prefer it if you left Gilbert here with me. His manners are more refined than that other Negro stable hand of yours. That large, coarse fellow makes me uncomfortable."

I was stunned to realize that she meant Eli. How could anyone not love gentle Eli? I longed to rise to his defense but I knew better than to contradict my elders, especially at the dinner table.

"If you wish, my dear," Daddy replied. "Eli can drive me tomorrow instead of Gilbert."

When the meal ended, Daddy and Jonathan retired to the library. I was about to follow my mother into the drawing room when Tessie suddenly stopped stacking the dirty dishes and pulled me aside.

"Missy Caroline!" Her eyes danced with excitement, as if something wonderful was about to happen. "Why don't you go along with your daddy tomorrow?"

"Go with him? Why?" The thought had never occurred to me.

"Nothing doing round here . . . besides, do you good to get out of this hot old city, meet your relations. . . ."

The more I pondered the idea, the more I liked it. I lived a lonely life, and I longed for a friend. Maybe my cousin with the impish grin could be a friend to me, like Grady had been.

"Would you come to Hilltop with me, too?" I asked Tessie.

"Oh, I would like that more than *anything*, Missy." Her smile made the chandelier seem dim. I glimpsed a longing in her eyes, and it aroused my curiosity.

"Have you ever been to my grandparents' plantation before?" I asked.

To my astonishment, her eyes seemed to grow even brighter as they filled with tears. "I born there, Missy. My mammy and pappy living there. I sure like to see them again. All my sisters and brothers there, too . . . if they ain't been sold off by now."

I didn't know what to say. Tessie had taken care of me since the day I was born. My entire lifetime had passed—and nearly half of her own—since she'd seen her family.

"Tessie, you should have told me. . . ."

She swiped at her tears. "Never had the chance before, I guess."

"I'll go ask Daddy right now."

The aroma of cigar smoke filled the library when I entered. Daddy and Jonathan were deep in conversation, discussing all the troubles out west in Kansas. "Are you sure?" Daddy asked when I told him I wanted to go with him. "It's a very long carriage ride out to the plantation, especially in this heat."

"It's hot here in Richmond, too." I didn't mention Tessie.

Surprisingly, Daddy turned to Jonathan. "What do you think?"

"I think it's a fine idea, sir," my cousin said. He winked at me as if we were conspirators.

When Daddy finally agreed, I could hardly contain my excitement. I ran outside to the kitchen to tell Tessie, then stopped short when I saw a strange Negro man filling our kitchen doorway. He stood as tall as Eli, and he had his arms all wrapped around Esther. She was sobbing and wailing as they rocked back and forth.

"What's wrong?" I asked her in alarm.

46

Esther unwrapped herself, and I saw a broad grin stretched across her face. "Nothing wrong, child. I happy to see my boy, that's all. This here's my son, Josiah."

He was not at all what I expected. Josiah was a grown man in his late twenties. He looked for all the world like a younger version of Eli—the same massive shoulders and broad chest, the same height and weight. But Josiah's handsome face had none of the gentleness and warmth of his father's. It was as if he'd been carved from cold black stone instead of rich brown clay.

"Pleased to meet you," I mumbled, then hurried inside to tell Tessie to start packing our things.

That night I was so excited about my trip to Hilltop I had trouble falling asleep. It was the first time I'd ever been excited about trying something new. I lay awake in bed a long time.

Later, not long after the downstairs clock struck ten, I heard a sharp *click* as if something hard had struck my bedroom window. I lay in the darkness, listening. Then I heard it again, the sound a hailstone makes when it strikes the glass. Tessie rose from her pallet, opened the shutters a crack, and peered out. Before I could ask what she'd seen, she grabbed her shawl and hurried out of the room, wearing only her nightclothes. When she didn't come back right away, I climbed out of bed and went to the window to see for myself.

Tessie stood in the shadows beside the carriage house, her white chemise bright in the half-moon's light. Josiah had her wrapped in his brawny arms, just as he'd clasped his mother a few hours earlier. Then he bent and began kissing Tessie's neck, and her soft laughter floated up to me in the quiet night. I quickly turned away, closing the shutters once again.

I left for Hilltop with my cousin Jonathan early the next morning, traveling northeast from the city on the Mechanicsville Turnpike.

Tessie rode on the driver's seat beside Josiah, but neither of them spoke a single word. In fact, they acted as if they were perfect strangers, never so much as glancing at each other. It made me wonder if I had dreamt the scene by the carriage house last night.

"Why doesn't your family ever come out to Hilltop?" Jonathan asked as we rode along beneath a scorching July sun.

"I don't know. Too far away, I guess."

Jonathan grunted derisively. "It's not *that* far—only three hours or so from Richmond by carriage. My father makes the trip into Richmond about once a month."

I wanted to ask why Jonathan's father never visited us, but I didn't dare. "Daddy talks about Hilltop sometimes," I said. "He told me it's the plantation where he grew up. That's all I know, though."

"Want me to tell you about it?"

"Yes, please."

He laughed, and when I asked him what was so funny, he shook his head. "You won't need your fancy city manners at Hilltop. . . . Anyway, my father is William P. Fletcher II, the older brother. He and Grandfather manage the plantation together. I mean, they did until . . ." He leaned his head back against the seat, struggling for control.

"You're very fond of your grandfather, aren't you?"

"He's your grandfather, too, you know," Jonathan said hoarsely.

I nodded, waiting until he could continue.

"Your father is the younger brother," he finally said. "He runs the business side of things in Richmond—operating the warehouses, selling the wheat or tobacco or whatever else we grow. Our fathers are supposed to be partners, but you'd never know it. They barely speak to each other. I don't know what that's all about exactly, but I have an idea."

"Tell me."

"Your father started buying and selling for other plantations besides Hilltop. He started importing coffee from South America and stuff from Europe and began making a lot of money. But I heard Grandfather say that his money is *tainted*. He won't touch any of it."

My stomach lurched at the thought of my daddy doing something wrong. Maybe I shouldn't be discussing such things with Jonathan.

"Anyway," he continued with a shrug, "none of that matters now. Grandfather is ill, so the family will all come together. Our fathers also have two sisters. Aunt Abigail is married and lives in Hanover County. Have you ever met her?"

I shook my head.

"You will. My brother was sent to fetch her. The youngest sister is Aunt Catherine, who married a planter from Savannah and lives down in Georgia. I sent her a telegram yesterday from Richmond, before I came to your house."

It felt strange to learn about all of these relatives for the first time. I repeated their names to myself so I wouldn't forget them—Uncle William, Aunt Abigail, Aunt Catherine.

"You have two more cousins at Hilltop besides me. My brother Will is the oldest; he's seventeen."

"How old are you?"

"Fifteen. We had a sister who died when she was just a baby, and another sister, Ruth, who died when she was eight. She would have been twelve by now if she'd lived. Then there's Thomas, the baby. He's six."

Jonathan began explaining to me how they used to grow tobacco at Hilltop but had switched to wheat because tobacco "used up" the soil. I was only half listening. Instead, I gazed at Josiah's broad back as we rode, remembering how I'd seen him kissing Tessie in the moonlight. Could Josiah be Grady's father? Eli said Josiah was born in Richmond, in our house, but I had no memory of him at all.

"When did Josiah come to live at Hilltop?" I asked when Jonathan paused for a moment. I hoped that the squeak and rattle of the carriage, the plod of horse hooves, would prevent Josiah and Tessie from hearing my question.

"There's a story behind his coming," Jonathan said. "Want to hear it?"

"Yes, please."

"When I was five I took a bad fall off my horse. Broke my collarbone, my arm, and my leg. The doctor fixed me up with splints and said I couldn't walk on my leg for at least a month. I got pretty bored lying around my room all day. When my father came to Richmond on business, Uncle George offered to send Josiah back home to carry me around. He said he was about to sell him at the slave auction so we may as well have him at Hilltop. Father wouldn't accept a gift from Uncle George, so he bought Josiah for me. Jo was plenty strong enough. Smart, too. He not only hauled me all around, he played dominoes and card games with me to keep me occupied until my leg healed."

"How old was he?"

"I don't know . . . late teens, I guess. Nobody keeps track of his Negroes' ages—and slaves don't know how to count. Anyway, I haven't needed to be carried around for ten years now, but Josiah and I are best friends. Couple of years ago, he started working as an apprentice to Hilltop's blacksmith, but I still send for Jo whenever I need someone to go hunting or fishing with, or just to ride around the countryside. I'll be going away to college in a few years and I want Jo to come with me as my manservant—although my father keeps threatening to make a field hand out of him because he's so big and strong. Says it's a waste of good manpower to use Josiah as a manservant, much less have him gallivanting around the countryside with me all day." He laughed, as if Josiah's future was of very little importance.

"May I ask him a question?" I asked.

"Sure, go ahead. Hey, Jo," he said, leaning forward, "Miss Caroline has a question for you." Josiah glanced briefly over his shoulder, then nodded curtly.

I hesitated, unsure how to begin. When I finally found my voice, my sentences all came out like questions. "Um . . . when you left

Richmond? And moved to Hilltop? Did you, um . . . did you miss Esther and Eli a lot?"

Josiah continued to stare silently ahead. I couldn't tell if he'd even heard me. Finally he shrugged his shoulders and mumbled, "Don't recall. Long time ago."

We crossed the sluggish Chickahominy River, and after a hot, dusty, three-hour ride over some of the bumpiest roads I'd ever traveled, Jonathan pointed to a weathered line of split-rail fences. "Those mark the edge of our plantation," he said. "We're almost there."

I saw slaves working in several of the fields we passed, their black bodies glistening with sweat in the heat as they bent to toil among the green plants. Pine trees lined the narrow road on both sides as we approached the house, forming a fragrant tunnel around us.

I fell in love with Hilltop at first sight. The white, two-story house sat atop a small rise, shaded by oak and chestnut trees and surrounded by fenced fields. The front facade had a peaceful elegance to it, with neat black shutters and four simple pillars supporting the portico. Josiah drove the carriage around to the rear of the house—to a smaller, plainer entry—and a yard that was alive with activity. A flock of chickens, geese, and other fowl scattered at our approach, along with a flock of small Negro children whose job it was to tend them. Nearby, their mothers scrubbed laundry in wooden tubs, draping the clean tablecloths and bed linens over bushes and fence rails to dry. Older children bustled back and forth hauling water and firewood.

As we drew to a halt, Jonathan's mother emerged from the house to scold him for driving the carriage into the yard and kicking up a cloud of dust. But she stopped mid-sentence when she saw me.

"Mama, this is Uncle George's daughter, Caroline," Jonathan said as he helped me from the carriage. "She's decided to pay us a visit along with her daddy—he's coming a little later."

"Welcome, Caroline. It's so nice to finally meet you." My aunt Anne's greeting was as warm as the summer day, but beneath the smile she looked very tired and careworn. She wore an apron and a plain, blue-checked work dress without hoops. Her graying, fly-away hair was gathered into an untidy bun on the back of her head. "You've caught me at a very busy time," she began, but Jonathan interrupted her apology.

"Don't you worry, Mama. You just go on back to whatever you were doing. I'll be glad to show Caroline around and keep her occupied till dinnertime. Her mammy can see to all of Caroline's things."

Inside, the plantation house was smaller and plainer than our enor-mous brick house in town. Jonathan explained that the original house, built by our great-grandfather, had only two rooms downstairs and two upstairs. Our grandfather had enlarged the house with a two-story addition on the west side. My Richmond house had five spacious bed-rooms—my mother's two-room suite, my father's adjoining bedroom, my room, and the empty nursery. Hilltop had only three modest-sized bedrooms upstairs, one for my aunt and uncle, one for the boys, and one that had belonged to the girls before they died. This latter room was where I was to sleep. After I'd freshened up a bit from the trip, I left Tessie to unpack my things while I went exploring with my cousin.

Downstairs, the double front and rear doors were left open all day to allow the breezes to blow through. The house had no library or drawing room like ours did, only the parlor to the left of the stair hall and the dining room to the right, where three slaves were busy setting the table for dinner. The parlor furniture was sheathed in cotton summer covers, like our furniture back home, but beneath the slipcovers I could see that their furniture was older and shabbier than ours. The door to my grandparents' room was closed, so Jonathan said I would have to wait until later to meet them.

Instead, he took me on a tour of the outbuildings, such as the kitchen, the dairy, and the smokehouse, all bustling with activity. More dark faces appraised me when we ducked inside a small work shed that housed a spinning wheel, a loom, and Hilltop's two seam-stresses. The kitchen, a short distance from the house, was similar to ours, with a loft upstairs where the house servants lived. It looked much too small to accommodate the dozen or so servants I'd already seen working in the house and yard.

"They don't all live here," Jonathan said. "Most of them live down on Slave Row."

"Where's that?"

"You can't see it from the house. I'll show you when we go down by the barn."

"Which of these servants are Tessie's parents?" I asked.

Jonathan gave me an odd look, as if I'd asked a very strange question. "I don't know. Who cares which Negroes are related to each other?"

I wanted to say that *I* did—that Tessie and Eli and Esther were like family to me—but I didn't. I could tell that Jonathan already thought I was very strange. And I wanted very much for him to like me.

Beyond the shady yard, pear and apple trees hung heavy with ripening fruit. Three young Negro girls about the same age as me were listlessly hoeing weeds in the fenced vegetable garden we passed.

"Hey there!" Jonathan called gruffly from the gate. "Those weeds are growing faster than y'all are chopping them." The girls worked a little faster as we watched for a moment. "If we don't keep an eye on these people constantly," Jonathan said, "they don't do a lick of work."

He led the way up the road to the weathered wooden barn and blacksmith's forge. The tall, windowless building alongside it was the tobacco shed; the crudely chinked log building, the corncrib. Cattle, sheep, and draft horses grazed in pastures behind more rail fences. Jonathan pointed to the cultivated fields in the distance, then to the dense green woods beyond. "We farm about six hundred acres in all," he said proudly. "And all of that forest land is ours, too."

I loved it—all of it. In spite of the busyness of farm life, there was a deep stillness here on the plantation that I'd never experienced in the city. The brush of wind in the treetops replaced the hectic rush of city traffic. Instead of smoking factories and warehouses crowded one upon the other, there were open spaces, green vistas, cloudless skies. I wished I could stay here forever.

Then Jonathan showed me Slave Row. Two rows of tumbledown shacks no sturdier than the corncrib faced each other across a littered dirt path. Jonathan said they were home to more than fifty of Hilltop's field slaves. I never would have believed that such ramshackle cabins were inhabited if I hadn't seen a handful of small children toddling in the dirt out in front and some ragged patches of vegetables growing in gardens in the rear.

"Oh, what a terrible place," I whispered.

Jonathan draped his arm around my shoulder and steered me away. "Come on. It must be nearly dinnertime. And I'll bet this carriage coming up the road is your father's."

They ate the big meal of the day at noon on the plantation and usually followed it with a short afternoon rest. But before Tessie and I went to our room to lie down that first day, my father took me into the downstairs bedroom to meet my grandparents.

"Grandmother is deaf as a fence post," Jonathan whispered in my ear as he followed us inside. "She has been for years, but she won't admit it."

Grandfather lay in bed with his eyes closed, gray-faced, unmoving. I'd never seen a corpse before, but he looked just like I'd imagined one would look. I wanted to run out of the room in fright. Jonathan took my hand in his and gave it a gentle squeeze.

Grandmother sat in a rocking chair near the bed, sewing. She was gray-haired and crabby-looking. She laid aside the needle and cloth when she saw us and stood. My daddy went to her.

"Hello, Mother." He rested his hands lightly on her shoulders and bent to kiss her cheek.

"George. You came." Her voice rasped harshly, her unsmiling expression never changed. At first my grandmother's greeting seemed cold, but then she reached up to touch Daddy's face, brushing a stray lock of his hair, and I recognized the love and tenderness in her gesture. Tessie fussed over me the same way.

"Mother, I brought my daughter with me from Richmond. I'd like you to meet her." He urged me forward. Up close, I saw that my grandmother had a mustache. She looked for all the world like Jonathan or my father dressed up in women's clothing and a gray wig.

"Who is this?" she asked, frowning.

"My daughter," he repeated, louder. "Her name is Caroline."

"What? She's from *Carolina,* you say?"

"No, Mother. That's her name . . . Caroline *Ruth*. She's named after you."

"After*noon*? I know it's afternoon! I just finished my dinner." I heard a sputtering sound and glanced over my shoulder. Jonathan was struggling to hold back his laughter—and barely succeeding. If he kept it up, I knew I would catch the giggles, too.

Daddy tried shouting. "No, *Ruth* . . . she's named Caroline *Ruth*—*your* name."

"Well, I should think I know my own name!" Grandmother said indignantly.

Daddy pushed me forward into her stiff embrace. I was taller than she was. Her arms and legs were so bony, it was like hugging a pile of kindling wood.

"Did you come by train from Carolina?" she asked me.

"N-no, ma'am," I stammered. "I came by carriage . . . from Richmond."

She frowned. "Rich men! They'll find it very difficult to enter the kingdom of heaven, I can tell you that. Don't put your faith in riches, young lady."

"Yes, ma'am . . . I mean, no, ma'am. I won't."

As soon as Daddy excused us, Jonathan and I fled the room. We fell into each other's arms in the hallway, laughing until tears came.

The afternoon was hot and still, as if nature were holding her breath. I was tired from the long trip, so Tessie and I went upstairs to my room for a nap. Aunt Anne sent a little Negro girl named Nellie upstairs to fan me while I rested, but I felt so sorry for the poor child, forced to wave her tired arms in the stifling heat, that I urged her to lie down on the floor beside Tessie. Nellie was sound asleep before we were.

"Have you seen your family yet?" I asked Tessie before drifting off.

"No, Missy," she whispered. "They all field hands. I have to wait till sunset, when they come in from the fields."

"May I go with you?"

"Down Slave Row? That's no place for Little Missy. Why you want to go down there?"

I couldn't explain why to myself, much less to Tessie. I suppose I remembered all the happy times I'd spent in our kitchen with Tessie and Grady, or out in the carriage house, talking to Eli, and I wanted to replace the image of Slave Row that I'd seen earlier with a happier one. I was certain that Eli would be down there, too, laughing and talking with Josiah.

"Jonathan already showed me Slave Row," I told Tessie. She didn't answer. I wondered if she had fallen asleep.

But later that night, while Daddy and the others were visiting in the parlor after supper, Tessie came to me and pulled me aside. "I take you down there now . . . if you still want to go," she said.

Tessie's family was truly happy to see her, but Slave Row wasn't a place of warmth and laughter like our kitchen back home. An atmosphere of weariness and wariness hung over all the cabins, so that even the small children seemed subdued. I caught a glimpse inside her family's unlit cabin, enough to see that it had a dirt floor and was nearly bare of furniture.

"You back here to stay, girl?" Tessie's mama asked as her family stood around their front stoop, visiting.

"No, my massa just come for few days." She wrapped her arm around me and pulled me close, as if sensing my uneasiness. "And my little Missy come long, too."

"Must mean Old Massa's dying if young Massa George come back here," Tessie's father said.

She nodded. "All the folk up the house think so. He in a real bad way, so I hear."

"Wonder what become of us when he die? You hearing anything, Tessie?"

"Don't know about that," she said. "But my massa, he got plenty money, so his family must have plenty, too. Probably no one have to be sold."

Tessie's father puffed on an old corncob pipe. "If you dream of Massa counting money, means someone gonna be sold."

Slowly, one by one, the other slaves ambled over to the cabin to greet Tessie and join the conversation. I didn't see Eli, but Josiah stood at a cautious distance, watching and listening. The young man beside him was shirtless, and when he turned around I saw ridges of ugly welts on his back, like a furrowed field. I couldn't stop staring.

"What happened to him, Tessie?" I whispered.

"Overseer's whip what happened." She turned my head away and held me close to her side so I couldn't see him.

As more and more people gathered near the cabin, I began to sense how uncomfortable they all were around me—and I began to grow uneasy around them. I couldn't understand why that was, why these servants were so different from our servants at home. For the first time in my life I felt out of place. I felt *white*. And I didn't like the feeling at all. I wiggled out of Tessie's grasp.

"I'm going back to the house now," I told her.

She looked over at Josiah. Their eyes met. "Then I going, too," she said.

"No, stay as long as you like, Tessie. I can walk back by myself."

I threaded through the crowd before she had a chance to follow me. But when I reached the last cabin I heard someone behind me say, "Peculiar little white gal, ain't she?"

CHAPTER

4

HILLTOP, JULY 1854

I awoke at dawn to the haunting sound of the conch shell, blowing to summon the field slaves. A few minutes later I heard a faint rumbling and recognized it as wagons rolling and the tramp of marching feet. Then, above the sound of roosters crowing and birds calling, I heard music—the song of the slaves. I never will forget that shivery, mournful sound.

Nobody know the trouble I see. . . . Nobody know but Jesus.

It was singing, yet it wasn't—it was weeping. And when the sound finally faded away, I realized that I was weeping, too.

My grandfather died that day. Aunt Abigail arrived in the afternoon with her husband, a minister, and he conducted the funeral service the following day. The plantation yard filled with carriages and the house overflowed with neighbors, all coming to pay their last respects. I had no idea how they'd heard the news. Hilltop was so huge that neighboring houses weren't even visible; the nearest town was miles away. But they came by the dozens, sharing words of consolation with my grandmother, embracing my aunts, somberly shaking hands with my daddy and uncle.

As I walked up the path through the woods to the family burial plot, holding my daddy's hand, a hot wind rustled through the branches all around me, carrying the fragrance of pine. A white picket fence separated the graves from the woods, the tombstones shaded by a massive oak tree, with branches that spread above us like gentle arms. Dozens of weathered tombstones marked the graves of my ancestors—people I didn't know. I did not feel any grief for a grandfather I'd never known. My daddy bowed his head, but his eyes, like his brother's, remained dry. Jonathan tried in vain to emulate the men, but he wept silent tears like the women.

When we returned from the gravesite, the slaves had a huge meal spread out on trestle tables in the yard. The lunch, too, was a somber affair. I stayed close to my father's side, listening as he discussed politics with the other men, until I grew tired of hearing about slave states and free states and a turbulent place called Kansas. Daddy didn't talk about my grandfather at all. Later, as quietly as they had come, the neighbors began to leave. My grandfather's funeral was the first I'd ever attended.

The next day was the Sabbath, and Aunt Abigail's husband conducted a church service for us on the plantation. The servants carried chairs outdoors for our family, setting them up in rows beneath the trees. They even hauled the parlor piano outside so Aunt Abigail could play hymns. Tessie, Eli, and all the other slaves sat on the ground or on handmade wooden benches behind us. The Negroes made up a much larger proportion of the congregation than us white folks. We sang "Rock of Ages" and "How Firm a Foundation." Then, after a prayer, Jonathan's father came forward to say a few words.

"I know many of you are concerned about my father's will," he said, addressing the slaves in the rear. "You may rest assured that it has been read and that his accounts are all in order. No one will have to be sold."

I looked over my shoulder to see if his words had relieved some of the tension I'd witnessed down in Slave Row a few nights earlier, but everyone seemed to be waiting for something more, as if collectively holding their breath. I nudged Jonathan, who was seated beside me.

"What's wrong with all the servants?" I whispered.

"Some of them are wondering if Grandfather set them free in his will."

"Did he?"

"Of course not. You've seen how big this place is. How could we run the plantation if we let the slaves go free?"

"I have inherited Hilltop and all its possessions," my uncle continued. "Things will go on just as they have in the past." I thought I heard someone behind me moan as Uncle William signaled for the service to continue.

The scripture text Aunt Abigail's husband read, from the book of Colossians, was a very familiar one: "'Servants, obey in all things your masters according to the flesh; not with eyeservice, as menpleasers; but in singleness of heart, fearing God . . . for ye serve the Lord Christ.'" I'd heard similar sermons preached in Richmond. But he surprised me by adding another verse from Colossians that I hadn't heard before: "'Masters, give unto your servants that which is just and equal; knowing that ye also have a Master in heaven.'"

I wondered what the Lord would say about Slave Row, if He would think it was "just and equal."

Cattle lowed in the distance as my uncle preached, leaves rustled in the treetops, my grandmother snored softly. My uncle told us that it pleased God when we obeyed His Word, that it offended Him when we disobeyed, and he reminded us that God's Word commanded us to obey our masters. "Look upon your daily tasks as the will of God," he said. "It's His will that some of you are slaves. Your earthly masters are God's overseers. Blessed are the faithful, those who are submissive, obedient. They will inherit the kingdom of heaven."

He had just concluded his sermon with a prayer when an elderly

Negro woman, as tiny and wiry as my grandmother, stood up in the back. "Preacher," she called out, "you say if I believe in Jesus I go to heaven? That right?"

"Yes, that's right." He glanced around nervously, as if unused to having his church services disrupted.

"I still be a slave in heaven?" she asked.

"Well . . ." He cleared his throat. "No one has ever returned from heaven, you see, to tell us what it's like. We have no way of knowing for sure—"

"But the Bible say heaven be paradise, ain't that right?"

He hesitated. "Well, yes. . . ."

"It ain't paradise for me if I still a slave."

I heard titters of laughter behind me from the other slaves. The preacher smiled weakly. "Well . . . now . . ."

"And I know it ain't paradise for white folks if y'all have to set down and eat that Marriage Supper of the Lamb beside us colored folk."

The slaves laughed out loud at her words. Several of my relatives squirmed in their seats. Jonathan's father stood, motioning for two of his house servants to remove the woman.

"Perhaps there's a white folks' heaven and black folks' heaven," my uncle said. "Then we'll all be happy."

Two Negroes had begun to lead the old woman away when she suddenly turned around and asked, "Then which heaven will all them little black children with white daddies be in?"

One of my aunts gasped. The gathering fell so silent I could almost hear the grass growing. Finally the preacher cleared his throat. He nodded to Aunt Abigail at the piano.

"My dear, the Doxology, please."

"What was that old woman talking about?" I whispered to Jonathan as the congregation sang "Praise God From Whom All Blessings Flow."

I don't know if Jonathan heard me or not. He didn't answer.

"Come for a walk in the woods with me," Jonathan said when we finished eating our Sunday dinner. His invitation sounded much better than an afternoon nap.

Of all the places to explore on the plantation, I grew to love the woods the best—the soft path of pine needles beneath my feet, the lush green vegetation, the fragrant scent of mulch and pine, the buzz and rattle of insects in the summer heat. Jonathan took my hand as we jumped from stone to stone to cross a small creek, and we walked that way, hand in hand, down the winding path. I felt very brave and adventurous. When we reached a small pond, a half-dozen frogs that had been sunning themselves along the muddy shoreline leaped into the water at our approach. We sat down to rest, side by side on the grassy bank, and counted seven box turtles perched on floating logs. Jonathan tossed acorns at the closest ones, trying to scare them into the water.

"I would have brought my pole and taught you how to fish if it hadn't been the Sabbath," he said after a while.

I tried to picture myself fishing and couldn't. "I don't think proper young ladies are supposed to go fishing—even when it's not the Sabbath."

"Who says?"

"The teachers at my school in Richmond. They would think it was scandalous for me to go hiking in the woods with you, much less go fishing. They're always trying to teach us what's proper and what isn't. Above all, we're supposed to remember that we're delicate young ladies."

"Doesn't sound like much fun at all," he said, laughing.

"It isn't. Where do you go to school?"

"Me? Right here on the plantation. Father hired a tutor to teach my brothers and me. He's away now for the summer."

We rose after a while and continued our lazy hike. Jonathan

pointed out many of the trees we passed—sassafras, willow oak, hackberry, sweet gum, Virginia pine, red cedar.

"Did your tutor teach you all those names?" I asked.

"No. Grandfather taught me."

I wondered if Grandfather had once taught my daddy the names of all the trees. And if he still remembered them.

Suddenly Jonathan stopped. He turned to me with a very serious look on his face. "You'd better wait back here where it's safe," he warned. "See that pit up ahead? We use it to trap wild animals. Who knows? There might be one trapped in there right now."

My heart leaped like a frog into a pond. "W-what kind of wild animals?"

"Oh, you know, wildcats, bears, panthers. . . ."

Fear froze me to the spot. The woods around me felt eerie and threatening. When something suddenly rustled in the bushes behind me, I ran into Jonathan's arms, clinging to him. "Take me home! I want to go home!"

To my surprise, he burst into laughter. "Oh, Carrie, I'm sorry. I was only teasing. There aren't really any wild animals."

I didn't want to let go of him until I was sure. "Th-then what was that sound?"

"I tossed a rock into the brush. I didn't know you'd be this scared. Honest, Carrie, I'm sorry." But it took him a minute to stop laughing. "You should have seen your face!" he sputtered. I managed to laugh along with him, mostly with relief.

"The pit is really our ice pit," he explained. "Come here, I'll show you. The servants cut blocks of ice from the river in the wintertime and bury them here, beneath the sand and leaves. They'll stay frozen a long time under there. That's how we have ice in the summertime."

I had to sit down by the edge of the pit until my knees stopped trembling. Jonathan dug up a chunk of ice and chipped off a few pieces with his pocketknife for us to suck on, wiping them clean with his handkerchief.

"You're a very pretty girl, you know that?" he said quietly. "I've never seen a girl half as pretty as you before."

I didn't know what to say. I also didn't know why my heart suddenly started to pound again, just as it had after Jonathan scared me.

"Come on," he said, reaching to help me up. "There's one more place I want to show you. I promise it's very safe."

"Promise you won't ever tease me again?"

"Well . . ." he said with a wide grin, "I promise I won't tease you again *today*. How's that?"

He led me a long way into the woods until we came to a small clearing in the middle of a grove of pines. The trees were very tall, surrounding us like pillars, the branches arching overhead like the nave of a cathedral. The atmosphere was as hushed and reverent as any church sanctuary back home, and every bit as beautiful. Even the wind seemed to whisper, so I did, too.

"I would love to live here."

"Then why don't you?" I looked up at Jonathan to see if he was joking. He wasn't. "You don't have to go home when your father does. We drive into Richmond every month or so for supplies. We can take you home at the end of the summer."

I sat down on a fallen log to think about the idea and to enjoy the gentle beauty all around me. I couldn't understand why my daddy would ever want to leave a wonderful place like Hilltop to live in Richmond. I decided to accept my cousin's invitation and stay here a while longer. I liked the plantation. But even more, I liked Jonathan.

My cousin was handsome, kind, and lots of fun to be with. We'd already become good friends. But what I was beginning to feel toward him was very different from the childhood friendship I'd shared with Grady. I didn't realize it at the time, but Jonathan was fast becoming my first adolescent crush.

I loved the feel of his rough hand in mine, the hard muscles of his arm as we bumped shoulders on the path. And as we sat side by side in the secluded grove, I wondered what it would feel like for Jonathan to kiss my neck the way Josiah had kissed Tessie's.

"Want an adventure?" Jonathan asked suddenly. "The Negroes are meeting here tonight. Want to sneak out and watch them with me? Your boy is going to preach."

"My . . . boy?" I was confused, thinking he must mean Grady.

"Yeah, your boy Eli. Don't you know he's the Negro folks' preacher? They're coming from all the neighboring plantations to hear him. But you can't tell anyone. It's a secret."

"Then how do you know about it?"

"I know lots of things." He stood, pulling me to my feet beside him. "So, do you want to sneak out tonight and watch or not?"

I fell asleep waiting for Jonathan, but as soon as I heard his soft whistle I was wide-awake. My heart began pounding when I saw him crouching outside on the porch roof, motioning to me through the open window. I never dreamed that I'd have to crawl around on the rooftop in the dark. But I'd already agreed to go on this adventure, and I was still wearing my clothes beneath the bedcovers. I tried to push aside my fear along with the mosquito netting that encircled my bed.

As I tiptoed across the room, I peered over at Tessie to see if my movements had awakened her. The lump on her pallet didn't move. In fact, she seemed unnaturally still. I looked closer and discovered that she'd padded her bed with pillows. Tessie was already gone.

Jonathan helped me climb through the window, and we crept across the roof to the ladder he had waiting. I closed my eyes and began to descend, careful not to look at the ground until I was standing safely upon it again. Then we raced across the dew-damp grass to the woods. I was excited—and terrified. The forest seemed much scarier at night, the sounds otherworldly. And walking down the narrow path in the dark was much harder, too. Jonathan gripped my hand tightly to keep me from stumbling.

"Are you sure there aren't any wild animals?" I asked.

"Just deer and skunks and raccoons and such. Nothing dangerous. The worst we might run into are hogs. They run wild until slaughtering time. Sometimes the boars can be mean."

"Do you think we'll meet any boars?" I hated that my voice shook.

"I brought my knife," he said, pulling it from his pocket to show me. "Don't worry, you're safe with me."

We heard the sound of singing in the distance long before we got there. The Negroes were meeting in the same pine grove we'd visited earlier that day. When we were a short distance away, Jonathan steered me off the main path and we cut through the dense brush, careful not to be seen or to make too much noise. I saw flickering lights from two or three torches, but the meeting was hidden from view by a wall of quilts, strung on ropes around the perimeter of trees.

"What are the blankets for?" I whispered.

"To deaden the sound so it won't carry back to the house."

"But why?"

"Don't you know? The slaves are forbidden to leave the plantation without their masters' permission. And they're strictly forbidden to gather in groups like this without white supervision."

"Even for a church service?"

"For any reason. If they're caught they could be whipped."

I remembered the man with the lash-scarred back I'd seen down on Slave Row. The thought of someone doing that to Eli's broad back sent a shiver through me. "You're not going to tell anybody, are you?" I asked Jonathan.

"Of course not." He started to move forward again, then stopped. "And just so you know, it's against the law to teach them to read and write, too."

I remembered once asking my governess if Grady could study my lessons along with me. She had been horrified. *"Those people can't learn things like this,"* she'd said. *"They don't have the same minds we do. You can't teach a dog or a horse to read, can you?"*

66

"*Grady isn't a horse!*" I'd protested.

"*He isn't white, either.*"

"But why is it against the law for slaves to read and write?" I asked Jonathan. He looked astonished by my ignorance.

"Because if the Negroes can communicate in writing, they'll plan all sorts of things—secret things. Next thing you know, they'll write up some false papers and use them to run away. You have to kill a Negro if he learns to read and write."

Eli had said they would kill a Negro woman if she told who the father of her child was. I didn't want to believe that either one of them was telling the truth.

"Come on," Jonathan said, "follow me." He crouched down on his hands and knees to crawl forward. I tried not to think about snakes as I followed. Jonathan found a sheltered place for us under a bush, where we could see beneath the wall of blankets. Grass and insects tickled my arms and face as we lay down on our bellies to watch.

I can't begin to describe the sheer joy I witnessed that night. I'd never heard such singing before—certainly never in a church. The sound of it took my breath away. It was so much more than mere singing—it was dancing, swaying, clapping, shouting. A celebration. I couldn't stop my toes from tapping to the elaborate rhythms as the slaves clapped and stomped and drummed.

I never wanted the glorious music to end. But gradually it calmed down, changing into some of the slow, mournful songs I'd heard the slaves singing early each morning on their way to the fields and coming home again at night. By the time the music died away altogether, the people had found places to sit on the ground or on logs and tree stumps. Then Eli stepped forward to deliver his sermon, and I thought my heart would burst with love and pride. He began in the quiet, gentle voice I loved so much, but as he spoke I sensed a dreadful, wonderful power rising up inside him, transforming him.

"Long time ago," he began, "God's people all be slaves—just like us. But pretty soon Massa Jesus hear them groaning down there in Egypt land. He hear how they suffering. He know how they yearn for freedom. That sound reach His ear. And it touch His heart. That's how I know He hears our groaning, too."

"Yes!" Some of the slaves began to shout and moan. "Hear us, Lord Jesus!" Eli continued to preach above the sound, spurred on by it, it seemed.

"Pretty soon the time come when Massa Jesus say 'Enough!' He say 'No more' to this slavery! He say 'Let my people *go*!'"

There were more cries and shouts of "Halleluia!"

Eli's voice thundered with power. "That's how I know time's gonna come for our freedom, too. Jesus know it ain't right to make people you property. It ain't right they sell us like a horse or a bale of cotton. Ain't right they whip us and treat us like animals. Massa Jesus see everything we suffering, just like He see them Israelites suffering in Egypt land."

"Yes!"

"Amen!"

"And if we keep praying . . . if we keep believing . . . He gonna do right by us, too. He gonna hear our cry! And He gonna set us *free*!"

The shouts and cries of joy rose in a great crescendo until I could barely hear Eli above it all.

"'Cause the Lord is faithful to His people! He's a just Lord! A loving God! He gonna set us free from our bondage! Oh, yes sir! One day very soon we gonna be free at last!"

Suddenly Jonathan gripped my arm. When I turned and saw the look of alarm on his face, I nearly cried out in fright.

"What? What's wrong?" He scrambled from our hiding place, pulling me back the way we had come. "What's the matter?" I whispered again when we were on the main path.

"Your boy is preaching rebellion! He's trying to start a slave uprising, telling them they'll all be set free. This is exactly why slaves aren't allowed to meet, don't you see? There's more of them than there are of us. They'll rise up and kill us all in our beds some night, just like Nat Turner's men did."

"What are you talking about?"

"A slave named Nat Turner started an uprising just like this, right here in Virginia. The slaves went from plantation to plantation one night, slaughtering white people in their beds—even women and children."

"Eli would never do that!"

"You're very naïve, Caroline. All it takes is one or two trouble-makers to start a mob. We can't let them plan a rebellion. We have to go warn Father."

"No, wait! That wasn't what Eli was saying. He wasn't telling them to rebel—"

"Caroline, we're wasting time!"

I was desperate to stop him. I couldn't let Eli get into trouble. I was certain my cousin had misunderstood. "Wait!" I pleaded. "Wouldn't it be better if we stayed a few more minutes and heard exactly what they're planning?" The shouting and singing had died down once again. Eli had resumed preaching.

Jonathan looked toward the clearing, then at the path home, then back toward the clearing again, as if trying to decide what to do. At last, he reluctantly agreed. "All right. We'll stay until we find out what their plans are."

We crawled back to our hiding place in time to hear Eli say, "Now, don't y'all be getting ahead of the Lord. That's what Moses try and do. He take matters in his own hands and he kill that overseer one day. Moses think he doing the Lord's work. But he ain't."

The grove fell silent. Eli had everyone's full attention. Even the women had stopped fanning themselves.

"Now, I know them overseers be mean men. I know they be hate-ful men. But we can't be deciding for ourself what God should do and who He should kill. We can't be telling God how to run His business. We got to wait for the fullness of time. We got to trust

God's mercy and justice. When time come for us to be free—and it will come! Oh, yes sir, it will surely come!"

"Preach it, brother!"

"When the time come for our freedom, we won't have to lift a finger against our enemies. 'Vengeance is mine, saith the Lord. I will repay.' We just have to sit back and watch—just like the Israelites sit back and watch. And God gonna send His plagues down upon this land. Grasshoppers . . . and hail . . . and ruined crops . . . and dying cattle. God gonna send His plagues on this here land while we just sit back. And in the end, when God finish showing white folks His power, our time finally gonna come! We gonna be *free!*"

This time there were no shouts. The people simply stared at Eli— unbelieving, yet yearning to believe.

"You say we not have to fight for our freedom, Eli?" someone in the crowd finally asked.

"Yes sir, that's what gonna happen. The Bible say it ain't by the sword that they won the land, nor did their own arm bring them victory. God do it for them, with His right hand, because He loved them. It ain't gonna be our power but God's power that set us free! And when He set us free, brothers and sisters, we be free indeed!"

The people were on their feet as one, clapping, dancing, shouting. Someone started singing a song about freedom. Above it all I heard Eli shouting, "'Some trust in chariots and some in horses: but we will remember the name of the Lord our God.'"

I felt the thrill I always felt at Eli's conviction and faith. Then Jonathan tapped my shoulder and motioned for me to follow him.

"You aren't going to tell your father, are you?" I whispered when we were back on the path again. "You heard what Eli said—they won't lift a finger."

"I heard, but . . . what did he mean? God isn't going to set the slaves free. Slavery is part of God's plan. It's in the Bible."

"But the story Eli told is in the Bible, too. God did set the Israelites free. And they didn't have to fight the Egyptians. Pharaoh let them all go free after the firstborn sons died."

Jonathan waved impatiently. "I know the story. But those slaves weren't Negroes. The black race is cursed by God. Their skin color is the mark of Cain."

"How can you think that way? You said Josiah is your best friend."

"He is. But he's still a Negro. And he belongs to me, just like Tessie belongs to you."

"She doesn't belong to me—"

"Okay then, to your father. They're our slaves, Carrie. Nothing is ever going to change that."

Jonathan and Eli couldn't both be right.

As I finally crawled back into bed that night, I decided I believed Eli. I hid the words he'd spoken in my heart. Still, I couldn't imagine what he'd meant when he said God would show white folks His power—ruined crops and dying cattle. I was one of those white folks. And even though Eli had said the slaves shouldn't lift a finger against me, his words scared me to death.

CHAPTER

5

The next morning at breakfast I asked Daddy if I could stay at Hilltop instead of going home with him. He considered it for a long moment without answering. "Please," I begged, "Jonathan and I are just becoming friends—and I don't have any friends back home."

"All right," he finally agreed. "But Tessie and Eli will have to come back to Richmond with me."

I knew Daddy needed Eli to drive the carriage home, but I couldn't understand why Tessie had to leave, too. I'd never been without my mammy before, and I didn't want to be without her now.

"Why, Daddy? Why can't Tessie stay here with me?"

"Because there are plenty of servants to help out around here. Tessie is needed back home." He wouldn't look at me when he spoke, and I had the feeling there was more to it than he was willing to say. But he had made up his mind, and I could tell that I wouldn't be able to change it. Before I'd come to Hilltop I never could have imagined being separated from Tessie. But my adventures with my cousin had made me stronger, braver. I decided to stay without her.

I ran upstairs to my room where Tessie was packing our things, and told her I was staying and she was going home. I bravely fought my tears as we kissed and hugged good-bye, then I hurried outside to say good-bye to Eli. As I neared the barn I heard his gentle voice, but it didn't sound like he was talking to the horses or to Massa Jesus. I peered around the open doorway and saw him deep in conversation with his son, Josiah. I waited outside, giving them time alone. But I couldn't help overhearing their conversation.

"There something I need you to do for me, Pa," Josiah said. "I need you to take care Tessie for me when you get back home. She my wife now. We jump the broom the other night."

"Son . . . you didn't!" Eli sounded shaken. "You know you can't marry Tessie without Massa's say-so. And you know for sure Massa Fletcher ain't giving it to you."

"I don't need no white man's say-so."

"Son, listen—"

"No! She's my wife now. Ain't no one telling me I can't marry the woman I love."

"Tessie's going back to Richmond with Miss Caroline and me," Eli said firmly. "So how you two gonna be husband and wife?"

"I plan on buying our freedom someday. I'm working as a blacksmith now. If Massa hire me out, I can earn my freedom doing extra work, then I move to town and make enough money to buy hers."

"You know my massa ain't never gonna sell Tessie to you. And you know why."

"She's my wife now!"

"Not without Massa's say-so she ain't. Son, the path you heading down lead to nothing but trouble. They get mad at you, they sell you south as fast as you can turn around."

"They wouldn't sell me—"

"They sold *Grady*!"

Something about the way Eli spoke those words—as if he still couldn't believe they were true—sent a shiver through me.

"Please, Josiah," Eli begged. "Don't act this way."

"I have to!" he shouted. "I'm not like you. I can't lay down and be a dog for the massa. I'm a *man,* not a dog!"

Eli grabbed his son's shirtfront and hauled him close, speaking right in his face. "Now you get one thing straight. I know I'm just as good as any white man. Ain't no difference between me and Massa Fletcher in God's sight. Bible say there neither slave nor free, but we all one in Christ Jesus."

Josiah shook himself loose. "If you believe that, then why you acting all *yes sir* and *no sir*? Why you letting them white folks treat you like dirt? How can you live with yourself?"

"Because Jesus is my massa, not Massa Fletcher, and Jesus tell me I have to turn the other cheek. He say do good to them that persecute me. Night before He died, He wash all them white men's feet, even the one who betrayed Him. And He say, 'Do just like me.' Jesus is God's *son* and the white folk treat *Him* like dirt! They whip Him till He half dead, then they crucify Him. Ain't no different than way they treat us. Jesus say, 'Take up you cross and follow me.' God knows how we're treated, Josiah. He put us where we are for time being and give us a job to do. And even if I can't see a reason why, I gonna do this job for Jesus. I gonna love white folks, whether they love me back or not, 'cause that's what Jesus tell me to do."

"How you know what Jesus say?" Josiah said angrily. "That's only what them white preachers say is in the Bible. They tell us that stuff to keep us low. I don't believe any of it. They lie to us."

"They not lying. That's what the Bible really say."

"How you know?"

"'Cause I can read it for myself!"

The shock of Eli's words seemed to rip through the air like a whip. The hair on my arms stood on end. *"You have to kill a Negro if he learns to read."*

Josiah stared at his father, stunned. Eli seemed shaken by his own confession, too. In a quieter voice, he said, "I know how to read, son. I have me a Bible of my own. Preacher man in Richmond give

74

it to me one time and I reading it every day. I know what it say. It say 'Love you enemies . . . return evil with good . . . bless them that persecute you.'"

I could tell Josiah wasn't listening. He shook his head as if dazed. "You never told me you could read."

"Well, now you know. I can."

Josiah's voice rose in volume. "Then why didn't you teach *me* how to read?"

"Son, I waiting all your life till you learn to control your temper. But you never did learn. If I teach you to read, I be killing you myself. I may as well be stabbing a knife in you. Devil get ahold of you and use your reading for his purpose, not God's."

As they stared at each other, I saw all the anger leave Eli's face. It was replaced by sorrow. "Josiah, I be going soon. I can't leave here with bitterness between us. Lord knows when I ever see you again."

Eli went to his son, embraced him. At first Josiah's arms hung limp at his sides. The two men were the same height, had the same wide shoulders and strong arms. One head of hair was black, the other gray. Slowly, Josiah lifted his arms and returned his father's embrace.

"Guard your heart, son," Eli said in a hushed voice. "That's what God looks at—your heart. Most folks look at the outside things, like the color of your skin. But God looks at your heart."

I settled comfortably into the rhythm of country life, enjoying the freedom of long, leisurely days, the excitement of new places to explore, and the contentment of my cousin's friendship. The carefree life I led wasn't typical of a woman's life on the plantation, though. Grandmother and Aunt Anne worked hard all day, everyday, overseeing the work that needed to be done. There was laundry to scrub, candles and soap to make, homespun cloth to be woven and dyed, then sewn into clothing for both the slaves and the family. The garden needed to be tended, the house cleaned, the food preserved, the cows milked, the butter churned, meat salted and smoked, and three hearty meals cooked and served each day. I wanted nothing to do with learning how to take charge of all that work.

I'd always been a bit of a tomboy when I'd played with Grady— before my teachers at the Richmond Female Institute tried to drum into me that proper young ladies didn't climb trees or wander through the woods or lie on riverbanks fishing. But for those few wonderful weeks at Hilltop, I didn't care about being a proper young lady. The Institute had taught my mother to be a lady, and I shuddered at the thought of living a life like hers. I loved the outdoors, and I didn't care one bit if my complexion turned as sunbrowned as Jonathan's. We explored the woods together, read books to each other beneath the trees, and simply gazed up at the stars and talked. I noticed that he was careful to keep me away from the harsher side of plantation life, such as the slaves laboring in the fields beneath the blazing sun, or life down on Slave Row, but one lazy, rainy day, as we sat in the parlor playing a game of dominoes, I asked him about the man I'd seen with the lash scars on his back.

"Our overseer isn't a cruel man," Jonathan replied. "He might yell and crack the whip a few times over everybody's head, but he would never give forty lashes like that unless it was absolutely necessary. My father would never allow his slaves to be abused."

"Then why did he whip that man?"

Jonathan hesitated, choosing his words as carefully as his next domino. "We caught him stealing bacon from our smokehouse. He had to be whipped in order to set an example. Otherwise, all the other slaves might start stealing from us, too. It's your turn," he added impatiently.

I studied my remaining dominoes, then played one. "I once saw slaves in Richmond wearing leg-irons and chains," I said. "Daddy told me it was because they'd tried to run away."

"Our people hardly ever try to run away. They know they have it good here. We take good care of them."

"But their cabins are so small, and they only have dirt floors, and—"

"The slaves don't care. They're used to it. They're not like us, Carrie." He was growing annoyed. I didn't know whether it was from our conversation or because he'd had to draw a half-dozen dominoes from the bone pile before finding one he could use. "Besides," he added, "our slaves are treated a lot better than the immigrants who work in the factories up north. Ever see where they live? And nobody gives them free clothing and food like we give our slaves."

I played another piece, then hid my last domino in my hand so he couldn't see it. "If the slaves are contented and happy, then why does everyone worry so much about them rebelling like Nat what's-his-name?"

"Some of the slaves are fools and very easily led. If another leader like Nat Turner came along, they might be persuaded to do anything." Jonathan groaned when he had to draw three more dominoes.

"No one could ever persuade Eli or Tessie to murder me," I said, playing my last piece.

Jonathan stood, sweeping the dominoes into the box with one hand as if wiping a slate. "I'd trust Josiah with my life, too. But there are more than fifty colored folk down in Slave Row and only half a dozen of us up here. We'd be fools to turn our backs on them." He was angry. And I knew it wasn't because I'd won the game. I decided never to talk about such things with him again.

The next morning, with the sun shining brightly again, Jonathan and his father left to attend a meeting at a neighboring plantation. Afterward, they were going to spend a few days drilling with the local militia—Jonathan's first time.

"Seems like I've been waiting all my life to finally join the militia," he said with a grin. He lifted an imaginary gun to his shoulder, aimed, and fired. "Can't wait to get my hands on a rifle for once, instead of Pa's old shotgun."

Jonathan's older brother, Will, was left in charge of the plantation for a few days. I hadn't gotten to know Will at all. He was more serious than his easygoing younger brother and told me flat-out that he was much too busy to entertain me in Jonathan's absence. Bored, I turned to my six-year-old cousin Thomas for companionship.

Thomas' playmates were the little Negro children who ran around the yard chasing chickens and running errands. They were delighted when I took charge of them, organizing their play, teaching them new games, reading stories to them beneath the pear tree. We quickly became friends, the younger children clinging to my skirts and fighting over whose turn it was to sit on my lap or hold my hand. I tried not to play favorites, but I couldn't help falling in love with Nellie, the pretty little Negro girl whose job it was to fan my grandmother as she sewed or napped in the sweltering heat of early August.

One day, Nellie's little brother Caleb somehow escaped from the old granny who usually tended the little ones down on Slave Row, and he followed her up to the plantation house. He couldn't have been more than two years old, toddling along behind her, naked as the dawn.

"Go on! Get back where you belong," Nellie scolded as my grandmother called impatiently to her from the house. But Caleb wouldn't go home, and every time Nellie took a step toward the back door to obey Grandmother, Caleb followed her, wailing loudly. "You can't come in the house!" she told him. "You ain't allowed!"

We always left the doors open, and I could see that he was going to follow her right inside. With my grandmother yelling threats, Nellie didn't have time to take Caleb home.

"Go on inside, Nellie. Hurry," I told her. "I'll take him back." I lifted the howling boy into my arms and headed down to Slave Row, soothing his tears as I went. He was a beautiful child, with smooth, ebony skin and dark, soulful eyes. Long before we reached his shack, I'd won a smile from him—and lost my heart to him.

From a distance, I heard babies crying in one of the cabins. Outside, two toddlers no older than Caleb played in the dirt street, unattended. Then the old Negro granny who had interrupted my uncle's church service emerged from one of the cabins. She peered beneath it, around it, then up and down the row calling, "Caleb! Caleb, where are you, child?"

"He's here, Granny. I have him."

She watched me approach, shaking her head. "That one always getting away from me. And I got my hands full today with all them sick babies."

She scooped up the two squirming toddlers and disappeared into the cabin. I followed her, carrying Caleb. "Go on, set him down here with these ones," she said, putting her two charges down on the dirt floor. "Time they eat something."

She chased a swarm of flies away from a wooden bowl, took a wedge of corn bread out of it, and broke off a chunk for each child. Caleb devoured his, then carefully picked up all the crumbs that had fallen in the dirt and ate those, too. Meanwhile, Granny turned her attention to the squalling babies. There were four of them—all naked, all crying at once—lying crossways on a mattress stuffed with corn shucks. She picked up the first baby, jiggling him in her arms, and ladled a spoonful of water into his open mouth.

"Got my hands full today," she repeated. "All four of 'em sick with fever."

I picked up one of the other babies, a little girl, and spooned water into her mouth like Granny was doing. The child's sweaty body was as warm as a baked potato and covered with a nasty-looking rash.

"You should bathe them in cool water," I told Granny. "It helps bring the fever down." That was what Tessie always did whenever I had a fever. Granny looked at me helplessly.

"How I gonna do all that and keep these others from running off, same time?"

"I-I'll help you. If you could fetch some cool water in a basin . . . and some clean cloths . . ."

Caleb clung to my skirt as I worked, wailing for more food. All I could find was the other half of the corn bread, so I divided it among the three children. Too late, I realized it was probably Granny's lunch.

She and I worked hard, bathing and rocking the babies—while trying to keep the three bigger ones from toddling away. I didn't realize how much time had passed until I heard the dinner bell ringing up at the plantation house.

"I have to go," I told Granny. "But I'll come back to help you this afternoon."

I hurried up to the house for lunch and found the dining room table spread with food—smoked pork, potatoes roasted in butter, green beans and tomatoes picked fresh from the garden that morning, soft white biscuits spread with melting butter, and sweet potato pie for dessert, still warm from the oven. My cousins Will and Thomas shoveled down their food as if it were their last meal. I couldn't eat a bite.

"What's wrong, dear?" Aunt Anne asked. "You're not getting sick on me, are you?"

"No, ma'am. I'm fine."

"Then you'd better start eating, or these boys of mine won't leave you a thing."

I ate. But I wrapped most of my lunch in my napkin, hidden on my lap, to bring down to Granny and the children. I was ashamed of myself for ever taking all this food for granted. I kept thinking of the slave who had been whipped for stealing bacon, and of the Bible verse my uncle had quoted: "Masters, give unto your servants that which is just and equal . . ." Dry corn bread hardly seemed equal.

"Aunt Anne, some of the little slave babies are sick," I told her when the meal ended. "May I please take some ice down there to help cool their fevers?"

"Our ice?"

"Yes, please. They don't have any ice of their own."

She frowned as if she was very annoyed, but I knew she didn't mean anything by it. Aunt Anne had a very kind heart. "You don't need to concern yourself with our slaves, Caroline. I'll go down after we have a little rest and see what I can do for them."

"Please, ma'am . . . I don't want to rest. I want to help the babies. They know me now. And I want to bring them my talcum powder. I think the rash must itch them."

She studied me for a long moment with the same expression Jonathan often gave me—as if what I'd said was very odd. "All right," she finally said. "I'll have one of the darkies carry down some ice for you. I'll come as soon as I can."

I bathed the babies, then soothed their itchy skin with talcum powder while Granny and the three older children shared the remains of my lunch. Two of the babies eventually slept, while the other two whimpered softly, exhausted from crying.

"They have measles," Aunt Anne said when she arrived a while later. "I pray to the Good Lord that you don't catch it, too, Caroline. I fear you've already been exposed."

For the next week, I hurried down to Slave Row early every morning to help Granny tend the sick babies. Unable to eat, they grew very weak. Caleb and the other two toddlers came down with measles, too, then my sweet little Nellie and another child her age fell sick. I nursed them all day and would have stayed all night if my aunt had allowed it. The children grew sicker and sicker.

"We should pray for them," I told Granny one day after my aunt had gone back to the house to prepare some more willow bark tea. Granny shook her head.

"We don't pray for our babies to live. All they'll ever know is misery and slavery. Much better if Jesus just take them home right now."

"You don't mean that! No mother would ever want her babies to die!" I thought of my mother, grieving for her dead babies.

"Well, these here mamas do. They know them babies better off in Jesus' arms than growing up to be a slave. Better she give them to Jesus right now than to the massa to be sold later on. Then she never have to wonder where her children are at, or if they suffering."

I lay in bed that night thinking of Granny's words. I wondered who suffered more—my mother, who knew her babies were in heaven, or Tessie, who didn't know where her child was or if she'd ever see him again.

The next day I didn't return to the cabin. I was sick with the measles myself.

Aunt Anne immediately sent for the doctor. Hovering over my bed day and night, she worried herself nearly to death until it became clear that I would recover. When Jonathan returned, she let him sit with me during the day, reading books to me, telling me all about the grand time he'd had with the militia, playing checkers with me when I finally felt well enough. He'd already had the measles.

"How are Caleb and Nellie?" I asked him one day. "And all the babies?" I had tried asking Aunt Anne but she only grew vexed with me for pestering her about them.

"Fine," he said offhandedly.

I threw one of the bed pillows at him in frustration. "You're not telling me the truth. I want to know the truth."

"You shouldn't get so involved, Carrie," he said, tossing back the pillow. "They're only slaves. You wouldn't be sick yourself right now if you hadn't meddled where you had no business meddling."

I felt pulled in two directions at once. I liked Jonathan and I wanted him to like me, but I hated the way he talked about the Negroes, the way he treated them. I knew it bothered him that I cared so much, but I couldn't help myself. I'd held and soothed and rocked those little babies. I'd fallen in love with Nellie and little Caleb. I needed to know how they were faring. I flung back the covers and lowered my feet to the floor.

"If you won't tell me the truth, then I'll just have to go down there and see for myself."

"Over my dead body!" He came out of his chair in a flash, scooped me up as if I weighed nothing at all, and dropped me back into bed. "Now listen," he said when we were both calmer, "the truth is, I don't know how any of them are. We've all been too worried about you to bother with them. But if you promise to stay put, I'll send for one of the Negro girls who lives down there. She can tell you what you want to know."

That afternoon one of the scrub maids came, a tall, dazed-looking girl about my own age. She showed no emotion at all as she stood in my bedroom doorway and told me the awful truth. "Nellie on the mend now, Miss Caroline. But Caleb and little Kate gone to be with Jesus. All four of them babies gone, too. No help for them, I guess."

All the grief that I'd felt over losing Grady returned, magnified tenfold. I wept and wept. I couldn't stop crying. Even when I was no longer sobbing out loud, the tears silently fell, all that day and into the night. It scared me that I couldn't seem to stop. It scared Aunt Anne, too. She sent for the doctor.

"Caroline has recovered from the measles," he told her. "But I think you'd better take her home."

I wept as I watched the servants pack my clothes, along with the bird's nest and the butterfly's wings and all the other treasures I'd collected with Jonathan. Uncle William would accompany me to Richmond tomorrow. I was sorry to go, yet I knew I couldn't bear to stay. Slave Row wasn't visible from the big house, but that didn't stop me from thinking about it.

Later that night, I awoke to the sound of voices in the next room. My aunt and uncle had left their bedroom door ajar, and I could hear them talking as they prepared for bed.

"Do you suppose her hysteria could have been caused by her

fever?" Aunt Anne asked. "She seemed fine the first few weeks she spent with us. A little skittish, perhaps, but she didn't cry like this."

My uncle's boots dropped to the floor, one after the other. "Her mother's the same way, Anne. Goes from one extreme to the other. She has terrible crying spells. It's a real shame, but it looks like the daughter is turning out to be the same way."

The thought of being just like my mother started my tears falling all over again.

"Poor George must certainly have his hands full with two of them like this," my aunt said. "I had only one of them and I was at my wits' end. Has he considered an asylum?"

"Heavens, no! George nearly took my head off when I suggested it." The bed creaked as one of them climbed into it. "No, my foolish brother wanted to marry that woman—the belle of all Richmond. I tried to warn him that she was high-strung, but he just had to have her. Now he's living with that mistake."

"Jonathan asked me if he could go to Richmond with you tomorrow," my aunt said after a moment.

"No. I already told him that he couldn't." The shaft of light from their doorway vanished as one of them snuffed out the light. "Caroline is a beautiful girl, Anne, in spite of her moodiness. She has a hypnotic quality about her—a vulnerability—that attracts foolish young boys like Jonathan. From now on, I don't want him anywhere near her."

I heard the haunting song of the slaves the next morning for the last time. As we drove past them laboring in the fields, I looked away.

6

RICHMOND, OCTOBER 1856

Back in Richmond, my life quickly returned to its old routine. I couldn't forget everything I'd experienced, but I managed to push most of it from my mind, packing away my disquieting thoughts and my grief like the dolls and other toys I'd outgrown. For the next two years, my mother's condition seemed to slowly improve. She spent more and more time downstairs in the drawing room instead of in her bedroom, and she even entertained guests for dinner once in a while. One afternoon when I came home from school, Ruby called me to my mother's sitting room.

Mother was smiling, and her curtains and shutters were open, but she couldn't seem to be still. She flitted restlessly around the small room, her hoop skirts swirling, her nervous hands picking up first one object, then another, quickly discarding them again.

"I have some wonderful news I want to discuss with you, Caroline. In private." Her voice had that frenzied breathlessness I'd grown to dread. "Ladies don't talk about such things in polite company, you know."

"What things?"

"You must tell no one, Caroline, but I'm finally expecting another child. I waited to tell you until the doctor was certain I was past the danger point. He says the baby is strong and healthy, and I'm not likely to lose it. But just to be sure, I must stay in confinement for the remainder of my time. I'm not even allowed to go to church."

I tried to act pleased, but the news terrified me. I recalled the terrible grief I'd felt after the babies died at Hilltop, and I worried about what would happen to my mother if her baby died. I tried to pray, putting all my worry into Jesus' hands, as Eli had taught me, but the worry and fear grew and swelled inside me even as the baby grew inside my mother.

One cold February day when Eli brought me home from school, the doctor's carriage stood parked by our front gate. Fear gripped my stomach in its fist and wouldn't let go. "Is Mother sick again?" I asked Eli.

"Better ask Tessie. She know."

"Is it time for Mother's baby?"

"Shush! Ain't fitting to talk of such things."

As soon as I came through the door, Tessie was waiting for me. "Where's Mother? Can I see her?"

"Now, you best stay down here, child, 'til the baby come."

I thought I could hear my mother moaning now and then as I waited nervously in the parlor. Tessie finally took me outside to the kitchen to distract me. Esther had all sorts of pots and kettles going in the fire, as usual, and the fragrant room quickly swallowed some of my fear in its steamy warmth. I sat down at the table across from Eli and watched the cold sleet wash down the windowpane outside.

"What's it like to have a baby?" I asked.

Esther rolled her eyes. "Ain't no picnic, I tell you that."

"What makes Mother cry out so?"

Eli leaped up from his chair and fled the kitchen.

"Hush, now," Tessie warned.

"Why won't anyone tell me?" I asked.

"Because it ain't fitting to talk about such things," Tessie scolded. "You find out when the time come. And I ain't gonna say no more about it, so quit asking."

When I heard Daddy's carriage arrive, I ran back through the cold sleet to the house. He immediately went upstairs to talk to the doctor, then came down again and asked Gilbert to pour him a drink. I went into the library to see him, but Daddy never did sit down in his chair. He paced nervously across the room to the window, looked out at the doctor's carriage, covered with slush, then paced back to his desk, over and over again. I grew tired just watching him.

"Is Mother all right?" I finally asked.

"The doctor says so."

I was afraid to ask about the baby.

Neither of us ate much of the supper Esther had made, but I saw Ruby carry up a huge tray of food for the doctor. The baby still hadn't come when it was time for me to go to bed. I slept poorly, listening to Mother's moans in the night.

The next morning, Tessie came to sit beside me on the bed, gently stroking my hair. "You mama had a little boy baby last night," she said softly. "But he all blue, just like the others. He in heaven now, with the angels."

"What about Mother?"

"She okay."

"Is she . . . is she going to die?"

"No, the doctor say she ain't gonna die. But I think she want to."

The doctor was wrong. Before nightfall, my mother was dead.

Mother's older sister, Martha, came down from Philadelphia by train for the funeral. Aunt Anne and Uncle William drove into town from Hilltop. Jonathan, who now attended the College of William and Mary, arrived by paddle steamer from Williamsburg. He wrapped his arm around my waist to hold me up as I stood beside Mother's open grave in Hollywood Cemetery. The gaping hole in the ground, the bare tree branches, the black mourners' clothes all looked stark against the frozen white ground. I had just turned sixteen, and my first grown-up dress, with long sleeves and proper hoops, was a black mourning gown.

That night after everyone else had gone to sleep, I slipped from my bed and went down the hall to my mother's room. Ruby sat all alone on the edge of Mother's neatly made bed, a single candle on the dressing table casting an eerie light. Ruby looked up as I entered, and I saw that she'd been crying.

"Ruby . . ." My voice sounded loud in the quiet night. "Ruby, there's something I need to know."

"You as pretty as she always was," Ruby murmured as I stepped closer. I cleared the knot of fear from my throat.

"The doctor said my mother was fine after the baby was born . . . but Mother died."

Ruby said nothing. I didn't want to ask the question out loud, but she wasn't going to make this easy for me.

"How . . . how did my mother die?"

Ruby shook her head as if she wanted both me and my question to go away. I knelt on the floor in front of her, face to face, taking her hands in mine.

"I came here to see Mother the day the baby was born. She didn't have a fever. She wasn't sick. . . ." I waited. "Please tell me, Ruby."

"Seem like . . . seem like maybe your mama make a mistake," she said in a tiny voice. "She not sleeping much, you know . . . and maybe she want to sleep. Laudanum pill always help her sleep, but maybe . . . maybe she take too many this time . . . by accident."

"Is that what you think, Ruby? That it was an accident?"

She closed her eyes. By the light of the single candle, I watched the tears roll down her cheeks. When she opened her eyes again, she smiled. "I glad they bury her little baby with her. Now he won't be all alone in that cold ground. Your mama so worried about that. Said a child need its mama." She squeezed my hands tightly, her eyes pleading, begging me to understand. "Your mama didn't want to leave her child all alone, Missy Caroline."

I wanted to understand, but I couldn't. I was her child, too. I needed my mother. And she had left me all alone.

My father seemed to age twenty years overnight. He wouldn't eat, couldn't sleep, and spent most of the time in his library, where Gilbert endlessly refilled his glass. Daddy and Uncle William had shouted at each other in loud voices the night before my uncle returned to Hilltop, but I didn't hear what they'd said. When it was time for Aunt Martha to return to Philadelphia, she and Daddy called me into the library one night. The sight of his grief-ravaged face brought tears to my eyes.

"I have business overseas, Caroline," Daddy said without preamble. "I'm sailing at the end of this week. Aunt Martha has offered to take you to Philadelphia to live with her for a while."

I couldn't find the words to tell him that I didn't want anything to change, that too many things had changed already. I felt this new loss as if it had already taken place. "I want to stay here, Daddy," I said desperately. "With you."

"I can't stay, Caroline." He glanced up at me, then quickly looked away. I knew I reminded him of Mother. I saw the resemblance myself in the mirror every morning. "I'll be gone for several months," he continued. "Your Aunt Martha doesn't think you should stay here alone."

"I won't be alone. I have Tessie and Eli and Esther. . . ."

"That's not an option," Daddy said harshly. "If you stay in Richmond you will have to board at school."

His words filled me with dread. I'd lost my mother, and now I was losing my daddy and my home, too. Aunt Martha came to me, slipping her arm around my shoulders, taking my hand in hers.

"Boarding schools are terribly lonely places, Caroline. After all you've been through, don't you think it might be better if you lived in a home for a while, with your family? I have two girls of my own who are about your age. They'll be company for you."

"The only other choice," Daddy said, "is to stay with my brother at Hilltop."

I didn't care for any of those choices. I knew I would hate boarding school—the cold gray hallways and barren rooms, standing in line for everything. I had no friends there—the other girls weren't like me at all. Nor could I go back to Hilltop with an aunt and uncle who thought I belonged in an asylum. My cousin Jonathan was away at college, and I didn't think I could stand being at Hilltop without him, living in the plantation house with papered walls and rich food on the table while the slaves lived in drafty cabins with dirt floors and cornshuck beds. I would never get used to seeing beautiful children like Caleb and Nellie hungry and sick, knowing their mothers were praying that they would die. That left Philadelphia as my only option—and I had no idea what to expect if I went there. Aunt Martha was as plump and plain as one of Esther's biscuits. She had none of my mother's beauty nor her shifting moods. She seemed kind.

She gently squeezed my hand. "Come to Philadelphia with me, Caroline."

"How long would I have to stay?"

"As long as you'd like. You can enroll in school with my girls."

"Could I come home again if I didn't like it there?"

"You'd have to agree to give it a reasonable amount of time," my father said. "It's not easy traveling back and forth at the drop of a hat. Especially after making all the arrangements for school."

"Why don't we say . . . at least until the school term ends in June,"

Aunt Martha said. "That's only four months away. Then we can see how you feel about staying longer."

In the end I agreed to go. I didn't seem to have much choice. Aunt Martha wanted to leave by the end of the week, which didn't give Tessie much time to pack our things.

"I've never ridden on a train before, have you?" I asked Tessie the night before we were scheduled to leave.

"No, I sure ain't never been on any train." Her voice sounded muffled, coming from inside the huge steamer trunk she was bending over.

"Are you excited, Tessie?"

She straightened, still holding a pile of folded clothes in her hands. She looked puzzled. "Excited? I ain't going on the train with you, Missy."

"What?"

"Oh, child . . . didn't they tell you? I staying here. I thought you knew."

I ran from the room, raced down the curved stairs, and barged into my father's library without knocking.

"I've changed my mind," I told him. "I don't want to go to Philadelphia."

It took him a moment to recover from my outburst. He looked disoriented, disheveled, the glass in his hand nearly empty. His shirt-front was wrinkled and stained, his usually neat hair unkempt, his face flushed. "It's too late now. I've purchased your train ticket, made all the traveling arrangements, notified the school. You're going to Philadelphia."

"You didn't tell me Tessie wasn't coming. I don't want to go without Tessie."

He looked away. "Well, I'm sorry, but Tessie can't go. It's out of the question."

"Why? Why can't she go?"

He tried to relight his cigar, but his hands shook so badly he couldn't strike the match. "People do things differently up north. They don't have Negro mammies, for one thing. And they don't care very much for people who do. The abolitionists and free Negroes will fill her head with crazy talk about running away."

"Tessie would never run away from me."

"Don't be too sure. It's different up there, you'll see. Tessie would be out of place, like a fish out of water. Ever see what happens when you take a fish out of water?"

"I need Tessie—"

"No! I need her here!" He picked up the whiskey bottle, sloshing it all over his desk as he poured another drink. This man wasn't my daddy. I couldn't bear to watch him toss back his head and drain the glass. I stalked to the door.

"You're sixteen now," he said as I reached it. "It's time you outgrew your mammy."

I stumbled up the stairs, trying not to cry. I was afraid that if I started I wouldn't be able to stop again. I would *never* outgrow my mammy. Hadn't Ruby been my mother's mammy all her life?

Tessie came to me as soon as I walked into the room. Her beautiful face was etched with concern. She rubbed my shoulders and stroked my hair, murmuring, "I thought you knew, baby. I thought they told you."

"Would you be a fish out of water if you went with me?" I asked, still fighting my tears.

"Is that what your daddy say?"

"Yes. And he said he needs you here." Her hands froze. She looked at me with an odd expression on her face, but it passed before I could define it.

"Your girl cousins won't have mammies in Philadelphia," she said, her hands caressing my shoulders again. "They be jealous of you if I there to fuss all over you. Best thing for you is to fit in, do like they do when you up north."

"But I'll miss you!"

She pulled me close, hugging me so tightly I could scarcely breathe. I heard sniffing and knew she was crying, too.

"Baby, you like my own child since the day you was born. I couldn't love you more if you my own flesh and blood. But you just about all grown up now. You be wanting a husband to share you room one these days, not an old colored woman like me."

I hugged her tightly in return, my tears finally falling. "You're not old at all. And I'll always want you with me, forever and ever."

But the mention of a husband reminded me that Tessie was secretly married to Josiah. They saw each other only rarely, but maybe she didn't want to go away to Philadelphia where she would never see him.

"I've made up my mind," I said firmly. "I've decided to go to Hilltop instead of Philadelphia. I'll go tell Daddy. He'll let you come with me to Hilltop."

She caught my arm in time to pull me back. "Listen, child. Your daddy won't let me go there, either. I certain of that."

"But why not?" Tessie didn't answer. I lifted her chin so I could see her face. "Is it because of Josiah? I know you're secretly married—"

"Hush your mouth!" Tessie's eyes went wide with fear. "Don't you ever say such a thing in this house!"

"Is that why Daddy sold Josiah to Hilltop . . . so you couldn't be together?"

She pulled me into her arms, smothering my words as if trying to smother flames. "Child, don't you go around opening doors that are better off closed and locked. It only lead to trouble—especially for Josiah. Forget you ever ask all these questions. Leave things the way they are. Promise?"

I nodded.

"You go on with your aunt to Philadelphia. Then, if you don't like it there, you can always come on home to Richmond again. And I be here waiting for you."

I watched Eli carry my trunk downstairs to the carriage the next morning and wondered who I would share all my troubles with in Philadelphia, who would answer all my questions. Gilbert was driving us to the train station, so this was the last time I would see Eli. The thought of saying good-bye to him made my heart ache inside, but when he returned to my room for the last load, I knew I had to try.

"I wish I didn't have to go away to Philadelphia," I said.

He nodded, his gray head bowed in grief. "I know . . . I know. Sure won't be the same around here without my Little Missy. No one asking me questions all the time . . . no one to drive to school. . . ."

I was a grown girl of sixteen, too old for a mammy, too old to sit on Eli's lap and listen to his stories. But when he finally looked up at me and I saw the love and the tears in his eyes, I was a child again. I ran into his arms. He hugged me as tightly as Tessie had.

"I'll miss you so much, Eli!"

"Me too, Little Missy . . . me too." When we finally let go, he wiped my tears with his thumb. "You remember to hide all them words I teach you in your heart . . . you hear?"

I nodded, tapping my chest the way Grady used to do. "They're in there, Eli."

"And anything too big for you, just take it to Massa Jesus."

"I will." I thought about Eli's terrible secret, the secret that could get him killed. I stood on tiptoe to kiss his bearded cheek and whispered, "Be careful, Eli." Then I turned away so I wouldn't have to watch him go.

CHAPTER

7

Philadelphia, February 1857

Our train arrived in Philadelphia in the middle of a blizzard. I'd never felt such cold, damp air before, or a wind that sucked away my breath the way this one did. My uncle, Judge Philip Hoffman, had come to the station with a driver and a sleigh to meet us, but I remember little else of that day except the bitter cold and my aching homesickness—a longing that had increased with every mile that separated me from Richmond and the people I loved.

In the months to come, I would visit all of Center City's famous landmarks and sights, but on that first day, places such as Penn Square and Independence Hall were hidden behind a blinding curtain of white. I knew we had crossed the Schuylkill River into West Philadelphia only because Uncle Philip told me we had. He was a portly, dignified man with receding hair and piercing eyes. I could easily imagine how his stern demeanor would strike fear in any criminals who stood trial before him, yet he was very gentle and kind to me. As we traveled through the storm, he asked me politely about my journey and the accommodations on the train. I couldn't answer;

my mouth and my heart seemed as frozen as the landscape. I was grateful when Aunt Martha signaled for him to stop with a gentle shake of her head.

The horses labored uphill through the snow, coming at last to a wealthy residential suburb and a large gray stone house that blended seamlessly with the snowy street and colorless sky. We were home.

The introductions passed in a blur. I learned that my cousins' names were Rosalie and Julia, but the Hoffmans employed more immigrant serving girls and chambermaids than I could ever hope to keep track of.

"I imagine you're tired from the long trip," Aunt Martha said when we'd finished a light supper. "Heaven knows I'm exhausted, too."

As I climbed the wide stairs to the large bedroom my cousins and I would share, Julia danced around me like a happy puppy, eager to please. A chambermaid had lit a blazing fire, and the bedroom was warm, the bed inviting. The maid, who barely spoke English, helped me shed my traveling clothes. The truth still hadn't sunk in that this room wasn't simply a place to rest for a night or two, but my home for the next few months, perhaps years.

"Don't overwhelm her, girls," I heard my aunt telling my cousins outside the door. "Remember, Caroline has recently lost her mother. Give her time to grieve."

As I crawled between the linen sheets, however, the sorrow I felt wasn't only grief for a mother I barely knew, a mother who had chosen to leave me, but a deep yearning for the beloved servants who had raised me and nurtured me, and who'd had no choice at all in our parting.

For the first month, the memory of Esther's fragrant kitchen, filled with all the people I loved, remained fresh and clear, a tiny pocket of solace and warmth amid the ice and cold of Philadelphia. I dwelt on those memories, fanning them like embers to keep them alive, anxious for them not to die—the sound of Eli's deep, rumbling voice as he talked to Massa Jesus; the touch of Tessie's dark hands as they gently soothed, caressed, loved. I kept thoughts of Virginia burning like tiny flames as I counted the weeks and the months until I could return.

The morning in March when everything changed began innocently enough—with Uncle Philip reading the *Philadelphia Inquirer* as he did every morning at breakfast. His choice to read rather than to give his full attention to my aunt was a constant source of friction between the two of them. Because of it, he'd developed the habit of reading a sentence or two aloud every now and then so his wife couldn't accuse him of ignoring her.

"I see Pierce Butler's mansion here in town is going up for sale," he said, adjusting his rimless spectacles. Aunt Martha's interest was instantly piqued.

"Oh? That's a lovely home. I know several people who might be interested in buying it."

"Well, it should sell for a bargain. It seems Butler ran up enormous gambling debts. But listen to this . . . this is truly tragic. 'A racetrack in Savannah, Georgia, was converted into a slave auction to dispose of 436 of Butler's Negro slaves. The unfortunate men, women, and children—who dubbed the event "The Weeping Time"—were sold to the highest bidder without regard for family ties, earning a total of $303,850 toward Butler's debts.' My! That should add fuel to the abolitionists' fires!"

"I'm sure that's an exaggeration," Aunt Martha said. "That seems like an awfully large number of slaves. I certainly don't recall any plantations around Richmond having that many, do you, Caroline? How many darkies does your uncle work with at Hilltop?"

"Um . . . about fifty." I could barely answer. I recalled the terrible anxiety that had gripped Hilltop's slaves after my grandfather had died, their tension and their fear as they'd waited, wondering who would be sold. I could well imagine the grief Pierce Butler's slaves must have suffered.

"I don't understand how people can *own* other people," my cousin Julia said, "much less buy and sell them like a new hat. That seems very wrong."

"That's because you girls were raised with servants, not slaves," my aunt replied. Her Virginia drawl, undetectable in most social situations, always became more pronounced whenever she grew annoyed. "Not every slave owner treats his people as callously as Pierce Butler did. Why, some of the slaves back home are just like family, aren't they, Caroline? And they certainly receive better treatment than the immigrants who labor in Northern factories. You've seen South Philadelphia where they live, Julia. Nobody provides those people with free clothing and food like we give our slaves."

I recalled my cousin Jonathan once voicing a similar argument.

"That may be true, my dear," Uncle Philip said, folding his newspaper. "But Northern factory workers are free to leave their place of employment whenever they choose. And they don't have their families torn from their arms like these poor souls did."

I pushed my plate away, unable to eat any more. The newspaper account had changed everything for me. The happy memories of home that I'd been keeping alive were suddenly overwhelmed by a flood of uglier ones—memories of dirt-floored shacks on Slave Row, of mothers who'd rather see their babies die than be sold, of the slave market on Fourteenth Street. And the still-vivid memory of Grady being dragged away, screaming for his mother.

I reread the newspaper account of "The Weeping Time" for myself after my uncle left for work, and I could no longer bear to think of home. The fire of longing that I'd nurtured had been coldly extinguished. I didn't want to go back to a place where 436 men, women, and children could be sold and separated from their loved ones like cattle. I wanted to forget that the people I loved—Tessie and Eli and Esther—were my father's property.

It proved easy to forget home, to lose myself in the rush and dazzle of life in Philadelphia. Everything about the city was frantic and fast-paced compared to Richmond, from the traffic that clogged the streets to the boisterous activity and lively visitors that filled and sometimes overflowed the house. My aunt and cousins were swept up in an almost endless series of parties, balls, and social gatherings, and I allowed them to carry me away with them. Since Cousin Rosalie and her mother were on a mission to find Rosalie a husband, every social occasion became a hunting expedition.

Rosalie was seventeen, a year older than me, and her life revolved entirely around meeting, wooing, and marrying the best possible "catch" in all of Philadelphia. As the daughter of a prominent, wealthy judge, she could well afford to be choosy. She was a very pretty girl—many said beautiful—with fine brown hair, hazel eyes, and the sort of fragile, delicate bone structure that made men rush to protect and assist her. But as I grew to know Rosalie, her excruciating perfectionism in matters of her clothing, her hair, and her toiletries—not to mention the importance she placed on her suitors' wealth and social status—diminished her beauty in my eyes. I grew to think of her as "pointy"; her nose and chin were pointy, her eyebrows as thin and as pointy as knife blades, her elbows and knees bony and sharp. But her tongue was by far the most pointed of all. I quickly learned to agree with her, to defer to her, and above all, to never, never outshine her.

Cousin Julia, who was still too young for a husband, wanted one anyway and flirted shamelessly, falling in love with a new beau every week. She was fifteen and still very much her father's spoiled pet. Physically, the two girls were as different as sisters could be. Julia was not fat, but everything about her was soft and full—her pouty lips, her pink cheeks, her dark brown eyes, her ample bosom. The latter was a constant source of jealousy on Rosalie's part, since she wasn't nearly as well endowed. Julia's golden brown, naturally curly hair was soft and full as well, and when she unpinned it, she looked as angelic as a cherub in an illustrated Bible. But her cherubic appearance belied her lively, unreserved personality.

Of course, we needed to be fashionably clothed for every social occasion, so Aunt Martha hired a dressmaker. She outfitted all four of us in day dresses for afternoon social calls and for entertaining callers at home, and in ball gowns for parties and evening affairs. I fell in love with the glamour and sway of taffeta petticoats and hoops, the swish and flow of fine silk skirts, the tickle of lace on wrist and neck. I became nearly as vain as Rosalie, primping and posing in front of the mirror, arranging my thick brown hair, admiring my tiny waist and high bosom. I was very pleased with the pretty, grown-up girl who gazed back at me. All this relentless activity helped me forget home, and as I watched my aunt in her unguarded moments, I sometimes wondered if it helped her forget, too.

Because I was somewhat of a novelty in Philadelphia—the Hoffmans' Southern cousin with her quiet, velvety drawl—the invitations poured through our mail slot. All my life I'd been painfully shy and fearful of new situations, and although that hadn't changed much, it proved no deterrent to my flowering social life. Rosalie was scheming and socially determined, fearing no one; Julia was lively and outgoing, fearing nothing; I simply floated in their wake. My natural shyness and reserve became part of my mystique as a Southern belle. And if the Hoffmans' cousin Robert was with me, I didn't even have to finish my own sentences—he finished them for me.

Robert Hoffman had become a fixture around our house that spring. He was Rosalie and Julia's cousin, not mine, and he lived on the same street that we did. Since his family was invited to most of the same social functions we were, Robert assumed the duty of escorting me. When the weather finally turned nice, he showed me all the sights of Philadelphia, sometimes riding on the new public horsecars that traveled the city streets on iron rails. Robert was fascinated with war, and no matter which site we visited—whether viewing displays of birds and insects at the National Academy of Sciences or strolling in Fairmont Park on a Sunday afternoon—his comments invariably turned into a lengthy monologue about the American Revolution or the second war with the British. Rosalie would tell him plainly to shut up. Julia would sigh and roll her eyes. And both would eventually wander away to leave me his sole audience.

Robert planned to attend West Point Military Academy in the fall, hoping to become a great army general, but I had trouble picturing him as a soldier. He had the same softness that Julia did, like a puppy that hasn't quite outgrown its baby fat. With his dark, glossy hair, swarthy skin, and soulful, down-turned eyes, he reminded me more of a mournful Spanish poet than a spit-and-polish military commander. His palms were sweaty, his monologues boring, and he danced as if his shoes were on the wrong feet, but I clung willingly to his arm, grateful that I didn't have to face new people and new situations all alone.

Robert escorted me to the extravagant ball that was given when the Academy of Music's opera house opened that year, but I quickly lost sight of him in the deluge of young gentlemen requesting the honor of a dance with me. I barely caught the first gentleman's name and a glimpse of his face before he swept me out onto the dance floor. Then the agonizing task of making conversation began.

"Good evening, miss. I don't believe we've had the pleasure of meeting before."

"Um . . . I'm Caroline Fletcher. Perhaps you know my uncle, Judge Philip Hoffman?"

"Caroline Fletcher," he repeated, imitating my Southern accent. "I must confess that I already knew that, Miss Fletcher. I just wanted to listen to your voice. I love the dreamy way *y'all* stretch out your words," he said, imitating me again. I excused myself and tried to flee the moment the music stopped, but I was immediately swept away by another would-be suitor.

"Judge Hoffman certainly lives with a house full of beauties," this one told me. "But I believe you're the prettiest one of them all. May I have the honor of calling on you sometime?"

I shook my head. His flattery did not gain my interest. "My uncle does not wish me to accept callers," I lied.

"I hear you're from down south, Miss Fletcher," my next dancing partner said. I'd forgotten his name the moment he'd told it to me.

"Yes. I'm from Richmond, Virginia."

"How many slaves do you own?"

"Why, I don't own any."

"Come now, Miss Fletcher. I'm not criticizing you or anything. I'm just curious to know what it feels like to own a few darkies."

"I really wouldn't know. As I've already told you, I don't own any Negroes."

"Say, you don't have to get in a temper. I've visited down south, and I understand how much your economy depends on slave labor." He lowered his voice to a murmur. "Tell you the truth, I'm on your side. I can't stand the way all these uppity free Negroes strut around Philadelphia."

I turned and walked away from him without even thanking him for the dance.

"You must have read *Uncle Tom's Cabin*," my next partner said. "What do you make of it? Are things down south really as horrible as Miss Stowe portrays them?"

"I'm sorry, but I haven't read the book."

"Oh, you should, Miss Fletcher. It's quite a vivid account. But then, you've probably seen firsthand some of the things she describes— husbands and wives sold to different owners, children separated from their mothers, slaves whipped . . ."

I wanted to weep. Everywhere I went, it seemed that people wanted to discuss slavery, yet they talked about it as if it was an abstract concept. It wasn't abstract to me. Slaves were real-life people with individual faces and souls. I knew some of those faces, loved some of those souls, and it broke my heart to be reminded of the truth about them—that Josiah and Tessie weren't allowed to be man and wife; that Grady had been torn without warning from his mother's arms; that Eli could be whipped for secretly preaching about Jesus in the pine grove or killed for knowing how to read.

"It's very warm in here," I said. "Would you mind fetching me some punch?"

"I'd be happy to, Miss Fletcher. You wait right here, now. And don't go wandering off with anyone else, all right?"

As soon as the gentleman disappeared into the crowd, heading for the punch bowl, I searched the sea of faces for Cousin Robert's. When I spotted him talking to an older gentleman in a military uniform, I fled to Robert's side like a drowning woman swimming for a lifeboat. I heard the end of his conversation, and thankfully it wasn't about slavery.

" . . . I'm just afraid there won't be any more battles left to fight by the time I get my officer's commission—" Robert stopped when he saw me. "Caroline? What's wrong? You're quite pale."

"Too much dancing, I guess. It's made me feel a little dizzy."

"Do you want to step outside for some air?"

"Yes, please."

"Will you excuse us, sir?" he asked the uniformed gentleman. Robert offered him a flabby salute before taking my hand. His palm was clammy, as usual, but I didn't care. I felt safe with him. He was always too busy talking about battles and wars to pester me with questions about slavery or the South.

"Are you having fun so far?" he asked after we'd stepped outside. Then, without waiting for a reply, he said, "I had the most interesting chat with Colonel Marshall. He fought in the Mexican War, you know, and he related several fascinating experiences. . . ." Robert talked on and on about the Mexican War for several minutes, but I wasn't listening. When he finally asked if I was ready to go back inside, I had a desperate idea.

"Robert, I really don't want to dance with anyone but you. Would it be terribly rude if we told everyone else to go away?"

His face registered surprise. For once in his life I think he was speechless. The balcony where we stood was quite dark, but I'm certain I saw his face flush with pleasure.

"Of course not, Caroline . . . d-dear. To tell you the truth, I really don't want to share you with all the others."

Robert was a terrible dancer. He held me awkwardly, and he kept treading on my toes, repeating, "Sorry . . . sorry." I didn't care. Each time another gentleman tried to cut in, Robert would proudly say, "Sorry, Miss Fletcher has promised all of her dances to me."

I hid in Robert's shadow for the remainder of the social season, knowing I would have to come up with a new strategy once he left for West Point. When that day finally arrived, Julia and I went with his parents to see his ship off at Penn's Landing.

"Promise me you won't marry someone else while I'm away?" he begged. He looked as somber as a soldier leaving for battle. I laughed at his sweaty earnestness.

"Don't worry. Rosalie would murder me if I dared to find a husband before she did." As he steamed away, gazing mournfully from the ship's rail, I wondered how I would ever get along without him. I decided to ask Rosalie for advice.

"For goodness' sakes, Caroline. I can't imagine feeling tongue-tied when I'm dancing with a suitor." I had broached the question as Rosalie sat at our dressing table, primping for a round of afternoon social calls. She took forever to get ready, and since there was only one mirror in our room, Julia and I rarely got more than a glimpse of ourselves. That day, I decided to stand behind Rosalie and peer around her as we both brushed our hair. She gazed at my reflection with pity.

"But your shyness is beside the point," she continued. "The unwritten rules of etiquette say that proper young ladies mustn't talk too much in the first place. We're supposed to *draw* the conversation out of our gentlemen."

"How do I do that? The only man I've ever talked to for any length of time is Robert. And he never runs out of famous battles to discuss."

"Don't judge all men by Robert." She dismissed him with a toss of her head and a flip of her hand. "Most men's favorite subject is themselves. Ask them a few questions, toss in a few *ooh*s and *ahh*s, and I guarantee they'll simply go on and on about themselves. You'll be lucky to get a word in sideways."

I tried her advice at the very next opportunity. Before the young man had a chance to say a word, I said, "Tell me about yourself." He didn't stop until the music did.

Along with their busy round of social obligations, my aunt and her family also faithfully attended worship services in one of Philadelphia's beautiful churches. It was the socially expected thing to do, the proper place to be seen—and a very lucrative place to engage in husband-hunting. The family pew had belonged to the Hoffmans since before the Revolutionary War, and pity the poor visitor who mistakenly sat there on a Sunday morning. Their church was very much like ours back home: the same hard, boxy pews; the same slow, somber organ music; the same stained-glass windows with their bronze plaques honoring generous donors; the same flowery oratory in the pastors' sermons, quietly lulling everyone to sleep.

Sometimes, in unguarded moments, I would recall the slaves' midnight worship service out in the woods behind the plantation, remembering its joy-filled music and Eli's heart-stirring sermon, and I'd almost wish I could go back there to clap and dance and sing about Massa Jesus. I'd promised Eli that I wouldn't forget all the lessons he shared with Grady and me, but after more than a year in Philadelphia, those memories were already fading like scenes glimpsed at sunset.

Then one Sunday morning the entire congregation was suddenly jolted awake. A new minister, fresh out of Yale Divinity School, arrived to fill in for our venerable old pastor who had taken ill. The young Reverend Nathaniel Greene shouted loudly enough to wake the dead in the churchyard, not to mention Aunt Martha. His sermon shook the chandeliers and the chancel rails and rattled the stained-glass saints and the drowsing deacons and dowagers. Blunt and raw, his wasn't a pretty speech, but it was electrifying in its passion. He spoke as though he really meant every word, the way Eli used to talk about Massa Jesus, as if He were a real live person. Rev. Greene's text from 1 Corinthians warned that the Lord "will bring to light the hidden things of darkness, make manifest the counsels of the hearts."

"What really motivates us as we go about our daily affairs," he asked. "Is it pride in our external appearance? The desire for wealth and recognition? Do any of us have a genuine desire to see the kingdoms of this world become the kingdoms of our God and of His Christ? We might hide the dimly illuminated recesses of our hearts from ourselves and from each other," Rev. Greene warned, "but the time is coming when God's light will shine in the darkness, bringing our motives to light!"

Those words were chilling enough, especially when I guiltily recalled how preoccupied I'd become with my clothes and my appearance. But when the pastor gripped the pulpit and fixed us with his impassioned gaze, his next words were met with pin-drop silence. "I'm speaking about the issue of slavery. You are either in favor of its continuance in these United States of America, or you will fight against it with all your heart and mind and strength until it is abolished. There can be no middle ground, no neutral territory between what's right and what's wrong, just as there is no compromise between light and darkness. What motivates *you*?" he concluded. "It's time to examine your heart. And then let's be about our heavenly Father's business."

My aunt and uncle didn't linger to socialize after the service—few people did. That's how shaken we all felt.

"Well! That young man certainly won't last long with our congregation," Aunt Martha declared at the dinner table. "Imagine! Trying to tell us how to live! That's not what church is for. Rosalie, pass the potatoes, please."

"What is church for, dear?" Uncle Philip asked quietly.

"Why . . . why, it's so that we will all feel uplifted, of course. It's to remind us that God is love."

"It seems to me that's precisely what that young man tried to do today—to remind us that God loves the Negro race as much as He loves ours."

Aunt Martha pushed her chair back, as if she was about to stand. "Don't start with me, Philip. You know I dislike slavery as much as you do. I gladly left it all behind when I moved up here."

"Out of sight, out of mind," I heard Uncle Philip murmur.

I stared down at my plate of roast beef in shame. I'd managed to push all the injustices I'd witnessed from my mind, too, but they hadn't gone away. I felt as though God was shining His light in my heart, just as Rev. Greene had warned, and I hated what I saw: cowardice.

"What we do outside of church is none of that young man's business," Aunt Martha concluded.

Uncle Philip gaped at her, his dinner roll halfway to his mouth. He seemed too stunned to speak.

"Mama," Julia asked suddenly, "may I invite Rev. Greene to afternoon tea on Thursday?" Julia's face wore the dreamy look she always got when she fell in love with a new beau. I guessed that she had now fallen for the young reverend. Had she even heard a word of her parents' conversation? Or Rev. Greene's stirring sermon?

"I think that would be a fine idea, Julia," Uncle Philip said before my aunt could reply. "I understand that Rev. Greene is originally from New York State. He probably doesn't know a soul here in Philadelphia."

Nathaniel Greene was the sole topic of Julia's conversation for the next four days. He had accepted her invitation to tea, creating the serious crisis of what she should wear for the occasion. I looked for a way to be excused from the event, terrified that he would see the darkness that was in my heart the moment he set eyes on me.

But of course I was expected to attend—to keep Julia from going into a swoon if for no other reason.

"What'll I talk about? What'll I say? What if my mind goes blank?" she worried. She needn't have. Rev. Greene descended from a long line of ministers and was well-practiced in the graceful art of taking afternoon tea with parishioners. He also had a subject that he never grew tired of discussing—abolition. It didn't take Julia long to realize that if she kept to that topic, she would have his full attention.

"I simply can't understand how people can *own* someone," she said, pouring him a third cup of tea. Then she made her first mistake. "My cousin Caroline is from Virginia," she said. "Her family owns slaves."

"Really?" He turned his attention to me as if I was a fascinating new species from an exotic culture. With his smooth-cheeked, boyish face and reddish-blond hair, he looked much younger than twenty-five. He would have made a more convincing schoolboy in overalls, playing hooky from school, than a minister in a dark suit and clerical collar. He even had freckles, for goodness' sake. But his first question unnerved me.

"I'd like to hear your view of slavery, Miss Fletcher."

"My . . . *view?*"

I remembered my first view of Slave Row, of the ramshackle cabins with Caleb and the other little children playing outside in the dirt. Then I pictured the view from my bedroom window that terrible morning, the wagon full of slaves in chains, Grady screaming as the men dragged him away.

"It's . . . it's horrible . . ." I couldn't finish. Tears sprang to my eyes before I could stop them. I dug in my pockets for a handkerchief and couldn't find one. Rev. Greene offered me his.

"Here . . . I'm so sorry, Miss Fletcher. I didn't mean to upset you." He rested his hand on my shoulder, patting it consolingly.

As I battled to regain control, Julia eyed me jealously. She seemed to be weighing the idea of bursting into tears herself, just so he would rest his freckled hand on her shoulder. In the end, she was wise enough to realize that the way to Nathaniel Greene's heart was to become an ardent abolitionist herself.

"How did you become involved in this very worthy cause?" she asked him, passing the plate of tea cakes one more time. "Did you live down south yourself?"

"No, I first joined the New England Anti-Slavery Society when I was in college and—"

"I had no idea there was such an organization," she chirped. "Might I join the society, too?"

He swiveled his full attention back to Julia. "Certainly, Miss Hoffman. We'd be pleased to have you. In fact, the American Anti-Slavery Society was founded right here in Philadelphia in 1833."

"Why, I had no idea. What is it that the society does, exactly?"

"Well, you see, the Declaration of Independence proclaimed freedom and liberty for all men, yet the Negroes are still enslaved. It says all men are created equal, yet the Negroes don't share that equality with whites. Slavery is a great evil, Miss Hoffman, and a curse to this great nation. It must be abolished. The Society believes it is our task to complete the unfinished work of the American Revolution."

Julia appeared horrified. "You don't mean going to *war*—with real *guns* and things!"

"Oh, no, no—nothing like that." He pulled a square lump from his bulging jacket pocket. I had assumed it was a Bible, but it turned out to be a good-sized packet of abolitionist tracts. He peeled off two and passed them to Julia and me. "The Declaration of Sentiments, written in 1833, reads that our principles 'forbid the doing of evil that good may come, and lead us to reject—and to entreat the oppressed to reject—the use of all carnal weapons for deliverance from bondage; relying solely upon those which are spiritual, and mighty through God . . . the destruction of error by the potency of truth—the overthrow of prejudice by the power of love—and the abolition of slavery by the spirit of repentance.'"

I stared at the words in disbelief. They were so similar to what

Eli had told his fellow slaves—that they wouldn't have to resort to violence, God would fight their battle for them. I wanted to learn more from Rev. Greene, but when I looked up, Julia was perched on the edge of her seat, gazing at him like a puppy with its master. I could see that he mistook her adoration as interest in abolition, especially when she said, "I would love to accompany you to one of your meetings sometime."

Rev. Greene beamed at her. It wasn't love I saw in his eyes but the excitement of a zealot who has just made a new convert. "There will be an anti-slavery lecture next week, in fact. It's being held at the Quaker meetinghouse in Germantown. I'd be very happy to escort you—and Miss Fletcher, of course."

I agreed to go, partly because I was genuinely interested, and partly because Julia never would have forgiven me if I hadn't. Her father wouldn't allow her to attend the lecture alone with an unmarried man, minister or not.

Uncle Philip let us take his carriage when the day finally arrived, and he instructed his driver to stop by the church to pick up Rev. Greene. The young reverend started lecturing us on abolition the moment he'd taken his seat beside Julia. His fanaticism reminded me of Robert's devotion to the subject of war.

"Since you are new to this area, Miss Fletcher, you may not know the history of where we are going today. Germantown was settled in 1683 by a group of Quakers and Mennonites from Germany. Its residents published some of America's first protests against slavery. Lucretia Mott, founder of the American Anti-Slavery Society, was a Quaker, and her husband organized free stores. Have you heard of those?"

"No . . . do tell me," Julia said.

From the rapt expression on her face, he might have been reciting love poems to her.

"Free stores sell only those products made with non-slave labor. Many of New England's most fashionable women are choosing to avoid southern-grown cotton for their dresses." I am sure Julia would have dressed in animal skins like a native for Rev. Nathaniel Greene.

All my life I had heard Scripture used to defend slavery, but at the lecture that day, for the first time, I heard the Bible quoted to oppose slavery. Jesus' commandments: " . . . whatsoever ye would that men should do to you, do ye even so to them . . ." and "love thy neighbour as thyself" applied to all of mankind, the speaker said. Slavery was a violation of the law of love and was therefore a sin. Taking our fellow man's freedom by force was not only cruel and unjust but also abhorrent to God.

"If you assume God will approve, then you don't know God," the speaker concluded, and I nearly rose from my seat and shouted, "Amen!" the way the people in Eli's congregation did. Those words finally explained the difference I'd always noticed between the way most preachers talked about God and the way Eli always talked about Massa Jesus. Eli knew God's heart.

As time passed, I grew more and more interested in the anti-slavery movement. Before long, I was no longer going for Julia's sake but to hear the lectures for myself. I couldn't get enough of them. The message of God's deliverance from slavery, which Eli had preached about in the pine grove years ago, suddenly seemed possible. And ordinary people like me could actually do something to help.

In the past, Julia's affections for her various beaux usually flamed and died fairly quickly, so I was surprised when they didn't this time. Her obsession with Nathaniel Greene grew stronger over time, even though he gave her no encouragement at all. I could have told her that the cause of abolition so consumed him that he had no room left in his heart for any woman—but I didn't. I wanted to attend every meeting I could.

We heard the famous Negro orator Frederick Douglass speak. We saw the lash marks on a former slave's back and heard the story of his daring escape. We learned about the Fugitive Slave Law, passed in 1850, and how any slave fortunate enough to beat the odds and escape could still be arrested up north and sent back into slavery. We met God-fearing people who risked fines and imprisonment to help escaped slaves reach safety in Canada.

But as time went on, a lingering discontent began to grow inside me. While a few individuals were actively trying to make a difference, most of us did little more than listen, shake our heads in dismay, then go on with our shallow lives. I finally voiced my thoughts to Nathaniel one day as we drove home from one of the meetings.

"Is all this talk really doing any good?" I asked him. "These speakers are preaching to an audience that already believes in abolition. What are they doing to change the attitudes of the slaveholders down south?"

"Well, our leaders hope that laws will eventually be passed in Congress and—"

"Laws? I think . . . I think that it's very easy for people in the North to support abolition because there aren't very many Negroes up here. And the ones who do live here are kept segregated from white people. They don't live in our neighborhoods, their children don't attend our schools. Even the pews in our churches are kept separate."

"Why, Miss Fletcher, I believe that's because—"

"Do you even know any Negroes, Rev. Greene? No one in my uncle's family does. Yet back home, Tessie and Esther and Eli and Grady were part of my family. As wrong as slavery is, our slaves' lives were woven together with ours in a complicated pattern—a pattern that often included genuine love. The North may have outlawed slavery, but it hasn't done away with bigotry and racism. Is the one condition any worse than the others?"

He smiled at me, the way a proud teacher will smile at his prize pupil. "I can see that you have a great deal of passion for the cause, Miss Fletcher."

His words struck me like a slap in the face. I suddenly realized what was missing in so much of the abolitionists' rhetoric and in so many of their hearts.

"Rev. Greene," I said in a trembling voice, "the Negroes are not a *cause*. They are *people!*"

CHAPTER 8

OCTOBER 1859

When my cousin Rosalie turned nineteen, she decided she must get married at once or risk being labeled an old maid. After a great deal of fuss and deliberation, she finally made her choice—the oldest son of a wealthy Philadelphia banking family. Her wedding was the premier social event of the season.

Cousin Robert arrived home from West Point and served as my escort. He had lost a good deal of his baby fat after one year at the academy, and he now sported a shadow of soft, dark fuzz on his upper lip that was supposed to be a mustache. But he still made an unconvincing soldier, even in uniform. Now he looked like a mournful Spanish poet dressed up for a costume ball. He walked and stood with his shoulders hunched, hanging his head as if he was about to apologize for some grave error. Julia made fun of him behind his back, but I was grateful for his arm to cling to at the wedding. He helped me thwart unwelcome advances from several of the groom's relatives.

Rosalie's wedding was the kind every girl dreams of—a gown like a fairy-tale princess's, a church fragrant with jasmine and roses, a glittering champagne reception, a wedding trip to Saratoga with a brand-new trousseau. Julia and I couldn't help being envious. When it was all over that night, our bedroom seemed very quiet and empty without Rosalie. Julia and I had the mirrored dressing table all to ourselves, but neither one of us could bear to sit there in Rosalie's place.

After we were both in bed with the lights out, I heard Julia sniffling. "Are you crying?" I asked.

"No!"

But when I tiptoed across the room and climbed into bed with her, I knew that she had been. "There must be a leak in the roof, then," I said. "Your pillow is all wet."

Julia's tears turned to giggles. We lay in the dark for a while, whispering about the day's events. Then Julia said, "Rosalie was so caught up in the wedding, I'll bet she never once remembered that she'd have to share a bed with a man tonight, dressed in only her chemise."

"Julia!" I was shocked. She laughed.

"Well, it's part of life, isn't it? And it's certainly part of marriage. Where do you think babies come from?"

"You shouldn't talk about such things. It isn't proper."

"Phooey! Who cares about being proper? Do you think Rosalie is in love with her new husband?"

"I never heard her say that she loves him. Just that she thought he'd make a good husband."

Julia sighed dramatically. "I could never marry a man I wasn't in love with, could you, Caroline? It would be awful to share a bed with him otherwise."

"I wish you would stop talking about . . . that."

"What? Sharing a bed with my husband?" She laughed at me again. "I sometimes pretend that my pillow is Nathaniel Greene and I hug it tightly all night. Who do you pretend yours is?"

"I . . . I've never done that."

"Haven't you ever been in love, Carrie?"

Hadn't I? I recalled the excitement of my infatuation with my cousin Jonathan years ago, how I'd wanted to spend every minute with him, how I'd thrilled to his touch. But I had long since outgrown those feelings. And I had felt nothing close to them since—certainly not with Robert, nor with any of the other men I'd danced with. I'd once heard love in Tessie's joyful laughter when she was with Josiah. I'd seen love in Julia's eyes when she gazed at Nathaniel. But I had never known it firsthand.

"I've never been in love," I said at last.

"Oh, poor you!"

Later, when I was back in my own bed, I tried hugging my pillow, pretending it was my husband. But the pillow had no face, and it seemed wrong, somehow, to even imagine such a thing.

The next day, Robert insisted on accompanying Julia, Rev. Greene, and me to our regular abolition meeting. As soon as we entered the assembly hall, we saw that it was not only packed, but also cloaked in an atmosphere of secrecy and danger. The guest speaker was a young Negro man named Peter Sullivan, a newly escaped slave. He was on his way to freedom in Canada, but he could be arrested and sent back to Mississippi if he was discovered speaking to us. Peter was a quiet, sullen young man whose smoldering resentment reminded me of Josiah. He had never spoken in public before, so the society's president interviewed him about his escape.

After a few preliminary questions the president asked, "What made you decide to take the risk and escape, Peter?"

"I leave after I find out who my father is." He stared at his feet, as if to hide his shame. "He a white man. . . . I find out Massa Sullivan my father."

I heard a collective gasp in the meeting hall. All the usual rustling and shuffling stilled.

"How did you find this out, Peter?"

He lifted his head, gazing out at the sea of white faces. But it was as if he was looking through all of us. "My mama tell me so. Ain't nothing she can do about him, either. Any time he want her, she have no choice."

I was certain that I wasn't the only woman who was blushing. Julia stared at the man, her mouth hanging open. Robert wiped his sweating palms on his thighs. I didn't dare look at Rev. Greene.

"Peter," the president said quietly, "I think the audience should know that your story is by no means unique. White masters have the right to use slave women for their own purposes any time they please, and many of these unions have produced mixed-race children."

A memory stirred from long ago—the old Negro granny at Hill-top, asking which heaven the little black children with white daddies would go to when they died. I hadn't understood the question at the time, but now that I did, I felt another rush of heat to my face. Surely not my Uncle William . . . surely not.

"So for most of your life, Peter, you didn't know who your father was?"

"Mama scared to tell me. She say a Negro woman be killed for telling."

I finally understood Eli's fear when I'd asked him about Grady's father. *"Never ask . . . They kill a gal if she tell."* I hadn't thought about Grady for a long time, but I let my mind wander away from this embarrassing subject and allowed myself to think about him now. The deep grief I felt at losing my friend was still there after more than six years. I missed him. He would be fifteen now and nearly grown. He'd been my only friend as I was growing up, except for Jonathan. I smiled to myself when I remembered how alike they were, the same sparkling dark eyes, the same mischievous grin.

"My skin nearly as light as Massa's white sons," I heard Peter say. "I know I can pass for white. That's how I escape."

Grady had been a very light-skinned Negro, too. A shade lighter than Tessie, several shades lighter than his ebony-skinned father, Josiah.

" . . . child cannot be lighter-skinned than his parents," the interviewer said. "And so a lighter skin shade, like Peter's, is an indication of mixed race. . . ."

His words hit me with the force of a physical blow. How could Grady be Josiah's son if his skin was so much lighter? As I struggled to work out a logical explanation, another thought forced its way into my dazed mind. My cousin Jonathan resembled my father. What if the reason Jonathan reminded me so much of Grady was because . . . because . . .

Cold dread rose up inside me. I began to tremble as if my entire body was trying to reject the thought. It couldn't be true. My daddy would never do such a terrible thing.

" . . . and so Peter's very own white father kept his son bound in the chains of slavery. . . ."

I couldn't breathe. I needed air. I stood to leave, to run out of the meeting hall, but when I took the first step I felt as if all the blood had drained from my body. The world went black.

I woke up outside in Robert's arms. He was sitting on the grass with me, frantically repeating my name. "Caroline! Caroline! . . . Please, God . . . Darling Caroline! What's wrong?"

I couldn't tell him what I feared. I could never tell anyone. The horror, the shame of it! Could Grady really be my half brother? Had Daddy sold Josiah to Hilltop so he could have my Negro mammy all to himself? I remembered how Tessie had blamed my mother for sending Grady away—my mother, who couldn't give Daddy a son of her own. I remembered Eli saying that Daddy would never sell Tessie, *"And you know the reason why."*

But worst of all was the horror of wondering if my father had sold his very own son—my brother—to the slave auction.

"No . . ." I murmured. "It can't be true. . . ."

"She's coming around," I heard Julia say. She was fanning my face with her handkerchief.

"Caroline, thank God! Are you all right?" Robert asked. I opened my eyes and gazed up at his worried face. Above us the tree branches flamed with fall colors.

"I'm okay," I whispered. But I wanted to weep.

Robert held my hand in his. "Dear one, what happened? You're trembling."

"It . . . it was warm in there. I needed air. I guess I fainted."

"I'll hail a cab," Rev. Greene said. "We'd better take Caroline home right away."

No one said much on the ride home, but when Robert and Julia hurried into the house ahead of us, calling for my aunt, Rev. Greene turned to me. "Do you need to talk to someone about this, Miss Fletcher?" he asked softly. "I will gladly listen and keep whatever you say in strictest confidence." I could tell by the pity in his eyes that he knew. Young Nathaniel Greene knew that it was the subject of the lecture that had upset me. I don't know why, but I felt compelled to lie to him. I needed to protect the people I loved—Tessie and Grady, and yes, even my daddy.

"There's nothing to talk about," I said, smiling weakly. "I've fainted before . . . usually when I haven't eaten, and I skipped lunch today. . . ."

Robert wanted to hover over me, but I sent him away and went to bed. I told Aunt Martha it was my time of the month. Julia knew it wasn't. She heard me weeping that night in the dark, unable to stop. She crawled into bed beside me and stroked my hair, the way Tessie used to do.

"Please tell me what's wrong, Caroline. It was something they said at the meeting, wasn't it? I confess I wasn't listening, I was watching Nathaniel. But won't you please tell me?"

"I can't. I can't explain it."

"Did talking about the South make you homesick?"

"Yes . . . I guess that's what's wrong." I clung to the lie as an easy way out, and Julia accepted it without question. When I finally managed to stop crying, she quickly changed the subject, probably hoping to take my mind off of home.

"I noticed something today," she said. "When you fainted, Robert nearly fainted, too. You should have seen his face, Carrie. He was so worried about you. And you probably don't remember what he was saying to you."

"No. I really don't remember anything."

"He's in love with you."

"No. Oh, Julia, no . . . that can't be true." I couldn't handle any more revelations.

"He is. Maybe he doesn't even realize it himself, but he is. Would you marry him if he asked you?"

"Julia, please . . . my head is throbbing."

"If you did, then you would be Caroline *Hoffman*. And you could live here in Philadelphia forever, and when I marry Nathaniel we could visit each other. Maybe we could even live next door to each other."

My fears about Grady were too much to handle. I didn't think I could deal with Robert's feelings, too. But it turned out I had to. Robert was waiting to see me in our parlor the first thing next morning.

"Caroline, I . . . I must speak with you. Alone." I felt sorry for him. He was stammering, flushed, terrified. If he barely had the courage to face a woman, how in the world would he ever face an invading army? "Darling, I've been so worried about you. . . ."

"I'm fine now, Robert. Honest, I am. It was very silly of me to faint like that."

He wasn't listening. I could see that he'd prepared a little speech and he would forge ahead with it to the end, a soldier charging uphill into battle. "I realized the depth of my feelings for you yesterday, and I can't go back to West Point tomorrow until I've talked to you about them. I can't . . . I can't bear the thought of you entertaining other suitors while I'm gone. This Rev. Greene—"

"I think you've misunderstood, Robert. I don't have romantic feelings toward him or anyone else. Julia is interested in Nathaniel Greene, not me. I go places with them as a chaperone."

"You're so beautiful, Caroline. You could have any man in Philadelphia, but . . . but you once asked to dance only with me, remember? And at Rosalie's wedding you let me monopolize all your time. Dare I hope that you share my feelings?"

Did I have feelings for him? Clumsy, boring Robert? He was well-meaning and pitifully sweet, my island of safety, my refuge. And after what I'd learned yesterday, I needed a safe place to hide more than ever before.

"Of course I'm fond of you, Robert."

"Would you . . . could you consider . . . a-an *understanding* while I'm away?"

I frowned. "An understanding?"

"I know that we can't make any formal announcements until I receive my army commission, but will you wait for me, darling?"

I saw a way out. I could stay in Philadelphia if I married Robert. I wouldn't have to face my father. Or Tessie.

"I'll think about it."

"May I write to your father concerning my intentions?"

"If you wish," I mumbled.

Robert lifted my hand to his lips and kissed it. "Thank you. Thank you, darling Caroline."

It was only after he'd sailed for New York that I recalled Julia's words and shuddered. If Robert was my husband I would have to share a bed with him, dressed in only my chemise.

On a cool autumn Sunday, midway through October, a subdued Nathaniel Greene stood in the pulpit of our church. "As you know," he began, "I've been very outspoken about the need for all of us to join in the fight to abolish slavery. That need hasn't changed. I still believe that God wants each one of us to decide what we should do to help. But a few months ago, a young woman asked me a simple question . . . and it has haunted me ever since. This morning I will ask all of you the same question: 'Do you even know any Negroes?'"

Julia elbowed me in the ribs. "He's talking about you, Caroline. You asked him that." I held my fingers to my lips to shush her. I wanted to listen.

"The young woman wanted to know why—if we believe all men are created equal—why we segregate Negroes into separate neighborhoods? Separate schools? And, God forgive us, separate church pews? In this City of Brotherly Love, why aren't these Christian brothers and sisters our schoolmates? Our neighbors? Our friends?"

Julia grabbed the back of my arm, unseen, and pinched. "You're *not* going to steal him away from me! He's mine!"

"Ow! I'm not interested in him, Julia."

"Well, he certainly sounds interested in you."

"Shh!" Aunt Martha's frown was stern. I rubbed my arm and tried to slide away from Julia.

"We've outlawed slavery here in the North, thank God. But as my friend so keenly pointed out, the things that have replaced slavery aren't any better. I'm talking about bigotry. And racism. Do *you* know any Negroes?"

As I glanced around at some of the faces in the congregation, I expected to see uneasiness, discomfort. But it surprised me to see anger. And opposition. Nathaniel must have seen them, too, but he courageously spoke his heart.

"The text for my sermon is found in the book of Isaiah, chapter fifty-eight. It says, 'If thou take away from the midst of thee the yoke . . . and if thou draw out thy soul to the hungry, and satisfy the afflicted soul; then shall thy light rise in obscurity, and thy darkness be as the noon day.'

"We've done away with the yoke of oppression here in Philadelphia. And many of you seated before me this morning have generously opened your purses and your wallets to support the cause of abolition. Why, then, does the shadow of bigotry and racism still darken our city?

"I believe it's because we've spent our money and not ourselves. I believe it's because we've served a *cause* and not the needs of the oppressed. Those needs include the need for fellowship, for friendship, for love." He gripped the pulpit and leaned forward, staring fearlessly at his disgruntled congregation. "If we want the light of Christ to shine in our darkness, then we must remember one thing: Our Negro brothers and sisters are not a *cause*. They are *people*!"

The next day at breakfast, Uncle Philip opened his newspaper and read aloud to us the shocking events that had occurred the day before, on that beautiful autumn Sunday, October 16, 1859. "'The following dispatch has been received from Frederick, Maryland, but as it seems very improbable, it should be received with great caution until confirmed. . . . An insurrection has broken out at Harper's Ferry, Virginia. A band of armed abolitionists have full possession of the U.S. Arsenal. . . . The band is composed of about 250 whites, followed by a band of Negroes who are fighting with them. . . . The telegraph wires have been cut. . . . It is reported that there has been a general stampede of Negroes from Maryland. . . . Many wild rumors are afloat, but we have nothing authentic at this time. . . .'"

A chill went through me. My cousin Jonathan and the other plantation owners had always feared another slave insurrection like Nat Turner's. But this time white abolitionists had led it. And now they had an arsenal full of weapons.

"Did you say *Virginia*, Daddy?" Julia asked.

"Yes. Harper's Ferry, Virginia."

She turned to me. "Is that close to where you used to live in Richmond?"

"I don't know where it is," I replied. My heart had begun to race as I did the arithmetic; my uncle and the overseer were the only white men left to defend the isolated plantation against more than fifty slaves.

The next day, the news was only slightly more reassuring. It wasn't a widespread rebellion as people had feared, but a small band of five Negroes and thirteen white men, led by a fanatical abolitionist named John Brown. They had seized the federal armory, the arsenal, and the engine house in Harper's Ferry, taking several hostages. The first man to be killed by Brown and his followers had been a free Negro; the first rebel to die had also been a Negro, a former slave who'd hoped to win freedom for his wife and children.

By Tuesday morning the insurrection was over. Ninety U.S. Marines, under the command of Colonel Robert E. Lee of Virginia, arrested Brown and the others and turned them over to the Virginia authorities to stand trial. I breathed a little easier knowing that all those weapons had been returned to the arsenal. But what continued to make me uneasy was the way the abolitionists praised John Brown for his courage and zeal. One newspaper called the incident "a great day in our history, a new revolution." Brown himself was called "an angel of light." I recalled what Rev. Greene had once told me about the abolition movement's nonviolent principles, and I wondered what he had to say about these unsettling events. I never had a chance to ask him.

I came home from an afternoon tea on Friday to find my father waiting in the parlor for me. He had arrived in Philadelphia unannounced. I couldn't believe my eyes when I saw him.

"Daddy? What are you doing here?"

"I've come to bring you home, Caroline." He opened his arms to me for a rare embrace, then rested his cheek against my hair. "I've missed you, Sugar. Two years is a long time."

"I've missed you, too, Daddy." I realized that it was true. I'd especially missed the sound of his voice, his gentle drawl. He looked so much better than he had when I'd left home, even though he'd lost weight and his hair had turned steely gray. But his gentle dignity and handsome face were unchanged.

"My, you're beautiful," he said, pulling back to gaze at me. "You look so much like your mother." His love for me shone in his eyes, and I remembered the loving way he used to look at my mother, the tender way he'd treated her. I always knew that his love for her was very deep, which was why his grief after she'd died had been so profound.

As I looked into my daddy's eyes I wondered how I ever could have believed that he'd been unfaithful to her. The idea seemed preposterous now. Daddy never paid any attention at all to Tessie. He and Grady looked nothing alike. It simply wasn't true. I must have been out of my mind.

At dinner that night, Daddy told my aunt and uncle that he planned to take me home right away. Uncle Philip laid down his silverware and stared at Daddy.

"This seems a bit sudden, doesn't it, George? Caroline has put down roots during the two years she's spent with us. She's flourished here. Do you really think it's wise to uproot her so suddenly like this?"

"Please understand that I'm very grateful for all that you've done for her," Daddy said, spreading his hands. "You've helped her—and me—through a very difficult time in our lives. But we're both past that now. She's my daughter. She belongs in her own home, in Richmond."

"Is it safe to go back there?" Aunt Martha asked. "I mean, with all the awful goings-on at that place ... Harper's Ferry ... ?"

Daddy frowned. "Of course it's safe. That was the work of fanatical outsiders, not native Virginians. Living in peace with our Negroes is a long-established way of life for us—you know that, Martha. Take your sister's servant, Ruby, for instance. You're aware of the bond of loyalty and love that existed between her and my wife. Can you honestly imagine our Ruby taking part in such a rebellion? It's the troublemakers from the North who threaten to upset that balance."

"We are not all fanatics like John Brown," Uncle Philip said, "any more than all slave owners are like Simon Legree."

Their voices had been gradually growing louder, harsher. Daddy took a moment to stop and carefully cut his meat. When he looked up at Uncle Philip again, I heard cold anger in his tone. "I've read some of the headlines that appeared in your Northern newspapers after this incident. The entire South is horrified that you would express sympathy and praise for a fanatic who tried to cause a slave insurrection. How can any thinking man endorse such an outrage?"

"So, that's why you've come for her, then."

"Yes. I don't want my only child influenced by that ungodly way of thinking. You're calling that maniac Brown a hero!"

"I've never called him that, George."

Daddy raised his hand in apology. "I'm sorry. I didn't mean to accuse any of you. But if even one person in the North defends that man, then it's time Caroline came home."

"Why not wait a bit and see what happens?" Aunt Martha said. "Maybe this will all blow over."

Daddy leaned back in his chair and gravely shook his head. "To the people in the North, John Brown is a hero. To the South, he's a murderous villain. Our differences are much too great, Martha. The dividing line between us is too clearly drawn. This won't blow over."

"You may be right," Uncle Philip said quietly. "But there is something we're all forgetting to consider—what would Caroline herself like to do?"

My uncle knew all about the anti-slavery meetings I'd been attending for the past year. He knew from the fervor of Rev. Greene's sermons what attitudes I'd been exposed to at those meetings. He turned to me.

"What would you like to do, Caroline?"

If it hadn't been for Nathaniel's courageous sermon, I may have drawn back at the thought of facing the darkness of slavery again. But then I recalled the verse he'd read from Isaiah: *"If thou take away from the midst of thee the yoke . . . thy darkness will be as the noon day."* I was tired of simply listening to anti-slavery speeches, tired of merely supporting a cause. My own words came back to haunt me—Tessie and Eli were not a cause, they were people.

I looked up at my daddy and said, "I want to go home."

CHAPTER
9

RICHMOND 1859

As our train neared the city and all the familiar sights of Richmond came into view, I knew that I was home at last. Gilbert stood waiting to meet us at the station, greeting me with a rare smile.

"Welcome home, Missy Caroline."

"Thank you, Gilbert. It's so good to be home."

He loaded all my trunks and hatboxes and carpetbags into the carriage, then Daddy asked him to drive to Hollywood Cemetery to visit my mother's grave.

The parklike graveyard was quiet and still. The crunch of gravel beneath the horses' hooves and wagon wheels was the only sound as we drove downhill from the entrance. Gilbert threaded the carriage through the maze of winding roads, beneath ageless trees in their fading fall colors, past the jumble of tombs and monuments, as he must have done countless times.

The James River was visible from Mother's grave site, with wooded Belle Isle floating serenely in the middle of it. As I stood silently gazing at her tombstone, I felt as though my mother had finally found the peace that had eluded her all her life.

"It's nice here," I said with a sigh.

Daddy nodded. Then he put his hat back on, and we drove away.

Hollywood Cemetery was west of downtown, our house on Church Hill east of it, so I was able to savor the sights as we drove up and down Richmond's hills on the way home. The brick buildings of Tredegar Iron Works sprawled near the canal, smoke rising majestically from its tall chimneys. I saw Crenshaw Woolen Mills, the Franklin Paper Mill, and a half-dozen flour mills whose names I couldn't recall. On the next hill, in front of the pillared capitol building, George Washington gazed southward from astride his bronze horse. Bells chimed the hour from nearby St. Paul's. I could see the curving James River in the distance, sparkling in the sunlight, and mules like toy figures laboring to haul packet boats up the Kanawha Canal. We rode through the business district, past shops and banks, past the Spotswood Hotel, past newsboys hawking the latest editions. I begged Daddy to drive past his warehouses so I could see the ships docked at Rocketts Wharf.

Richmond wasn't enormous and frantic and loud, like Philadelphia, but lovely and dignified, a proud queen perched on her hills. And best of all, everywhere I looked I saw a wonderful mixture of black faces and white faces.

As the horses labored up Church Hill, the spire of St. John's came into view, and I knew I was nearly home. Then I was standing in our front hallway at last, and Tessie was running out to meet me, looking even more beautiful than I'd remembered. She hugged me so tightly I thought my bones would snap, but I never wanted her to let go.

"I hardly know you, baby," she wept as we hugged and cried. "You all growed up."

"Oh, Tessie! I've missed you so much! I'm never going away again."

"Is that our gal?" Esther cried as she hurried in from the kitchen. She took a long, tender look at me before swallowing me in her ample embrace. "Land sakes, honey! You growed some bosoms while you was gone. Looks like it gonna take a mighty strong wind to blow you to Washington, D.C. now!"

We were all laughing and crying, even shy Luella. My mother's maid, Ruby, cried the hardest. "I just knew you gonna be as pretty as you mama someday. Oh, it so good to have you back."

But someone was missing. I felt bone-chilling fear when I looked around and realized that Eli's beloved face wasn't among the others. "Where's Eli?" I asked.

"He's wanting to see you real bad," Esther said, "but he don't have clothes that's good enough to wear inside the big house."

I flew out the back door and down the walk to the carriage house. Eli stood in the doorway, tall and proud, waiting for me. His hair and beard had turned nearly white while I was gone, but his arms and shoulders were as sturdy and strong as ever. I fell into those arms and smelled the wonderful scent of horses and leather as I rested my face against his broad chest.

"I'm home, Eli."

"Oh, yes . . . thank you, Massa Jesus! This place sure be dark and dreary without our Little Missy. Maybe now the sun finally gonna shine around here again."

I was home, and the longer I was, the more certain I became that some of the stories they told in those meetings up north were exaggerated. I felt thoroughly ashamed that I'd ever entertained such an outrageous idea about my father and Tessie. Josiah had been sold to Hilltop around the time Grady had been born—perhaps as a punishment for his behavior with Tessie. As for the color of Grady's skin, I must have remembered wrong. He hadn't been any lighter than Tessie, had he? Besides, she'd borne no other children since Josiah had been sold.

But even if some of the abolitionists had exaggerated, I still knew that slavery was very wrong. I had brought a large box of anti-slavery pamphlets back to Richmond with me, convinced that if I simply talked to people, simply explained to them what I'd learned from the Anti-Slavery Society up north, many people would listen to reason.

On a cold November day, I headed down to the mercantile district to do some shopping, carrying a bundle of tracts in my bag with the intention of dropping them off in the stores I visited along Main Street. I was about to step into the milliner's shop when I heard a loud shout and looked up to see a dark-haired man in his mid-twenties running toward me, chasing a little Negro boy. They were just a few yards away from me when the stranger finally caught the child by the arm. The boy kicked and flailed desperately as he struggled to free himself, but he was ragged and thin, no more than eight years old, and a pitiful match for the well-dressed, well-built man who had him in his grip.

Without a second thought, I swung my bag at the man's head as hard as I could. "Stop that! Let go of him!"

The man was more than a foot taller than me, so I missed his head and struck the back of his shoulder instead. He released the boy, more from surprise than from the force of the blow, and the child raced away. Breathless and angry, the man whirled around to face me, and I found myself looking into the bluest eyes I'd ever seen—wide and clear and as cold as mountain ice. He blinked in surprise when he saw who had struck him, and I noticed the thick, dark lashes that fringed his eyes.

"Listen now," he said when he'd recovered from his surprise. "What do you think you're doing?"

"How dare you treat a child that way? You have no right to use force against a defenseless boy just because he's a Negro!"

"That boy is a thief. I caught him stealing fruit from that vendor over there, but now he's gotten away, thanks to you." The man's dark brown hair had become tousled during the struggle, and he raked it from his high forehead with an angry thrust of his hand. His hair was thick and fashionably long, covering the tops of his ears. A curving mustache and trim beard hid his chin.

His anger unnerved me. I didn't know what had ever possessed me to interfere in this affair, but I was suddenly very sorry that I had. "Y-your slave wouldn't be forced to steal . . . if . . . if you treated him fairly," I stammered.

"He is not my slave."

A gust of wind suddenly blew, and I realized that some of my tracts had spilled out when I'd swung my bag. They were starting to blow away.

"Oh no!" I scrambled to retrieve them, but running and bending were awkward in my billowing hoop skirt.

"Allow me," he said. The angry expression smoothed from his face as he remembered his manners. He crouched on the sidewalk and began gathering my papers. But as he stood, straightening the pamphlets into a pile, he read what they were. His anger returned in an instant. "What sort of trash is this?" he demanded.

His startling eyes pinned me, and my heart began to race. I wanted to run, but I also wanted to stand up for what I believed. "Y-you might benefit from reading one of them, sir. They clearly explain that slavery is a sin, and that it is abhorrent to God. It is impossible for a Christian to defend it."

"Listen now. You're breaking the law. Don't you know you could be arrested for distributing this propaganda?" I could see that he was growing angrier by the minute. I was afraid of him, but my own rising anger fueled my courage.

"No, I'm quite certain that I still have the right to freedom of speech here in America. And freedom of the press."

"Each state has the right to enact its own laws," he said coldly, "and in the state of Virginia, it is a felony to distribute abolitionist material."

I had no idea if he was telling the truth. My heart raced faster. "First you try to arrest a poor, starving child, and now you're threatening to arrest me? Am I to believe that you're a policeman, sir? Or do you make it your habit to run around Richmond taking the law into your own hands?"

"It's the duty of all law-abiding citizens to stop people who are breaking the law. I was merely trying to help the grocer recover his goods and to help you avoid arrest—not to mention help retrieve your disgusting pamphlets. It seems I've had nothing but abuse from you in return for my efforts."

"Well, it's your fault the pamphlets fell out in the first place."

"Oh, I see. Is it also my fault that my shoulder was in the way when you decided to swing your bag at my head?" He shoved the tracts into my hands, then dusted off his own as if they'd become contaminated. "I wash my hands of you. If you're arrested for distributing contraband, you'll have no one to blame but yourself."

"I have not distributed a single one of these!"

His brows lifted in surprise. It made his eyes appear wider still. "Excuse me, but most people don't need a dozen copies of the same tract for their own reading purposes."

"I don't see how it's any of your business what I do with them."

He folded his arms across his chest. I hated it that his height enabled him to look down on me. "Your accent tells me you're from Virginia," he said, "but your actions speak otherwise. Listen now. If you're visiting our fair city, I only wish to warn you, as a gentleman, that folks in Richmond don't take kindly to such interference with our Negroes. Nor do we appreciate people spreading abolitionist propaganda. Good day."

He strode away so quickly that I would have had to either shout or run after him in order to have the last word. I began walking back to where Eli waited with the carriage. The encounter had left me too angry and shaken to continue with my shopping. Had the boy really been a thief? And was it really against the law to distribute anti-slavery pamphlets?

Eli looked surprised to see me back so soon. He hurried to help me into the carriage. "Back already? Shopping all done? Hey, now . . . what's wrong, Missy Caroline?" I was nearly nineteen years old, but I had a ridiculous urge to sit on Eli's lap and cry.

"Take me home, please."

"Sure thing, Missy. Right away."

He maneuvered the carriage through the crowded streets and up the hill toward home. By the time the steeple of St. John's church came into view, I was beginning to calm down, but I still longed to talk to Eli like I used to do when I was a little girl, telling him all my troubles, listening to his gentle wisdom. When he drew the carriage to a halt beside the gate and helped me down, I hesitated, unsure of how to begin. Eli made it easy for me.

"Now, Missy Caroline . . . anything you want to tell me, you know I listen."

"Can . . . can we go inside the carriage house and talk?" A cold wind was blowing up from the river, and the air had turned chilly.

"Sure thing, Missy. I be going in there to unhitch these horses anyway." He opened the double doors for me, and I watched from inside as he climbed up into the driver's seat and drove the carriage in behind me. I was a little afraid of the horses and kept a respectful distance, but Eli treated them as if they were his children, gently patting their flanks, rubbing a favorite spot on their necks, talking quietly to them as he unhitched their harnesses. He would wait patiently for me to speak my mind. And I knew he would listen carefully to everything I said.

"When I lived up north," I began, "I met a group of people who are working hard to end slavery. One of the reasons I wanted to come home was so that I could work to abolish slavery down here." I waved the pile of windblown pamphlets that I still clutched in my hand. "See these? They explain what the Anti-Slavery Society believes. They spell it out so clearly. If I could just get people to read them and see the truth, I know they would change their minds."

Eli examined a spot on one of the horses' necks where the harness had rubbed. "That what you try and do today?" he finally asked. "Change folks' minds?"

"Yes . . . but I only talked to one person. And he threatened to throw me in jail." I exhaled angrily at the memory. "I don't know what I did wrong . . . or what to do differently next time . . . or how I should go about this. I need your advice, Eli."

He had removed one of the harnesses, and he held it in his huge hands, rubbing the smooth leather with his thumb as he studied me. "Seem like it be a mighty hard thing to change someone's mind," he said. "Most folks won't change their mind unless they have a change of heart first."

"Well, then . . . how do I change their heart?"

"You can't, Missy Caroline," he said gently. "Only Massa Jesus can change folks' hearts."

"How does He do it?"

Eli hung up the harness and led the horses into their stalls. When he was finished, he walked back to where I waited and leaned against the carriage wheel. "If a person's heart is soft and tender toward God—like yours, Missy Caroline—I think his heart get changed pretty easy. But if folks' hearts is cold and hard, like a stone—well, only fire can melt stone."

He looked down at his feet for a long moment, then lifted his head to face me again. "Seems like God gonna have to bring an awful lot of folks through the fire before we see their hearts changing any."

I wrote to my cousin Jonathan, who was in his last year of school at the College of William and Mary, and told him that I was home. The trip from Williamsburg wasn't too far by steamer, so I invited him to visit me whenever he was in Richmond. Jonathan had always had a tender heart, and I hoped for an opportunity to preach abolition to him. He'd once told me that he owned Josiah, and I had the crazy idea that if he recognized the truth about slavery he would set

Josiah free. At the very least, he might recognize Josiah's marriage to Tessie and allow them to spend more time together. But I knew I'd have to take Eli's advice and proceed slowly after my disastrous experience with the stranger I'd met on Main Street.

Jonathan came to see me several times that fall, and I was happy to discover that my cousin hadn't changed one bit. Of course he was older and taller, a grown man now, with a silky brown mustache. But he was still lanky and lively and every bit as mischievous as he'd been as a boy. He came to the house one afternoon when he was home for Christmas vacation, and he was so excited that he grabbed me by my waist, lifted me up in the air, and whirled me around saying, "Congratulate me, Caroline! I'm in love!"

"Put me down," I said, laughing, "and tell me who the lucky woman is."

"Her name is Sally St. John—Sally, Sally, Sally!" he sang. "The most beautiful name, the most wonderful girl I've ever met . . . after you, of course. When I'm with her I feel drunk with joy."

"I'm not sure you're sober right now," I laughed. "Come on." I took his hand and led him into the parlor to sit down. "I'll have Esther bring some coffee and maybe a bite to eat, and then you can tell me when the wedding is going to be."

He didn't sit. His face was suddenly a mask of tragedy. "You don't understand. I can't eat. I'm too lovesick. And there is no wedding date. Every man in Richmond is in love with Sally. She lives in a tower in a castle on a distant hill, and I must embark on a quest to woo and win her." He pulled an imaginary sword from its scabbard and waved it in the air. "But I must be victorious! I simply cannot live without her!"

I grinned up at him. "You're quite insane."

"I know. Insanely in love." He suddenly dropped to one knee in front of the sofa and took my hand in both of his. "Dear Caroline, I've come to ask for a favor. I need your help on this valiant quest."

"Get up, you crazy fool."

"Not until you promise to help me. Sally has invited me and a dozen other fellows to her Christmas party next week. Please, please, I beg you to come with me."

"Wait a minute. If you're in love with Sally, why are you inviting me to her party?"

"Because you're beautiful, Carrie. If I arrive with you on my arm it'll make Sally insanely jealous. In fact, every man there will be jealous. One look at you, and the other men will toss Sally aside like yesterday's newspaper. I'll have her all to myself, don't you see? She loves the thrill of conquering men's hearts. And she always wants what she can't have. If I bring you to the party, I'll win her heart and destroy the competition in one simple stroke."

"Get up," I repeated, pulling him onto the sofa beside me. "Your plan will never work."

"It will! I know it will! Please say you'll help me. I'll do anything you want in return."

"Anything?" If I had Jonathan in my debt, maybe I could bargain with him on Tessie and Josiah's behalf. I dreaded the thought of socializing with strangers at a Christmas party, but I made up my mind to do it for Tessie's sake. "All right," I said. "I'll help you on one condition. I'm going to give you a booklet, and you have to promise me that you'll read it. And that you'll really think about what it says and not simply get angry and toss it aside."

"Sure, I'll do anything." I gave him one of my tracts and he stuffed it into his coat pocket without even glancing at it. Then Jonathan fairly raced to the door, obviously eager to leave before I changed my mind.

"I'll pick you up for Sally's party at eight o'clock on Saturday," he called. Then he left again as if carried away by a whirlwind.

On the evening of Sally St. John's party, I put several pamphlets in my reticule before leaving home, planning to give one to every gentleman who asked to dance with me. If I didn't convert anyone, at least the tracts might scare away unwanted suitors.

Sally's ornate house in the fashionable Court End district was enormous, glittering with all the trappings of great wealth. As our carriage stopped beneath the *porte cochere,* a half-dozen liveried servants rushed out to assist us.

"Are you sure you aren't in over your head, Jonathan?" I asked.

"She's filthy rich, I know. Her family owns a couple of flour mills, and who knows what else. But I don't care a thing about her money. Her father can keep all of it. I just want Sally."

"That's very noble, but how will you ever afford to keep Sally in the style to which she's accustomed? I mean, Hilltop is nice, but it's nothing like this."

Jonathan wasn't listening. He had spotted Sally, greeting her guests in the soaring entrance hall. Behind her, a sweeping staircase decked in candles and greenery seemed to float toward the second floor with nothing supporting it.

"Isn't she beautiful?" Jonathan sighed.

She was. Sally St. John wore a magnificent gown of rose-colored silk that must have taken twenty yards of cloth. It dipped daringly low off her shoulders, revealing skin like white rose petals. Her hair was the color of honey, and her vivacious green eyes sparkled like the jewels around her neck. My face was probably just as pretty as Sally's, but my shyness made me seem cold and withdrawn. Sally's vibrant personality, her effortless warmth and bubbling charm, made her irresistibly beautiful.

"Why, Jonathan Fletcher," she exclaimed when she spotted him. "I'm so glad you could come!" He might have been the honored guest the entire party had been waiting for.

"Merry Christmas, Sally." Jonathan acted very cool as he gallantly kissed her hand. I saw no sign of the lovesick boy who'd come to me begging on one knee.

"Who is this *darling* girl you've brought with you?" she asked as she sized me up. I didn't see "darling" in her eyes. Sally had the alert look of a competitor at a sporting event, eyeing her opponent before dashing off for the prize. I was amazed to discover that Jonathan had been right; Sally was jealous of me. His plan just might work.

"This is my dear friend Caroline," he replied. "She's been attending school in Philadelphia for the last few years and has finally returned home to stay."

"I'm pleased to meet you," Sally said. But she wasn't.

It was probably Jonathan's plan to make Sally think we were sweethearts. And although it would have been perfectly acceptable for first cousins to court each other or even to marry, I noticed he hadn't told her my last name or that I was his cousin. He and Sally talked for a moment about mutual acquaintances and events I knew nothing of. Then he quickly turned his full attention back to me.

"I'm so sorry, darling. Forgive me for boring you. I promised that you would have me all to yourself tonight, and you will."

As Jonathan and I moved toward the drawing room, Sally caught his arm. She wore a sweet, strained smile on her lips, a green glint of jealousy in her eyes. "You will save one dance for me, won't you, Jonathan?"

"If Caroline will let me." He smiled at me, not her, and we swept into the ballroom.

The servants had moved most of the furniture out of the vast drawing room and transformed it into a ballroom. I'd never seen such an opulent room before, or such a high-ceilinged one, even in Philadelphia. Acres of fringed silk draperies, swags, and jabots adorned the windows. Plasterwork embellishments in the latest neo-classical designs decorated the walls. Brilliantly patterned carpeting stretched from wall to wall, and four huge chandeliers, each bearing dozens of candles and hundreds of crystal prisms, bathed the glittering room with light.

"I never realized what a clever actor you are," I whispered as Jonathan took me into his arms to dance.

"It's working. Sally is jealous, isn't she? Now, Caroline, don't be angry with me, but when the time is right, I'll need to leave you and dance with her, just one time. Is that all right?"

"Did you read the booklet I gave you?"

He struck his forehead with his fist dramatically. "The booklet! Forgive me, Caroline, but I was so excited about tonight that all I could think about was Sally. I promise I'll read it the moment I get home."

Jonathan was such a charming clown it was impossible to be cross with him. As an escort, he was much more suave and dashing than Robert had been, and as the evening progressed, I never once regretted my decision to accompany him. Jonathan and I danced together, explored Sally's gardens and the first floor of her house, spied on the other couples, and sampled the canapés and fruit punch. The evening reminded me of our adventures on the plantation when we were young, only now we were dressed in formal evening clothes.

When we weren't dancing, Jonathan's friends gathered around waiting to be introduced to me. I didn't feel a bit nervous. Jonathan not only made me feel brave, he made the evening fun.

"Is Sally watching?" he would ask every now and then. Nearly every time I looked, she was watching him, even though a host of suitors flocked around her at all times like birds at a feeder—all except for Jonathan. He paid no attention to her at all. Perversely, she wanted what she couldn't have. I could see that Sally enjoyed the thrill of the quest as much as Jonathan did.

"Clever boy," I said. "Yes, she's watching. Your idea is working like a charm."

"I'm going to dance with her now," he told me later that evening. "I'll leave you with my good friend Roger. He's been dying to dance with you."

"No, don't do that," I said quickly. "I'd rather sit down for a while. My feet ache."

"All right, then. I'll be back for you in a little bit."

We parted, and I headed toward the door to a smaller parlor

where guests could rest between dances. But I was looking over my shoulder, watching Jonathan approach Sally instead of watching where I was going, and I suddenly collided with a man as I stepped into the room. Some of his punch spilled down his shirtfront.

"Oh, excuse me," I said.

I looked up and found myself face-to-face with the stranger I had argued with on Main Street.

"You again!" I said in surprise.

"I might say the same thing—and in the same tone of voice—if I wasn't a gentleman." He took out his handkerchief and dabbed his shirt. "I suppose I should be grateful that you weren't armed with your bag."

I realized that I was blocking the doorway and stepped aside. "Excuse me. Did you want to go back into the ballroom?"

"No. As a matter of fact, I'd just stepped in here to sit down when you plowed into me. It would seem that you are a dangerous woman to cross paths with."

There were only two empty chairs in the room, and they were side by side. My feet ached from dancing, and I wasn't about to let this oaf deprive me of a chance to sit. He was evidently as stubborn as I was, because he followed me over to the corner and took the seat beside me. His insulting manner brought out the worst in me. I wanted to insult him in return, letting him know I despised him for the way he treated Negroes, if for no other reason.

"So, have you grown tired of fluttering around Sally like all the other men?" I asked. "Or isn't she giving you the time of day?"

He frowned slightly. "Sally St. John? She's not my type. I've never cared much for women whose sole concern is themselves—women who prattle on and on about outward things, such as hair and jewelry and clothes."

I tried not to blush when I recalled how vain I'd been in Philadelphia—before I joined the Anti-Slavery Society. "I'm surprised you came to her party at all if you have such a low opinion of her," I said.

He looked at me for a long moment before replying. "My parents adore Sally. I came to the party as a favor to them. Are you a friend of hers?"

"I don't know her at all. I'm here as a guest of someone who knows her."

"Ah! And I'll bet you saw this as a golden opportunity to pass around your abolitionist propaganda." I felt my anger build as his arrow hit its mark. "Let me give you some advice," he continued. "I know Sally's parents quite well, and you would be insulting a highly respected Richmond family if you distributed your garbage in their home. I know for a fact that they have always treated their slaves very kindly."

"There's more to the matter of slavery than kind treatment," I replied. "Just because they don't whip or abuse their Negroes doesn't make it right to own them. Slavery denies people the right to benefit from their own labor. Poor whites can work hard and eventually get ahead—immigrants do it all the time. But no matter how hard a slave works, he is still in the same place. The only people who benefit from a slave's hard labor are his white owners."

"Listen now. When one of Sally's servants comes over here, I dare you to take him aside and ask him if he's content."

"There would be no point at all in doing that. He'd say he's content because he's been trained to give white people the correct answers. But let me ask you this—if the slaves in Virginia are so content, why are slave owners so terrified that they'll join up with zealots like John Brown?"

"Because most Negroes are ignorant and superstitious. They're like little children. They can be led to rebel very easily."

"It's not their fault that they're ignorant. If we provided them with an education—"

"Don't be naïve. It's been scientifically proven that the Negro race is inferior."

"Oh! That makes me absolutely furious!" I longed to tell him about Eli, but I didn't dare. "I've seen educated Negroes up north who were employed in all walks of life. Frederick Douglass is an eloquent speaker and a gifted journalist. And I've also met plenty of ignorant white people, too."

"I'll wager you've never been to the Dark Continent and witnessed the ignorance and barbarity of native Africans. The 'school of slavery' here in America has civilized the Negro race and brought them true religion."

"I don't believe you would know the first thing about true religion. The Bible says that anyone who claims to be in the light but hates his brother is still in the darkness. If there is a Dark Continent, sir, it's this one."

As we argued, his blue eyes grew darker and darker, like approaching storm clouds. Suddenly they flashed with anger. "Is it Christian of you to toss Scripture around and condemn all slaveholders without knowing the truth about them as individuals? Would your God like it that you pass judgment on people before learning the truth, the way you passed judgment on me when you saw me chasing that Negro boy? Is yours a God of grace or judgment?"

I suddenly recalled a line from the Anti-Slavery Society's aims— *the overthrow of prejudice by the power of love.* Once again, I knew that I had failed miserably. And with the same person, no less.

"I have never met anyone quite as infuriating as you," I said for lack of anything better to say. "And if you believe in a God of grace instead of judgment, then why didn't you buy that poor child an apple instead of trying to arrest him for stealing one?"

I saw Jonathan stroll into the room, and I rose to leave. "There you are, darling," I said as he moved toward me.

He must have noticed our angry faces because he wrapped a protective arm around my shoulder. "Is something wrong, Caroline?"

I lifted my chin and smiled sweetly. "No. Nothing at all."

"Good. Come dance with me, then. They're playing a waltz."

My anger slowly cooled as I drifted around the floor in his arms.

"That man I was speaking with in the parlor . . . do you know him, Jonathan?"

"I never saw the gentleman before."

"Oh, believe me, he's no gentleman. How did your dance with Sally go?"

"Perfect!" He whirled me around in joy, grinning like a fool. "She gave me permission to call on her."

I kept a wary eye out for the infuriating stranger, but I didn't see him again for the remainder of the evening. He didn't come into the ballroom to dance, nor was he at the buffet table later, when dinner was served. He must have left the party early, because he wasn't in the foyer when we all said good-bye to Sally sometime after midnight. I might have been able to forget him altogether if I'd been able to stop thinking about his magnificent eyes.

I had a silent conversation with him as Tessie helped me take off my gown and get ready for bed. I thought of all the things I wished I'd said, and I planned all of the things I would say to him the next time. The next time? Would there even be a next time?

"I certainly hope not!" I mumbled as I dove beneath the covers. But that wasn't quite true. Why was I rehearsing all these arguments if I wasn't going to see him again? *Just in case,* I assured myself.

Then came the harder question—did I want to see him again?

"Certainly not!" I said aloud.

"If you gonna talk to yourself all night," Tessie said from her bed in the corner, "then I guess I better go sleep someplace else."

"Sorry. It's just that he makes me so angry."

"Who does? Your cousin?"

"No, not Jonathan. That . . . that *man!*"

"What man is that, honey?"

I didn't even know his name.

10

RICHMOND 1860

January seemed to last a long time that year. I didn't venture downtown very often because of the bad weather, nor did I have any more adventures with Jonathan, who had returned to college. But no matter how hard I tried, I couldn't stop thinking about Sally St. John's party and my second encounter with the blue-eyed stranger.

On a blustery day in February—long after I should have forgotten the man—I sat at the table in my bedroom, trying to compose a letter to Robert at West Point. But I found myself remembering my argument with the stranger instead.

"Negroes are ignorant and superstitious," he had said. *"It's been scientifically proven that the Negro race is inferior."*

"That's just not true!" I said aloud.

Tessie looked up from her sewing. "You talking to me, honey?"

"No . . . I was talking to that horrible man."

"The one you writing the letter to?"

"No, not Robert . . . *him!*" I tossed down the pen, leaving a blob of ink on my sheet of writing paper.

"Well, I just an ignorant old mammy . . . but I ain't seeing any man in this here room."

I was so angry I stood up. "You're not ignorant, Tessie. And that's exactly what I told him, too. It's not your fault you've never had an education."

Tessie stared at me, bewildered, then returned to her sewing. "I just gonna mind my own business, now. Ain't nobody knows what you talking about, except yourself."

"I can prove it, too. Come here, Tessie."

She looked up at me in alarm. "Now, why you want to make me talk to a man who ain't there?"

"I'm not. I'm going to teach you to read and write."

Tessie looked frightened. "What earthly good that gonna do? Don't you know colored folk ain't allowed to read and write?"

"No one will ever know except you and me." I went to her chair beside the fireplace and took her hand, pulling her to her feet. "Please, Tessie. This will prove it to him. I know I can teach you."

"This gonna make you happy, honey?" she asked, stroking my cheek. "Because you know I hate to see you moping around here, talking to yourself."

"It will make both of us happy. You'll see. Come on, sit down at the table."

With a good deal of pushing and prodding, I got Tessie seated, then I wrote her name for her in block letters. I explained how each letter had a sound, how the *S* made a sound like a snake, and so forth. Then I gave her the pen and coaxed her to copy her name herself.

Tessie did her usual share of good-natured grumbling and grousing—"Don't see what good this gonna do. . . . Don't see how this make folks happy. . . ." But I could tell she was pleased with herself. She learned very quickly. By the end of the hour, she had filled several sheets of paper with boldly printed lines of TESSIE. She had also remembered how to write it without looking at my copy.

"You a good teacher," she said when we finished our first lesson.

"This is only the beginning," I told her.

"Oh no . . ."

"Yes. We're going to have a lesson every afternoon, and before long, you'll be able to read and write as good as anyone."

"If that's what you want, honey," she said hesitantly. "But now there something I have to do. And don't you go getting mad at me for doing it."

I watched as Tessie carried her work over to the fireplace and solemnly fed every last sheet into the flames.

Jonathan returned to Richmond along with the spring weather. He showed up on my doorstep one sunny afternoon, begging me for another favor. "Sally has agreed to meet me at the fairgrounds for a picnic on Sunday, but her father insists that we be chaperoned. Won't you *please* come with us, Caroline?"

"No, not this time. I would hate being a third wheel. Besides, I don't think Sally likes me very much."

Jonathan wasn't listening. And he wouldn't take no for an answer. As he continued to wheedle and beg, telling me all the reasons why I was his only hope, I suddenly remembered the bargain we had made the last time I'd done him a favor.

I interrupted his pleas to ask, "Did you ever read that booklet I gave you?"

"What? Oh . . . yes . . . it was very interesting." He wore the guilty look of a naughty boy. "Why don't you come on the picnic this Sunday and we'll discuss it?"

"You're lying. You didn't read it."

"Caroline, don't you and I always have fun when we're together?"

"Well, yes. . . ."

"And you won't be a third wheel. Sally's brother is supposed to be arriving home from Washington sometime this week. We'll ask him to be our fourth. Please say you'll go out with us."

"But you know how hard it is for me to talk to strangers. I'm not very good at socializing. And I certainly don't want to be stuck with some shallow, self-centered brother of Sally's."

Jonathan refused to yield. He was madly in love, he claimed, and I was his only means of seeing Sally. As he continued to beg and plead, I remembered my mission—change one person at a time. If Jonathan wouldn't read my pamphlet, maybe Sally's brother would. Besides, if Jonathan was further in my debt, perhaps I could bargain on Tessie and Josiah's behalf.

"All right," I said at last. "You owe me *two* favors . . . and her brother better not bore me to tears, or I swear I'll go straight home."

"I love you!" he said, hugging me. "When Sally and I have our first daughter, we'll name her after you."

"If you want to thank me, read the material I gave you," I called. But he was already out the door.

Jonathan and I arrived at the fairgrounds first and waited on a bench near the entrance for the St. Johns to arrive. At least I waited on the bench. Jonathan was so feverishly excited that I gave up trying to get him to sit down, let alone converse with me. If this was how people in love acted, I hoped it never happened to me.

"That's Sally's carriage!" he shouted when he finally spotted the matched team of horses trotting toward us.

"Calm down," I said, laughing. "You're dancing, and there isn't even any music."

The carriage pulled to a stop. The coachman stepped down to open the door. Sally alighted first, then her brother. When I saw who he was, I wanted the earth to open up and swallow me.

Him again!

I felt my cheeks burning as Sally and Jonathan made the introductions. "I'd like you to meet my cousin, Caroline Fletcher."

"This is my brother, Charles St. John."

An icy silence followed their words. Charles and I both knew we were supposed to be polite, to say things like "how do you do?"

and "pleased to meet you," but we coldly stared past each other for what felt like an eternity.

When Charles suddenly began to laugh, I felt insulted. Jonathan and Sally gaped at him, mystified.

"Tell us the joke, Charles," Sally said.

I made the mistake of looking into his eyes and my heart turned traitor on me, galloping as foolishly as a spring colt in a wide meadow. It was the first time I'd seen laughter in his eyes, and it made them startlingly bright, like the blue in a rainbow.

"You have to admit this is quite ironic," he said when his laughter died away. "I had no idea you would be the mysterious cousin, and I can see by your reaction that you had no idea I was Sally's brother." His smile was so radiant, his face so transformed when he wasn't scornful or angry, that I smiled weakly in return.

"Do you know each other?" Sally asked.

"Miss Fletcher and I have never been formally introduced until today. But we have bumped into each other before."

"I remember now," Jonathan said. "Weren't you having some sort of disagreement at Sally's party?"

"Oh, Charles, you're not going to spoil this nice afternoon for me, are you?" Sally said, pouting.

"I wouldn't dream of it," he said smoothly. "Truce, Miss Fletcher?"

"Of course."

He offered his hand, and I shook it. His grip was warm and firm. A tight little knot in the pit of my stomach seemed to come unraveled at his touch, and I hated myself for reacting to him.

"I'm not hungry yet," Sally decided. "Let's stroll around the fairgrounds for a while before we eat." Jonathan picked up the picnic basket that the St. Johns had brought, and Sally took his other arm. They started down the path ahead of us, Jonathan's head bent lovingly toward her as they talked.

Thankfully, Charles didn't offer me his arm. As we walked down the path behind them, I decided to take Cousin Rosalie's advice and ask him about himself. I learned that he was five years older than me, that he'd graduated from Virginia University in Charlottesville, and that he would probably manage his father's flour mills one day. But he also loved politics, and he was currently working as an aide to one of Virginia's senators, traveling with him to Washington whenever Congress was in session.

I told Charles about my father's business, about my cousin's plantation, and how I'd attended school in Philadelphia for the past two years.

"Ah! So, that explains it," he mumbled.

"Explains what?" But I knew exactly what he was going to say.

"How you became brainwashed with all that anti-slavery propaganda."

"Nobody brainwashed me. I'm perfectly capable of thinking for myself."

"Let me guess, they had you read *Uncle Tom's Cabin,* and—"

"For your information, I have never read it. I didn't need to. My experiences with slavery right here in Virginia were enough to—"

"Your experiences should have told you that Miss Stowe's book is filled with melodramatic exaggerations."

"Have you read it, Mr. St. John?"

"I wouldn't be caught dead—"

He stopped short when Sally suddenly pushed between us. "Charles, stop this!" Her voice was hushed with embarrassment.

I had forgotten myself in the heat of the argument, but as I looked around I was shocked to discover that Charles and I had been standing in the middle of the path, shouting at each other. People were staring at us. I felt mortified. Charles looked shaken.

"If you two can't be civil, then please have the decency to be quiet," Sally said.

"Fine," I replied.

"Of course," Charles agreed.

Sally took Jonathan's arm again, but they walked behind us this time, ready to douse the flames if the sparks began to fly. Charles shoved his hands into his pockets. "It has turned out to be a beautiful day, hasn't it, Miss Fletcher?" I was surprised that the spring flowers didn't wither at the ice in his voice. But I could be coldly polite, too.

"Yes, it's a lovely day, Mr. St. John."

We continued in that vein until Jonathan found a peaceful spot on the grass for us to spread our blanket. As we ate lunch, Charles gradually revealed a very charming side of himself, a side I'd certainly never seen before. "I'd like to hear more about your work in Washington," Jonathan said.

"Tell them about the time you met President Buchanan," Sally coaxed.

"Right. My shining moment in the presence of greatness," he replied. I heard gentle laughter in his voice and saw that conceit and self-importance were not part of his nature. Instead, Charles possessed the rare quality of being able to laugh at himself. "I was attending a reception at a Washington hotel," he began, "and the president mistook me for the British ambassador's attaché. I didn't know what to do. It was a huge gathering, and President Buchanan took me aside to ramble on and on about some trade agreement he was negotiating. I couldn't be rude and interrupt him, so I just kept nodding my head. But then he asked me what I thought. I didn't know whether I should embarrass the president of the United States by pointing out that I wasn't the attaché, or simply mimic a British accent and say, 'I think it's a jolly good treaty, old boy!'"

Charles' imitation of an Englishman was so amusing that I couldn't help laughing. "So what did you do?" I asked.

"Luckily, I spotted the real British ambassador just then, so I said, 'There's the ambassador, Mr. President. He's much more qualified to speak to this issue than I am.'" Charles used his phony British accent again, and we all roared with laughter.

"Is that the tightest spot you've ever been in, in Washington?" Jonathan asked.

"Politically, perhaps. But my most dangerous experience occurred the time my landlady lost her cat."

"Tell us, Charles," Sally begged. Charles had such an amusing manner of storytelling, mimicking all the voices and gesturing dramatically, that he might have been a stage actor. I found myself leaning toward him, listening attentively.

"Well, I had just returned to my boardinghouse one afternoon, when my landlady came running out to the front hallway, wringing her hands and begging for my help. Mrs. Peckham is such a sweet little white-haired lady, so small and frail—and at least a hundred years old—so of course I offered to help her any way that I could.

"'My poor little kitty cat has been missing for three days,' she said, 'but I heard her crying this morning. I think she's trapped up in a tree.'

"Now, I'm no cat-lover," Charles said, "but I do take pride in being chivalrous. Her cat was, indeed, about halfway up the oak tree in front of the boardinghouse. So, like a good Southern gentleman, I removed my hat and coat, fetched Mrs. Peckham's ladder from the tool shed, and began to climb. Wouldn't you know, the blasted cat saw me coming and climbed higher and higher to get away from me? By the time she ran out of branches to climb, the ladder was far below me, and we were both teetering at the very top of the tree. The limbs were a bit thin to bear my weight, so I swayed in the breeze like wheat in the wind.

"Well, I finally succeeded in catching the animal, but she fought like a wildcat, scratching and hissing at me. I was already hanging on to the tree for dear life, and I knew I couldn't hold her and climb down at the same time, so I did the only thing that came to mind: I unbuttoned my shirt, stuffed the cat inside, and buttoned it up again.

"Dreadful mistake. She had claws like razor blades, and she wanted her freedom, so she proceeded to slice my chest into ribbons. Of course, Mrs. Peckham was watching all this from below and singing

152

my praises as a hero. So I had no choice but to grit my teeth, ignore the pain, and start climbing down.

"By the time I reached the ladder, the cat had worked her deadly way around my body and was now shredding my back. I was in such a hurry to end my torment that I accidentally kicked the ladder over in my haste to get down. Tiny, frail Mrs. Peckham couldn't right it again, so she tottered off, in her doddering way, for help.

"I couldn't wait. The lowest branch was about fifteen feet above the ground, but I figured if I broke my neck in the fall, at least it would end the misery the cat was inflicting on me. And with any luck, the cursed cat would die, too. I swung from the branch with both hands and dropped to the ground—spraining my ankle in the process. I didn't care. That pain was nothing compared to those needle-like claws. I quickly unbuttoned my shirt, wrenched the blasted cat off my back, and bundled her up inside the shirt like a sack of potatoes.

"By the time Mrs. Peckham returned with her handyman—who probably should have been sent to retrieve the stupid cat in the first place—I must have looked a sight: sitting on the ground, shirtless, my body bleeding and cut to ribbons.

"'Look like the overseer done whipped you good, Mr. St. John,' the handyman said. He took the bundle away from me and carefully opened it to present the cat to Mrs. Peckham. That's when I got the biggest surprise of all.

"'Why, Mr. St. John!' she exclaimed. 'That's not my kitty!'"

By the time Charles finished his story, I was laughing so hard I had tears in my eyes. I couldn't believe he was the same obnoxious man I'd argued with earlier. And I couldn't believe that I was having such a good time with him. But when Sally and Jonathan left the two of us alone on the blanket and went to feed the leftover cake to the ducks, the fireworks soon started again.

"Have you picnicked here at the fairgrounds before?" Charles asked me casually.

"No, I never have."

"Isn't it nice to see so many people enjoying the fine spring weather?"

"Yes, it is." But I'd noticed that all of the couples strolling the paths that afternoon were white. It angered me that educated people like Charles couldn't see how wrong that was. I simply had to speak my mind. "It's too bad, Mr. St. John, that in this beautiful land of freedom, the Negro population of Richmond is not allowed a day of rest or the pleasure of a stroll."

His eyes narrowed. "Listen now. Don't start . . ."

"The truth leaves you without defense, doesn't it?"

"I have a perfectly good defense, but why waste my breath?"

"Ha!" I said. "I'd like to hear you try to defend the fact that slavery deprives people of their basic rights and freedoms."

"Why bother? You people don't listen anyway. All I ever do in Washington is argue with Northern abolitionists, and it doesn't do a bit of good."

"That's because they're right and you're wrong."

"No, it's because you've all been brainwashed with a bunch of overblown rhetoric—"

"Stop it this instant!" We looked up to see Sally standing over us, hands on hips. "Honestly! If you two won't stop bickering, then we'd better go home."

Charles held his hands up in surrender. "Sorry. Don't let me spoil your day. I promise I won't say another word."

"Me either!" I folded my arms across my chest.

"Well, that will make for a cheerful afternoon," Sally said. "Pack everything up, Jonathan. Charles, fetch the carriage. I want to go home."

"No, Sally, wait!" Jonathan pleaded. "Let's give them one more chance."

But Sally refused. Long before the afternoon should have ended, she and Charles were gone. Jonathan was so upset with me he didn't say a word on the ride home, and he refused my invitation to come into the house. When he drove off without saying good-bye, I comforted myself with the thought that he wasn't likely to beg me for any more favors.

The worst part of that whole disastrous day was the fact that I couldn't stop thinking about Charles. Half of the time I would argue with him in my head, and the other half of the time I would be remembering his smile or the sound of his laughter—and then that breathless, dizzy sensation would come over me again, the way it had when he shook my hand. I hated myself for being attracted to such a horrible man—for laughing at his stories and for enjoying myself at least some of the time that I'd spent with him.

As I lay tossing in bed that night, I could still hear the sound of his drowsy voice and the habit he had of saying, "Listen now . . ." I groaned aloud.

Tessie got up and came over to sit on my bed. "May as well tell me what's bothering you, or neither one of us gonna get any sleep tonight."

I sat up to face her, sitting cross-legged. "He is the most infuriating man I've ever met!"

"Jonathan?"

"No. Charles St. John. I hate him! I never want to see him again! I've been arguing with him in my head, thinking of all the things I should have said, and now I know exactly what I intend to say to him the next time I see him."

"I'm just an old mammy, but . . . why you gonna talk to him again if he annoy you so?"

"Because I want to forget him, but I can't get him out of my mind. I hope I never see him again, but I'm so afraid that I won't see him. He has me so confused, Tessie! I wish he would go back to Washington and . . . and drown in the Potomac River!"

"Guess this here James River ain't good enough to drown him."

"No! I mean, yes! Tessie, I'm not even making sense, am I? What's wrong with me? I shake all over when I'm with him, even before he makes me angry. My heart starts going crazy, and I can't catch my breath, and he makes me laugh—yet I can't help arguing with him."

"Let me ask you, honey. That young man who keep sending you letters from West Point?"

"You mean Robert?"

"Uh huh . . . does he do all this 'heart messing' and 'body shaking' with you?"

Not once. Nor had any other man I'd ever met. I shook my head.

"How you feel about that Yankee man?" she asked.

"I feel . . . I feel sorry for Robert. And I feel safe with him."

"You want to wake up beside him every morning?"

I remembered my cousin Julia asking me the same thing. The thought horrified me. "No," I told Tessie.

"Well, then. That's your answer."

"What? What's my answer?"

"You not in love with this Robert."

"Well, I'm certainly not in love with Mr. St. John, I can tell you that! He's insulting . . . and . . . and obnoxious and . . ."

"What he look like? He as ugly as he is mean?"

"No, he's not ugly at all." My voice suddenly quivered with emotion, and I didn't know why. "He's . . . he's . . ." I saw his face in my mind, the way he looked when he laughed and told stories, not when he was angry.

"He's what, honey?"

"Well . . . he would be a handsome man if he weren't so obstinate!" I covered my face and cried. I didn't even know why.

"Mm, mm, mm," Tessie soothed as she gathered me in her arms. "Sure do make it hard to hate a man when he's handsome."

She let me cry for a while, but as my tears began to fade, she asked, "What you and this man arguing about all the time?"

"Slavery. He defends it! Can you imagine? He thinks it's perfectly acceptable!"

A smile tugged at the corners of Tessie's mouth. "Seem to me

156

Cousin Jonathan, your daddy, and just about every white man in Virginia think the same thing. You arguing with all of them, too?"

"No," I answered meekly.

"Honey, if you looking to find a Virginia man who think like a Yankee, you gonna die an old maid. Guess you better marry that Robert fellow while you still got the chance."

I recalled what she'd said about Robert. I wasn't in love with him. But how had she known? "What's it like to fall in love, Tessie?" I asked.

She gazed into the darkness for a long moment, then her smile widened. "Well, when you see that certain man you heart flies like paper on the wind—don't matter if you just see him one minute ago or one year ago. When you with him, ain't nothing or nobody else in the whole world but him. You might be walking down the same old street you walk on every day, but if you with him, your feet don't hardly touch the ground anymore, like you just floating on a little cloud. And, honey, you want his arms to be around you more than you want air to breathe."

"Is that how you feel about Josiah?" I asked. She nodded silently. "But you hardly ever see Josiah. Have you ever thought about finding another man?"

"Most people very lucky if love come around once," she said quietly. "Better not be letting go of it, thinking there be another chance."

I knew that my father's grief had healed when he decided to take an active part in Richmond society again. As more and more invitations arrived at our house, he sometimes asked me to accompany him in my mother's place.

"It's hard for me to believe, Caroline, but you are old enough to be married already," he told me one day. "I think it's time I introduced you to some suitable families."

Half of the time I worried that I'd run into Charles St. John at one of these functions, the other half of the time I was disappointed when I didn't. Then one night, nearly a month after the picnic, I accompanied my father to a political fund-raising ball at the governor's mansion. I was standing near the punch table when Charles appeared out of nowhere and stood in front of me.

"Dance with me."

There was nothing gentlemanly about it. But it was a command. I wanted to refuse, but I couldn't stop myself from moving into his arms. It was the first time Charles and I had ever held each other, and my knees trembled so badly I could scarcely move.

"Listen now," he said after a moment. "If I believed in witches I'd swear you were one." There wasn't a trace of humor in his voice. He stopped moving and drew back to look at my face. I'd never seen a bluer pair of eyes before. They smoldered like blue flames.

"Come on, Miss Fletcher, fight with me. Make me angry."

"Why?" I asked in a tiny voice. I was afraid I was going to cry.

He looked away and started dancing again. "Because maybe then I can stop thinking about you day and night."

I knew exactly how he felt. I decided I would do it; I would give him one last fight, ending this obsession once and for all.

"Do you believe that Negroes can accept the Gospel?" I asked quietly.

"Certainly."

"Then wouldn't that make them our Christian brothers and sisters? The Bible says we can't love Christ and hate our brother."

"I don't hate Negroes."

"Maybe not. But if you loved Christ, you couldn't stand to drive past the slave auction on Fourteenth Street, knowing what's going on in there to some of your Christian brethren."

He danced silently to the music for a moment, then said quietly, "I don't have an answer to that. I'm sorry."

He pulled me closer. His grip on my hand and my waist was firm, possessive. I'd danced with dozens of men before, but I couldn't recall

158

ever being so aware of a man holding me, so conscious of his nearness or the strength of his presence. Everything inside me seemed to be vibrating, as if I stood inside a clanging alarm bell.

When the music ended, we moved apart. I waited for him to thank me for the dance and walk away, yet I was terrified that he would. I had no awareness of the room, the people, or anything else that was going on around me, just Charles standing in front of me, his eyes studying my face. He hadn't let go of my hand.

"What are you doing to me, Caroline?" he asked softly. "Do you know I've actually found myself thinking about some of the things you said? And some of the stupid things I said—like the Negroes being an inferior race. I don't really believe that. I've been wondering which one of us has been brainwashed with overblown rhetoric."

I don't know how long we stood that way. I felt breathless, disembodied, as if I were floating—not only from his words but also from his nearness. It was just as Tessie had described it.

"I argue about slavery all the time in Washington," Charles continued. "I can do it in my sleep. But I'm not used to debating with a woman—especially such a beautiful woman. And to be frank, I've rarely known one who had anything intelligent to say about political matters. You've turned my comfortable world upside down, Caroline. And I'm forced to admit that you were right about at least one thing—I should have bought that little Negro boy an apple."

I was so moved by his words, so captivated by his extraordinary blend of humility and charm, that I couldn't speak. Suddenly, Jonathan's friend Roger bounded over and tapped Charles' shoulder, breaking the spell.

"Excuse me. May I have the next dance with you, Miss Fletcher?"

I had to decide. If I accepted this dance with Roger, then Charles would probably walk away, perhaps for good. If I refused it, Charles would know that I had feelings for him. I thought of Tessie's words about not having a second chance with love, and I made my choice.

"I'm sorry, Roger, but Mr. St. John has the next dance."

Charles closed his eyes, briefly, as Roger walked away. I heard him exhale. "What do we do now?" he asked when he opened them again.

"Maybe we could stop arguing for once and listen to each other."

He pulled me into his arms again and waltzed me smoothly around the dance floor. For a long time neither of us spoke, then Charles said, "There is some truth in your arguments about slavery, but they are too simplistic. Besides, this dangerous rift between North and South is not about slavery. It's about states' rights."

"But the right they want to preserve is the right to hold slaves."

"Slavery is necessary to the South's economy."

"True, but that doesn't make it morally right."

His grip on my hand tightened. I could sense that he was waging a struggle within himself. "Even if we agreed to abolish slavery tomorrow," he said, "what would the millions of Negroes do with their freedom? Where would they live? How would they support themselves? The abolitionists have never come up with a sensible plan. And don't give me that nonsense about Liberia—do your slaves all want to move back to Africa?"

"No, but surely our lawmakers in Washington could come up with a better plan if they put their minds to it. The Negroes deserve the right to have dreams of their own, to live with their families, to know that their children won't be sold out of their arms."

"Listen now. Not every slave owner is that cruel."

"If even one of them is, then it's wrong. Have you ever befriended a Negro, Charles?"

"My family has always treated our servants well. I was very fond of the mammy who cared for us when we were small."

"But are you friends with anyone now, as an equal? Have you listened to his thoughts and dreams?"

"Truthfully? No. Have you?"

"Yes. That's why I feel the way I do. It's not because I've swallowed all of the abolitionists' propaganda. It's because of Tessie and Eli. I wish you could meet them."

He seemed to wrestle with the idea for a moment before saying, "I think I'd like to."

When the waltz ended, Charles steered me out of the noisy ballroom, his hand resting lightly on my back. I felt as though I no longer had any bones in my legs. We found a quiet corner outside on the terrace where we could talk.

"I wasn't sure we could do it," I said.

"Do what?"

"Talk to each other for more than five minutes without fighting. But see? Nearly twenty minutes have passed, and you haven't told me once how infuriating I am."

He smiled. "I knew the first day we met that you were an unusual woman. I'd certainly never met one before who was as outspoken as you—not to mention one who went around clubbing suspected slave drivers with her bag. I thought you were just parroting empty words, Caroline, but you aren't. You really believe what you say. You really care. I'm sorry I misjudged you."

"Will you forgive me for allowing the Negro boy to escape?"

Charles laughed out loud. "Certainly. But that little thief is still loose on the streets of Richmond, you know. It would serve you right if he snatched your purse right out of your hand one day."

I smiled up at him in return. "I'll take that chance."

Charles looked at me for a long moment. He seemed to be drinking me in, the way a thirsty man gulps water. "Who did you come to this fund-raiser with tonight?" he asked at last.

"My father."

"I'd like to meet him. I'd like to ask him if I may escort you home."

My father was very pleased when Charles asked for permission to court me. "The St. Johns are one of Richmond's finest families," Daddy said proudly.

"Not to mention, one of the richest?" I teased.

"Well now, that never hurts, either. But let's not forget what's really important—"

"That I'm growing very fond of Charles?"

"No," he said, laughing, "that he's a good Southern Democrat."

Charles and I went everywhere together that summer—to musical recitals and dinner parties, to the theater, and to countless political functions as the upcoming presidential election grew closer and closer. As my feelings for him deepened, so did the guilt I felt concerning Robert Hoffman—especially when Robert's unanswered letters began to pile up on my desk.

I realized that my cousin Julia had been right; Robert believed he was in love with me. I'd continued writing to him regularly since returning to Richmond, but now that I was falling in love myself, I knew that it was unfair to string Robert along with false hopes. I sat down at my desk one day and wrote him a long, honest letter, gently explaining to him that we no longer had an "understanding."

At the same time, I wrote to Aunt Martha, asking her to help cushion the news. I felt relieved, but a little worried, when Robert's letters stopped immediately. I eventually received a very cool note from my aunt saying that she and Robert had talked, but she gave no indication of how he had received the news. My cousin Julia stopped mentioning him in her letters.

I had much bigger things to worry about that fall. The United States that I loved so much seemed on the brink of a terrible crisis. The race for president, like John Brown's uprising, revealed a nation bitterly divided over slavery. The Democratic Party had split in two, with Northern Democrats nominating Senator Stephen Douglas of Illinois, and Southern Democrats nominating Kentucky's Senator John Breckinridge. The Republicans chose a compromise candidate named Abraham Lincoln, who pledged to halt the spread of slavery in any states that joined the Union in the future but promised not to interfere with slavery in the states where it already existed. I thought Mr. Lincoln's position was a fair compromise; Charles disagreed.

"Lincoln's views are unacceptable," he insisted. "Once our slave states are outnumbered in Congress, we will no longer have fair representation. The North could enact any laws they pleased."

"Is that why South Carolina is threatening to secede if Mr. Lincoln is elected?"

"Yes, that's exactly why. America broke away from Great Britain for the same reason—her interests were not being fairly represented."

"Do you think it will come to that, Charles? Another revolution?"

"I pray not."

But when Abraham Lincoln won the election—with only forty percent of the popular vote—Charles and I both felt a sense of dread. Not a single slaveholding state had voted for him.

Charles and I still disagreed over slavery, but we were able to discuss it without arguing now. He listened to my opinions, and that drew my heart to him. He admitted that slavery was unjust, and I admitted that abolishing it immediately would not only destroy the South's economy but would leave millions of slaves unequipped to deal with their immediate freedom. Charles was kind and fair to his family's slaves, even if the bonds of love that existed between Tessie and Eli and me were missing.

Tessie and I continued with our reading lessons in the afternoons, and she made excellent progress. Within six months, she could read simple stories and write down the sentences I dictated to her, even though her spelling was poor. She remained very fearful of being discovered, however, and every afternoon she would make me repeat my promise not to tell a soul what we were doing before she would agree to read or write a single word. What had begun as a way to prove Tessie's equality to Charles would forever remain our secret.

But I no longer felt compelled to prove anything to him. Charles had admitted to me that some slaves could undoubtedly learn how to read, but he felt quite strongly that they should not be educated. Even though we often disagreed, Charles and I were convinced of one thing: our growing feelings for each other were much stronger than our political differences.

Late that year, on December 20, Charles' family hosted a Christmas party in their enormous home. All of Richmond's high society was invited. As I waited for Charles to arrive to escort me, I couldn't help recalling his sister Sally's party, just one year earlier.

"So much has changed in a year's time," I said to Tessie. "I wonder what I'll be doing a year from now?"

She was watching for Charles' carriage from my bedroom window, but she turned to smile mischievously at me. "Think you'll be waking up beside your Mr. St. John by next Christmas?"

The subject still made me blush, but the thought made my heart race. "I . . . I hope so," I said shyly.

Tessie clapped her hands together and laughed out loud. "That prove it, then! My baby girl in *love*! And here come Prince Charming's carriage now."

I heard it, too. I waited for the ring of the door chimes, the sound of Charles' footsteps in the foyer, his languid voice as he greeted my father. They never came. "What's taking him so long?" I asked.

Tessie peered out the window again. "He standing out in back . . . talking to Eli."

"Let me see." I went to the window and saw them there, deep in conversation—Charles dressed in formal attire, Eli in ragged stable clothes. They were the same height, and they faced each other, eye to eye. The discussion seemed to last a long time. Then, to my amazement, Charles extended his hand to Eli. Tears filled my eyes as they shook hands with each other. Never before had I seen a well-bred Southern gentleman shaking hands as equals with a Negro.

"Hey, now! Stop that crying!" Tessie scolded. "Your eyes gonna be all puffy and red."

"I can't help it. I love him, Tessie."

"Well, didn't I just say that, honey?"

When I came down the stairs and saw Charles waiting for me,

I knew I wanted to spend the rest of my life with him. He took my hand and kissed it, his lips lingering for a moment. He tenderly rested his bearded cheek against the back of my hand, then kissed it again.

"You look beautiful," he said.

I had no sensation of my feet touching the ground as I floated out to his carriage. We settled in the back, side by side, for the drive downhill to his home in Court End.

When he said, "I want to give you your Christmas present a few days early," my heart began to pound with joy and anticipation. Charles pulled a small, wrapped box from his pocket. My fingers trembled so badly I couldn't unwrap it.

"Need help?" He smiled and took it from me again. Inside was a magnificent ruby ring in what looked to be a very old platinum-and-gold setting. "It was my grandmother's ring," Charles said. He paused for the space of a heartbeat, then said, "Will you marry me, Caroline?"

I wanted to shout my answer from the top of the capitol building, but I couldn't seem to raise my voice above a whisper. "Yes, please." I sounded like a small child accepting a cookie. Charles laughed and pulled me into his arms as I battled to control my tears.

"Listen now. I believe I've finally found a way to render you speechless," he said. "I should have tried this months ago. Here, try it on and see if it fits." He slid the ring onto my left hand. It was a perfect fit. "I asked your father for permission to marry you a few days ago," Charles said. "He gave us his blessing. Would it be all right if we announced our engagement at the party tonight?"

I wanted the whole world to know, but all I managed to say was, "Yes. It would be wonderful." Then another thought occurred to me. "Is . . . is this what you were talking to Eli about tonight?"

"You saw us?" For a moment, Charles seemed embarrassed. "Actually . . . yes. I know what a good friend Eli is to you, and I thought . . . well, I thought I'd like to have him as my ally. He gave us his blessing, too."

I could no longer control my tears. I hugged Charles tightly, unable to express in words how much his gesture had moved me. He understood me well enough to know that Eli's blessing meant as much to me as my father's.

Charles' parents stood next to Daddy at the party later that night to announce our engagement. We would be married next July. The guests applauded the news. All of Richmond's leading citizens stood in line to congratulate Charles and me and wish us well. Many remembered my mother and spoke fondly of her. But I couldn't help wondering if a few were worried, for Charles' sake, that I would turn out to be like her.

Sally had tears in her eyes as she hugged me. "I'm so pleased that you'll be my sister," she said. We had become friends now that she no longer viewed me as her rival. She was fond of my cousin Jonathan but was reluctant to limit herself to only one beau.

Jonathan offered his congratulations, too, along with a hug and kiss. "I must say," he grinned, "this is one match I never would have bet money on, judging by your first date."

In the midst of this dizzying joy, Mr. Jennings Wise, editor of the *Richmond Enquirer*, arrived at the party two hours late. It quickly became apparent that he brought startling news. "We received a late bulletin over the wire this evening," he said. "It came in just as I was leaving the office. South Carolina has officially seceded from the Union."

The news wasn't entirely unexpected, but it rocked the gathering nevertheless, bringing the merriment to a temporary standstill. Even after Mr. St. John told the orchestra to continue playing, and urged us all to enjoy the evening's celebration, everyone gathered in small, worried groups, discussing the secession in hushed whispers. I couldn't help feeling afraid. I had seen firsthand the deep rift between North and South after the events at Harper's Ferry. Now that the first state had broken away, I wondered if anything could stop an avalanche of splintering states.

"Something terrible has begun tonight, hasn't it?" I asked Charles.

"We don't know that," he replied, but I read the concern in his eyes.

"Do you think there will be a war?"

"That depends on how Washington reacts. Every state joined the Union voluntarily; they should have the right to leave it again if the Federal government no longer represents their best interests."

"Will Virginia leave the Union, too?"

He sighed. "There's not a lot of support for secession at the moment. But listen now. We can only live our lives one day at a time—and this is our special day. Come with me, Caroline."

He took my hand in his and led me outside to the terrace. The night was warm for December, but still cold enough to make me shiver in my ball gown. Charles took off his coat and wrapped it around me before pulling me into his arms. He held me tightly. Suddenly all that mattered was this moment.

When I stopped shivering, he pulled back to gaze at me with his beautiful eyes. "I love you," he said. Then he bent his head toward me and kissed me for the first time. I felt the brush of his beard on my face, the pressure of his hands on my back, the warm touch of his lips on mine, and I knew that Tessie's words were true—I wanted Charles' arms around me more than I wanted air to breathe.

11

RICHMOND 1861

At the beginning of the new year, 1861, I began to include the *Richmond Enquirer* as part of Tessie's daily reading material. Each morning after Daddy finished with the paper and left for work, Tessie and I would huddle near the fireplace in my bedroom and read aloud the latest news to each other. Then we would spend the rest of the day preparing my wedding trousseau and filling my hope chest. But throughout the month of January, the news we read grew more ominous, my future as a bride less certain. One by one, five more states followed South Carolina's lead and seceded from the Union. Texas joined them on the first of February.

"Where're all these places I reading about?" Tessie asked one morning. "They near Richmond?"

We went downstairs to the globe in Daddy's library, and I showed her where to find the Confederate states: South Carolina, Georgia, Florida, Alabama, Mississippi, Louisiana, Texas. Then I showed her Virginia—sandwiched uncomfortably between the North and the South. Richmond was less than one hundred miles from Washington, D.C.

"What you think gonna happen here?" she asked.

"I don't know. Everything is changing so rapidly—and you know how I've always hated change."

"Oh yes, I do know that for sure."

I gave the globe a spin, setting it in motion. "I used to believe that the United States was strong and that nothing could ever shake our great country. But this flood of hatred between North and South is spreading faster than I ever imagined it would."

Tessie nodded. "It look like we all gonna drown in it pretty soon."

By the time Abraham Lincoln was inaugurated as president in March, the renegade states had created a new government in Montgomery, Alabama, with a written constitution guaranteeing the autonomy of each state. They'd selected Jefferson Davis, the former Secretary of War, as president of this new Confederacy. So far, Virginia still hadn't joined them.

I helped Tessie read President Lincoln's inauguration speech in March as we sewed yards of lace on my bridal gown, and his words sent a chill through me. Lincoln promised not to interfere with the states that already had slavery, but he clearly believed that no state had a legal right to leave the Union. He said he hoped the crisis could be resolved without resorting to warfare, but he vowed to preserve the Union no matter what.

The idea of war was unthinkable to me, yet events seemed to be drifting dangerously close to one. At my engagement party two months previous, the rising tide of unrest seemed far away from Richmond. Now my familiar world felt threatened, the future precarious and uncertain as the floodwaters rose higher, inching closer to Virginia.

I turned to Charles for reassurance. He was now taking part in a state convention that was meeting to decide whether or not Virginia would secede. So far, the delegates had proceeded very slowly, leaving everyone waiting anxiously for news.

"There are three factions within the Virginia convention," Charles explained to me one day on our carriage ride home from church. "Those who favor immediate secession, those who want to stay in the Union, and those who want to work out a compromise."

"Which faction do you represent?"

"I'm not an official delegate," he said. "I'm only assisting Mr. Randolph, but he favors compromise."

I felt slightly reassured when Charles told me in early April that the convention had voted nearly two-to-one against a motion to secede. For now, it looked as though Virginia would remain in the Union. But that was soon to change—so swiftly, in fact, that we were all unprepared.

Late one Saturday afternoon in mid-April, I had been entertaining Charles' relatives—Sally, his mother, and two of his aunts—for afternoon tea, planning the guest list for my wedding, which had been set for July 20. My visitors had just departed a few minutes earlier, and I was helping Tessie gather the dessert plates and teacups when my cousin Jonathan burst into my parlor in his usual whirlwind fashion.

"Is Sally here?" he asked breathlessly.

"No, you just missed her. In fact, it's a wonder you didn't bowl her over on the front walk."

"Have you heard the news?" Jonathan's face was serious, not smiling. I was almost afraid to ask.

"What news?"

"Big news, Caroline. The South Carolina militia has fired on Union troops at Fort Sumter. The war has begun."

I groped behind me for the nearest chair and slowly sank down onto it. "No . . . that can't be true. No one would be stupid enough to start a war against his own countrymen."

"But it is true. All of Richmond is in an uproar. Come downtown with me. This is something you won't want to miss. We'll pick up Sally and then head over to the newspaper office to find out the latest."

As Josiah drove us downtown, I silently prayed that the news would prove to be a false rumor. But when I saw the streets near Capitol Square jammed with carriages, my fears deepened.

"Where is this fort where it all started?" I asked.

"Fort Sumter? It guards Charleston Harbor."

Even though Charleston was far away from us, I gripped Jonathan's hand for reassurance. "How bad is this?" I asked. "Do you think the fighting will spread?"

"All I know is that South Carolina's heavy artillery began bombarding the Union fort, demanding surrender."

Our carriage slowed to a near halt in all the traffic. Impatient, Jonathan ordered Josiah to drive down back alleyways and side streets to reach the St. Johns' mansion. When we finally arrived, Jonathan and I went inside to fetch Sally. She was thrilled with the idea of witnessing something new and exciting and readily joined us.

As we were leaving, Charles arrived. His quiet self-assurance had a calming effect on me. I felt ready to face anything with him beside me. He bent to kiss my cheek, and his clothes and hair carried the fragrant aroma of cigars from his endless meetings.

"Have you heard about Fort Sumter?" Jonathan asked him.

Charles nodded. "A messenger interrupted our meeting with the news, so we decided to adjourn. I was just coming home for our carriage to drive over to the *Enquirer*."

"Come with us," Jonathan said. "That's where we're going." We all climbed into the carriage, and Josiah drove back toward the business district.

"Do you know any details about Fort Sumter?" Jonathan asked Charles when we were on our way.

"I heard that the Mexican war hero, General Beauregard, is in charge of the rebellion. He refused to allow a U.S. ship to deliver supplies to the Federal garrison, then demanded their surrender. When they refused, South Carolina's artillery opened fire."

I felt a heavy weight sink to the bottom of my stomach at the thought of men firing at each other. But across from me, Sally could barely sit still.

"This is so exciting!" she said, clinging to Jonathan's arm. "How long do you think the battle will last?"

He covered her hand with his own. "Probably until the fort runs out of ammunition." I could tell by the satisfied smile on his face that he would be glad if the battle lasted forever as long as it meant having Sally snuggled beside him.

By now, the area around the capitol was so packed with carriages that none of them could move—including our own. Many downtown businesses had closed, and people flowed into the streets as the sidewalks grew overcrowded, making the congestion worse. Josiah couldn't make any headway at all with Jonathan's carriage.

"Listen now. Maybe we'd better get out and walk," Charles finally said. "I don't think we're going to be able to get any closer."

We left Josiah and the carriage stalled on Ninth Street and threaded our way through the mob. Charles held my hand so we wouldn't become separated. A huge crowd had gathered around the *Enquirer*'s offices, waiting for the latest dispatches to come over the wire. As fast as the editors received news by telegraph, someone shouted it from the windows.

" . . . Confederate forces have forty-three batteries stationed around Charleston Harbor . . . They have poured more than three thousand shells into the fort . . . The bombardment began more than thirty hours ago. . . ."

Finally, not quite an hour after we arrived, the stunning news came: "Union troops at Fort Sumter have surrendered! Fort Sumter has surrendered!"

The cheer that went up from the crowd was deafening. Jonathan shouted along with them while Sally hopped up and down, clapping her hands. Charles didn't cheer, but he looked pleased. I couldn't understand why Jonathan or anyone else in Richmond would cheer. Virginia wasn't part of the rebel government, we were part of the

United States—and the United States had just been bombarded into surrender. I cupped my hands around my mouth and shouted up at Charles, "Why are they cheering?" He led me around the street corner away from the mob so we could hear each other. "Why are they cheering?" I repeated.

"Because the South has won the first battle. The Federal forces have backed down. It's a great victory for the Confederacy."

"I know, but what does that have to do with us here, in Richmond?"

His expression sobered as if he realized the import of his words as he spoke them. "I guess it shows that Richmond's sympathies are with the South. It may not take much to push the convention toward secession now."

"Jonathan said that a war has begun."

"He's right. It certainly has begun in South Carolina. They've declared their independence and forced Union troops out of their state. How far Lincoln is willing to pursue this remains to be seen."

Jonathan and Sally suddenly rounded the corner, hand in hand. "What are you two doing back here?" he asked. "Come on, we're missing all the fun."

We could already hear strains of brass music and the rattle of drums in the distance. A carnival atmosphere had gripped the city, so I pushed my fears aside for the moment, gripped Charles' arm, and joined in. The crowd pulled us along as it surged down the street toward the river, following the music.

A few minutes later we caught up with the armory band. They had donned their militia uniforms and were marching down Cary Street to the popular tune "Dixie's Land." The effect of the martial music, the sound of bugles and drums, was instantly intoxicating. A surge of pride and patriotism flowed through us until it became impossible not to tap our feet or march in step. Even my pulse seemed to match the cadence of the snare drums.

Someone held a handsewn Confederate flag aloft, and the crowd, which had grown to more than three thousand people, turned down

Fifth Street and headed toward the Tredegar Iron Works near the canal.

The sprawling complex of brick buildings billowed steam and smoke, symbolizing Virginia's industrial power and might. Not only did the foundry produce cannon, naval guns, shells, and railroad iron, but the buildings themselves seemed to represent impregnable strength. Someone ran the Confederate flag up the pole on top of the building, and the crowd cheered wildly. The band played "The Marseillaise," anthem of the French rebellion. Liberty for the South seemed within reach.

Tredegar's proprietor, Joseph Anderson, delivered a speech, followed by more cheers. Then Virginia's attorney general stood up to speak, reminding the crowd that the cannons that had brought victory at Fort Sumter had been made at Tredegar's, right here in Richmond. I had to cover my ears at the mob's deafening roar of pride and approval. Meanwhile, some Virginia militiamen had hurried to the armory and hauled out the weapons for a one-hundred-gun salute. Cannon boomed for more than an hour, rattling store windows and shaking the ground beneath my feet. Across the city, church bells rang endlessly from every spire and steeple. All around us, people embraced each other and danced with jubilation. Jonathan hugged Sally tightly, then lifted her in the air and whirled her around.

"Isn't this wonderful?" Jonathan shouted, his voice hoarse from cheering.

"Yes! Yes!" Sally laughed, gripping him for dear life. Her cheeks were flushed with excitement, rosier than any rouge could have made them.

I didn't understand what Jonathan meant. The atmosphere was certainly more thrilling than any Fourth of July celebration I'd ever seen, but I could see nothing wonderful about the inauguration of a war. Charles had added his own shouts of "Yes!" and "Hear, hear!" to some of the speeches, but he and I were much more subdued than the others. Still, we couldn't help feeling the electric charge of exuberance that filled the air, nor could we help being swept away by it all.

We followed the multitudes back up the hill to the *Enquirer*'s offices for more speeches, including a stirring one by editor Jennings Wise. The crowd—and the traffic jams—swelled to even greater proportions as people arrived from the surrounding countryside, drawn by the clamor and noise.

I scarcely noticed that darkness had fallen. Bonfires and torches lit the city, lamps blazed in the windows of every house. We walked through the teeming streets like people in a dream, following meandering torchlight parades bearing Confederate flags; stopping to join groups singing on street corners or giving speeches; watching rockets blaze and flare above the glittering river.

Later, we followed a brass band and a wagon draped with banners to Governor Letcher's mansion on Capitol Square. The masses chanted for the governor, shouting "Letcher! Letcher!" until he finally appeared. Everyone hushed to hear his words.

"Thank you for the compliment," he said sternly, "but I must be permitted to say that I see no occasion for this demonstration."

Waves of surprise, then anger, rippled through the crowd as he spoke. Letcher said that he did not recognize the flags they were flying, that they had no right to take the artillery from the armory, and that they should put it back immediately. Virginia was still a state of the Union, he insisted. Then, after telling us all to go home, he bowed slightly and returned inside.

The mob hissed as if Letcher was a villain in a melodrama. Someone shouted, "Aim the cannon at the governor's mansion!" and the crowd roared with laughter.

The gathering gradually split into smaller torchlight parades, fanning out from the square in all directions. My feet ached. It seemed we had walked for miles, and I was growing exhausted. Sally looked tired, too.

"It's getting late," Charles said. "We'd better take you ladies home."

As we made our way across the square toward Ninth Street in search of Jonathan's carriage, we saw a group at the capitol building raising the rebel Stars and Bars in place of the Stars and Stripes.

"It looks as though Virginians aren't going to wait for your convention to vote on secession," Jonathan said with a grin. "Tonight, the people have spoken." Even from where we watched across the square, the shouts that greeted the Rebel flag were uproarious.

"Some of them certainly have spoken," Charles said quietly. "But we still believe in democracy here in Virginia, not mob rule . . . and I know that a good many people in the western part of the state don't share these sentiments."

We walked uphill, searching for our carriage. My emotions felt as worn-out as my legs. It was so easy to be caught up in the frenzy of the crowd, to rejoice over the victory at Fort Sumter, to feel pride for the part Richmond had played in making the cannon, to feel stung by the governor's cold, dampening words. Yet part of me didn't want Virginia to leave the Union and take the dangerous path toward war. I found myself hoping that cooler heads would prevail at the convention, that Charles would help Virginia reach a comfortable compromise without resorting to armed conflict.

It seemed as though everyone was choosing sides between North and South and that I must soon do the same. But I felt too confused to choose, my loyalties painfully divided. Virginia was my home, the United States my country.

We finally found Jonathan's carriage. Hours had passed since we'd left it, but Josiah still sat tall and proud on the driver's seat, waiting for us. I felt sick inside at the tremendous waste of it all—how a man as intelligent as Josiah could be forced to wait endlessly on someone else's whim, as if he had nothing better to do, as if he was as mindless as the horses that had waited along with him.

"Oh, poor Josiah. He's been waiting all this time." My voice trembled as the last strand of my frayed emotions threatened to break.

Charles gave me a puzzled look. "Most carriage drivers spend a great deal of time waiting. I'm sure he's quite used to it."

"I know, but it seems so unfair. We can run all over the city, following the crowds and the excitement, while he's forced to wait here for hours, just because he's a slave."

Charles frowned. "It has nothing to do with the fact that he's a slave. It's part of his job, Caroline. Don't carriage drivers up north have to wait, too?" I could tell that he was annoyed with me, but then his tone and his expression softened as he decided to make light of it. "Listen now. Sometimes my job requires me to spend long hours waiting, as well. In fact, I've been waiting two months for this blasted convention to reach a decision. After what happened today, maybe they finally will."

I knew he was right. I recalled seeing long lines of carriages in Philadelphia, waiting for a party or some other social gathering to end. The emotion-filled day must have made me overly sensitive. I started to climb into the carriage behind Sally and Jonathan, but Charles stopped me.

"Caroline . . . ?" His fingers caressed my cheek while his eyes searched mine, as if to see if his words had offended me. "I agree that some plantation slaves have a difficult life," he said gently. "But our servants lead pretty good lives, don't they?"

I glanced up at Josiah, but his stony expression was unreadable. I wanted to explain to Charles that Josiah and Tessie were in love, to ask Charles how he would feel if we were prevented from living together in marriage, as they were. But I didn't say anything. Charles was a good man who genuinely hated injustice. It wasn't his fault that he'd been raised to accept slavery as a natural way of life, just as Daddy and Jonathan and everyone else in Richmond had been. The fact that I sometimes saw things differently could never alter the fact that I loved him.

"Yes, Charles," I said. "They're treated well."

On Sunday, Daddy and I joined the St. Johns for worship services at St. Paul's Church. Across the street in Capitol Square, the Rebel flag had been removed from the capitol building, and the United States flag waved in the breeze above it once again. Most of the excitement over the surrender of Fort Sumter had died away, but a cloud of suspense seemed to hover over the city as everyone braced for the next thunderclap.

Nearly every pew in church was filled with people, and I knew that nearly every heart, like mine, was filled with a mixture of excitement and anxiety. Even so, most people avoided discussing the latest news and talked of spiritual matters, as was fitting and proper on the Lord's Day. Daddy and I joined Charles' family for a lovely Sunday dinner, and it was as if Sumter had never happened as our conversation focused on simple pleasantries.

Monday's news plunged us all back into the maelstrom.

Every newspaper in the nation trumpeted the appalling headline—President Lincoln had declared war on the South. To prove his resolve, he had called for an army of seventy-five thousand men to put down the rebellion. I desperately needed Charles to reassure me that Virginia would not become involved in this conflict, that our wedding would take place in July, that we would begin our new life together just as we'd planned. But Charles was gone all day and half the night as the state convention met in the capitol to debate secession.

When I read the newspaper on Tuesday, all remaining hope for neutrality dissolved. Lincoln's secretary of war had demanded that Virginia do its share to quench the Southern rebellion by sending three regiments of soldiers to Washington. Governor Letcher refused this demand. He must have had a change of heart since the night Fort Sumter surrendered, because he told President Lincoln that his request "has inaugurated civil war."

I waited all day Tuesday for Charles to come, then all day Wednesday. Sick with anxiety, I sorted through the items in my hope chest, folding and refolding linen sheets and damask napkins, wondering if I'd ever have a chance to use them. Tessie threatened to lock the chest and take away the key.

"You gonna have them nice things all worn out before you ever use a one of them," she scolded.

Charles finally arrived at our house early Thursday morning, exhausted after a sleepless night of debates. I quickly dressed and hurried downstairs without taking time to pin up my hair. The news he brought Daddy and me was anything but reassuring.

"Late last night the convention reached a decision," he said wearily. "Virginia has joined the Confederacy. We've seceded from the Union."

Charles' usually neat clothing was rumpled, his shoulders bent with fatigue. He seemed almost too tired to stand. Daddy invited him into the library, where he collapsed into a chair.

"It's war," he said. "We're in this fight now. There is no way to avoid it."

Outside, the April morning was peaceful and serene. Blossoming trees showered the grass with pink and white petals. Spring flowers pushed through the warming soil. No armies marched, no cannon boomed, no battle cries disturbed the sound of birdsong. The very idea of war seemed preposterous.

"What changed the delegates' minds?" Daddy asked. "The victory at Fort Sumter?"

Charles sighed and shook his head. "President Lincoln tipped the scales against himself when he called for soldiers from Virginia. When it comes right down to it, the Virginia militia simply can't turn against their fellow Southerners. If we have to fight and die, then it will be for the states' right to govern themselves, not for Northern tyranny."

I listened, sick at heart, while they discussed the secessionist vote. Charles explained how most of the opposition to secession had come from western Virginia. Daddy offered his scathing opinion of the gangly despot who had taken over the White House.

"Let's all have some breakfast," I said when I could no longer stand listening to the disturbing conversation.

"Thank you, but I really can't stay," Charles said. He slowly stood, as if getting up out of the chair required the last of his strength. My father stood as well and crossed the room to shake Charles' hand.

"Thanks for stopping by with the news," Daddy said. "Now if you'll please excuse me, there's something I must attend to." Daddy left, closing the library door behind him. He had given Charles and me a rare moment alone.

Charles opened his arms to me and I rushed into them. He held me closer, more tightly than ever before. I felt his heart thumping as I wept against his chest.

"Listen now," he murmured. "Everything's going to be all right."

I pulled away to look up at him. "Is it really, Charles? Promise? Because right now I feel like nothing in our lives will ever be the same."

He didn't answer. Instead he lowered his mouth to mine and kissed me. But it wasn't the warm, tender kiss he'd given me four months ago on the night we were engaged. This time his lips were possessive. His hands caressed my back, then became lost in my unbound hair. For a few brief moments, I forgot that the world was crumbling around us as I kissed him in return.

When he finally pulled away, we were both breathless. "I love you, Caroline," he said hoarsely. "That's one thing that will never change."

Then, before either of us wished, he turned and left.

By the end of the day, the Confederate flag flew above the capitol. All business was suspended as news of Virginia's secession spread. Cannon fired, bells rang, people rushed to and fro, shouting and cheering in the streets, just as they had after Fort Sumter surrendered. Jonathan came to the house to fetch me after supper, and we drove downtown to pick up Sally and Charles.

Throughout that warm, spring evening of April 19, a magnificent torchlight procession illuminated the city of Richmond. Bands played, crowds cheered and sang as they paraded down Main Street; rockets and Roman candles exploded and blazed. Once again, we listened as a succession of orators delivered impassioned speeches about the War for Southern Independence.

"I predict that in less than sixty days we will capture Washington," one of the speakers said. Someone shouted from the crowd, "No, thirty days!"

I prayed it would be so. Charles and I were to be married in just ninety days.

After the first few hours, I found the excitement enervating. Charles also seemed drained after missing a night's sleep. His enthusiasm, like mine, had been subdued all evening. When we came upon a deserted park bench near Capitol Square, we sat down to rest for a few minutes, away from the clamor and noise of bands and speeches.

"You don't seem to be rejoicing like everyone else," I said.

He raked his hand through his hair. "I'm tired. This has been the longest week of my life."

I turned toward him on the bench so I could see his face. It appeared shadowed and gray, not from the night all around us, but from a restless anxiety deep inside him. "What's going to happen?" I asked softly. "Please be honest with me, Charles. I know we're at war, but . . . how will it all end?"

He wouldn't look at me. For a long moment he didn't reply. Instead, he held my hand in both of his, gently toying with the ruby ring he had placed on my finger. "You deserve to know the truth," he finally said. "I don't think we can possibly win this war."

A rocket flared and boomed close by. Charles looked up at me, and his face was momentarily illuminated in sparkling light. "The Northerners have more manpower than we do, more resources, more guns. Compared to them, the South does very little manufacturing.

We're dependent on imported goods, yet we have no navy to protect our harbors. We'll need cannon, arms, ammunition—but aside from Tredegar, there are few factories to produce them. Our transportation and supply networks are horribly inadequate. Five different railroads serve Richmond, but they are different gauges, and none of them connect properly with the others. It's that way all over the South. . . ."

I touched my fingers to his lips to stop him. I didn't want to hear anymore. There was another question I needed to ask, but I dreaded his answer. I turned away, afraid I would read the truth in his eyes before I found the courage to ask.

We sat in the dark for several minutes, watching the excitement that swirled around us. I felt wonderfully detached from it all, as if Charles and I floated magically above it, invisible, safe. But he brought me back to earth again when he sighed and said, "Listen now. If you're rested, we should try to find the others. I think it's time we headed home." He started to rise, but I stopped him, my need to know suddenly greater than my fear.

"Are you going to fight in this war, Charles?"

He paused, then said, "I have to."

"Why? Why can't we go abroad for a while? Let's live in London or Paris or someplace else until this ends."

"Virginia is my home," he said quietly, "not London or Paris. I have to fight to defend it. To protect you, my family, my friends."

"Can't you fight some other way? The new government will need leaders; can't you run for office?"

"There are plenty of experienced politicians for that. They're stepping all over each other, in fact."

"What about your father's mills? Won't there be a greater demand for flour—"

"We're at war. I have to fight."

"But you just said you didn't believe we could win."

"Maybe not. But I do believe in the cause."

"The *cause*? How can you say you believe in this cause?" I was growing panicked at the thought of Charles taking up a gun, fighting, dying. "You've admitted to me that slavery is morally unjust—"

"Caroline, listen now . . ."

"How can you fight for the right to preserve slavery?"

"This war isn't about slavery. It's about giving Virginians—not the politicians in Washington—the right to decide what goes on in Virginia. We're fighting for the freedom to govern ourselves, just as our ancestors did during the first Revolution. All we want is independence, to be left alone to—"

"To continue slavery."

"No. To govern ourselves."

"So you're going to pick up a gun and march off to war? You're going to fight against a more powerful enemy, knowing you can't possibly win?" I was trembling all over with dread and fear. Charles took both my hands in his and held them tightly against his chest, speaking calmly to soothe me.

"They were outmanned and outgunned during the last revolution, too. George Washington, Thomas Jefferson, James Madison . . . a handful of courageous men from Virginia weren't afraid to defend themselves against a stronger, despotic government. Right here in St. John's Church, Patrick Henry said 'Give me liberty, or give me death!' They all fought to win our freedom the first time. Now I have to fight to keep that freedom."

"Please don't go to war, Charles."

I have to," he said softly. "I have to stand up for what I believe."

I lowered my head and closed my eyes as my tears began to flow. Charles gently took my face in his hand and lifted my chin. "Caroline, look at me . . . Remember the day we first met, how you clubbed me with your bag? I was much bigger and stronger than you were, but you believed that I was wrong to chase that boy, and you decided to stand up for what you believed. You must have known you couldn't possibly defeat me in a brawl, didn't you? But you had to do something, you had to try. It's the same with this war. We have to try. Besides," he added, smiling slightly, "you did win the war, Caroline. You won my heart, my love . . . my life. Who knows, maybe the South will win, too."

I clung to Charles on that park bench in Capitol Square, not caring if it was improper, my face pressed tightly against his chest. He held me, gently rocking me, as cannon fire and church bells and Roman candles filled the night with noise, drowning out the comforting sound of his heartbeat.

"I don't want to lose you," I wept.

"You can't lose me, Caroline. I'm yours forever."

By the time Jonathan and I returned home it was late. It didn't take much to convince him to spend the night in our guest room. I found Tessie waiting in my room with a lamp lit to help me undress.

"What's all the noise and carrying-on about this time?" she asked as she unpinned my hair.

"Virginia has left the Union. We're going to war against the Northern states."

"They celebrating that?"

I nodded wearily as she ran the brush through my hair.

"I think you've had enough of this here celebrating," she said, pointing to the mirror. "See how pale you are? You all worn out. Look like they dragged you down Franklin Street behind a team of horses."

My eyes filled with tears. "Charles is going to fight."

The brush froze in Tessie's hand. "You mean in the war? What about your wedding?"

"I don't know."

She bent over me to hold me in her arms. I allowed her to soothe me for a minute, then I gently pulled away. "Josiah is here," I told her. "He and Jonathan are spending the night. I think you should go be with your husband."

For a moment she looked taken aback. "Well . . . we'll see about that later. Let me get you tucked away in bed, first."

"No, you go now, Tessie. Time is much too precious to waste. I'm a grown woman. I can get undressed by myself."

"You sure?"

"He's your husband. You belong with him."

I stood at my bedroom window after Tessie left, gazing outside into the night. A light shone from the carriage house and I knew that Eli was inside, taking care of Jonathan's horses. I watched him passing back and forth in front of the window as he worked, barely visible through the veil of new leaves and tree branches, and I felt the same helpless anger I'd felt the night I'd seen Josiah waiting for us on the carriage seat. He and Eli were grown men, human beings, with lives that didn't deserve to be wasted on someone else's whim.

I thought I understood how they must feel. I had also lost control over my life, my future. I was forced to submit to a war I neither believed in nor wanted, powerless to act while others decided my fate. Charles could go to war, fight for control, take action to win back the freedom he felt was being stolen from him. But the war could rob me of my wedding day, my husband, my tranquil future in Richmond, Virginia—and like Eli and Josiah, I could do nothing about it. We could only stand by and wait.

I hadn't changed out of my dress yet, so I slipped my shoes back on and went outside to talk to Eli. He was scooping feed into the trough for the horses, but he stopped when he saw me and ambled over to where I stood.

"I hear there's big news going around. They talking about a war."

"It has already started. Charles told me tonight that he's going to fight in it."

"He's a good man, Missy Caroline. Your Massa Charles a real good man."

"I know. But now all the plans we had for a life together ..." I paused, battling to control my tears. I didn't want to cry. Eli waited patiently until I could trust myself to speak.

"The world I know has changed, Eli. It finally sank in tonight that war is inevitable. The men I love will all go off to fight—some of them might die. My life will never be the same as it was two days ago, and I want it all back."

"I know," he murmured. "I know."

"I'm so afraid of what lies ahead. We're at war. It doesn't seem like it right now, but the war has begun, and now there's an enemy out there who wants to destroy me and my loved ones and my way of life. I don't feel safe anymore. I think of all the things I took for granted and might no longer be able to do, things like walking in the park or visiting the plantation. Will I ever get married, Eli? Have a home? Be a mother? My security and stability are all gone, all changed, and I can never get them back. I can't even go to bed without the fear of what tomorrow will bring. I feel so helpless."

"That's a terrible feeling, Missy Caroline. I sure know it is. From the moment I born I ain't never had any power over my own life. I never knowing about tomorrow, if I be living here or if I be sold to auction like little Grady. They snatch away the people I love, like Grady and Josiah, and there's nothing I can do about it. But I ain't telling you all this so you feel sorry for me. No, I telling you so maybe you can face it like I do ... so maybe you can lay down your head at night and not worry about tomorrow."

"What's your secret, Eli?"

"Ain't no secret at all. It's right there in the Bible—you give your life to Massa Jesus. You stop trying to control everything and to figure everything out, and you let Him do all the figuring. That way, if it's God's will I be set free tomorrow, then I be set free. If Massa Fletcher sell me to auction tomorrow, I know it ain't because it's Massa Fletcher's idea; Jesus must be wanting me down there for some reason, so I better get on down there and do it. The Bible says men got plenty of plans in his heart, but it's always the Lord's plans that win. Right now it's your plan to marry Massa Charles, have a bunch of little babies, live happy-ever-after. But that might not be God's plan. Can you live with that, Missy?"

I couldn't lie to Eli or to myself. "No. I would be very angry with God."

"That's why we struggle. Until we can pray, '*Thy* will be done in earth, as it is in *heaven*,' we gonna have a whole lot of sleepless nights. We want to make our own plans and then pray, '*My* will be done, if you please Massa Jesus, in earth, as it is in *my* plans.' You got to put your life in Jesus' hands. Trust that in the end, whatever happens, He still in control."

"I can't. I don't have as much faith as you do."

"Faith don't come in a bushel basket, Missy. It come one step at a time. Decide to trust Him for one little thing today, and before you know it, you find out He's so trustworthy you be putting your whole life in His hands."

"That's the problem—my whole life has been turned upside down. What's going to happen to all of us?"

"God's gonna have His way, Missy Caroline, that's what's gonna happen. God always have His way."

APRIL 1861

Two days later, I was still thinking about Eli's words when I attended Sunday worship services at St. Paul's Church with Charles and his family. The minister, Dr. Minnigerode, was careful not to use God's pulpit to preach politics, instead praying for His wisdom, for calm hearts, and for peace to prevail. The tranquillity of that beautiful sanctuary, the reassuring words of Scripture, and the hymns that spoke of God's love and faithfulness helped me forget the ugly reality of war for a while. But when the appointed Old Testament Scripture for that Sunday was read, I sensed a ripple of excitement pass through the congregation. *"But I will remove far off from you the northern army, and will drive him into a land barren and desolate. . . ."*

People nudged each other, exchanging glances, as if the scheduled reading from the book of Joel was prophesying a Southern victory. But weren't people in the North gathering in their churches this morning, too, asking for God's blessing on their cause? Which side was right? God couldn't be on both sides, yet both sides prayed to Him, believed in Him. I had worshipped in both places, and I knew that there were faithful Christians in the North as well as the South who trusted Christ and looked to Him for guidance. How was He supposed to choose between them?

Near the end of the service, as Dr. Minnigerode asked us to bow for the closing prayer, the harsh clanging of the alarm bell sounding from the tower across Ninth Street on Capitol Square destroyed the morning's tranquillity. It rang the signal for danger—two peals, a pause, a third peal—over and over again, shattering the quiet noon hour.

"What is it, Charles?" Mrs. St. John asked. "Why is that bell ringing?"

He sat on the edge of his seat, alert, listening. "It's signaling danger. All able-bodied men are supposed to go to the armories and find out what the emergency is."

The church was thrown into confusion as people sprang to their feet. Many of the men briefly embraced their wives before stepping toward the aisles and hurrying from the sanctuary. Charles gripped my hand in his for a moment, then left to join the others. He'd had no time to reassure me, to say "don't worry" or "everything will be all right." Perhaps he knew his words would be spoken in vain. Judging by the pale, frightened faces all around me, I wasn't the only woman who feared for her loved ones.

When all the men of fighting age had departed, the rest of the congregation made its way outside into the warm spring sunshine. "Wait here," Charles' father told us. "I'll go over and see if I can learn anything." We watched him walk across the street to the bell tower, his steps slowed by rheumatism.

Sally held my hand while we waited. "I'm so scared! Aren't you, Caroline?"

"Yes," I admitted. I longed to run home to Tessie and Eli for comfort, but I couldn't leave until I knew the danger we were all facing. After what seemed to be an endless wait, Mr. St. John limped back with his report. He spoke calmly, but his anxiety was evident in the way he quickly herded us toward the carriage.

"Governor Letcher ordered the alarm to be sounded," he said. "Let's start home, and I'll tell you what little I know on the way."

So much traffic jammed the streets as people raced about that we probably could have walked the few blocks to the St. Johns' mansion faster than it took us to drive there. But once we were all settled inside the carriage, Mr. St. John told us what was wrong.

"The U.S. warship *Pawnee* has been operating in Norfolk Harbor for the past few weeks. The governor received a report this morning that it's currently moving up the James River toward Richmond."

"Daddy, no!" Sally cried. "Can't we stop it?"

"Well, it won't be easy to stop a warship, but we're certainly going to try. We're mustering the militia, the Richmond Howitzer Battalion, the Fayette Artillery . . ."

"How could the Yankees move to attack us so quickly?" Mrs. St. John asked. "We just announced our secession a few days ago."

"I know, I know. They were prepared, we weren't. We haven't had time to equip any shore batteries, so we have absolutely no defenses between here and Norfolk. We can't stop the *Pawnee* from sailing up to our doorstep."

"What will the ship do once it's here?" I asked shakily.

When her husband hesitated, Mrs. St. John said, "It's all right to tell us, dear. We need to know."

"Well, I imagine they'll bombard us from offshore. Richmond is one of the South's most industrialized cities. They'll try to demolish Tredegar Iron Works . . . perhaps destroy the entire city."

"Your flour mills?" Sally asked. He shrugged helplessly.

Our vulnerability and impotence made me sick with fear, not only for my own safety but also for Charles'. Did the governor expect him and the other men to stand on shore with rifles, facing an armed warship's cannon? How could we have entered a war without any defenses?

When we finally reached the St. Johns' house, Charles' father invited me to stay and wait for the latest news with them. Their cook had prepared an enormous Sunday dinner, but I was too ill with worry to eat any of it. I begged Mr. St. John to let his driver take me home.

"If you wish," he agreed, "but I insist on escorting you there myself."

It took nearly a quarter of an hour to drive less than three blocks to Broad Street. It seemed that every man and boy in Richmond had crowded into the streets, trying to join up with the city's militia. Most of the men still wore their Sunday finery, and nearly everyone bore arms. I saw all manner of guns, from dueling pistols to Revolutionary War relics. The volunteers appeared pitifully inadequate and disorganized, certainly no match for a U.S. warship.

Mr. St. John pointed to the capitol roof as we passed the square. "See there? Those are lookouts watching for the *Pawnee*. I've heard you can see as far as the first bend in the river from up there. We'll have a few minutes' warning, at least."

As we made our way east toward Church Hill, we were forced to stop again as a troop of soldiers crossed the street, marching in somewhat of a military fashion, their bayonets fixed. I searched the rows of faces for Charles' but didn't see him.

"Where are you headed?" Mr. St. John called from the open carriage window.

"Rocketts Wharf," someone replied, "in case they send a landing force." As if facing an armed warship wasn't bad enough, now I had to face the possibility of marauding enemy soldiers overpowering our haphazard forces and invading the city.

The traffic thinned once we started up Church Hill, and a few minutes later we passed St. John's Church. All my life I had heard the story of how Patrick Henry had spoken his famous words, "Give me liberty or give me death!" in that church just a few blocks from my home, but I had never before thought about what they meant. Charles had quoted them to me only a few nights earlier, saying he would willingly fight to keep his freedom. But freedom to do what? I still didn't understand what Charles would be willing to die for.

When I reached home, Daddy thanked Mr. St. John for escorting me and invited him inside. I left the two of them in the library, discussing the impending invasion, and fled upstairs to the safety of Tessie's arms. She tried her best to calm me, but every time I looked at the engagement ring on my finger and thought of Charles facing a warship, I was forced to battle waves of nervous hysteria. I knew the afternoon would stretch ahead of me endlessly as I waited, facing the terror of the unknown.

"How about we do something?" Tessie finally said. "Take your mind off your troubles instead of sitting here fretting."

"I . . . I wouldn't be able to do anything. My hands are shaking too badly to do any needlework or—"

"Not that kind of something. How about I practice my reading? I ain't never gonna get any better if I don't practice."

Her offer surprised me. It was the first time she had ever asked for a lesson. Even though she was making wonderful progress with her reading and writing skills, her reluctance and fear had remained very strong, her written work invariably thrown into the flames at the end of each session. But this time Tessie had taken the initiative, and before I could respond to her offer, she had already fetched her latest textbook, the Bible, and was opening it to where we had left off in the Book of Psalms.

"'Unto thee lift I up mine eyes,'" Tessie read, "'O thou that dwellest in the heavens. Behold, as the eyes of servants look unto the hand of their masters, and as the eyes of a maiden unto the hand of her mistress; so our eyes wait upon the Lord our God, until that he have mercy upon us. Have mercy upon us, O Lord, have mercy upon us . . .'"

At dusk, Tessie went down to the kitchen to fetch me a tray of food. A few minutes later, someone knocked on my door.

"Missy Caroline?"

"Come in, Ruby."

"Tessie tell me you upset on account of Massa Charles going off to fight that big ship." She stood close to the door, shuffling nervously from one foot to the other.

"Yes . . . What is it, Ruby?"

She held out her hand, offering me something. "These here laudanum pills always help you mama when she upset."

They were also what had killed her. Tears filled my eyes at this reminder of my own weakness. I recalled my last night at Hilltop and my aunt and uncle's worried whispers that I would turn out to be just like my mother.

Ruby set the container of pills down on my dresser, then hurried away. As I stared at the medicine in the gathering twilight, a faint booming sounded in the distance. I recognized the sound. I'd heard it during two nights of celebration. Cannon fire.

The *Pawnee*.

Terror rose up inside me until I thought I might suffocate. The war was only beginning, but I knew that I couldn't live with such overwhelming fear every day until it ended. I saw only two choices. I could turn to the pills as my mother had, or I could turn to God, as Eli did. *"As the eyes of servants look unto the hand of their masters . . ."* The laudanum was certainly a quicker solution, but Eli's peace was genuine, enduring. I picked up the tin of pills and hurled it across the room into the darkness, unwilling to end up like my mother. Then I fell to my knees beside my bed.

"Oh, God, I can't live like this," I prayed. "The city is defenseless. I'm helpless. I can't protect the people I love. Help me trust you, God. Help me believe that you love Charles as much as I do, that you'll always do what's best for him. I want to trust you, Lord, but it's so hard. So very hard. Please help me. Please help me pray 'Thy will be done.' Help me to really mean it, Lord."

Eli was right; God didn't instantly reward me with a bushel basket of faith. But by the time I whispered "Amen," I felt strong enough to get through this night without my mother's laudanum. I would probably have to pray this way every day, perhaps several times each day, but that was the only way to face this war—one day at a time. *"...as the eyes of a maiden unto the hand of her mistress..."* I would have to look to God to teach me daily lessons of faith, just as Tessie had trusted me to teach her.

By the time Tessie returned with a bowl of Esther's chicken soup and some hot biscuits, the cannon had stopped sounding in the distance. My knees were no longer trembling.

"What you doing sitting here in the dark?" Tessie scolded. She set down the tray to light a lamp. "You come on and sit down over here, honey. Try and eat a little something." It surprised me to discover that I could do it, that the spoon didn't shake in my hand.

I prayed for a long time before I fell asleep that night, and as I did, I realized that I had always been utterly dependent on God for every breath I took, every breath Charles took. Why had it taken a crisis like the *Pawnee* to make me see it, to drive me to my knees?

I fell asleep reciting a verse from the psalms that Eli had made Grady and me learn years ago to ward off our nightmares: "'I will both lay me down in peace, and sleep: for thou, Lord, only makest me dwell in safety.'"

Charles arrived the next morning just as Tessie finished helping me dress. I ran down the stairs and into his arms. "Charles! You're safe!"

He surprised me by lifting me up and whirling me around two times before setting my feet on the floor again. It was something Jonathan might have done. Charles' fine Sunday clothes looked disheveled and stained, but he was smiling.

"Yes, aside from spending a cold night on the hard ground, I'm safe."

"I heard cannon fire last night, just as it was growing dark. Was it the *Pawnee*?"

Charles laughed out loud. "No, that was our own artillery. We were testing it. There never was any warship steaming up the James River."

"What?"

"It was all just a wild rumor. The *Pawnee* left Norfolk, but it's probably halfway to Washington by now."

"Oh, Charles. All that fuss and worry for nothing?"

He laughed again. "I guess so."

Esther walked into the foyer with my breakfast tray just then, on her way upstairs to bring it to me. She halted when she saw Charles, and her face broke into a wide grin.

"Why, Massa Charles. If you ain't a sight for sore eyes. Our Missy awful worried about you. But you get on in that dining room and sit yourself down now, you hear? You gonna let me feed you this morning, and you ain't gonna argue, because I can hear the gears in your belly grinding clear across this hallway."

"Yes, ma'am." He smiled and gave a mock salute as he agreed to stay for breakfast. Daddy joined us at the dining room table. As Esther piled food in front of us, Charles told his story.

"After we all arrived at the armory and they distributed the weapons, we headed down to Rocketts Wharf to engage any enemy landing forces. Later, they decided to station part of us downriver a few miles, below the city. We were all so tense and edgy it's a wonder someone didn't shoot off his own foot. At least those of us who've trained with the state militia knew how to handle a weapon—although I'm not sure bayonets and musket balls would have done much good against a warship.

"We spent the night camped on the river, waiting, only to learn early this morning that it was all a false alarm. The *Pawnee* did leave Norfolk Harbor yesterday, but it headed out into Chesapeake Bay and, presumably, up the Potomac."

"More ham and biscuits?" Esther asked as she bustled into the room with another tray.

Charles held up both hands. "You're only feeding one soldier,

Esther, not the entire army. Although that's not such a bad idea. Would you like to come along and be our commissary cook?"

"If I do that, Missy Caroline never would eat nothing," she said, setting the platter in front of me. "Then she just might blow away one of these days." Esther disappeared through the door again.

"So all that fretting was for nothing," I said with a sigh.

"No, it did accomplish one important thing," Charles said, cutting into another slice of ham. "It showed us how ill-prepared we are to defend ourselves and this city."

"Well, we only voted to secede a few days ago," Daddy said. "We can hardly expect to be prepared so soon."

"If the enemy's military leadership had been on their toes," Charles replied, "they would have sent the *Pawnee* upriver and blasted the Tredegar Iron Works into oblivion before we had a chance to build a single cannon. You can bet we'll start constructing shore batteries now and mining the James with torpedoes."

Daddy sipped his coffee, then leaned back in his chair. "Have you made any immediate plans, Charles?"

Charles' eyes met mine for a moment before he answered, as if giving me time to prepare myself for his response. "I plan to enlist right away in the Richmond Light Infantry Blues."

"Ah, yes. That's an old, highly regarded unit," Daddy said. "A very distinguished outfit."

Charles nodded. "I'm continuing a family tradition. Some of my ancestors fought with the 'Blues' during the first revolution." He sighed and removed his napkin from his lap, folding it carefully and placing it beside his empty plate. "I have a feeling that yesterday was only a taste of what's to come. Virginia is likely to become a principal battleground during this war, not only because we're so close to Washington, but because Richmond is one of the South's few industrial centers."

"I think you're right," Daddy said. "In light of all this, may I ask . . . what have you two decided about your wedding?"

Charles looked at me again. "We haven't decided anything, sir. I still want very much to marry Caroline. But I think, unless the war ends before July . . . I think we will be forced to postpone it for a while."

In the weeks that followed, Charles became part of a stampede of volunteers who lined up to enlist in the Confederate Army. Jonathan joined him in filling the ranks of Richmond's Light Infantry Blues. I drew a small measure of comfort from the fact that the two of them were together, watching out for each other. Jennings Wise, editor of the *Enquirer* and son of our former governor, was named the Blues' captain. Jonathan's older brother, William, joined an artillery unit.

Even as I watched my loved ones put on uniforms, take up arms, and train for battle, I clung to the irrational hope that it would all prove to be another false alarm like the *Pawnee* incident. As the spring days quickly passed, that hope grew more futile.

With the declaration of war, I could no longer receive letters from my cousins up north. I often thought about the two years I'd spent with them, and I couldn't help imagining all the young men I'd danced with in Philadelphia lining up to kill all the young men I knew in Richmond. Cousin Robert Hoffman would soon have his wish to fight in a war fulfilled. What disturbed me was that he might be fighting against Charles. I only wished I knew how—and when—this ugly conflict would end.

The Richmond I once knew changed rapidly during those early months of war, doubling in size within a matter of weeks. Refugees from Baltimore who were loyal to the South streamed into Virginia after Federal troops occupied their city. Hundreds of unfamiliar faces filled the streets as young men raced to the city to enlist. Colleges and schools were forced to close for lack of pupils and teachers. Young boys, turned away from the army because of their age, complained that the war would be over before they had a chance to fight. Every passenger train that pulled into one of Richmond's depots brought more soldiers, all of them eager for war. When a trainload of troops from South Carolina arrived, people from all over the city flocked to the station, cheering wildly for the heroes of Fort Sumter.

The young men who arrived to enlist came from all walks of life—laborers and lawyers, farmers and factory workers, miners and merchants. Sally would call out to them from her carriage window, asking where they were from. Their varied answers amazed me. "Mississippi, ma'am . . . Texas . . . Florida . . . Missouri." Seeing their enthusiasm, one might have guessed they were going to a picnic, not a war.

Army encampments soon sprawled in all directions around the city, with men bivouacked in places like Monroe Park and the fairgrounds where Charles and I had our disastrous first date. From the top of every hill, white tents were visible in the distance, dotting the landscape like mushrooms.

As the spring evenings warmed and lengthened, many of Richmond's ladies made it their habit to ride out to the fairgrounds after dinner to watch the evening dress parades. Sally was one of them. She coaxed me into coming with her to watch Charles and Jonathan drill. The central fairgrounds above the city had been transformed into a vast instruction camp where Colonel Smith and his young cadets from the Virginia Military Institute drilled the new recruits. We saw gentlemen in top hats and frock coats drilling side by side with barefooted sharecroppers in muslin shirts. Suppliers simply couldn't keep up with the demand for uniforms and boots.

Those early days of parade drill often resembled a comedy routine. Inexperienced soldiers would mix up the commands, causing them to pivot in the wrong direction, march straight into each other, and even accidentally whack each other in the head with their rifles as they turned. Eventually everyone learned to form a column for long marches, to dress the line, and to form a line of battle in any direction. Once they'd mastered those commands, they were ready to be trained for larger tactical maneuvers. The men also had to learn the nine steps required to load and fire their weapons, although ammunition was too precious to waste on practice.

"I have something for you," Sally said on one of our first trips to the fairgrounds. She leaned close to pin a rosette of palmetto leaves onto my lapel.

"What is that?"

"It's a secession badge. Everyone's wearing one. It's a symbol of patriotism for the Confederacy."

The thought of it made me uneasy. I still considered myself an American, so it seemed disloyal to support the Confederacy. Yet when I thought of Charles going off to fight the enemy, American soldiers would be trying to kill him, American warships would be bombarding my home.

Sally didn't seem as bothered by divided loyalties as I was, nor did she notice my unease. As we sat on our folding stools near the edge of the field that evening, watching the maneuvers, she kept up a steady, patriotic monologue.

"Just look at all those wonderful, brave men. Aren't they courageous souls? When I see their bravery and determination it makes me so proud to be a Virginian. I want our men to know I'm behind them all the way. No sacrifice we're asked to make is too great for the cause. I'm willing to do whatever I can here on the home front to support them, aren't you, Caroline?"

She turned to me for my assent, but I didn't know what to say. Instead, I pointed vaguely toward the ranks of men and said, "Are they the 'Blues'? Do you see Charles and Jonathan anywhere?"

"No, I don't think that's their unit." Then she returned to her speech. "The North will back down and leave us alone, you'll see. They're all cowards, afraid of a fight. Why, I read in the Richmond papers that they can hardly get anyone up there to volunteer—and even then it's only for ninety days. If they ever do attack us, we'll lick them in no time. Everybody knows Billy Yank won't fight. Besides, our cause is just."

Sally talked very bravely, but I wondered how she—how I—would react if faced with another scare like Pawnee Sunday. What would we do if the next threat was genuine?

One evening when Sally and I were at the parade grounds, she grew especially excited as she pointed to a tall, distinguished-looking man with graying hair and beard watching from the sidelines.

"Look! That's Colonel Lee . . . I mean *General* Lee! He's in command of all the Confederate forces in Virginia. Isn't he a good-looking man?"

Robert E. Lee was indeed a striking man. Tall and broad shouldered, probably in his mid-fifties, he had a handsome, well-proportioned face with calm, composed features. His military bearing was commanding and dignified, yet not cold or stern as many career military men sometimes were.

"I read in the news that Mr. Lincoln offered him the command of all the Union armies," Sally said, "but he refused."

I had read that, too. Lee, the hero of Harper's Ferry, said he couldn't fight against his birthplace, his home, his family. Since he had graduated from West Point—had been the academy's superintendent, in fact—he would now be fighting against many of his former colleagues, friends, teachers, and even students like Robert. I sympathized with Colonel Lee's dilemma. People I loved lived in the North, too. But like Charles, Lee was determined to fight for the South. At least I could be thankful that Charles and Jonathan would be under Lee's capable leadership.

By late spring, Tennessee, North Carolina, and Arkansas had joined Virginia and the other secessionists, bringing a total of eleven states into the Confederacy. The new government voted to move its capital from Montgomery, Alabama, to Richmond. We would be the "Washington, D.C." of the South. I thought our city was already filled to capacity after the earlier influx of soldiers and refugees, but now it nearly burst its seams as politicians and government officials, along with their families, arrived from all the other Southern states. I couldn't imagine where we would put them all.

President Jefferson Davis arrived on May 29, moving into the Spotswood Hotel until his new executive mansion, not far from Charles' home, was ready for occupancy. The city celebrated his arrival in grand style, decorating the hotel and nearly every house in Court End with the Stars and Bars in his honor. They held a reception for him at the governor's mansion the following day. I accompanied Sally, her mother, and the rest of Richmond's fashionable ladies in greeting President Davis in the forenoon; the men's reception was in the afternoon.

"Wasn't that exciting?" Sally said as we made our way back to her house afterward. "Think of it! We've met the *president!*"

"He isn't much to look at," Mrs. St. John said with a sniff.

"Well, neither is Mr. Lincoln, Mother," Sally said. "The point is, none of us except Charles has ever met a president before, and now here we are, living in the nation's capital!"

I had endured the reception as if it was just another dreary party, but as I listened to the two women talking, reality began to set in. Not only was I being forced to face a war I dreaded, but I also lived in the capital city of a new nation. Overnight, Richmond had become a symbol of the rebellion, and for the enemy, the ultimate prize of war. The familiar Stars and Stripes no longer flew from every flagpole. In fact, I no longer lived in the United States of America. The city around me might look familiar, but I now resided in a foreign land.

What worried me most was the fact that nobody I knew seemed to grieve over this loss the way I did. The man I loved was even willing to die for the right to create a new nation, fly a new flag. What was wrong with me that made me so different?

I continued my prayers each morning and night—or whenever fear began to strangle me—asking God to help me through whatever the day might bring. And as summer neared, routine life in Richmond quickly adopted a new rhythm. Our days began with the distant sounds of reveille and the rattle of drums, calling soldiers to duty; they ended with evening taps. Throughout the day, the sound of martial music and the tramp of marching feet served as background accompaniments to everything we did.

As soon as a company of soldiers was sufficiently drilled in military exercises, they would be transferred wherever the Confederacy needed them, defending one of the enemy's three possible invasion routes to Richmond. General Joseph Johnston and his forces were positioned in the Shenandoah Valley, guarding against a western attack. General Beauregard, hero of Fort Sumter, patrolled the northern approach and the rail route from Washington, D.C. to Richmond. Colonel Magruder was in charge of the peninsula, keeping an eye on the Union troops who still held Fortress Monroe, less than seventy-five miles southeast of Richmond.

As the newly mobilized troops marched through the city toward their assignments, the ladies of Richmond would send them on their way with cheers and blown kisses and fluttering handkerchiefs. Sally believed that it was our patriotic duty to support our men by join- ing in as many of these farewell marches as possible. She somehow found out where and when the men would be departing and made a determined effort to show up along the parade route, plowing forward in rain or shine, towing me in her wake as if she was a mule and I was a barge on the Kanawha Canal.

I found it difficult not to weep as I watched young men, family men with small children, saying farewell to the people they loved, reluctantly releasing them from their arms after a final, lingering embrace, then marching from sight, full of resolve and determina- tion. We all knew that many of the waving, cheering women would never see their departing soldiers again, and behind our smiles our hearts were as heavy as cannonballs.

Inevitably the day came when Charles and Jonathan completed their training. The Richmond Blues entered into Confederate service as part of the First Virginia Infantry. On the day before they departed, Captain Wise granted Jonathan a short leave to visit Hilltop. Jonathan stopped by my house on his way there, so excited, so full of life and the lust for adventure, that it was hard to imagine that anything terrible could happen to him. Wouldn't he always be this vibrantly alive?

"I've come to dance with you one last time before I go," he announced, then he swept me into his arms and waltzed me around the foyer, singing "I Dream of Jeannie With the Light Brown Hair."

"See, my dear?" he said when he had whirled me into a state of dizzy laughter. "We've always made great dancing partners, haven't we? Promise you'll write to me, Caroline. Promise me you won't waste all your ink on Private Charles St. John."

"Of course I'll write to you. And I'll pester Sally every day to make sure she writes to you, too."

"You are a sweetheart. Listen, I have to go—"

"Already? You just got here."

"Sorry, but would you do me one more favor? Would you tell Josiah to be ready to leave by the time I get back from Hilltop tonight? He's coming with me."

"Wait a minute. Coming with you . . . where?" I was confused. Josiah had been living here in town with us while Jonathan trained. Tessie had been dreading the day when the training ended and Josiah would be sent back to Hilltop. "Isn't Josiah going home to the plantation with you?"

"No, I've decided to take him off to war with me. My unit is going north to establish defensive positions along the Washington rail routes. We could use a good, strong set of muscles to dig entrenchments."

The absurdity of his plan infuriated me. "You're fighting for the right to keep Josiah a slave—and you have the nerve to ask him to *help* you?"

"Calm down, my dear little abolitionist," he said, taking my hands.

"Yes, I finally read your pamphlet, so I know you're one of *those*." He grinned, as if it were all a merry joke. "Josiah won't be fighting in any battles. He'll be quite safe behind our lines—which is more than I can say for yours truly. Besides, I'm certainly not the only soldier who's bringing his boy along."

"*Boy?* Josiah is a man, not a boy!"

"It's only a figure of speech. . . . Come on, Caroline, don't be mad at me. Who knows when we'll see each other again?"

Once again, his charm won me over, just as it always had in the past. I reached up to touch his cheek. "I could never stay mad at you."

"Then how about one last hug good-bye?"

I held him fondly in my arms—and in my heart. "Be safe, Jonathan," I whispered. "Please. Please. Be safe."

Charles came later that evening to eat dinner with us. Esther vowed to fill him with enough food to last until the war ended, then she made a valiant attempt to do just that.

"Please, no more," Charles finally begged. "My uniform buttons are about to pop off, and I haven't a clue how to sew them back on."

"I'm sorry, Massa Charles, but I do love to see you eat. You a man with an appetite, just like my Josiah. Little Missy here don't eat enough to keep a bird alive. Ain't no fun feeding her at all."

After dinner, Charles and I walked outside through the drawing room doors and into the balmy evening. Tomorrow was the last day of June. If it weren't for the war, we would have been married in three more weeks. I was sickened at the thought that this was our last evening together, that neither of us knew when—or if—we would ever see each other again. We walked wordlessly through Eli's garden, never noticing the carefully tended boxwood or lacy crepe myrtle, oblivious to the scent and beauty of the flowers we passed. Charles didn't stop until we reached the shelter of the magnolia tree near the rear of our yard, the tree I'd climbed so often with my friend Grady. We ducked beneath its low-hanging branches, then stood once again beside the trunk. There, hidden behind a curtain of thick, glossy leaves, Charles bent to kiss me.

"You have no idea how much I want to make you my wife," he murmured as we clung to each other afterward. "It should be our life together that's just beginning, not a war."

"Then let's get married, Charles—now, tonight. I don't care about a big wedding, I want to be your wife, if only for one night."

He pulled back to look into my eyes. "I can't do that to you. I won't. If anything should happen to me—"

"Don't say it!"

"Listen now. If anything should happen, I don't want to leave you a widow."

"I want to be your wife."

"I know. But let's get this war behind us first. Let's begin our marriage in happier, more hopeful times."

Our final moment together had come. I tried to study every detail of his face in the moonlight, memorizing it. We had exchanged photographs, but a picture wouldn't help me recall the exact shade of his eyes or the texture of his hair. It couldn't offer me the same assurance of love that I felt every time he looked at me.

He gave me one last kiss, one final embrace. "I love you," he whispered.

"Please don't go," I begged as I held him for the last time.

"Caroline . . . please don't ask me to stay."

He tore himself from my arms, tearing my heart from its place, as well. I watched him hurry away.

He looked back once when he reached the garden gate—the same gate they'd dragged Grady through—but the night was too dark for me to see Charles' face.

Jonathan returned for Josiah later that night. When all three men were gone, Tessie and I wept in each other's arms. We didn't speak. There were no words to say. We both knew the thoughts and emotions that filled the other's mind and heart. The color of our skin didn't matter, nor did the fact that she was my slave and I was her mistress. We each loved a man, and now we each felt the same pain, knew the same fear at his leaving.

The day after Charles left, I began practicing the piano again, using music as an outlet for my hoarded emotions. Concentrating on the notes took my mind off the war, if only for a few hours each day. I was in the parlor one afternoon, so intent on learning Mozart's "Turkish March" that I didn't hear my father return home early from work. I don't know how long he stood listening in the doorway, but when I finished the piece, he applauded softly.

"That was excellent, Caroline."

"Is there a reason why you're home early?" My heart had changed tempo the moment I saw him there. It accelerated when Daddy moved a small parlor chair next to the piano and sat down beside me.

"May I talk with you, Sugar?"

"What's wrong?"

"Nothing's wrong. But I've reached an important decision today, and I'd like to share it with you."

"You aren't going away to war, too, are you?"

He smiled, and for a moment I saw my childhood daddy again, the man with the familiar, cockeyed smile and uplifted brow. "No . . . no, I'm not going to fight. This war came ten years too late for me. But there is a way I'd like to help the Confederate effort." I stared down at my hands as I waited, my heart beating a quickstep.

"You've read in the papers about 'Operation Anaconda,' haven't you, Sugar? How the U.S. Navy intends to close all our Southern ports?"

I could only nod and wait, fearing what he was about to say.

"Lincoln thinks he can strangle us to death by cutting off all our supplies. Frankly, I think it will be quite impossible for seventy-odd

Union ships to patrol more than three thousand miles of Southern coastline. Still, it's clear that Richmond has already begun to feel the effects of blockade."

Anyone who had shopped downtown lately had noticed the blockade's effects, not only in the higher prices but also in the growing scarcity of many consumer items. Richmond relied on imported goods. Everything came from outside the South, from tin pots to teacups, from our hairpins to our shoes. In the months ahead we would quickly learn to either make do, do without, or make it ourselves.

"Is the blockade interfering with your business, Daddy?"

"It is, but that's not the point. I met with President Davis today. He said the government is having trouble importing the military equipment we so desperately need. England is willing to sell us their Enfield rifles, but we need ships to get them here."

"Are you going to loan President Davis your ships?"

"Sugar . . . I'm going to sail to England with them myself."

"He's asking you to be a blockade-runner? Daddy, no! It's too dangerous!"

"The president didn't ask me to go—I volunteered." I tried to protest, but Daddy wasn't listening. "There's nothing useful for an old man like me to do around here. Besides, importing things is my job, Caroline. I'm good at it. I've done it for nearly twenty years."

"But not with the U.S. Navy trying to shoot you out of the water!"

He reached to take my hand in his. "It's a very big ocean. We'll be transporting the rifles from England to Bermuda, first. The odds are very good that we'll never even encounter the Navy. The freight steamers that run from Bermuda to our Southern ports are small enough and swift enough to outmaneuver the Union ships."

I felt too numb to absorb what Daddy was telling me. I only knew that I was about to suffer yet another loss. "How long will you be gone?" I finally asked.

"I'm not sure. I'll probably return home from time to time, but I plan to make runs for the Confederacy for as long as I'm needed.

It's not just for arms. We also need tools, medicine, things like that. And if I can carry a load or two of cotton to England on my way over for the rifles . . . well, so much the better."

I felt too overwhelmed to speak. Daddy was leaving. Like Charles and Jonathan, he was willing to risk death for the Confederacy. He rose from his chair and stood over me, resting his hands on my shoulders.

"You mustn't worry, Sugar. I have a good man to manage my affairs here in Richmond. I've instructed him to give you whatever funds you need to live on."

"I'm not worried about money."

"Good. You shouldn't be. I know I can rely on you to run the household and oversee the servants for me while I'm away."

I looked up at him. "First Charles left me . . . and now you? I'll be all alone."

"You won't be alone," he said gently. "You'll have Tessie and Eli." I heard something sad and wistful in his tone, almost as if he was envious of the relationship I had with them. And he was right, of course. They wouldn't think of leaving me alone and defenseless.

When the terrible day finally arrived and I had to say good-bye to Daddy, he called all of the servants into his library with us to give them their final instructions.

"You are all fine men and women," he said as they stood in a line in front of him. "I've seen the kindness and . . . yes, the love you've shown my daughter. I'm leaving her in your hands, trusting you all to take good care of her. If anything should happen to me, you will become Caroline's property according to my will. She's free to do whatever she wishes with you." As Daddy walked down the row of servants, saying a few words of farewell to each one, all six of them stared mutely at their own feet.

"Luella, I know you'll do just as fine a job for Caroline as you've always done for me. Gilbert, thank you for your faithful service. Be strong. Ruby, take good care of Caroline, for her mother's sake. Esther, you've been an excellent cook . . . and so much more. Eli, it's easier for me to leave, knowing my daughter is in your very capable hands. Tessie . . ." He paused, and I was amazed to see that Daddy was battling his emotions. "Tessie, thank you . . . for everything."

His farewell speech alarmed me. It sounded as though he was saying good-bye forever. "You'll be back in a few months, won't you, Daddy?" I asked when we were alone.

"Yes, Sugar. God willing, I'll be back. Until then . . . may He keep you in His care." Then Daddy left, just as Charles and Jonathan had. All I could do was watch helplessly as the war continued to swallow up everyone and everything I had ever loved.

13

My stomach rolled with the wheels of the carriage as Gilbert inched the horses forward several more yards, then stopped again. We sat in a long line of carriages, waiting to disembark beneath the St. Johns' *porte cochere* for the sewing-society meeting. I was in no hurry to arrive. Before leaving home that hot July morning, I had watched from my bedroom window as Luella and Ruby washed laundry in wooden tubs in our backyard. I'd seen them each grab one end of a linen sheet and twist in opposite directions to wring all the water from it. That's the way my stomach felt now—as if someone had grabbed both ends and was twisting it into knots.

Up ahead, the matrons and belles who had already alighted from their carriages greeted one another, their laughter as bright and dry as the sun. I dreaded joining them. It had been easier to face these wealthy society ladies when I had Charles' arm to cling to. And since I had little in common with the young women my own age, I usually tried to float, unnoticed, in Sally's sociable wake. But Sally would be our hostess today; I could hardly expect her to tow me behind her like a lost child. The next several hours were certain to be torturous.

As volunteer soldiers continued to pour into Richmond, the production of Confederate uniforms fell far behind the demand. The few textile mills and manufacturing plants that we did have were able to produce the cloth and cut it into pieces with patterns, but with so many men enlisting, they lacked the manpower to sew the pieces together. In order to help the cause, every fashionable ladies' society—previously devoted to frivolous amusements—was being transformed into a sewing society. The one that Sally and her mother had invited me to join was among the city's most prestigious.

At last Gilbert rolled our carriage to a halt beneath the *porte cochere*. "All right, Tessie," I said with a sigh. "Let's go."

She stared at me as if I'd lost my mind. "Now, you know I ain't allowed to go waltzing through that door with you. You seeing any of them other fine ladies waltzing in there with their mammies? Door I use is around back."

She was right, of course. While many of the ladies had brought along one or two of their maidservants, and some had even brought their Negro seamstresses to help, the slaves gathered at the rear servants' entrance, not the grand foyer.

The inequity added to my feelings of guilt. I already felt bad for asking Tessie to come and ashamed for being here myself. By helping the Confederacy, it was as though I was helping Tessie and the others remain slaves. I had criticized Jonathan for taking Josiah with him, but wasn't I doing the same thing?

Jeremiah, the St. Johns' porter, opened my carriage door and stood waiting to help me down. A half-dozen carriages stood in line behind mine. "Go on, honey," Tessie whispered. "I see you inside."

I buried my feelings behind a false smile and walked into the house with the other women. In their brightly colored outfits and billowing hoop skirts, they reminded me of a bouquet of multicolored asters and chrysanthemums. You would never guess from this fashionable display of summer dresses and flowered hats that the price of cloth had skyrocketed due to the blockade, or that new straw hats could scarcely be found at any price. Sally wore the most expensive dress of all. Made from plaid silk, it required several more yards of material than a plain fabric would because the plaid on all the seams had to be matched. I had the urge to shake her—to shake all of these women. Was I the only one who saw that our lives would never be the same?

Mrs. St. John herded us all into her huge drawing room, and at least the changes in our lives were more evident in there. The furniture had been rearranged, transforming the room into a workshop, with every belle and society matron transformed into a seamstress. Those who owned sewing machines had brought them, and the clatter and whir of treadles and gears served as background music.

Nearly every woman, including myself, wore a chatelaine fastened to her waist, carrying her needles, scissors, thimble, and measuring tape. But few of us had ever done more than simple embroidery work, hemstitching, or needlepoint, and our delicate fingers weren't accustomed to pushing needles through heavy wool uniform jackets and trousers. I began with the relatively easy task of binding buttonholes and sewing on buttons, but even so, my fingertips were roughened by dozens of pinpricks by the end of the afternoon. In the weeks ahead, our hands as well as our fingers would be stiff and bleeding from stitching through heavy sailcloth as we sewed tents and overcoats.

The women talked of nothing but war, thought of nothing but war. Every one of them had a loved one in uniform—a husband, a father, a brother, a son, a sweetheart. As I listened to them talking about how difficult it was to be separated from them, I glanced down at Tessie, sewing quietly on a stool beside me. She had suffered this pain nearly all her life—separated from her parents, from her husband, from her son. What right did all of us privileged ladies have to discuss our current experiences as if they were unique when beside us sat slave women who had known this aching sorrow for many years?

"I admit that I've led a spoiled life," Sally said, entering the conversation. "I never would have *dreamed* that I'd be doing such a menial task as this. But I must say, I'm *proud* to do it. If our men are willing to do their part, then I'm willing to do mine."

"That's right," the woman beside her said. "If we want freedom for our country, then we have to fight for it. We can't expect someone else to do it."

"All of the noble women of Virginia stood beside their men in 1776," an elderly dowager said. "I'm proud to say that their self-sacrificing spirit has been passed down to us."

"We may be called upon to sacrifice more than our time or our pride in the months ahead," another woman added somberly. "I know what an enormous sacrifice it must be for you, Mrs. Randolph, to send all five of your sons off to fight."

Mrs. Randolph quickly blotted a tear with her hankie. "My boys are not cowards, so I must be brave, as well. I sent them off gladly. Their country needs them."

I had hated to watch Charles go; I couldn't imagine watching a beloved son, a child I'd nurtured from infancy, march off to war. For a second time I thought of Tessie, of how she must have felt to watch her son being taken away against her will.

Then, like a changeable wind, the conversation turned to another aspect of the war, our first victory. Mrs. Goode told us about the letter her son had sent describing last month's skirmish at Big Bethel Church.

"The Yankees sent troops up the peninsula from Fort Monroe—more than four thousand of them—thinking they could drive us out of our fortifications and move inland. But my Daniel said our boys fought like wildcats. We drove them back, that's for certain, even though our boys were outnumbered nearly four-to-one." The society ladies of Richmond gave a modest little cheer.

"God's favor is always on the side of justice," Sally said. "Even if we're outnumbered, heaven will protect the Southern cause."

Her words brought an even more enthusiastic response. When the applause died away, Mrs. Goode said, "It also shows that our enemies are cowards who will run at the first chance."

"That's right," everyone agreed. "Billy Yank won't fight."

"Johnny Reb will, though. It's our homeland that's being invaded."

When the room quieted again, Mrs. Randolph asked, "Have any of you been downtown yet, to see all the Yankee banners we captured at Big Bethel? They're on display in the store windows."

"I've seen them," Mrs. Taylor bragged. "And I also saw them parading the prisoners right down Main Street. I got my first good look at a real live Yankee."

"Frankly, I'd much rather see a dead one," Mrs. Goode replied. Everyone laughed except me. I had been picturing Robert in his U.S. Army uniform.

As the afternoon wore on, the drawing room grew increasingly hot, the scratchy wool uniforms like blankets in our laps. Even with all the windows and double doors thrown open, we perspired in the heat, our needles slipping through our sweaty fingers. The St. Johns had equipped several of their slaves with palmetto fans and stationed them around the room to keep the air circulating. But when the young Negro girl standing behind Sally and me grew weary and paused to rest, Sally turned around with a frown and pinched her leg.

"Sally! That's no way to treat a child," I admonished her without even thinking.

"But it's hot in here," Sally said, pouting. "She's supposed to keep fanning."

"She's been fanning us for nearly an hour." I kept my voice low, hoping no one else would hear me. "Your arms would be tired, too, by now. And she's just a little girl."

"Caroline, she's a slave."

"That's no excuse to treat a person unkindly."

At first Sally seemed annoyed that I had interfered. But when she glanced over her shoulder again, she saw that the girl had tears in her eyes. "Sit down and rest a minute, Lucy," she said with a sigh. Then Sally turned to me. "I don't even realize I'm being unkind. I hardly think of them as persons. I'm sorry, but I was raised not to see them."

Now it was my turn to be ashamed of my behavior. Admonishing my hostess had been rude. I mumbled an apology of my own and tried to disappear into the sofa cushions.

By now the discussion had turned to another topic—the traitorous Yankee sympathizers who lived in western Virginia. Unwilling to secede from the Union, they had seceded from Virginia instead, forming a new state.

"There are probably Northern sympathizers living right here in Richmond, too," Mrs. Taylor said. "If we're not careful, they'll be stabbing us in the back and passing secret information to the Union government."

"That's why the city council passed a new ordinance this week," Mrs. Goode said. Her husband served on the council, so she prided herself on being among the first to know the council's business.

"What ordinance is that, dear?" Mrs. St. John asked.

"It's called the 'Suspicious Persons Law' or something like that. We're supposed to be on the lookout for people who express Northern sentiments or opinions. If we discover such a person—man or woman—it's our duty to inform the mayor immediately so he can have them arrested."

"My goodness," Mrs. Randolph said. "Isn't it frightening to think such traitorous persons could be living right here among us and we wouldn't even know it?"

Mrs. Taylor gave her a withering look. "Don't be naïve, Clara. Any fool could tell."

"How? How could they tell?"

"Why, just open your eyes and look around. Notice who isn't cheering along with everyone else. Pay attention to the person whose enthusiasm seems a little . . . false."

I felt my cheeks begin to burn. I had not been among those who'd cheered the Confederate victory at Big Bethel a few moments ago or the capture of Yankee prisoners. But I wanted to run from the room when Mrs. Taylor's daughter Helen spoke next.

"Another way to tell is if they're Negro-lovers."

The room went momentarily silent. My heart thumped against my corset stays. Helen Taylor had fancied herself Charles' sweetheart before I came along. Neither she nor her mother had ever forgiven me for "stealing" Charles away. Too late, I realized that Helen was sitting close enough to Sally and me to have observed our conversation over the little slave girl.

"Traitors are always Negro-lovers," Helen repeated. She and her mother exchanged looks. My instincts urged me to run, to plead dizziness or nausea or some other excuse and leave while I still had a chance, but I didn't know how to escape the tightly packed circle of women without causing a scene. When Helen directed her next question to me, I knew it was too late to run.

"I understand that you once lived up north, isn't that right, Caroline? And don't you still have relatives living up there? I suppose they're all fighting for the Yankees now."

"None of them are fighting," I said shakily. "My aunt and uncle have two daughters."

"I've heard that Philadelphia is a hotbed of abolition activity," Mrs. Taylor added. "I pity you for having to live in such a place. Poor girl—I'll bet they tried to fill your head with their anti-slavery ideas." All of the ladies had stopped sewing, waiting, as women will, for a fresh scrap of news to feed the gossip fires. I had to say something.

"My aunt Martha is a native Virginian." My voice sounded tiny, apologetic. "She was born and raised right here in Richmond."

"Well, how do *you* feel about the slavery issue?" Helen asked. "Do you agree with the Yankees that it's an *evil institution*?"

I didn't answer. I couldn't answer. I was a coward. I had returned from Philadelphia determined to spend myself on behalf of the oppressed and to let my light rise in the darkness as the Scripture

216

urged me to do. I had once prided myself on being outspoken with Charles and helping to alter his way of thinking. But now I remained silent. Sally did, too, even though she knew the truth.

"Come now, speak up, Caroline," Mrs. Taylor said. "You must have an opinion."

As I vainly searched for a way out of the trap, Mrs. St. John suddenly cleared her throat as if about to make an important announcement. "Ladies," she said, her voice dripping gentility like honey, "perhaps you've forgotten that Caroline was forced to move to Philadelphia after her mother's tragic death. And I think you've also failed to notice that the dear girl is now sitting here among us, pricking her own fingers raw to help the cause. But maybe I should also remind you that she is engaged to my son, Charles. If her loyalty is in question, then so is his."

Mrs. St. John finished her little speech with a prim smile, then turned to one of her maidservants. "You may serve us our tea now, Katy."

When the grueling afternoon finally ended, I returned home, ashamed. Today was only the sewing society's first meeting; I would have to return tomorrow and the next day, working several times a week until the shortage of uniforms eased. I would have to face the same women, the same questions. Mrs. Taylor's suspicions would be confirmed if I didn't return to support the Southern cause. And I couldn't lie to myself and vow to speak out bravely the next time. I would be just as cowardly tomorrow and the day after as I had been today.

Tessie wisely said nothing on the way home. As ashamed as I was of my behavior, I knew that the only way I was ever going to figure out what to do about it was to talk to Eli. I remained inside the carriage after Tessie climbed down. I stayed until Gilbert drove us inside the carriage house and unhitched the horses. When all the others were gone, Eli ducked into the back of the carriage and sat down beside me.

"You planning on sleeping out here?" he asked gently.

I nodded, biting my lip to keep from crying.

"Must be something awful bad happen if you gonna be living in the barn from now on."

"I don't know where I should live, Eli." My tears began to fall, but Eli waited, patient as always, until I could speak. "Some people up north are working so hard to end slavery," I finally said. "John Brown may have been misguided, but at least he put his convictions into action, even though it cost him his life. I want to help end slavery, too, but everyone else in Richmond is working very hard to keep it. I don't want to leave my home, but as long as I'm living here and working alongside the other women, I feel like I'm condoning slavery—like I'm helping their cause."

"You want to tell me what happen today?"

"One of the women came right out and asked me, in front of all the others, how I felt about slavery, if I thought it was an evil institution. I didn't answer her, Eli. I'm so ashamed of myself now. I wasn't afraid to tell Charles how I felt, but today I didn't say anything at all to those women. Not one word."

His mouth twitched with a playful smile. "Tell you the truth, I'd rather face Massa Charles any day than a whole roomful of women." He made me smile in spite of the situation, but my guilt quickly returned.

"It's worse than that. They were talking about a new law the city council passed. Citizens are supposed to report people who sympathize with the North. Anyone who's against slavery might be a spy and could be arrested."

"That what would happen if you spoke out today? They throw you in jail?"

"I don't know. But I was afraid someone would report me as a suspicious person. I was scared." I continued staring down at my lap, twisting my hands, too ashamed to face him. "When I first came back to Richmond I was committed to speaking out. I wanted to serve God—but now I feel like I've let Him down. I'm nothing but a coward."

Eli sighed. "That ain't no surprise to God, Missy Caroline. He know exactly what's inside each one of us. Now you know it, too. And that's good."

"How is that good?"

"The Bible ask if a leopard can change its spots? Answer is *no*. Leopard can't change its spots—unless couple things happen. First, that leopard has to look in a mirror and see her spots need changing. Then she has to figure out she can't change them all by herself. But God sure can."

"So . . . I should pray for courage? Then what, Eli?" I finally lifted my head, looking up into his gentle brown eyes. "Maybe I'll be brave enough to give my opinion tomorrow, but what if Helen Taylor reports me and I end up getting arrested? What good will I be to God in jail? Maybe I should have stayed in Philadelphia, where people don't have slaves. Maybe I should go back there now and work for the side that's trying to end slavery instead of sewing Confederate uniforms."

"I don't think so, Missy Caroline," Eli said, shaking his head. "You know the story of Queen Esther? Lord put her in the palace among all them unbelievers for a reason. She have a job to do for Him—when the time's right. I think Massa Jesus send you up north, then bring you back here for a reason, too. But I think you have to wait until the time's right. God gave Esther courage so she could walk right into that throne room saying, 'If I perish, I perish.' But then she waited. She invite that king to dinner two times before she speak her mind. Wasn't because she scared. She waiting for the Lord to say, 'Now, Esther! Now's the time!'"

"So if they ask me my opinion again tomorrow . . . what should I say?"

"Nothing. Because even if you tell them what you believe, you ain't gonna change a single woman's mind, are you?"

"No, probably not."

"Don't go running ahead of God. He's gonna tell you when the time's right. Then whatever you do gonna make a difference. And one more thing—Queen Esther asked all her servants to pray with her. We be praying with you, Missy Caroline. You know we be praying."

I lived in a continual state of suspense that July, not only waiting for the war to begin in earnest but waiting for God's call to act. Tessie and I read the story of Queen Esther, and the words of Scripture seemed to shiver through me: "And who knoweth whether thou art come to the kingdom for such a time as this." I felt as though I was waiting to be called into battle, just as the two huge armies that were mustering near the Potomac waited for the battle that was certain to come.

Sally dragged me downtown for the Fourth of July celebrations, which included an eleven-gun salute—one for each state in the Confederacy. "Come on, Caroline. Show a little excitement," Sally urged when she noticed that I wasn't clapping and cheering like everyone else.

"I'm very tired," I said—which was true. "I've been so worried about Charles that I haven't been sleeping."

The next day Tessie and I read in the paper that in Lincoln's Fourth of July speech he had asked Congress for 400,000 soldiers and four hundred million dollars to wage war. The Northern armies rallied behind the cry "Forward to Richmond." Their goal was to conquer our city before the Confederate Congress had a chance to assemble for the first time on July 20. The newspapers also announced the answering cry of the Rebels—"Independence or Death." I felt like a passenger on board a ship that had become unmoored, floating toward certain disaster.

I did return to Mrs. St. John's sewing society but remained wary of Helen Taylor and her mother. As we worked, I sensed a new mood of anxiety among the women, barely concealed behind a façade of busy hands and idle chatter. The strain of waiting for news—with both longing and fear—was evident in our brittle voices and unsteady hands. This mood of apprehension thickened and settled over all of us, becoming as oppressive as the humid July air. Then the production of uniforms was suddenly halted and we were put to work at a new task—preparing bandages.

Early one evening after supper, Charles' father drove up Church Hill to pay me a visit. I invited him into Daddy's library and asked Gilbert to pour him a drink. My nerves jumped as I made small talk, waiting for him to come to the point of his visit.

"You've heard from Charles, I suppose?" he asked as Gilbert offered him one of Daddy's last few cigars.

"Yes, I've had a few letters. He and the others are well, but they haven't had much time to write, between marching for days on end and digging fortifications."

"He's probably eager to get the fighting underway, eh?"

I nodded, unwilling to share everything that Charles had confided—how unprepared he had been for the heavy marching and other privations of army life; how the suspense and the fear of the unknown ate at him like a disease; how he agonized over what he would do when he faced enemy fire for the first time and he would be forced to aim his weapon at another man.

"I certainly do envy all these young men," Mr. St. John said, settling comfortably into Daddy's chair. "If only I was younger and not crippled with this blasted rheumatism, I would love to join them. As it is, there's nothing much I can do besides serve in the Home Guard."

"That's an important job, too," I said, not insincerely. "The Union forces would like nothing better than to capture Richmond."

"You're right. And that brings me to the reason why I've come." He took a long, fortifying drag on his cigar, then exhaled, his words filling the room along with the smoke. "General Lee has spent the past few days inspecting the fortifications around Richmond. Sad to say, he has declared them woefully inadequate. He wants to construct a better system of defenses, but as you can guess, there is a serious shortage of manpower at the moment. One solution has been to use free Negroes."

"As volunteers?"

He studied me over the rim of his glass as he took a long drink. "No. As conscripts. But we are providing them with food and the same monthly wage our army privates receive. I don't think it's unfair to ask Negroes to defend their own homes, do you?"

"I suppose not."

"That leads me to the first difficult request I'm forced to make. You see, there aren't nearly enough free Negroes. We need more laborers. I understand that you have several male slaves—"

"Two. We only have two."

"Yes . . . well, if you could send even one of them, the Confederacy would be grateful." He puffed on his cigar for a moment before continuing. "My second request is for horses, and I'm afraid this isn't a voluntary matter. The army needs every one you can spare. You will be reimbursed, of course . . . but I'm afraid you must relinquish them."

How would I ever tell Eli? Those horses were as dear to him as pets. "How soon do you need them?" I asked.

"If you could have everything ready by tomorrow morning . . ." He finished his drink, rather than his sentence, and set the glass on Daddy's desk. "One final request. Your boy Eli has a reputation as one of the best hostlers in Virginia. Word is he knows more about what's wrong with a horse and what to do about it than anyone around. The Confederacy could use him. Please think about donating him to the cause."

"I . . . I will consider it."

I don't recall saying much else as Mr. St. John hoisted himself from the chair and bid me good-night, promising to return in the morning for my answer. If Daddy were home, he probably would have done his patriotic duty immediately, emptying the stables and sending both Eli and Gilbert away with Mr. St. John that very night. But Daddy wasn't home. I was the one who had to make the decision, and I couldn't bring myself to order either man to go off with the Rebels to defend his own enslavement. I wrestled with the decision for a while; then, not knowing what else to do, I went out to the carriage house to find Eli and Gilbert. I told them about Mr. St. John's requests.

"I don't know anything about horses," I admitted. "I have no idea how many we need to keep or which ones we should give to the army. But what's even worse is that I don't want to order either one of you to go away with these men unless you want to go. What . . . what do you think? What should I do?"

Eli's calm expression never changed, but Gilbert was visibly upset. He frowned at Eli, making angry sounds, and shifted from foot to foot in agitation.

"What's wrong, Gilbert?" I asked.

"Ain't the way it works," he replied. "Ain't our decision. Missy supposed to tell us what to do, then we do it. We your slaves."

"Well, suppose you weren't slaves. What would you recommend that I do?"

"I still your slave," he said stubbornly. "Missy supposed to give me orders."

But that was precisely what I was trying to avoid—giving orders. It frustrated me that I was forced to become the very thing I hated—a slave driver. Then I had an idea, born of desperation. If I was stuck with the system of slavery, then I would have to play by its rules.

"All right, Gilbert. Here are my orders: I demand that you and Eli decide how many horses we need and which ones to sell. I also order you to decide how many male slaves are needed to do the work around here and who can be spared for the war effort. I'll need your answers before morning." I stalked to the door, then turned around and added, "That's an order."

I heard Eli laughing as I slammed the carriage-house door. He still had a playful smile on his face when he and Gilbert came to the servants' entrance an hour later to tell me their decision. "We reckon that the one little mare is all you need to get around town," Eli said. "She can pull the buggy instead of the big carriage. 'Specially since Missy don't weigh much more than a sack of feathers. It pains me to say it, but you can sell the other three horses."

"What about the . . . the other matter?"

"I ain't going, Missy Caroline," Eli said gently. "I promise Massa Fletcher I watch out for you and I determine to do that. You more important than horses. But Gilbert, here . . . he says he gonna go help with the digging."

"Are you sure, Gilbert?" I'd never known the wiry little man to do much manual labor. He was Daddy's valet, our butler, our carriage driver. I guessed his age to be in his early forties. "You don't have to help the Rebels, you know. They're fighting for the right to keep slaves."

Gilbert squared his shoulders. "I ain't doing it for them. I promise Massa Fletcher I watch out for you and take care all his things. I don't know what them Yankee soldiers do if they come here, but I ain't intending to find out. This seem like something Massa would want me to do." I held back my tears until the two men left, then braced myself for yet another loss.

Mr. St. John led our horses away the next morning. Then Tessie, Ruby, and I stood on the front steps and watched Gilbert march off with the Home Guard and a troop of free Negroes, carrying Eli's garden spade over his shoulder like a rifle.

14

I awoke on the morning of July 20 with the realization that today would have been my wedding day. Sally remembered, too, and she drove up Church Hill to invite me to join her in attending the Confederate Congress, convening in Richmond for the first time. "It'll help take your mind off things," she promised.

"But I don't want to take my mind off Charles. I can't, not even for one moment. I . . . I don't know how to explain it." How could I explain the illogical notion I had that it was my loving thoughts, the strength of my will, and my prayers that kept Charles alive—just as a drowning swimmer, treading to stay afloat, dares not stop paddling for a single moment?

"I understand," she said simply, and she stayed all day with me, instead. We laughed, shared confidences, and dreamed of our futures once the war ended. I talked about Jonathan and reminisced about Hilltop. Sally told me stories about Charles' boyhood. As the lazy summer sun finally sank from sight, we felt as close as sisters—which we would have been if it weren't for the war.

Sunday, July 21, was a warm, tranquil day. I went to services at St. Paul's with Sally and noticed two things: that the worshippers were almost exclusively women, and that President Davis wasn't in his usual pew, halfway up the main aisle on the right-hand side. I later learned that while we had passed the Sabbath afternoon in peaceful conversation, enjoying a leisurely lunch and an afternoon stroll down the boulevard, the first bloody battle of the war had raged near Manassas, Virginia, on a creek called Bull Run.

As I had knelt in the hushed beauty of St. Paul's to recite the Lord's Prayer that morning, I'd had no idea that Charles crouched in a muddy ditch, silently reciting the same prayer as he watched masses of enemy troops march steadily toward him like a dark blue wave. I didn't know that his lips had turned black from ripping open countless powder cartridges with his teeth, or that his voice had grown hoarse from shouting the Rebel yell, or that his hands had trembled with fatigue and hunger by the end of the day. I hadn't pictured him bravely fighting a relentless enemy—loading and firing, then loading again, even as the sun blazed down and his shoulders ached and enemy bullets whizzed past his head. I didn't see him advancing forward, the earth shaking, fire flashing from the barrels of enemy rifles aimed at him, his eyes red and watery with smoke and dust. I couldn't know that his ears rang from the deafening din until he could no longer hear the command signals, and that the Confederate line around him had faltered and fallen back. Nor did I know how he'd watched so many of his friends suddenly drop beside him, writhing, screaming, dying, and he'd stumbled over their bodies as he'd retreated. While I'd sipped mint tea, Charles had witnessed death in combat for the first time, the nauseating sight of a man's body torn apart, his guts spilled.

The first news came to us on that quiet Sunday in Richmond when Charles' father hurried home from Capitol Square late in the afternoon. "The fighting began this morning near Manassas Junction," he told us. "It has been going on all day."

I prayed as I never have before and later learned that a miracle had occurred as General "Stonewall" Jackson's brigade held the hill at the center of the Confederate line, and General Johnston's reinforcements arrived, and the tide of battle changed in the Rebels' favor. Charles knew the dizzying euphoria of victory as he raced forward behind a fleeing enemy, kicking aside their discarded haversacks and cartridge belts and blankets, strewn along the road.

Charles' father returned to the capitol to await more news, for the telegram that finally arrived saying, "Night has closed on a hard-fought field. . . . Our forces have won a glorious victory." General Beauregard, the hero of Fort Sumter, had routed Union General McDowell.

As Monday dawned, wet and dreary, I wondered if it had all been a dream. Could it really be true that the South had won a great victory so close to the Union capital? Sally and I waited in her carriage outside the *Enquirer* office for more news, with rain drumming steadily on the carriage roof, dripping from the building's eaves, and running down the cobbled streets. Slowly the reports arrived, not only confirming our great victory on that bloody Sunday but also telling of a spectacular Union rout. The Yankees had panicked and fled before the Rebels, littering the road with equipment and baggage as they retreated to Washington in a stampede. Spectators who had driven out on that lovely Sunday afternoon to watch the battle had been nearly trampled by their own retreating soldiers. The cries of "On to Richmond" were silenced by cries of fear that their own capital might now be threatened with invasion.

I overheard many of Richmond's politicians speculating that Lincoln would sue for peace as a result of this stunning loss. After experiencing such bloodshed so close to their own homes, the people up north would lose heart for war.

Sally and I hugged each other in joy, knowing that we wouldn't be able to truly celebrate this good news until we learned whether or not Charles and Jonathan were safe. Any victory, especially a hard-fought one, meant casualties. After receiving the news, we returned home—while many of Richmond's citizens began making preparations for the avalanche of casualties that was certain to follow.

On Tuesday I went to the central depot with all the other women to await news of our soldiers. Rumors circulated that a list would be posted, company by company, naming the men who had been wounded, who were missing, and who had died in battle. Sally and I waited, clutching each other's hand.

The train from Manassas finally arrived, returning President Davis to the city from the battlefield. Along with him came the first victims of the conflict. The dead arrived in pine boxes, stacking up at the depot in alarming numbers, awaiting shipment home. The wounded arrived on crutches and on stretchers and on makeshift pallets—more and more of them every hour. As I stood scanning their shocked, pale faces, praying that I wouldn't see Charles' among them, I overheard one of the doctors pleading with Mrs. Goode's husband, a city official, to find more places to care for them all.

"The Medical College Hospital is full," the doctor insisted. "You can't send us any more."

"All of the other hospitals are overflowing, too," Mr. Goode replied. "What am I supposed to do?"

"You must find more places for them."

"Where?"

"I don't know . . . take them to homes or schools or hotels, even warehouses—someplace where they're out of the sun and the dust. Someplace where they can rest and get a drink of water."

Everywhere I looked the wounded men lay, waiting on the train platform and on sidewalks and even on the city streets. Some of the men moaned and wept and begged for morphine or a drink of water, men with missing limbs and savage wounds and filthy, blood-soaked bandages. I was staggered by the knowledge that we didn't have enough hospitals to care for them all, enough ambulances to transport them there, enough doctors or nurses or beds or medicine.

Sally closed her eyes against the terrible sight, refusing to budge from our place near the ticket office as we waited for the casualty list to be posted. I longed to run home, but my greater need was to search for Charles and Jonathan among the mangled bodies. I forced myself to walk between the rows, searching each exhausted face, looking for a Richmond Blues insignia on each uniform. Some of the men grabbed the hem of my skirt as I passed, pleading for help, for mercy, for the assurance that they weren't going to die. By the time the list arrived, and I learned that neither Charles St. John nor Jonathan Fletcher was on it, I knew that it would be a long time before I could erase the horror of this day from my mind.

As I clung to Sally, weeping and thanking God for Charles' safety, the doctor I'd seen earlier suddenly interrupted us. "Ladies, please. I need your help . . . these men need your help."

"We're not nurses—" Sally began.

"You don't need to be. Please, just help me. Talk to the men, reassure them." I saw the fatigue on the doctor's distraught face, the bloodstains on his hands and coat. From what little I'd seen on the platform, I knew that he faced an overwhelming task.

Sally backed away from him. "I can't . . ."

He gripped her arm, refusing to let go. "I noticed that you were looking for someone's name a moment ago. A boyfriend? Husband? Brother? Suppose he was one of these wounded souls, lying on a train platform in a strange city. Wouldn't you want some kind, compassionate woman to help him? I'm not asking you to tend their wounds. Just give a soldier a drink of water. Help someone write a letter home—especially the ones who are dying. Help me feed the men who can't feed themselves. Talk to them, encourage them. . . . Please."

"Sally, we have to help him," I said. "You know we do."

The doctor's shoulders sagged with relief. "Thank you." He relinquished Sally's arm, and after directing us to the City Almshouse where a makeshift hospital was being organized, he hurried away to intercept another group of women and beg for their help.

The scene at the City Almshouse so overwhelmed me that I staggered against the doorframe for support. Mutilated men lay wall-to-wall on the bare floor, leaving scarcely enough room to walk down the rows between them. Every square inch of floor space was filled, yet still more injured men continued to arrive, filling the yard outside, waiting for someone to die and make a space for them inside. Blood stained the soldiers' bandages, their clothing and faces, the floors, even the doorposts as bodies flowed in and out in a steady stream. I'd never seen so much blood in my life.

The matron seemed grateful to see us, but she had little time to spare for instructions, let alone pleasantries. "Start with that room," she said, pointing to a smaller room off the main hallway. "Most of them haven't eaten in two days, a lot of them need water. You'll have to help some of them feed themselves." She appraised Sally, whose beautiful face had turned the color of paper, and added, "Talk to them, miss . . . smile for them."

We rolled up our sleeves, fetched the food and water, and set to work. But less than a minute passed after we'd entered the stifling room before the mingled smells of sweat and blood and sickness made my gorge rise. I battled to hold it down. As soon as the injured men saw us, they began clamoring for our help, moaning, whimpering. Dozens of them had survived amputations at the field hospitals, and as the morphine finally wore off, they screamed in shock and pain at the loss of their arms, their legs.

The first soldier Sally approached broke into anguished sobs, weeping, "My leg! Oh, God! They cut off my leg!" and Sally collapsed in a faint on top of him.

I ran into the hallway, calling for the matron. "Please, somebody help my friend, she's fainted!"

The nurse gave me a withering look. "Push her aside and help the injured man." She hurried past me toward another room.

I found smelling salts in Sally's reticule and revived her. When she finished vomiting into her handkerchief, I rinsed her face with the washcloth meant for the soldiers.

"I can't do this," Sally wept. "I can't look at those horrible amputated arms and legs. . . ."

"Don't. Look at his face. Pretend that he's Jonathan or one of your other beaux." My voice gentled. "Because someday he might be."

In the end, Sally stayed. We worked until late that afternoon, until neither of us could stand on our feet for another moment. If we had stayed until we were no longer needed, we would have been there for weeks.

That terrible day, I watched men die for the first time. Some of them struggled and grasped to hold on to life until the very end; others relinquished it with a peaceful sigh, a final exhaled breath. As Sally and I finally stepped outside into the thick July heat, I recognized that my own life hung from God's hand by a slender silver thread. Its fragility made it no less precious in His eyes, but it pointed to the need to treasure it, to protect life at all costs.

Injured men crammed the yards and sidewalks outside the almshouse, some of them too weak to swat away the flies that swarmed around their wounds. Like so many other Richmond ladies that day, I gave an ambulance driver my address, and by nightfall my drawing room was filled with wounded men to nurse and feed.

"Lord have mercy on their souls!" Esther said when she saw their wretched condition. Luella and Eli carried every mattress and cushion in the house down to the drawing room, every pillow and blanket they could find. Esther cooked gallons of soup, which was all that many of the invalids could manage to eat. Ruby tore some of our linen bed sheets into strips for clean bandages, and Tessie volunteered to change and dress their wounds, nearly fainting herself the first time she saw the damage that a Minie ball could inflict. Eli spent the next several nights sleeping on the floor alongside the men, the only one of us strong enough to help a man turn over.

Along with my work at the almshouse, I now endured all-night vigils at home by the soldiers' bedsides, making sure that no one had to spend the last hours of his life alone. On one such night, I sat with a young soldier named Wade, from Mississippi. I knew from the fetid smell of his shoulder wound and the ominous streaks that radiated from it like spokes that he would probably die. Wade knew it, too, and he struggled to die manfully, without weeping. He'd told me he was eighteen, but I didn't believe him. The soft fuzz on his cheeks and his trembling youthful limbs told me that he couldn't possibly be more than sixteen. Lying down made it difficult for Wade to breathe, so Eli helped him sit up, supporting him in his strong arms.

"Would you like us to pray with you?" I asked.

"I used to go to Sunday meetings. . . ." Wade mumbled. "Haven't been in a long time. . . ."

"That doesn't matter right now. God is always willing to hear your prayers."

Wade nodded weakly and closed his eyes. I held his hand in mine and signaled to Eli to pray.

"Oh, Lord Jesus," Eli began, "we ask you to—"

"No . . . no . . ." The boy began thrashing, tossing his head from side to side.

"Wade, what is it? What's wrong?"

"I don't want that nigger praying for me!"

I was too outraged to speak. I dropped Wade's hand, waiting for Eli to drop the boy to the floor and leave him there to die. Instead, Eli rested his hand on my shoulder to calm me.

"Go on, Missy Caroline, you pray for him."

"I can't." My voice shook with fury and contempt.

"Yes, you can, and you best do it quick."

Somehow, I managed to do it. I prayed and recited the Twenty-third Psalm until Wade finally grew calm and slipped into unconsciousness. Then I stood and fled to Daddy's library. I was trembling from head to toe. Eli followed a few minutes later, carrying the lamp.

"You all right?" he asked.

"I don't understand people like him. How could he say such a thing to you? And why did you make me pray for him after what he said?"

Eli set the lamp down on Daddy's desk. "That boy will have to face God pretty soon and give an accounting for all the hate he storing away in his heart. But you and I better not be storing any in ours. Let it go, Missy Caroline—right away, before it take root. Else we be just as bad as he is. The devil wants us to be like himself—telling lies and hating people. Jesus wants us to be like He is—loving our enemies and praying for them. Who you gonna be like?"

I sank into the chair behind my daddy's desk, then leaned forward to rest my elbows on it and covered my face. "It's too hard," I mumbled. "All this work, night and day, with scarcely a moment's rest—and then some of them are so ungrateful . . . insulting!" I exhaled, expelling my anger in a rush of air. When I felt calmer, I said, "Listen, Eli, you don't have to do this anymore. Go home and go to bed. You've been working harder than any servant should be expected to work."

I waited for him to leave, but Eli didn't move. When I finally lowered my hands and looked up, he was standing in the same place in front of the desk, gazing down at me.

"Some of these men never once thought about Jesus their whole life," he said. "But they crying out to Him now cause they hurt and afraid. Jesus wants to answer them. He wants to help that poor dying boy out there, but the only arms and the only voice He has is ours."

I covered my face again, feeling very small and ungracious compared to Eli. "I can't do this anymore."

"You have to," Eli said.

"Why?" I sounded like a petulant child, but I didn't care. "Who says I have to?"

"Jesus is our Massa, and He say so. We're here to serve Him, not the other way around. Your daddy ain't saying to me, 'Sit yourself down, Eli. Tell me what you want to eat. Let me wait on you.'"

"I thought the Bible says I'm God's child."

"Comes a time when every child has to grow up and get about his father's business. Cousin Jonathan and Massa Charles . . . didn't they grow up and go to work for their daddies? Time you grow up, Missy Caroline. Your heavenly Father needs you to be His servant."

I was exhausted and demoralized and discouraged. All I could think to say was, "It's too hard."

"You bet it's hard. Even Jesus struggled all night in the Garden. He didn't want to die. But He prayed, 'Not my will, but thine, be done.' A servant does what his massa says and goes where his massa sends him and doesn't quit until the job is done."

I closed my eyes, thinking, *Tomorrow. I'll start all over again tomorrow.* But Eli wasn't finished.

"Every day a servant goes to his massa and finds out what he supposed to do that day. If a servant is in the middle of something and Massa calls his name, he don't say 'just a minute'—he drop whatever he doing and he run to stand before the massa and he say, 'Here I am.' Every morning we need to ask the Lord, 'This where you want me today? This what you want me to do?' If it is, then that's where you have to be, and that's what you have to do."

"All right, Eli," I said with a sigh. I knew he was right. And I knew I would have to pray about everything he'd said. But right then I simply wanted to be alone, to lay my head down on the desk and weep. "You may go now," I told Eli. "I need some time alone."

"No, Missy Caroline," he said gently. "You coming with me. That poor boy gonna die, and Massa Jesus wants you and me to be with him."

Eventually, the deluge of wounded soldiers receded, the makeshift beds in our drawing room emptied. The nursing shortage in Richmond's hospitals eased when women arrived from all over the South to nurse their wounded husbands, sweethearts, and sons. Tessie and

I read in the news that the Confederate Congress had given credit to "The Most High God, King of Kings and Lord of Lords, for the triumph at Manassas." Congress was convinced that the Union would never continue the war after this stunning defeat.

But the war did continue, slowly spreading to other parts of the country. We read of another Confederate victory at Wilson's Creek in Missouri and then a victory at Ball's Bluff, here in Virginia. More captured Yankee prisoners arrived in Richmond, adding to the hundreds that had been captured at Manassas. No one knew what to do with them all. Some of the vacant tobacco warehouses on the waterfront near Daddy's warehouses had been converted into prisons, but when they quickly overflowed, the prisoners were confined on Belle Isle in the middle of the James River. From Mother's grave site in Hollywood Cemetery, I could see row upon row of tents and makeshift shacks dotting the six-acre island and thousands of wretched, blue-uniformed men milling around.

In August, Union forces captured Fort Hatteras in North Carolina. This meant that our blockade-runners could no longer use this important route, cutting off the flow of much-needed supplies. I didn't worry as much about the rising prices or the empty store shelves as I did about Daddy. His work had become even more dangerous now. And we hadn't heard from him since he'd left home in July.

"Your father has an important job to do overseas," Mr. St. John assured me as we walked home from St. Paul's one beautiful fall day. We had been walking a lot more since the war began, but Richmond enjoyed a long spell of beautiful Indian summer weather that year, making our walks pleasant. "It's more than just English rifles he's after," Mr. St. John continued. "England and France depend on the South for their supplies of cotton and tobacco. If we can convince those nations to back our cause and join the war on our behalf, the North will have to concede defeat."

"You think my father is part of this effort?"

"President Davis is preparing to send diplomats to Europe to negotiate an alliance. But he needs men like your father to keep the trade ships running in the meantime. He's doing a very important job."

In November, the Union Navy intercepted the British mail steamer *Trent* on the high seas and captured the two Confederate diplomats, James Mason and John Slidell, en route to Great Britain for President Davis. The British were so outraged by this assault on one of their ships that it seemed as though the *Trent* affair might finally persuade Great Britain to support the South. But President Lincoln recognized the danger of such an alliance and ordered the two diplomats to be released with an apology to England. The Rebels' hopes were disappointed once more. The war continued. Gilbert returned home again, his digging finished for the winter, and we welcomed him as a hero. But I still heard no word from Daddy.

When wintry weather finally arrived, bringing bone-chilling rain and frigid blankets of snow, the women in Mrs. St. John's sewing society turned to knitting. I had never knitted in my life, but I learned how to that winter; the need for warm hats, gloves, scarves, and socks for our soldiers was critical. As we crowded around the fireplace in the St. Johns' smaller parlor, I pictured Charles and Jonathan huddling inside their leaking tents, shivering beneath thin blankets. Hospitals began filling with soldiers again—not casualties of battle but victims of diseases such as pneumonia, typhoid, and dysentery, which spread through the army camps like biblical plagues.

Two years ago, Jonathan and I had celebrated Christmas together at Sally's party. Last Christmas, Charles and I had celebrated our engagement. This Christmas, Esther sent our turkey and all the trimmings to Jonathan, Charles, and the other "Richmond Blues," dug in for the winter in northern Virginia. I tried to put on a brave face in public as my clumsy fingers gripped the slender knitting needles and wrestled to master the basics of knitting and purling. I managed to turn skeins of yarn into oddly misshapen socks and mittens, but only Tessie knew how many tears I silently shed in my room.

15

MARCH 1862

A gust of wind rattled the shutters outside my bedroom window one cold morning in March, then whistled down the chimney. But it was the words that Tessie had just read from the book of Philippians that made me pause in my knitting to look up at her, not the blustery wind. "Wait . . . read that again, Tessie."

"'Let this mind be in you, which was also in Christ Jesus,'" she read. "'Who, being in the form of God, thought it not robbery to be equal with God: But made himself of no reputation, and took upon him the form of a servant. . . .'"

"A servant," I repeated. "That's what Eli was trying to tell me last summer when we nursed all those wounded soldiers. God wants us to be His servants."

Tessie shook her head as if she couldn't believe the words either. "Eli always telling us colored folk that Massa Jesus understand us, that He a servant, too. But I ain't believing it until I read this."

"You and the others have an advantage over me in this area," I said, returning to my knitting. "You already know how to be good servants, how to obey your master. No wonder Eli understands Jesus so much better than I do."

Tessie turned back to the Bible and read, "'He humbled himself and became obedient unto death, even the death of the cross. . . .'" I stopped her again so I could ponder that thought. *Would I be willing to obey God, even in the face of death?*

My thoughts were suddenly interrupted by the sound of footsteps pounding up the stairs and Gilbert shouting, "Missy Caroline! Missy Caroline! Come quick! Come see who's here!"

When I opened my bedroom door, I couldn't believe the look of joy on Gilbert's face. "Come see!" he repeated, and he bounded down the stairs again, ahead of me. When I reached the landing, I saw the front door flung wide open and my father standing in the foyer with his satchel at his feet. I ran downstairs to embrace him.

"Daddy! I can't believe you're finally home!"

"I can hardly believe it myself, Sugar. I had quite a time getting here, let me tell you."

"Thank God you're safe."

When Daddy finally released me, Gilbert was still grinning. As he took Daddy's hat and overcoat from him, the other servants began gathering shyly in the foyer to have a look at Daddy, as if they'd forgotten what he looked like.

"Welcome home, Massa Fletcher," Tessie said softly, and Daddy smiled.

"Here you are home again," Esther moaned, "and ain't a bite of meat to eat in this whole house. I'm sorry, Massa Fletcher, but we ain't had nothing but fish for days and days. Beef you buy in the market cost a fortune, and even then it's about as tender as Eli's old shoe."

Daddy chuckled. "Fish will be just fine, Esther. In fact, Eli's shoes would probably taste fine, too, if you cooked them. Ah, it's good to be home!"

The servants went all out for Daddy, setting the dining room table for lunch, even though it was just the two of us, and uncorking a bottle of wine from the cellar. "Ain't too many bottles left," Gilbert explained, "since all them wounded soldiers Missy took in needed it so bad. But this here is a celebration."

Esther set a bowl of potatoes in front of Daddy. "We eating a lot of potatoes, these days. Ain't no butter to put on them neither, so I had to fix them with vinegar and bacon."

"They smell wonderful," he said.

"Don't your daddy look good?" Tessie whispered as she set the platter of fish in front of me. "Don't he, though? All that ocean sailing and salty air must agree with him."

Eli came to stand in the dining room doorway, hat in hand, to welcome Daddy home and to explain to him why his stables housed only one little mare. "You made a good choice," Daddy told him. "I would have done the same thing if I had been home."

When we all finished telling Daddy our stories and explaining what had gone on in his absence, he leaned back in his chair and said, "You've had quite a time of it here while I was gone, haven't you? But you've all done very well. My thanks to you."

"I'm so glad you're home," I said. "Now you can make the hard decisions from now on."

He reached for my hand, frowning. "Caroline, I can't stay. I'm leaving again in a few days." I stared at him, unable to speak. "I came back to apply for a government commission as a privateer."

"Daddy! That's the same thing as being a pirate."

He laughed. "I suppose Mr. Lincoln and his friends might see it that way, but I consider myself part of the Confederate Navy. Our privateers have already made a big impact on the war effort, raiding Northern ships. And, of course, any goods my ships manage to seize will help the South, too."

What my father planned was much worse than running the blockade. Attacking Union merchant ships on the high seas was considered piracy, and captured privateers faced execution. "Please don't do this," I begged. "It's too dangerous. If you're caught they'll kill you."

"Then I guess I'd better not get caught." He smiled, trying to make light of it, but when he saw my expression he sobered. "Caroline, don't make me feel any worse than I already do for leaving you. I would gladly heed your wishes if this were peacetime. But we're at war, and every man—every woman, for that matter—has to do what he feels called upon to do. For Charles and Jonathan, that meant going off to fight. For me . . . this is something I really feel I have to do."

I nodded and pretended to understand. Charles, Jonathan, and now Daddy were all willing to risk death for the Southern cause—but I still didn't see how it was worth dying for.

"Besides," Daddy continued, "President Davis had a showdown with Lincoln last November over his treatment of captured privateers. Davis threatened to execute a captured Federal officer for every privateer Lincoln executed. Lincoln finally backed down. Privateers are treated like any other prisoners of war now."

"That's a very small comfort, Daddy."

"I know. But you can be proud that your father is about to become part of the Confederate Navy, Sugar. Did you read in the papers how we took on the Union fleet last week—and won?"

I had read about it, but Daddy was so excited about our victory at Hampton Roads that I let him retell the story of how the Confederate ironclad *Virginia* sank the Union's most powerful warship, the *Cumberland*, then set the *Congress* on fire and drove the *Minnesota* aground. When the Union ironclad *Monitor* arrived the next day, the *Virginia* battled her for four and a half hours before the duel ended in a draw.

"Our sewing society has been making sandbags all week," I said. "We're sending them to General Magruder to fortify Yorktown against the Federal fleet."

Daddy raised his fist and cheered. "Bravo! And bravo for Magruder. He has the Feds fooled into thinking he has a lot more men at Yorktown than he actually does. If the enemy fleet knew we only have about eight thousand men there, they would have sent landing parties and taken the city a long time ago."

I thought about his words as Esther brought in a pecan pie for dessert—Daddy's favorite. If the enemy knew how weak we were, maybe they could attack quickly and end the war before there was any more bloodshed. More than anything else, I wanted the war to end before the men I loved had to die.

"Now, this ain't gonna taste near as good as usual, Massa Fletcher," Esther warned as she set the pie in front of Daddy. "Seeing as I had to make it without real sugar. Ain't no sugar anywhere in Richmond, just sorghum."

"When I come back, Esther, I promise I'll bring you a whole boatload of sugar."

"You going away again, Massa Fletcher?"

"Yes, I can only stay for a couple of days."

"Well, you make sure you bring yourself back safe, you hear? And don't be worrying about bringing me no sugar."

Daddy waited until Esther left the dining room again before turning to me, his expression serious. "The Federals are coming, Caroline, make no mistake about it. McClellan's army is going to come after Richmond. The northern approach didn't work for Mc-Dowell last summer, so they're going to try moving up the Peninsula this time, between the James and York Rivers. Word has it that more than one hundred thousand soldiers are on their way to Fortress Monroe by ship—the largest army ever assembled on American shores."

My stomach rolled over at the thought of such a huge army. "How many men do we have?"

"Not nearly that many. But Joe Johnston's troops are going to be heading down to the Peninsula pretty soon to help Magruder."

"That means ... Charles and Jonathan?"

"Right. Our troops held their own against the Feds at Manassas last year, and they'll do it again if they have to. You'll be safe here in Richmond, I promise." I would think about his promise many times in the months ahead.

Daddy stayed less than a week. The government moved swiftly to commission him as a privateer. Then, as abruptly as he had arrived, Daddy was gone.

On a mild spring day, the first Sunday in April, the Army of the Potomac passed through Richmond on their way to the Peninsula. We had been expecting them for days and preparing parcels of food for their arrival, but the news first reached us at noon, at the close of our church service.

"Trainloads of General Longstreet's men have been arriving from Fredericksburg all morning," a city official told us as we lingered on the portico outside St. Paul's. "The poor souls have traveled nearly twenty-four hours without food. They're half-starved."

"Where are they now?" Mr. St. John asked. "Do you know if the Richmond Blues are among them? My son, Charles?"

"All I know is that they're marching through town to Rocketts Wharf. They're heading down to the Peninsula from there by steamboat."

The calm of Sunday morning turned into chaos as people rushed around in all directions, searching for their loved ones, desperate to get parcels of food to them. I had come to church in my own buggy that morning, so I left the St. Johns to their own plans and hurried off to find Gilbert.

"Take me to Rocketts Wharf," I told him. "Hurry! If Charles hasn't arrived yet, we can wait for him down at the wharf." I was afraid that I would be too late, that I'd already missed him.

Gilbert drove as if our lives depended on it, maneuvering the little buggy through back lanes and narrow alleys to avoid the worst of the traffic and the columns of men who were tramping through the streets. Bands played and women tossed spring flowers in greeting, and while it was reassuring to see so many thousands of soldiers, I couldn't help remembering that a year had passed since we'd celebrated the first shots at Fort Sumter. The war, which many thought would be over in thirty days, had dragged on for a year with still no end in sight.

The wharf was a sea of milling, gray-clad men. If Charles was among them, I didn't know how I would ever find him. I only knew that I had to try. I climbed down from the buggy without waiting for Gilbert to help me.

"Drive home and fetch the food I packed," I told him. "And bring Tessie back with you so she has a chance to see Josiah."

Gilbert surveyed the vast host of soldiers and shook his head. "Ain't right to leave you here all alone, Missy. All these men . . ."

"I'll be fine. Just hurry, Gilbert."

I started running toward the dock before he could stop me, pushing through the swarming men, scanning their faces, calling Charles' name, asking for his company. Then above the rumble of voices I heard him calling.

"Caroline! Caroline, over here!" I caught a brief glimpse of Josiah and of Jonathan waving to me. Then I spotted Charles plowing a path through the crowd as he hurried toward me. I'm not sure I would have recognized him if he hadn't been calling my name.

His body looked leaner and more muscular than I remembered, his dark hair overgrown and badly in need of a barber. His beard, always so neatly trimmed, was long and scruffy. But his beautiful eyes were the same, his face as handsome as I'd remembered, even with windburned cheeks and a new network of lines etching the corners of his eyes.

We both halted when we were a few feet apart and drank in the sight of each other from head to toe. The gray uniform coat he'd had tailor-made a year ago was wrinkled and worn at the cuffs. A rip in his right sleeve had been crudely patched. His trousers were baggy-kneed, the hems caked with dried mud. The soles of his scuffed boots testified to miles of hard marching.

Charles gazed back at me, his eyes as soft as blue flannel. "You're even more beautiful than your picture," he said. "Your letters keep me going, Caroline. I read them over and over." He slid his knapsack with his blanket roll off his shoulders as he talked and leaned his rifle against it. Water sloshed in his canteen as he lifted the strap over his head to remove it. Then he opened his arms to me.

"Let me hold you, Caroline." The gray wool of his jacket felt rough against my cheek. It smelled of woodsmoke and gunpowder and sweat. "I want to memorize what it feels like to have you in my arms," he murmured, "and the scent of your hair, your skin."

We might have been the only two people on the wharf as Charles held my face in his hands and kissed my forehead, my temples, my neck. I felt the strength in his arms as he held me tightly to himself, the warm pressure of his body against mine. Neither of us wanted to let go. I listened to his heartbeat and the sound of his breathing, remembering the delicate thread of life that held both of us to this earth. I had watched that thread break so many times now—watched helplessly as a heart ceased to beat or a last breath was drawn—and I willed life to fill Charles, to remain in him.

"When I left home," he said, "I didn't think it was possible to love you any more than I already did . . . but I do."

"I love you so much!" I told him, but I don't know if he heard me as the blast of a steam whistle drowned out my words.

"That's my ship," he said.

"Charles, don't go!"

He clutched me tighter still. "Listen now. God willing, I'll be back to hold you again soon." He bent down, and his lips briefly kissed mine. It was all we dared do in such a public place. I sensed his reluctance as he finally released me from his arms.

"Where are they sending you?" I asked as he retrieved his gun and slung his knapsack over his shoulder.

"Yorktown."

My stomach rolled like a wave at his words. *"One hundred thousand enemy soldiers."*

"Don't go . . ." I whispered.

As the call came to begin boarding the ship, Sally and her carriage driver arrived with food. She filled Charles' arms with sacks and parcels, so he wasn't able to hold me or squeeze my hand a final time. I reached out once more to touch his cheek, his hair. "I love you."

"I love you, too, Caroline." He walked backward as far as he could, unwilling to lose sight of me, then ran up the ramp and dropped his packages so he could crowd near the ship's rail and wave.

The soldiers gave the Rebel yell as the boat steamed from the dock, and the sound of it—bold and defiant—shivered through me. I waved until my arms ached and Charles' boat finally disappeared from sight. Then, as I turned away to wipe my tears, I saw Tessie hurrying toward the dock, searching for Josiah. Too late.

Charles remained in besieged Yorktown, sixty miles away, for nearly a month while McClellan's massive army assembled nearby. When the report came that the Federals were moving their heavy guns into place to fire on Yorktown, I spent every spare moment in prayer for Charles' safety.

Such dreadful news filled the newspapers throughout the month of April that Tessie begged me not to read it anymore. "It just making you upset, honey," she insisted. "Where's the good in knowing what's happening in all them places if you can't change anything? I wish I never learn to read about such terrible things."

We read about the battle in Shiloh, Tennessee, and the incomprehensible loss of eleven thousand soldiers. Four days later, Fort Pulaski surrendered, leaving the Savannah harbor undefended. A week later, Fort Macon in Beaufort, North Carolina, was lost. Then, at the end of the month, came the staggering loss of New Orleans and the lower Mississippi River.

"I want this awful war to end, Tessie." *Dear God, when will it end?* I had little time to worry about those faraway places as the enemy pressed closer and closer to Richmond. While McClellan's army prepared to move up the Peninsula, two other Union forces inched closer to Richmond, one moving south along the Rappahannock River, the other approaching in the Shenandoah Valley. During the first week of May, rumors spread throughout the city that our troops had evacuated Yorktown and had moved to defend the entrenchments around Richmond. I didn't learn about the fierce fighting that had taken place in Williamsburg, or the danger Charles had been in, until I received his letter a few days after the battle.

We knew the Federal guns were in place, ready to bombard Yorktown, and that it was useless to stay and defend the city any longer. On the night we evacuated, our batteries rained fire on the enemy throughout the night to cover our retreat. My company was part of the rear guard and among the last to leave. The next day when the Federals discovered that we were gone, they pursued us, catching up with us at Williamsburg and attacking my division.

We battled them from sunrise until sundown—outnumbered and outgunned—but we drove them back. When the enemy finally withdrew, we waited until dark, then marched all night toward Richmond. I have never been so weary in all my life, nor have I ever fought so hard and marched so long without food. You can see by my shaky handwriting that I am still weak with exhaustion. But the thought of what we are fighting for keeps me going—the knowledge of the freedoms we stand to lose . . .

Charles' letters were precious to me, but this time his words made me so angry that I crumpled up his letter and threw it across the bedroom. Then I pulled out a sheet of stationery and composed an angry letter to him in return.

I told him how furious I was with him for risking his life for such a hopeless cause. The South was wrong, the "freedom" he was fighting for—the "freedom" to hold people as slaves—was a moral outrage. Couldn't he see the terrible devastation he was bringing upon our land, the tragic waste of life? I told him to read his Bible, the book of Exodus, and see how Pharaoh had hardened his heart against freeing his slaves until even his own officials begged him to let them go, saying, "Do you not yet realize that Egypt is ruined?" The South was slowly being ruined, and I was so afraid that Charles would die, just as all of Egypt's firstborn sons had died. I didn't want to go on living without Charles.

In the end, I carefully straightened all the wrinkles out of Charles' letter and threw my own letter into the fire instead.

A week after Yorktown, the Confederates evacuated our naval base at Norfolk, withdrawing more of our forces up the Peninsula to defend Richmond. When I read that the Rebels had destroyed their most powerful warship, the ironclad *Virginia*, rather than see her fall into enemy hands, I thought of how devastated my father would be by this news. The *Virginia* couldn't navigate the shallow waters of the James River, nor could it get past the Union blockade into the open sea, so the decision had been made to destroy her.

Now Richmond faced a new threat. I learned of it when Mr. St. John drove up Church Hill late one afternoon to warn me.

"Caroline, you must pack your things and get ready to leave the city," he said. Gilbert had shown him into Daddy's library, but Mr. St. John was too agitated to sit down, too distraught to accept even a glass of brandy or one of Daddy's last few cigars.

"I'm sending Sally and my wife to safety outside Richmond tomorrow," he said. "You must get packed and go with them, Caroline."

"Leave the city . . . why?" I backed into the chair Gilbert had offered Mr. St. John as my knees suddenly went weak. "What's going on?"

"The evacuation of Norfolk means that the mouth of the James

River is now wide open to the enemy's fleet. There is the very real possibility that Federal gunboats are going to sail up the river to bombard Richmond into surrendering. We've planted torpedoes and obstructions in the channel, but our last river defense at Drewry's Bluff is only half-finished. No one knows if her guns can stop the ironclad *Monitor*. And the *Monitor* will likely come with an escort of gunboats. You must evacuate."

I couldn't grasp what he was saying. Thousands of displaced persons had crowded into Richmond from the surrounding countryside, seeking refuge. I had always pitied these homeless souls, alone in a strange city. Was I now to become one of them, looking for shelter in an alien city?

"But . . . where would I go? This is my home . . . I have no place to go."

"President Davis already sent his family south to Raleigh, North Carolina, by train. I managed to purchase three of the very last tickets on a train that's headed there tomorrow morning."

"What about all of our servants?"

He shook his head. He was going to leave them all here to die.

"I can't run away and leave Tessie and Eli."

"They will be fine, Caroline. The Union army won't hurt them. But there's no telling what the Yankees will do to you and the other women if you stay. Besides, if the warships do get through, the state legislature plans to reduce this city to ashes rather than let it fall into enemy hands. Congress has adjourned, and most of its members are fleeing. Don't you see? You must evacuate. Charles would never forgive me if I let anything happen to you."

I felt too numb with fear to argue with him. I agreed to meet Sally and Mrs. St. John at the depot early tomorrow morning. Then I ran upstairs to ask Tessie to help me pack.

"You doing the right thing," she assured me as she calmly filled a trunk with all the belongings I would need. On my own, I wouldn't have known what to bring and what to leave behind. I couldn't think past my panic. "Them St. Johns will take good care you—almost as good as I would," she soothed. "Most important thing, you be safe."

"What about you and Eli and the others? If it isn't safe for me to stay here, how in the world can I leave all of you? They plan to burn the city down—if the Federals don't blast it to smithereens first."

Tessie paused to look up at me, and her beautiful face showed no trace of fear or worry. "We be safe, baby. Don't you know Eli will be praying up a storm? Massa Jesus gonna take care us."

"I just wish there was someplace safe where you could go, too."

She took my hands in hers and gave them a gentle squeeze. "Honey, I wouldn't leave here if you had a hundred train tickets. Someday, after the Yankees win, my boy, Grady, gonna come home looking for me, and I plan on being here when he do."

It was the first time Tessie had mentioned Grady since they'd taken him away nine years ago, the first hint she'd ever given of the hope she'd nurtured all those years. I fell into her arms, grieving for her, with her.

"Oh, Tessie, if there was anything I could do to bring Grady home again, I would gladly do it. When this war is over, I promise I'll move heaven and earth to find him for you."

We held each other for a few more moments. Then, as if sorry she had allowed me to glimpse her hope, Tessie freed herself from my arms and resolutely resumed her packing. "I want you to go see Ruby, now," she said. "Ask her which of your mama's necklaces and things was special to her, so you can take them with you for keepsakes."

I wrote a long letter to Charles by candlelight, then spent a sleepless night waiting for dawn. It was very early when Gilbert loaded my trunk onto the buggy and drove me to the depot, but even at that early hour, traffic jammed the roads. Columns of soldiers marched about while people fled Richmond in droves, scattering in all directions and by every conceivable means of transportation. Wagons and carts and even wheelbarrows were headed south across the James River bridge; flatboats floated west up the Kanawha Canal, all heaped with boxes, trunks, satchels, and all kinds of household goods. In downtown Richmond, businesses were closed and boarded, houses deserted. As we passed Capitol Square, we saw workers removing boxloads of documents from the government buildings. The fear etched on every face seemed contagious, the panic barely contained.

The scene at the depot was one of complete chaos, with people dashing to and fro, shouting and clamoring for tickets that couldn't be purchased at any price. As I watched from the buggy seat, a feeling of great calm suddenly filled me. Why was I running away? I had been praying for God's help and strength every day since the war began—why would He desert me now? Couldn't He protect me here, as He would protect Eli and the others, just as easily as someplace else?

When Gilbert started to climb down from the buggy, I stopped him. "Leave my trunk, for now," I told him. "Wait here. I'll be right back."

The train was already at the station, taking on coal, working up steam. Passengers hovered close, waiting for the signal to board, even though the train wasn't scheduled to leave for another ten minutes. I found Sally and her parents on the platform, watching anxiously for me.

"Caroline, finally," Sally said, exhaling. "We were so afraid your carriage would get stuck in that awful traffic and you'd miss the train."

"Where's your trunk?" Mr. St. John asked. "Did your boy check your baggage already?"

"Please don't be angry with me," I said, "but I'm not going with you."

"Now, see here," Mr. St. John said, "I feel responsible for you, seeing as your father is away. I really must insist that you go. This may be your only chance to reach safety."

I shook my head. "I'm not afraid to stay here. This is my home. I would be much more afraid to be a refugee without a home, far away from my loved ones."

All around us, the volume of agitated voices suddenly swelled to a roar as the bell on the locomotive began to ring. The conductor pushed through the crowd, calling ticketed passengers to board. As people began mobbing the train cars, Sally and her mother looked desperately from the train, to me, to the train again.

"Come with us, Caroline. Please," Sally begged.

"I can't," I told her, shaking my head. "Good-bye...." I turned and hurried away, knowing how eager the women were to leave Richmond, knowing that Mr. St. John was too lame to run after me.

Gilbert was pacing nervously beside the buggy when I returned. "You wanting this trunk now, Missy? Seems like that train's about to leave."

"It is, but I won't be on it. I'm staying here."

"Oh, Missy Caroline . . . I don't think—"

"Take me home, Gilbert." I mustered my bravest smile and added, "That's an order."

Even though I knew I had made the right decision, the suspense of waiting for the Union gunboats to arrive, waiting for the shelling to begin, was terrible. I kept my own trunk packed and made all the servants pack their things, too, so that if the city did burn to the ground we would all have a few essentials. Then we gathered in the parlor to wait.

"You thinking we might go out to Hilltop if things get bad?" Tessie asked.

"No, Hilltop won't be any safer than Richmond—in fact, it might be worse. Enemy troops are heading right up the Peninsula in that direction. And that's where all our men are dug in, waiting for them."

I played the piano for everyone while we waited. Tessie and I took turns reading the Bible aloud. We knitted. Luella and Ruby did some mending. Eli prayed.

Not long after we had all eaten a little lunch, we heard the unmistakable sound of cannon booming in the distance. Unlike the night of the *Pawnee* scare, the cannonfire didn't stop this time. Instead, the volley of explosions built and intensified, rattling the windowpanes and echoing off Richmond's many hills. Drewry's Bluff, the last fortress guarding the city, was a scant seven miles south of where we sat on Church Hill.

The battle raged for more than three and a half hours. I felt each blast in the pit of my stomach. But while we could tell from the thunderous sound that the fighting was very fierce, the shelling didn't seem to be drawing any closer to the city. We continued to pray.

As evening fell, the sound of artillery fire slowed, then finally stopped. We all looked at each other. The silence was as heavy as the cannonading had been.

Esther stood. "Enough of this nonsense. Kitchen fire's gonna go out if I don't tend to it."

As she strode away, chin held high, Eli began to laugh. "Seems like fear is a more powerful enemy than the Yankees."

We learned the next day that the Union fleet had not been able to get past the eight Confederate guns at Drewry's Bluff. For now, Richmond was safe. But more important, my own faith had won a victory over my fear.

Throughout the month of May, General McClellan's massive army made its ponderous way up the Peninsula through torrential rain and oozing mud. We all knew that the two armies were about to clash, and city officials were determined to be better prepared to handle the thousands of casualties this time. Our latest sewing project was to stitch yards and yards of ticking material into mattress covers for the three-thousand-bed Chimborazo Hospital, on the hill just east of my home. That's what Tessie, Ruby, and I were doing one afternoon when we heard a carriage arrive at our door.

"Sounds like we got company," Tessie said. She started to rise, but I quickly stood instead.

"No, let me go."

I lived in dread of the day that a messenger would arrive with news of my father, or of Charles or Jonathan, but delaying the news would never change it. I laid down my sewing and hurried to the door behind Gilbert. It wasn't a carriage that was drawing to a stop out front, but a battered farm wagon, its wheels caked with mud. It took me a moment to recognize the tired, bedraggled-looking people climbing down from it. They were my grandmother, my aunt Anne, and my young cousin Thomas from Hilltop.

Their driver and the two Negro maidservants accompanying them were coated with mud clear to their waists from pushing the mired wagon out of ruts. I opened the front door wide and welcomed my family inside as Gilbert led the horses, the wagon, and the dripping servants around to the back door.

"Where's George?" my grandmother demanded to know before I could utter a word of greeting.

"He . . . he's not home, Grandmother. My father's ships sailed last March, and we—"

"Where's George?" she repeated. "Did any of these useless servants tell George I'm here?"

"George isn't home, Mother Fletcher," Aunt Anne shouted. I remembered then that my grandmother had been nearly deaf when I'd met her eight years ago. Judging by the way she peered all around with her eyes squinted and her head thrust forward, her eyesight was probably failing, too.

"What? This isn't George's home?" Grandmother said. "Where are we, Anne? You said we were going to George's home."

"This is George's home, but George isn't home," Aunt Anne shouted.

"Stop repeating everything! Is this George's home or isn't it?"

"Yes," Aunt Anne and I both shouted together.

"Then why doesn't somebody tell George I'm here?"

Aunt Anne looked at me helplessly.

"George is at work," I shouted in a moment of inspiration.

"Of course . . . at work." Grandmother reached for my arm and let me help her to a chair in the parlor. She was alarmingly thin and frail, her skin as fragile as tissue paper. "Make me a pot of tea, Ellie," she told Ruby, who was watching all of this, wide-eyed.

"Yes, ma'am," Ruby replied and scurried out to the kitchen. But where she was going to get tea was a mystery to me. We'd had nothing but steeped blackberry leaves to drink for months.

"You're looking very well, Mary," Grandmother said. It took me a startled moment to realize that she was talking to me—and that she had mistaken me for my mother.

"Um . . . Mary was my mother. I'm her daughter, Caroline."

"Where is Caroline? At school, I suppose?"

"No, *I'm* Caroline," I shouted.

"I haven't seen that child in ages," Grandmother said as she leaned back in her chair. "You'd think George would bring his only child out to Hilltop once in a while to see me, wouldn't you? Where is George?"

I looked to Aunt Anne for help, but she simply shrugged and said in a hushed voice, "Caroline, please forgive us, dear, for arriving unannounced, but we had no one to send ahead of us. The Negroes would have all bolted over to the enemy, thinking they'd be free, if we had let them out of our sight."

"I don't mind at all. And I'm sorry for not welcoming you properly. Please, would you like something to eat, or maybe a place to rest or freshen up?"

"I'm not hungry, but perhaps Mother Fletcher would . . ." We both turned to ask Grandmother, but her eyes were closed and her head had lolled to the side, resting against the wings of the chair. She was snoring.

Aunt Anne and Cousin Thomas ate the light lunch Esther had quickly prepared, while Tessie and Luella readied the upstairs bedrooms for our guests. Gilbert hauled their luggage up to their rooms.

We decided that Grandmother and her maid would sleep in Daddy's library, since climbing the stairs was difficult for her.

"Hilltop is on the far side of the Chickahominy," Aunt Anne explained as she ate, "and since the Confederate lines are on this side of the river, William thought it wise to send us to safety. The Federals are advancing, and the plantation will soon be in enemy hands."

"They're that close?" I asked, my stomach doing a slow, queasy turn.

"Yes, I'm afraid so."

"I wanted to stay home and shoot Yankees," young Thomas said, "but Father wouldn't let me." They were the first words he had spoken since he'd arrived. I calculated his age to be fourteen, nearly the age Jonathan had been the first time we'd met. But Thomas had none of his older brother's curiosity and wiry vitality. Instead, Thomas was plump and lethargic and seemed content to sit and stare out the window all day. If he had stayed at Hilltop to shoot Yankees, I don't know how he would have summoned the energy to reload the shotgun.

"William insisted on staying at the plantation," Anne continued. "Heaven only knows what the Yankees will do with him. He's the only one left, except for the slaves, but he didn't want to abandon our home."

"You are all very welcome here, Aunt Anne. Stay as long as you'd like."

"We don't want to be a burden to you. Your servants will find some produce in the wagon and the last of our hams. We'd rather you got them than the Yankees."

"You have no idea what a blessing it will be to have real food again. Eli dug up his flower garden and planted vegetables this spring, but all we've harvested so far are some greens. Your food is a godsend."

She smiled ruefully. "You may change your mind about what a godsend we are after you've lived with Mother Fletcher for a few days. But you know, out of all of us, I feel the most sorry for her. The war has changed everyone's life—probably forever—but we're still young enough to adjust, to start all over again if we have to. I pray to God that the war doesn't take my husband or my sons, but at least the decision to engage in this folly was theirs to make. Mother Fletcher didn't choose any of this. And now the quiet life she always had with her family, living on her own land, is gone—and no one can help her understand why."

A few days later, early in the afternoon, a great rumble, like the roll of thunder, suddenly shook the house. Deaf as she was, Grandmother awoke from her catnap and said, "You'd better tell the servants to close the windows, Anne. It's thundering."

The skies were gray and overcast, but there weren't any thunderclouds. Aunt Anne and I looked at each other as the rumbling booms grew louder. "It's artillery," I told her.

"Is it the war?" Thomas asked, looking up from the house of cards he was constructing. His mother nodded. "Tarnation! I want to fight, too, Ma, like Will and Jonathan. I'll bet it's grand."

I knew better. The only thing *grand* was the scale of the slaughter. Every boom of the cannon meant men's bodies were being blasted into pieces in a hail of canister shot and shrapnel.

We walked outside into the still, humid afternoon and listened. The fighting was the closest I'd ever heard it, just east of us. We felt the ground quaking. In the quiet moments between cannon blasts, we could hear the hollow clatter of gunfire, like bones rattling.

The horrific thundering finally stopped that evening, then resumed the next morning. By the time the battle ended the following afternoon, a long line of ambulances and farm wagons was already rolling into the city carrying the wounded and the dying.

"I'm going to Chimborazo Hospital to help," I told Aunt Anne after lunch. She stared at me in surprise.

"You always did have a tender heart, Caroline. I remember how you nursed those little colored babies through the measles. But frankly, it surprises me that you're able to go to such a dreadful place and see . . . that sort of thing."

I forced myself to say what I had been thinking since the artillery fire began. "Charles and Jonathan are fighting out there somewhere. These soldiers might be from their company. If I don't go and help them, who will?"

"I'd like to join you," she said simply.

Chimborazo resembled a scene from Dante's *Inferno*. I lost what little lunch I had eaten after I glimpsed a dying soldier whose entire lower jaw had been blown away. But from the men who were less seriously wounded, whose faces I cooled with water and whose thirst I helped ease, I learned that yesterday's battle had been fought at Seven Pines, a few miles east of the city. Charles, along with the First Virginia Infantry, had taken part in a Confederate assault that attempted to push back the Union forces. The engagement had been successful the first day, then ended in a bloody draw the second. Among the wounded was the Rebel commander General Joe Johnston.

Before returning home, Aunt Anne and I drove downtown together, holding our breath and each other's hands as we scanned a list of the four thousand men who had been killed, wounded, or taken prisoner. We sagged against each other in relief when we saw that Jonathan and Charles were not on it.

"You've changed, Caroline," Aunt Anne said as we drove back up Church Hill afterward. "You've become a very strong young woman."

I shook my head, my tears of relief still falling onto my lap. "No. I'm not strong at all. The fact that this war is so close terrifies me. Reading those lists and waiting to hear news of my loved ones is an agonizing ordeal. I'm not strong at all, Aunt Anne . . . but I'm learning to lean on a God who is."

16

JUNE 1862

All of Richmond was a hospital again. I spent every spare moment during the next week caring for wounded soldiers at Chimborazo Hospital. Then one quiet afternoon after the crisis eased and the hospital no longer needed me, a messenger came to our door. The man was gone again before I could hurry out to the foyer, but Gilbert handed me the note he had brought, scribbled on a folded scrap of greasy brown paper.

> *Dear Caroline,*
> *I know that we are supposed to be at war with each other, but I cannot believe you would consider me your enemy. In Philadelphia, we were once dear friends, and I appeal to you now on the basis of that friendship.*
> *I am being held here in Richmond as a prisoner of war. My fellow prisoners and I are suffering under dreadful conditions. Many of us are ill and near starvation. I remember your kindness and your Christian charity, and I ask for any shreds of mercy that you can*

spare my comrades and me. I am confined in a warehouse known as Libby Prison, in the east building.

Sincerely,
Lieutenant Robert Hoffman
United States Army

Eli and I went down to Libby Prison together. We parked the buggy on a side street and walked across the vacant lot beside the building beneath a broiling sun. The brick tobacco warehouse, which overlooked the canal, consisted of three conjoined buildings, four stories high, filling half a city block on the corner of Cary and Dock Streets. A faded sign, "L. Libby & Son, Ship Chandlers," which had been hung by former owner Luther Libby, gave the prison its name. Behind the barred windows on the upper floors, I glimpsed shadowy figures, passing like ghosts. The sentries standing guard outside made Eli raise his arms as they searched him, then they searched the basket of food he carried. They directed us to Major Turner's office on the ground floor.

The first thing I noticed was the smell. I had thought the hospital odorous, but Libby Prison's hot, stifling air reeked—worse than any charnel house—of filth and death and human waste. I had to pull out my handkerchief and hold it over my nose and mouth to keep from gagging.

Major Turner scrambled to his feet when we entered his office. "Miss, you have obviously come to the wrong place. Let me escort you—"

"No, thank you, sir," I said firmly. "I have come to Libby Prison to see one of your inmates."

"Out of the question."

I felt an immediate dislike for Major Turner. He hadn't even taken the time to consider my request. Not much taller than me, Turner had a boyish face and a permanent frown—adopted, I guessed, to make himself appear more manly. My first impression was that he was a bully, and I determined to stand up to him—backed by Eli, of course, who towered over the man.

"My name is Caroline Fletcher," I said. "My father is George Fletcher, owner of several warehouses in this district and recently commissioned by President Davis as a Captain in the Confederate Navy. My fiancé is Charles St. John, serving with the First Virginia Infantry. Surely you've heard of the St. John family, Major Turner? Proprietors of the city's largest flour mill and one of Richmond's most prominent families?"

"What is your business here, Miss Fletcher?" His voice was high-pitched, boyish.

"I've learned that a relative of mine is imprisoned here. I've come to see him on a mission of charity."

"Leave your package. I'll see that he gets it."

"I don't intend to leave until I've spoken with him, sir."

Turner's frown deepened. "This prison is not a suitable venue for social calls. We do not have the proper facilities for visitors to—"

"Then I'll wait until a suitable room is prepared," I said, seating myself on the chair in front of Major Turner's desk. "I would hate to bother President Davis at such a busy time as this, just for a request to meet with my cousin. But I will do it, sir, if you force me to." I saw Turner's resolve weakening and added, "My cousin's name is Lieutenant Robert Hoffman. I believe you'll find him in the east building."

The guards readied a small storeroom on the ground floor and escorted Robert inside. The windowless room quickly filled with his stench. I would have run forward to embrace him but he held out both hands, stopping me with a cry of horror.

"No, Caroline! No! I'm crawling with vermin!"

The skin on his hands and neck was scaly and raw from ringworm and scabbed insect bites. As I stepped closer I could see lice moving through his black hair. Robert was pale and thin; dark circles rimmed his mournful eyes. His infested hair was long and matted and dirty, his face unshaved. But he smiled and briefly gripped my fingers in a quick, reassuring squeeze.

"I'm sorry. I didn't mean to startle you. But heaven knows how I would defile you if we embraced."

"Robert . . . I . . . I don't know what to say. . . ." I could barely speak, barely see him through my tears. He was so horribly changed, a figure from a nightmare. Yet his voice, his sweet nature, were the same.

"You don't need to say a word, Caroline. Just your beautiful presence . . . the fact that you came . . . they will sustain me for a year."

The major had provided us with two wooden benches. Robert and I sat down, and I gave him the basket of food I had brought. It was meager fare by pre-war standards—a square of Esther's corn bread, some cold boiled potatoes, a piece of leftover fish, a slice from one of Aunt Anne's hams that we had been stingily doling out—but the sight of it, the aroma of it, caused Robert to break down and weep.

"I'm sorry . . . I'm sorry," he repeated as he vainly tried to wipe his tears. "I don't know what's come over me . . . forgive me. . . ."

I longed to hold him, to comfort him, but I didn't dare. I silently cursed the war, the stupidity and hatred that had reduced gentle Robert to such a state. "It's okay," I murmured. "There's nothing to forgive."

The food trembled in Robert's hands as he slowly began to eat. He lifted each bite to his nose first, closing his eyes and inhaling, before tasting each morsel. I knew by his appearance that he must be half-starved, but he took his time eating, allowing his shrunken stomach to adjust to food again.

"How long have you been here?" I asked.

"Since early last November. I was part of a Federal expedition that crossed the Potomac at Ball's Bluff, above Leesburg, Virginia. We were ordered to probe the Rebels' defenses, but they proved stronger than we expected. The Rebs drove us back to the river, then mowed us down as we tried to get into our boats and escape." He paused, struggling with his emotions. "I . . . I surrendered my unit rather than watch everyone die. Even so . . . I lost too many men."

He looked down, concentrating on his food as if to distract himself. Robert had been raised in a wealthy home with the finest of table manners, but I watched him eat fish with filthy hands, then lick every precious drop of oil and juice off his fingers.

"The Rebels marched us through their lines to the rear," he said when he could continue. "I was angry, humiliated. The war had barely begun and I was already a prisoner. They marched us double-quick, but I observed all their defenses, their reserves and artillery and gun emplacements. When the guards looked away, I hid my money, my watch, and any other valuables I owned in my clothing. I was glad I did. They found some of my money when they searched me, but not all of it. One of the Rebel guards took my haversack with all my rations, then tried to pump me for information in exchange for food and other favors. Another stole my boots and gave me his worn-out shoes to wear in their place.

"As we traveled south, more prisoners from other captured units joined us. I remember marching through one small town along a river and all the young boys came out to pelt us with stones and manure as we passed. The women jeered and spit at us. When we finally arrived in Richmond, they separated the other officers and me from the enlisted men and brought us here. I don't know what they did with my men . . . I hope they're being treated better than we are."

"They're being held on an island in the middle of the James River," I said. "It's called Belle Isle. You can probably see it from the windows that overlook the canal." I didn't tell him that he and the other officers were fortunate to be housed inside a building, that the only shelter the enlisted men had against the winter's cold and the summer's heat was a tent.

"I've watched men die in this place," Robert said. "I've seen others lose their minds. It can easily happen in this hellhole where men who are ill and delirious scream all night until we wish them dead.

We have no doctors, no medicine. All of us suffer from dysentery. At times I've been so sick with the fever and shakes that I believed I might die. I've often wished that I would."

Robert had saved the corn bread for last, as if savoring it for dessert. He held it close to his chin, careful not to drop any crumbs, but when one accidentally fell to the floor he quickly snatched it up and ate it. I remembered watching the little Negro children at Hilltop do the same thing, eating off the dirt floor.

"You can't imagine how slowly time passes here, Caroline. Every day is the same. We fight to spend a few moments at the window, just to watch the boats on the canal out front, and the traffic crossing the bridges, and the trees and fields and rolling green hills across the river. We're not allowed to look out of the windows on the other side. The sentries shoot at us if we do."

"It's just as well," I told him. "The view is only of rooftops, chimneys, warehouses, vacant lots—nothing worth getting shot at to see."

"For entertainment, we sometimes capture lice off our heads and hold races with them. The winner gets the lump of salt pork in the soup if there happens to be one. This place is filthy beyond imagining. The Negroes sweep the floor and slosh water across it twice a week, but that's all the cleaning that's done. We have water but no soap. At night, I sleep jammed into a room with one hundred other men, back to back on the bare floor, like herring in a box. Our daily rations are corncob bread and bean soup flavored with rancid salt pork and garnished with white worms. On special occasions we get tough, boiled beef. At first we all pooled our money and bribed the guards into buying us extra rations, but our money has finally run out. We were hoping for a prisoner exchange, but with the fighting so close by, there's not much hope of an exchange now. In fact . . . there's not much hope at all in this godforsaken place. That's why I wrote to you. I'm sorry . . . but it was either that . . . or go mad."

Robert's eyes met mine and I saw his utter despair. I remembered how eager he'd been to study at West Point, how he'd longed to

distinguish himself in battle, and I could well imagine the staggering cost to his pride to have the woman he'd once loved see him in
such a state. I tried to spare him the remnants of his dignity by not
allowing my pity to show.

"I'm glad you wrote," I told him. "It's good to see you again."

"I gave the guard my pocket watch to deliver the note to you. It
was the only thing of value I had left. I was afraid you might have
fled to safety when the war started, and I hoped for your sake that
you had. I'm glad for my sake that you didn't."

"Richmond is my home. I couldn't leave here."

"Julia wrote and told me you were engaged." The pain I saw in
Robert's eyes was so intense I could barely keep from looking away.

"Yes. Have . . . um . . . have you met anyone, Robert?"

He didn't seem to hear my question. "Is your fiancé fighting for
the Rebels?"

"Yes. . . . yes, he is. Charles believes that he is fighting for the
South's freedom."

"Are you a Rebel, too?"

"No. I . . . I'm not for either side."

One of the guards suddenly pounded on the door, startling me.
"Your time's up, Miss Fletcher." I rose to my feet as the key rattled
in the lock and the door swung open.

"I'll be back in a few days, Robert. I promise. I'll bring you another parcel."

He didn't stand, as if hoping to stretch out our visit for as long
as he possibly could. His eyes hadn't left mine. "Your fiancé and the
others are deceiving themselves, you know. The Rebels aren't fighting
for freedom, they're fighting for the right to keep slaves."

"Let's go," the guard shouted. "On your feet."

At last Robert slowly stood. He handed me the empty basket. "I
know that you believe slavery is wrong, Caroline. But maybe what
you don't realize is that if the South wins . . . if your fiancé wins . . .
then slavery wins, too."

I returned to Libby Prison to visit Robert a few days later, bringing him some newspapers and a few books to read—*Les Misérables* by Victor Hugo and my collection of works by Sir Walter Scott. I also brought him my father's chessboard, a bar of soap, and Mother's fine-toothed ivory comb to help get the nits out of his hair. Major Turner gave up trying to dissuade me after my third or fourth visit and routinely sent for Robert, locking us in the storeroom for our allotted half-hour. Within a few weeks, Robert looked stronger, saner, and a good deal cleaner than he had on our first visit.

One day he set the food aside instead of eating it right away and leaned forward to grasp my hands. "We need to talk, Caroline. I have a favor to ask of you." He kept his voice low, as if not wanting the guard to overhear him. "Some of my fellow inmates are newly imprisoned, captured after the latest fighting at Seven Pines. They've told me what's going on out there—and now I'm going to tell you. General McClellan thinks he's facing vast numbers of Confederate troops. He's moving too cautiously, waiting for another forty thousand reinforcements to arrive before he attacks. But the men who have passed through enemy lines on the way here know the truth about the Confederate forces. They know how badly outnumbered you are. If we had a way to get that information back to the Union lines, McClellan might stop hesitating and attack." He paused, gripping my hands tighter still. "Caroline . . . we need you to deliver this information to them."

I yanked my hands from his grip. "*Me?* Are you out of your mind?"

"Shh . . . shh . . . Listen, if you carried the reports to McClellan, you could help end this war. If the North wins a decisive victory, if we capture Richmond, the war would end tomorrow. President Lincoln's only goal is to restore the Union."

I wanted to run from the room, run from the ugliness of what he was suggesting, but I was too stunned to move. "You can't possibly ask me to betray the Confederate Army. Charles is out there in one of those trenches defending Richmond. It would mean betraying the man I love . . . betraying my cousins . . . my own father. . . ."

"If the war ends quickly, there would be less chance of any of them dying."

"No, Robert. I can't help you. I won't."

"I know how you feel about slavery, Caroline. If you don't help me, then you're betraying your own convictions. You're helping to keep hundreds of thousands of people in slavery."

I stood, ready to flee, but my legs trembled so badly I couldn't take a single step. "I came to help you as an act of charity," I said. "I never expected you, of all people, to take advantage of my kindness by asking me to do such a terrible thing."

"Terrible? Wouldn't it be a greater crime to compromise your beliefs? To betray your God?" He paused. "Here, take this, Caroline." He shoved a small, pocket-sized Bible into my hands.

"Why? What is this?"

"Look at it carefully. On all of the blank pages and between the lines, my fellow officers and I have written everything we saw and remember of the Confederate forces defending Richmond. We've signed our names and ranks to these intelligence reports."

"I won't take it," I said, throwing it down on the bench.

Robert calmly removed all of the food from the basket I'd brought, then put the Bible inside in its place. "Take it home and burn it, then. You're condemning all of us to death if it's found in here." He pushed the basket into my hands. We stared at each other for a long moment. When he spoke again, his voice was gentle. "I'm told that if you travel beyond the Confederate lines for a mile or two, our Union pickets will likely intercept you. Give them the book and ask them to take it to the proper authorities. That's all I'm asking."

"That's *all*? How dare you ask me to do this?"

"I dare because I know what you believe. I know you're convinced that slavery is wrong. 'Have nothing to do with the fruitless deeds

266

of darkness, but rather expose them.' And I know that you were once committed to doing whatever you could to abolish this evil institution."

I left the prison so upset that Eli immediately asked me what was wrong. I waited until we reached home, then told him in the privacy of our carriage house. "Robert asked me to help the Yankees. There's information written in this Bible that he says could help the North win the war. He wants me to deliver it to them."

"Guess you're not wanting to do that?"

"I can't. I would be helping Charles' enemies, betraying him. This information might endanger his life."

Eli's warm brown eyes met mine. "If your mind's made up not to do it . . . then why you still upset?"

I looked away, remembering Robert's words. "Because if I don't do it, I'm helping the South win . . . which means I'm helping all of you remain slaves. Don't you see? Either way, I'm a traitor."

Eli exhaled. "You in a hard place, Missy."

"Could Charles and Daddy be wrong, Eli? Is God on the Yankees' side? And if so, what about all the people in my church who are earnestly praying to God, asking Him to help the South win? How can I expect my own prayers to keep Charles and Daddy and Jonathan safe?"

Eli pulled up a wooden stool and motioned for me to sit down on it. But he remained standing, pacing a bit as he took his time replying.

"There's a story in the Bible about when Joshua getting ready to fight the battle of Jericho. He cross over the Jordan River, all alone, and he meet the angel of the Lord, carrying a sword. Joshua ask, 'Whose side you on, ours or the enemy's?' Angel said, 'Neither one. I'm on God's side.'

"God's gonna have His way in this war, Missy, just like He have His way at Jericho. He ain't on neither side, North or South. But there are things He needs to get done and battles He wants to win in folks' hearts—up north and down here. People on both sides better not be praying for their wills to be done, because God don't answer them kind of prayers. They better pray that *His* will be done."

Eli paused as he stopped beside my stool, then he crouched in front of me so we were eye to eye. "When the angel of the Lord tell Joshua he's on God's side, Joshua do the right thing. He fall on his face and say, 'What does God want his servant to do?' Joshua decide to serve in God's army and fight God's battles instead of trying to get God to fight his battles."

"Neither the Yankees nor the Rebels are my enemies," I said. "I don't believe in either of their causes. Could this . . . could this be the time you warned me would come? Do you think God has prepared me 'for such a time as this'?"

"That depends. You making up your mind to be His servant?"

"I don't know . . . I don't think I can betray Charles. But if I don't help Robert, then I'm betraying you and Tessie. How do I decide?"

"The decision isn't who you gonna help and who you gonna betray. The decision is whether or not you gonna listen for God's voice and do what God telling you to do. Might be something as silly as marching around Jericho in circles. Or it might be as hard and as dangerous as helping the enemy, like Rahab did."

"How do I know what God is saying? How do I know what He wants me to do?"

"God doesn't change His mind. What has He already told you about the North and the South, about right and wrong? What do you feel in here, deep in your heart? What is the real battle God wants to fight?"

"Slavery. God hates slavery." I didn't even have to think about it. "He loves you the same as He loves me. He doesn't see the color of our skin. It's wrong for anyone to own another man."

"Did He speak that to you from His Holy Word?"

"Yes," I said in amazement. "Yes, He did. He said we should do away with the yoke of oppression and spend ourselves on behalf of the hungry and oppressed."

"Then the only thing left to decide is whether you gonna be His servant and say 'Here I am,' and go do the job He give you to do—or not."

I now knew what that job was. Robert had spoken the truth when he'd said that if the South won—if Charles won—then slavery would win, too.

"But what about Charles and Jonathan and Daddy?" I wasn't sure if I was asking Eli or God.

"It's a hard thing, Missy, but Jesus say sometimes a man's enemies are in his own household. He say anyone who loves his family more than Him ain't fit for the kingdom."

"But Eli, I'm scared. I can't just walk over to the Union lines and hand them this book, can I? I won't even be able to get a travel permit out of Richmond unless I have a good reason for going. Besides, a man got caught spying for the North right here in Richmond a few months ago, and they hanged him."

Eli didn't reply at first. As I watched him pull himself to his feet and pace a few more steps, I recalled the verse Tessie had read—how Jesus was obedient even unto death. Queen Esther had said, "If I perish, I perish." My father and Charles were willing to die for the cause they believed in. Was I?

"This ain't something you can do on you own strength," Eli finally said. "Any more than Joshua can make those walls of Jericho fall down all by his self. You either do this with God's help or not at all. But once you make up you mind to trust Him, He gonna provide a way to get the job done. You'll see."

I lay awake praying for a long time that night—just as I had on so many other nights since the war began. An even greater fear than losing my own life was my fear of losing Charles. My actions could very well cause his death. Worse, if he found out I'd helped his enemies, he would surely hate me.

The hall clock struck midnight before I finally found the courage to tell God I would do His will, regardless of the cost. Then I lay awake for two more hours, trying in vain to think of a plausible excuse to apply for a travel permit. I fell asleep before I could concoct a plan. But when my grandmother's servant frantically shook me awake early the next morning, I knew that God had provided a way.

"Missy Caroline . . . Missy Caroline, please wake up," she begged. "You got to come help me with your grandmother."

I struggled to wake up after a too-short night, feeling groggy and disoriented. "Why? What's wrong?"

"Lord have mercy, Missy Caroline . . . I think your grandmother is dead."

Aunt Anne went to the provost marshal's office with me to apply for a permit to travel to Hilltop. She pleaded our case more convincingly than I ever could have. "My husband would never forgive me," she said, "if I buried his mother in any other plot of ground except the family graveyard at Hilltop, beside her husband."

"Don't you know that your plantation is likely behind enemy lines by now?" the marshal asked.

"Yes, I know."

"The Yankees may not allow you to come back to Richmond once you cross over."

"I don't care. It was mostly for my mother-in-law's sake that we came to Richmond in the first place. My husband didn't want her to see what the Yankees would do to Hilltop."

In the end, the Provost Marshal reluctantly granted us permission, adding my name and Eli's to the permit, and giving it to Aunt Anne to sign. When I read the document on the ride home, I nearly fainted with relief and gratitude that the marshal hadn't asked me to sign my name to it: *Permission is hereby granted to Mrs. William Fletcher, Miss Caroline Fletcher, and their slave, Eli Fletcher, to visit Hilltop Plantation upon their honor not to communicate, in writing or verbally, any fact ascertained which, if known to the enemy, might be injurious to the Confederate States of America.*

I sent Eli out to purchase a plain pine coffin. The other servants washed and dressed Grandmother and combed her feathery white hair. Eli tenderly lifted her tiny body into the casket.

"God forgive me," I murmured as I placed Robert's Bible beneath her folded hands.

Young Thomas threw a temper fit when he learned he had to stay behind in Richmond, so while Aunt Anne soothed him, I gathered my servants out in the kitchen and asked them to pray for Eli and me. Then, when the coffin was finally loaded onto Aunt Aunt's farm wagon, we headed out the Mechanicsville Turnpike toward Hilltop.

The three-hour journey to the plantation took more than four hours as Confederate troops stopped us repeatedly along the way, searching the wagon, the coffin, and all of our clothes and belongings. But no one thought to search the Bible I'd placed beneath Grandmother's stiff, folded hands. When we finally reached the last Confederate picket line, the officer in charge begged us not to go any further.

"The Yankees are not gentlemen, Miss Fletcher, they're animals. I'd hate to tell you what they might do to a pretty young lady like you."

"I appreciate your concern. But Eli won't let us come to any harm."

The officer pulled me aside, whispering, "I don't want to disillusion you, but that boy is going to bolt for freedom as soon as you cross over to the other side. All the Negroes do. They think the Yankees will set them free."

"Not Eli. He won't leave us."

The man gravely shook his head as he helped me climb back into the wagon. He obviously believed he was sending us to our deaths. "I wish you all the luck in the world, ladies. You're going to need it."

Eli snapped the reins and we headed down the road into no-man's-land. When we'd traveled about a mile, Aunt Anne said, "This is our land. We're on Hilltop's property now."

I thought I recognized the road to Hilltop from when I'd visited years ago, but the driveway, now deeply rutted from heavy use, was no longer shaded by an arch of pine trees; it was bordered by a row of stumps. The sultry afternoon seemed much too quiet and still. No slaves labored in the barren fields, no animals grazed its pastures. The split-rail fences that had once bordered Hilltop's land were gone, torn down to reinforce the Confederate trench-works. I had seen obstacles made from sharpened stakes protecting those trenches from enemy assaults, but I'd had no idea that Hilltop's beautiful forest land had been denuded to provide those stakes. I shivered in the eerie silence. I had the feeling we were being watched.

Just as Hilltop's barn came into sight, a dozen blue-uniformed soldiers sprang out of the bushes on both sides of road. Their guns were aimed at us.

"This plantation is my home," Aunt Anne explained. "I've returned to bury my husband's mother in the family graveyard."

The process of being searched seemed much scarier this time, since our Confederate travel permit was now worthless. Afterward, the soldiers confiscated the wagon and drove it up to the house, ordering us to walk in its dusty wake. On the way, we saw row upon row of white tents in the distance, covering Hilltop's wheat fields as far as we could see. Slave Row looked deserted. The once-bustling yard behind the plantation house was deserted, too. Even the flock of poultry had disappeared.

The Yankees had billeted their officers in the plantation house and wouldn't allow us inside. A Colonel Drake eventually appeared at the back door to speak with us. He sent one of his men for Uncle William, who emerged under close guard from what had once been the weaving shed. My uncle received the news about his mother's death as if enduring one more blow to an already bruised body. Aunt Anne clung to him, holding him up as Eli pried open the casket for a final glimpse.

"I'll dig the grave for you, Massa Fletcher," Eli said, "if you show me where."

"Yes ... thank you ... of course," he mumbled. "May I ... ?" he asked, turning to the colonel.

Drake nodded. "Fetch them a shovel from the tool shed," he told one of his men.

I stayed behind with the colonel as Aunt Anne and Uncle William trudged into the denuded woods, leading Eli to the graveyard. As soon as they were out of sight, I lifted the coffin lid, which Eli had left loose, and retrieved Robert's Bible. The task God had given me seemed almost too easy. Still, as I handed the Bible to the colonel, I couldn't escape the feeling that I was handing over Charles' life.

"This is for you," I said, placing the book in his hands. "My aunt doesn't know about it, but it's my real reason for coming. It's from one of your captured officers, Lieutenant Robert Hoffman."

"Who? Where did you get this?"

"I've been to see Robert in Libby Prison in Richmond. He and his fellow inmates filled these pages with their observations of the Confederate defenses as they passed through the lines. Please make sure that it gets to the proper Union authorities."

He opened the Bible and read one of the handwritten pages, then looked up again, to stare at me. I could tell by his expression that he thought me a traitor. I certainly felt like one. I sank down onto the back step, my energy suddenly spent.

"Why are you doing this?" he asked.

It took me a moment to recall the reason. "Because ... because I believe that slavery is wrong."

"But you're a slave owner."

"My father is. I'm not." When I thought of all the things the servants did for me each day, all the things I didn't know how to do for myself, like plucking a chicken or kindling a fire, the distinction seemed absurd. I quickly changed the subject. "If you could please arrange it, Colonel Drake, I would like to return to Richmond before dark."

Drake quickly sent three of Hilltop's remaining slaves into the woods to help Eli dig. They nailed Grandmother's casket shut and lowered it into the grave. Aunt Anne wept quietly as Uncle William read from the Scriptures in a weary voice.

"I want to stay here with you, William," Aunt Anne said when the funeral ended.

My uncle shook his head. "The fighting is going to start soon. And you still have Thomas to think about." They were offered no privacy as they said good-bye.

Colonel Drake and three of his men escorted us as far as no-man's-land, then turned back without another word. We were soon approaching the Confederate lines once more. The Rebel soldiers held us for more than an hour, asking us to recall everything we had observed of the Union forces and where they were deployed. When we finally reached home late that night, I felt numb.

"If I did the right thing, why do I feel like such a traitor?" I asked Eli.

I saw compassion in his eyes as he looked at me for a long moment. "I know what this cost you today," he said. "Me and Esther and Tessie are grateful for what you trying to do for us. But now you best stop listening to your feelings, Missy Caroline. Can't never go by your feelings. Got to go by the word of the Lord."

CHAPTER 17

I had no way of knowing if the information I'd smuggled to Colonel Drake had helped the Union forces or not. I waited, along with the rest of Richmond, for the dam to break, for the thin Confederate lines to cave in and the massive Federal army to engulf us. I prayed that Robert was right, that this battle would be the one that would end the war.

Two days after we returned from Hilltop, Aunt Anne and I were eating our breakfast when the boom of cannon shattered the quiet June morning. It rattled the windows and shook our teacups in their saucers.

"That sounds very close," Aunt Anne said.

"It is."

The cannonading continued to rumble, swelling into a ceaseless, thundering roll. We could see the chandelier swaying and feel the ground shaking beneath us. If I could have driven out to the battlefield and pulled Charles to safety, I would have gladly done it.

The battle lasted all day. There was no escaping the sound of it or the constant shuddering reminders that somewhere close by, men were being blown to pieces. We later learned that the battle at

Chickahominy Bluff had been a scant five miles away. The Union army had been close enough to count Richmond's church steeples, until the smoke of battle obscured them from view. None of us needed to wait for the morning newspaper to know that a terrible battle raged and that the city was in great peril.

When Thomas learned that Mr. St. John and many of Richmond's other citizens were driving out to watch the fighting, he begged to go with them, threatening to steal my little mare and ride out bareback if we didn't let him go. To appease him, Eli carried a stepladder up to the balcony off my father's room, and we all climbed up to the roof to peer through Daddy's spyglass.

Confederate encampments stretched around the edges of the city, their tents covering the ground like a blanket of snow. Above the treetops to the northeast, a haze of smoke was visible on the horizon, lit from beneath with flashes of fire like summer lightning. The sulfurous smell of gunpowder hung in the air. Wagons, soldiers, and horses jammed the roads leading toward the road we had just traveled to get to Hilltop. Along with the steady rumble of artillery, the wind carried the crack and sputter of gunfire. I tried not to imagine bullets raining down on Charles in a deadly shower.

We could also see the endless line of ambulances laboring up Broad Street to Chimborazo Hospital, just east of us. I needed to go there and help—if for no other reason than to assuage my conscience. Eli had warned me not to trust my feelings, but he hadn't been able to tell me how to deaden them. Knowing I wouldn't be able to sleep, I spent the evening hours at the hospital, working late into the night.

Early the next day, the sounds of battle began all over again, the artillery resounding endlessly from Richmond's hills. The carnage was unimaginable. By the end of the second day, all of Chimborazo's three thousand beds were filled, as well as the floor space between them. The ambulance drivers continued to dump their cargo of mutilated men at the hospital, regardless of the fact that we were full, and returned to the battlefield for more. The hospital was comprised of one hundred fifty small, whitewashed buildings, spread out over a forty-acre plateau; when these facilities overflowed, the administrator ordered tents to be set up. These also quickly filled, forcing us to lay the wounded on the ground between the tents. Richmond had set up more than forty hospitals, large and small, but they still overflowed with the deluge of wounded that week.

The plague of flies that tormented all these poor, suffering souls seemed biblical in its proportions. Many soldiers survived their wounds and hasty field amputations only to be killed by one of the diseases that quickly spread in the suffocating heat. There were not enough bed sheets in all of Richmond to tear into bandages, not nearly enough drugs to deaden the pain, not enough help for the exhausted doctors who wept as still more ambulances arrived. Eli worked tirelessly beside me, lifting soldiers out of the ambulances in his brawny arms, carrying away the bodies of men who had died, making room for more. Gilbert drove Aunt Anne's farm wagon back and forth from the battlefield all day, heaping it with wounded.

"I seen too many young men die today," Eli told me with tears in his eyes. "They in the prime of they lives . . . Such a terrible waste."

I couldn't even speak of what I'd seen and experienced. By the end of the third day I returned home mute, certain that I'd never find the courage to return to the hospital again. Only the loving nourishment of Esther's meals and Tessie's enfolding arms gave me the strength to go back.

The battles continued the next day and the next, lasting an entire week. Each morning I gathered my courage to drive downtown and read the casualty lists. The stench of death in the sweltering city was so horrific I had to travel with a handkerchief pressed over my nose and mouth. The city couldn't dig new graves and bury the dead fast enough, and the corpses quickly swelled and stank in the heat as they piled up.

"Look away, Missy Caroline," Gilbert warned whenever we had to pass an open wagonload of the dead, headed for Hollywood or Oakwood cemeteries. With so many casualties, there was scarcely time for proper burial services as neither the clergy nor the grave-diggers could keep up.

If General McClellan had received the information I'd brought, he hadn't taken advantage of it. I was amazed to learn that the week-long battles hadn't begun because he and his massive army had finally attacked us, but because our own Confederate forces under General Lee had launched an offensive strike, determined to push the Federals back down the Peninsula. I was even more amazed when the sounds of battle gradually receded in the distance day after day. The largest army ever assembled on American soil was, in fact, retreating—from Mechanicsville to Gaines' Mill, to Savage's Station, to Frayser's Farm, and finally to Malvern Hill. From June 25 to July 1, Lee had attacked and won in battle after battle. His only defeat had come in the last battle at Malvern Hill, where Confederate troops bravely charged up an open slope and were mowed down wholesale. According to General Daniel Hill, "It was not war—it was murder."

General Lee halted his offensive after Malvern Hill. But I couldn't comprehend the news that McClellan continued to retreat, all the way to Harrison's Landing and the safety of his gunboats on the James River. By summer's end, he and his vast army were preparing to leave the Peninsula.

Once again Richmond had been spared—but there were no victory celebrations this time. Far too many people were in mourning. The price of victory had been costly—twenty-one thousand Confederate soldiers killed, wounded, or taken prisoner that terrible week. It seemed that every family in Richmond knew someone who had been among the casualties. Miraculously, my loved ones had been spared. After what I'd done, I knew I would never forgive myself if Charles had been killed.

I didn't have time to visit Robert that terrible week, or the next. But when the long hours at the hospital finally eased, I returned to

Libby Prison with a parcel of food and some more books. I couldn't help feeling angry with him.

"I did what you asked me to do, but the war didn't end," I said without a word of greeting. I knew that I was unfairly discharging my stockpile of grief and disappointment at him, but I couldn't stop myself.

Robert was incredulous. "You did? You really delivered it?"

"Yes. I carried your Bible across to the Union lines and gave it to a colonel named Drake. But a fat lot of good it did for me to turn traitor. Your precious army is in retreat."

"Retreat? But . . . that can't be true."

"Oh, it's true, all right. At the rate they're running, they'll be back in Washington before the leaves fall. According to all the newspapers, Lincoln has replaced General McClellan."

Robert looked as though I had punched him in the stomach. "Caroline . . . I don't know what to say. I mean, that's what the jailers told us . . . but we didn't believe them. We thought it was idle boasting. How could our army be defeated? And why are they retreating? We have the Rebels outnumbered. . . ."

"Here's the paper," I said, tossing it to him. "Read it yourself."

"No . . . no . . ." The paper fell to the floor as Robert slumped down onto the bench and leaned against the brick wall. For a moment, I thought he might start banging his head against it. Too late, I realized that a Union victory would have meant his freedom.

"McClellan let us down," he mumbled. "We put all our hopes in him . . . and he let us down."

I reached for his hand. "I'm sorry, Robert. I'm so sorry. I thought you knew."

"What's wrong with our leaders?" Robert shouted. He thrust my hand aside. "What are they doing? What are they afraid of?"

"Robert, listen to me—"

"How long do they think we can stand it in this place?" The despair I saw in his eyes made me suddenly afraid for him.

"Tell me what else I can do to help," I said as calmly as I could. "I want this war to end as badly as you do. Tell me what to do."

Fury quickly replaced the despair I'd seen in his eyes. "I need to go back and fight. Help me escape."

The idea terrified me. I knew I couldn't possibly help Robert escape, but I didn't dare destroy his hope a second time. "H-how? Do you have a plan?"

"If I think of one, will you help me?"

"I'd like to help you . . . if I can," I said carefully. "Now, here, why don't you eat the food I brought you?"

I stopped bringing Robert the newspaper for a while. I was afraid he would become even more depressed than he already was if he read how Union troops had retreated once again after a second battle near Manassas Junction in August. Charles and Jonathan had marched north with General Longstreet to take on the Union forces under General Pope. The second battle they fought at Manassas had proved even bloodier than the first, but once again our Confederate forces had been victorious.

And once again I breathed a sigh of relief as Sally and I read the casualty lists together. She and her mother had returned to Richmond along with the Confederate Congress once the Peninsula crisis was over. Aunt Anne and Thomas had returned to Hilltop. Except for the chronic shortages of food and the constant worry over Charles, my life had resumed its normal wartime routine.

In his next letter, Charles told me how hard he and the other men had fought at Manassas, and how some of Stonewall Jackson's men had thrown rocks at the enemy when they'd run out of ammunition. Then we learned that the Confederates had kept going, marching north into Maryland to invade Union territory.

The next time I visited Robert he confronted me. Before the door to the storeroom had even swung closed, he asked, "Is it true what the guards are saying? They've been taunting us, telling us that the Rebels have invaded the North. Is it true?"

I could only nod as I sank down onto the bench. Robert was a different person when he was angry.

"How many men does Lee have? What's he after? Why won't you bring me a newspaper?"

"Because I knew that the news would upset you—as it obviously has. I come here to be a comfort to you, Robert, not to make you angrier and more frustrated than you already are."

"All right . . . all right . . ." he said, calming himself. "Tell me what's going on."

"There has been a second battle at Manassas—"

"At the same battlefield? Who won?"

"The Confederates did. Your General Pope underestimated the size of our forces and had to retreat—"

"Again? What's wrong with those fools?"

I saw his anger building dangerously. With every Union defeat, it seemed as though Robert relived his own defeat and what he called his "shameful" surrender at Ball's Bluff. I decided to pour out the rest of the news all at once and get it over with.

"The Rebels crossed the Potomac River into Maryland on September the fourth. A lot of people in that state are Rebel sympathizers, and the papers say some of them might enlist in the fight. We need more soldiers after our losses here last summer. The South is also hoping that Britain and France will support their cause, and a victory on Northern soil might finally persuade them to help us. Besides, General Lee knows that a lot of Northerners will lose heart for the war if blood is shed on their own soil this time."

Robert's restless frustration was painful to watch. "You have to help me get out of here," he said. It had become his desperate, unending refrain. "Please. I want to go back and fight."

I avoided telling Robert for as long as I dared that the Federal Arsenal at Harper's Ferry had fallen to General Stonewall Jackson's men. He would find out soon enough when some of the twelve thousand captured Union prisoners arrived at Libby Prison. Then, two days later, I heard about the horrific battle that had been fought at Antietam Creek outside Sharpsburg, Maryland. Sally and I went downtown to read the casualty lists, and for the first time I felt helpless disbelief when I saw what I had long dreaded seeing—my loved ones' names.

Among those listed as killed in action was Jonathan's older brother, Will Fletcher. His entire eight-man artillery squadron had been struck down together. And Jonathan was listed among the wounded.

Sally and I had both seen enough wounded men over the past year to expect the very worst. Even so, when the casualties from Antietam began to arrive, Sally and I rose before dawn each morning, determined to meet every train and ambulance coming into Richmond until we found Jonathan. Just as we were about to leave on our daily round of searching the second morning, Esther hurried into the foyer to tell me that her son, Josiah, had arrived at my back door bringing news. We ran outside to him.

"Where's Jonathan? Is he all right?" I asked without a word of greeting.

Sally was right beside me. "Is he still alive?" she asked.

Josiah's dark face was unreadable. "Massa Jonathan been shot, Missy. I'll take you to him and you see for yourself."

I wanted to ask about Jonathan's injuries, but I was afraid—and not only because I dreaded the answer. Josiah still inspired fear in me, in spite of the fact that he now looked like a walking mountain of rags. His anger had always seemed barely controlled, like a banked fire that might burst into flames at the slightest breath of air. I avoided saying any more to him than I had to.

Josiah had walked up Church Hill to my house, so we decided to drive to the hospital in Sally's carriage, which was waiting outside. Josiah climbed up beside the driver to direct him. Josiah didn't know the name of the hospital, but it wasn't huge Chimborazo.

By the time we pulled up in front of Winder Hospital on the city's west side, Sally was distraught. "You go in the room first, Caroline.

I can't bear to look. I've seen so many mangled bodies, and if dear, sweet Jonathan looks like that . . . if he's mutilated . . ."

"All right. Stay out in the hallway," I told her. "I'll go in." I couldn't hide my annoyance. I don't know why she thought this was any easier for me. I had loved Jonathan since we were children.

I found him lying on a straw-filled pallet beside hundreds of other soldiers. His eyes were closed, his face paper white. I'd seen so many faces like this before, so many thousands of blood-soaked bandages, but this time tears came to my eyes. This time it was Jonathan. The left side of his tattered uniform was stained brown with crusted blood, the sleeve torn away. Blotches of fresh red blood colored the dressing around his arm. I quickly counted all four of his limbs. None of them ended in a bandaged stump.

"Thank God," I said aloud. I sank to my knees beside him.

Jonathan opened his eyes. He smiled when he recognized me. "Hello, beautiful. Are you here to dance with me?"

"Not today." I took his uninjured hand in mine. I could hardly speak. I'd seen so many wounded men who hovered near death that I was grateful beyond words to see that Jonathan was very much alive. "How are you? Can I get you anything?" I finally asked.

He shook his head. "They already told me they're low on morphine. I'm okay. . . ."

"Thank God," I repeated.

"Yes, thank God it's only my left arm," he said, exhaling. "Thank God it was only a bullet and not a Minie ball. Hurts like the devil, though."

I'd seen what the dreaded Minie ball could do, shattering bones and mutilating limbs so badly that the wounds almost always required amputation. Even so, I could tell by Jonathan's sweaty brow and white lips that he was in a great deal of pain.

"Doctor says the bone is broken but not shattered," he told me. "The bullet severed some sort of artery, though, and I guess I lost a lot of blood. Good thing Josiah got me to a field hospital in time."

"I've seen a lot of wounds, Jonathan. You're very fortunate that it didn't do more damage than it did."

"That's because the bullet had slowed down considerably by the time it hit me."

"I don't understand. . . . How do you know that?"

"Because it went through the neck of the man kneeling beside me first. Killed him." He paused, biting his lip, then said, "My arm should heal if it doesn't get gangrene or erysipelas."

"That's why we're going to take you out of here and nurse you at home." I turned to the door, remembering Sally. I motioned for her to come into the room. "In fact," I told Jonathan, "I brought you your very own private nurse."

Sally began to weep as she knelt on the floor beside him. "Oh, Jonathan . . ." Jonathan wrapped his free arm around her and pulled her close.

I stood then and went out to find Josiah so he could carry Jonathan to the carriage. I heard men moaning, weeping, and knew it could have been so much worse. He might have lost an arm or a leg as so many of these men had. And I silently thanked God that it wasn't Charles lying dead beside Antietam Creek instead of Will.

It took a few more days for my cousin Will's body to arrive in Richmond. The battle at Sharpsburg had accumulated more casualties than any single battle to date, but they wisely chose to send the living home first. Jonathan quickly improved thanks to Esther's cooking and Sally's constant nursing. He was still weak on the day Eli and I came back from the train station with the coffin, but he insisted on going to Hilltop with us for his brother's funeral.

I hadn't let Jonathan read that morning's newspaper. I didn't want him to know about the stunning announcement President Lincoln had made after declaring Sharpsburg a Union victory. When Tessie had read the headline—*Lincoln Vows to Free Slaves in Rebel States*—she'd wept tears of joy.

"Read the story out loud to me, honey," she begged. "I can't see the words for all these silly tears."

"Let's go out and share it with the others." We took the newspaper outside to the kitchen, and I read it aloud to all the servants. According to Lincoln's proclamation, the slaves in all of the rebelling states would be emancipated as of the first of January, 1863.

"Tell me in plain English what that means," Esther said.

"Means that if the North wins this war," Eli told her, "we all be set free. There be no more slavery down here."

"Grady gonna be free, too?" Tessie asked, still wiping her eyes. "He gonna be able to come home?"

"Yes, he surely will."

I slipped outside as they hugged and rejoiced, knowing that I had no right to share in their joy. For me, the stakes had been raised. It was now more important than ever that the North win the war. "Here I am," I whispered. I was willing to do whatever God asked me to do.

I waited to break the news to Jonathan until we had secured a travel pass and were on our way to Hilltop in a borrowed wagon. He would not rejoice over Lincoln's Emancipation Proclamation.

"Can't you see what he's doing?" Jonathan asked. "Lincoln knows he can't beat us any other way, so he's dangling freedom in front of our slaves, hoping they'll rise up against us."

"Why is a slave uprising always your biggest fear?" I asked. "Maybe Lincoln is doing it because it's the right thing to do. I know you don't agree with me, but slavery is morally wrong. Other civilized nations have realized it. Great Britain outlawed slavery thirty years ago and—"

Jonathan groaned. "Oh, no. I'll bet that's another reason Lincoln did it. We were this close to winning England's support," he said, holding his thumb and forefinger an inch apart. "Our victory at Antietam could have clinched it. But now Lincoln is claiming a victory and making the war into a moral issue by tossing in slavery. England will never support us now."

I decided not to argue with him. We were both much too emotionally drained. As Jonathan raged on and on about Lincoln and the slaves and "those cowardly Yankees," I let him vent his feelings without comment. But after we passed the picket lines and crossed the Chickahominy, nearing Hilltop's property, he forgot everything else as he viewed his desolated plantation for the first time.

"The trees . . . Caroline, where are all the trees?"

The devastation was even worse than before the Seven Days' Battles, before the two clashing armies had rampaged across Hilltop's fields and blown what little remained of its forests into matchsticks with their artillery.

"All our fences . . ." he murmured. "All our livestock. Our crops . . . there should be crops in those fields, ready to harvest. . . ."

"The barn is still there," I said with relief when it came into sight. "And there's your house. At least they didn't burn down your house." But as we drove into the yard, I saw that the room that had once been our grandparents' had been badly damaged by cannon fire, then crudely repaired.

Jonathan's parents emerged from the house as our wagon drew to a halt. I watched them appraise Jonathan's bandaged arm and the pine coffin in the wagon bed with stunned expressions, then slowly comprehend the reason for our visit.

"Oh, God . . ." Aunt Anne moaned, her hands covering her mouth. "Please tell me that's not Will . . . tell me that's not my son. . . ."

I felt as though I had dealt her and Uncle William the final, killing blow. As I looked at their stricken faces, I knew that regardless of who won this war, neither of them had the strength to restore Hilltop to what it once had been. All but three of their slaves had fled with the Yankees. Inside, their gracious home had been ravaged by months of hard use by careless soldiers, the lovely carpets and furniture and oil paintings stained and scarred and spoiled beyond repair. If my aunt and uncle lived carefully, they might scrape together enough food from the pillaged garden and orchard to provide a bare subsistence through the winter. But the Hilltop of my childhood had been destroyed.

I cried as we buried Will beside his grandparents and younger sisters, crying not only for him but also for everything else that was lost. In a way, Will was one of the lucky ones. His suffering was over.

When the funeral ended, Jonathan and I walked down the path to where the pine grove had been. All that remained of the beautiful, quiet sanctuary were weeds and tree stumps and the charred remnants of Yankee campfires.

Jonathan had managed not to weep as his brother was buried, but now I saw tears fill his eyes as he kicked at the remains of a Yankee campfire, scattering the half-burned logs and showering his pant leg with ashes.

"I curse them all!" he shouted. "The Yankees who did this to my land don't deserve to live. I could kill every last one of them with my bare hands." I suddenly realized what Jonathan must have understood all too well as he'd viewed the desolated plantation: Hilltop would now be his one day—what was left of it.

"Don't you know that Egypt is already ruined?" I murmured.

"What?"

"Do you remember the night you brought me here to listen to the slaves' worship? Eli preached that night. Do you remember what he said?"

"Vaguely. I remember it sounded seditious."

"He said that God had heard the slaves' cries, and He was going to set them free—just like He had once set Israel free from the Egyptians. He told them the Negroes wouldn't have to lift a finger . . . that God was going to send plagues on this land to show the white folks His power, and in the end, all the slaves would go free."

"Our slaves weren't set free, Carrie—they ran away. And the

Yankees are breaking the laws of their own land when they help them. The Fugitive Slave Law says—"

"Lincoln's proclamation of freedom cancels that law."

"Only if the North wins. And they aren't going to win. We pushed them all out of Virginia once, and we'll do it again if we have to."

"You don't get it, do you?" I said sadly. "By the time Pharaoh finished his showdown with God and the slaves were free, Egypt was ruined. I imagine it looked a lot like Hilltop looks right now."

"Shut up!" Jonathan shouted. I knew he was furious with me, but I said what needed to be said, regardless.

"The final plague came on the night of Passover, when all the firstborn sons—"

"I said, shut up!" He grabbed my shoulder with his free hand, as if he wanted to shake me. "Isn't it bad enough that my brother is dead? How dare you imply that this was God's will? The Yankees are the ones who killed him, Caroline! The Yankees!"

"I'm sorry." I tried to hold him, but he pushed me away.

He started down the path toward home, refusing my help, but he paused long enough to turn around and ask bitterly, "Does Charles know you're a Negro-lover?"

18

NOVEMBER 1862

"The Union Army is going to try again," I told Robert that November. "A new general named Burnside is moving his forces south to try to take Richmond. But first he'll have to get past the Army of Northern Virginia."

"That includes your fiancé's regiment?"

I nodded. I didn't want to discuss Charles, but Robert seemed determined to follow his movements as closely as I did. It was as if he enjoyed tormenting himself by comparing Charles' triumphs to his own failures.

"The first battleground will probably be Fredericksburg," I said.

"Where's that?"

"About halfway between Washington and Richmond."

Robert paced the tiny storeroom, as if he was the commanding general, plotting strategy. If I hadn't known him so well, known that discussing battles and military maneuvers had been his passion since youth, I never would have had the patience to indulge his questions.

"Have you ever been to Fredericksburg?" he asked.

"No. It's really very small—no more than five thousand people. But I know it's on the Rappahannock River."

"Who has to cross the river, the Yankees or the Rebels?"

"The Yankees do. I heard Mr. St. John and the other men discussing it after church last Sunday. The city is on our side of the river. They're planning to destroy all the bridges before the Yankees get there."

"Of course. We will be expecting as much. We'll have to construct pontoon bridges. And we'll have to control the high ground to do it. Are there any hills nearby?"

"Robert, I'm sorry, but I really don't know. I've never been there." I didn't dare tell him that refugees were already fleeing Fredericksburg and coming to Richmond for safety. He probably would have begged me to interview them. "I did hear the men talking about Marye's Heights, but don't ask me where that is."

"Burnside will have to move quickly," Robert said. "That was McClellan's problem—he moved too slowly, and . . ." He stopped suddenly, staring at me with an expression of amazement on his face. "Caroline! Of course!"

"What?" I was certain he was going to spout off more battle strategy, so I wasn't prepared for his next words.

"You could find out what else the Rebels are planning. You could deliberately place yourself in a position to overhear their strategy, like you did at church. Didn't you tell me your fiancé's family is high society? You could wine and dine the generals and other high officials. No one would ever suspect that a woman was paying attention. Do you know many of the Confederate bigwigs?"

I hesitated. "President Davis goes to St. Paul's church—Charles' church. So does General Lee when he's in town. I have met a few majors and colonels and such, but—"

"But what?"

I felt the same revulsion I'd felt before delivering Robert's Bible—as though I was betraying Charles. St. Paul's was his church, and

I had only begun attending there because of his family. They were also the ones who had introduced me to all the ranking officers I knew. To do what Robert was asking would mean betraying the St. Johns' trust.

The guard knocked on the door just then, telling me my time was up. I was relieved. "I don't know if I can do what you're asking or not," I told Robert. "You'll have to give me time to think about it."

I gathered up my things and hurried away. I really didn't want to think about what Robert had asked me to do. I was sick to death of this war and all the difficult decisions I'd had to make, all the impossible things I'd been forced to do. I was tired of feeling torn between conflicting loyalties, choosing between my love for Charles and my love for Tessie and the others. When the nation split apart, my life had been ripped right down the middle along with it.

I emerged from the prison into the cold November afternoon, wanting nothing more than to run home and hide. But when I looked across the street to where Eli had parked the buggy, I was shocked to see Mr. St. John standing there alongside him, waiting for me.

My first response was a stab of shame, as if Charles' father had somehow overheard my conversation with Robert and read my thoughts and had come to accuse me. But I realized that was impossible—and then a towering fear rose up inside me, overshadowing everything else. He must have come with news of Charles.

The pain that suddenly filled my chest was so intense I pray I never feel it again. Without thinking, without looking, I rushed across the street to him. I might have been run over by a carriage, for I never even looked.

"Oh, God . . . has something happened to Charles?"

For a moment, Mr. St. John seemed taken aback. "No . . . no, I'm not here about Charles." He saw how badly he'd frightened me and quickly apologized. "I'm sorry, I didn't mean to scare you, Caroline. I haven't heard from Charles."

I leaned against the buggy and closed my eyes, overwhelmed by the same sickening nausea I'd felt after I'd seen Will's name and Jonathan's on the casualty lists. I honestly believed I might faint.

Eli gently took my arm and helped me up onto the carriage seat. "Easy, Missy. Better sit down a minute."

"I'm very sorry," Mr. St. John repeated. "Are you all right?"

I nodded. "As long as Charles is okay, I'll be fine."

"Well . . ." He cleared his throat. "What I've come to discuss with you is very serious, but it has nothing directly to do with Charles' safety. Would you prefer to drive home and talk about this?"

"I don't know . . . tell me what it's about."

"It has to do with Libby Prison." He tilted his head toward the building across the street.

"The prison? Tell me now."

He sighed, then studied the ground for a moment as if searching for words. "It has recently come to my attention that you have been a regular visitor there, and frankly . . . well, I was shocked to hear it. I didn't believe Major Turner when he first told me you went there, but he suggested I drive down and see for myself. And so I have."

I was dumbfounded. "I've never tried to keep my visits a secret from you . . . or anyone else."

"I understand you're visiting a specific prisoner?"

"Yes, my cousin Robert Hoffman. Why?"

"Just how is this man related to you . . . if I might ask?"

I couldn't believe he was interrogating me this way. My heart continued to pound as my fear slowly transformed into anger. I struggled not to show it. "Robert is related by marriage. My mother's sister—who grew up here in Richmond—married Philip Hoffman, Robert's uncle. They were kind enough to take me into their home in Philadelphia after my mother died. That's where I met Robert. He is nothing more to me than a cousin, no different than my cousin Jonathan."

Mr. St. John's eyes met mine. "I'd like to ask you not to visit him anymore."

"Why? All I do is bring him a little food and some reading material. Conditions in that place are deplorable."

"From now on your boy can deliver the parcels. Major Turner will see that your cousin gets them."

"That's not the point. Doesn't the Bible say we're supposed to visit the sick and those who are in prison?"

"Does Charles know you're going there to see that man?"

I shook my head. I don't know why I'd never told Charles, but I hadn't. At first, it didn't seem important. After I'd carried the Bible to the Union lines, I was afraid to tell him, afraid my guilt would bleed between the lines, staining my letters with it. I could no longer meet Mr. St. John's gaze.

"Listen, Caroline, I'm sure your intentions are innocent enough. But in many people's eyes, your actions are scandalous. The fact that you're helping an enemy soldier calls your loyalty into question. Visiting a man in close quarters without a proper chaperone puts your reputation at risk. I'm going to ask you again for Charles' sake—and for the sake of your own reputation—please stop coming here to the prison."

For a long moment, I couldn't speak. He was right, of course. I would have to send Robert a note in my next parcel, explaining why I could no longer come. I sat with my head bowed, staring at my hands for such a long time, Mr. St. John interpreted my silence as acquiescence and got ready to leave.

"Thank you for understanding. Good day, Caroline."

I finally looked up, and this time my eyes met Eli's. There was no anger in them, no reproach, yet I knew before I even asked his counsel what his answer would be.

"Mr. St. John . . . wait!"

He turned and slowly limped back as I climbed down from my carriage.

"I'm sorry, but I have to refuse your request. I will write to Charles myself and tell him all my reasons for visiting Robert. And Eli will stay right beside me from now on as a chaperone. But I believe that obeying Christ is more important than worrying about what other people think. Robert is not an enemy soldier but a prisoner, a friend suffering inhuman conditions. Jesus said that whatever we do for the least of our brethren, we do for Him."

Mr. St. John turned so abruptly and walked away that I wasn't able to see his face. But I saw Eli's. And his smile could have lit up the darkest prison cell.

I wrote to Charles that evening, telling him the same things I'd told his father. I asked for neither his permission nor his blessing but concluded by saying that if he were ever captured, I would pray that the women up north would show their enemies the same Christian kindness I was showing to Robert. Two days later, I gave the letter to Jonathan to deliver. He was returning to the warfront, the wound to his arm finally healed. Sally and I went to the train station to see him off.

The moment Jonathan's train disappeared from sight, Sally gave up all pretense of bravery and fell into my arms, weeping. I rode home with her, trying my best to comfort her. The servants brought tea and pulled one of the parlor sofas close to the fire so we could warm ourselves after our farewell on the chilly train platform.

"I don't know what's wrong with me," she said, wiping her eyes. "I didn't carry on like this the last time Jonathan left."

"Sally . . . have you fallen in love with him?" I asked gently.

She began weeping all over again. "I've spent so much time with him these past few weeks, talking to him, taking care of him . . . and he is the sweetest, most wonderful man I've ever known. If anything happens to him . . . if I never see him again . . . I don't know what I would do or how I would live."

I gathered her in my arms, soothing her the way Tessie always soothed me. "I think you've answered my question. You're in love with him. And if it's any consolation, Jonathan has been in love with you for three years." I smiled, but she was too distraught to return it.

"What am I going to do, Caroline? How can you stand not seeing the man you love, having him so far away? And in so much danger?"

"I can't stand it. I hate it. I know you've always supported the war, but I wish it would end right this minute, before one more person has to die."

"I think I understand why you've never cheered like everyone else," Sally said as she blew her nose. "I can't believe I was naïve enough to think the war was glorious."

"War may not be glorious, but it does take courage to stand up for your convictions like Jonathan and Charles are doing. That's what my father told me before he left. He said every man—and every woman—needs to do what they feel is the right thing to do in this war."

"Is that why you visit your Yankee friend in Libby Prison?" Sally asked. She spoke just above a whisper.

I shivered, but not from the November chill. "Yes . . . how did you hear about Robert?"

"My father. He's furious with you."

"Because I refused to stop going there?"

"Yes, and because everyone in Richmond is talking about you. Helen Taylor and her mother are spreading gossip about you all over town. Daddy hates a scandal."

"Did your father also tell you why I refused? That it's because the Bible says when we visit those in prison it's as if we're visiting Jesus himself?"

Sally reached for the teapot and poured each of us a cup of tea. She wouldn't look at me. "You have to understand my father. He's used to getting his own way. He was very angry with you for not leaving Richmond with us last May. This incident at the prison only made matters worse. He feels responsible for you. You should try to smooth things over with him, Caroline."

"How? He won't be happy unless I stop going to the prison altogether, right?"

"I suppose not. But he's threatening to write to Charles about you."

I shivered again. "Let me ask you a question. If your father was angry with Jonathan . . . if he forbade you to see him . . . would you marry him anyway?"

Sally set her cup on the tea cart before answering. "I could never have imagined going against Daddy's wishes before the war started. But I also couldn't have imagined working with all those wounded men at the hospital. Now, after all we've been through . . . yes. I would marry Jonathan whether Daddy approved or not."

I closed my eyes in relief. "I hope your brother feels the same way you do."

The battle we had all been expecting took place at Fredericksburg on December 13. Once again, the victorious Confederates halted another Union drive to take Richmond. And once again, Sally and I joined with the other women of Richmond in the heartbreaking ritual of reading the casualty lists. Neither Jonathan nor Charles was listed among the more than five thousand names.

My relief was profound. Then I saw the disappointment on the face of every slave I passed on the streets and realized that for them, a Confederate victory was a defeat, their freedom that much further in the future.

I dreaded facing Robert for the same reason. He had been certain that General Burnside would succeed where the others had failed and that any moment now, Union troops would pour into the city, liberating him and his fellow prisoners. "Is it true about Fredericksburg?" he asked the moment he saw me, and I knew he must have heard about it from the gloating guards.

"Yes, it's true. Fredericksburg was another Union defeat. I brought you the newspaper if you want to torture yourself with the details."

He pushed it away. "I have a plan, Caroline."

"It's too late. The battle is over and done with. The snow is falling, it's freezing outside, and there probably won't be any more fighting until spring."

"Not a battle plan," he said, shaking his head. "An escape plan." His eyes were unnaturally bright. I'd never seen such frenzied agitation in them before, and I was frightened for him. I glanced at Eli, who now accompanied me on each visit, then sank down onto the bench.

"I'm listening."

"Good. Because I'm going to need your help." He pulled his bench closer, speaking barely above a whisper. "I'm going to dig a tunnel. I know that sounds impossible, but I think I've figured out a way to get into an unused part of the basement by burrowing down through the chimney. What I need from you is the layout of the area surrounding this place so I'll know in which direction to dig and how far. You need to find a place where I can come out of the tunnel without being seen by the sentries."

"Robert . . . if you're caught—"

"I know! I know!" he shouted. "You don't need to say it!" Then he took control of himself again and lowered his voice. "I know the risks. But I need to make up for all my stupid mistakes at Ball's Bluff. I need to get back into the war and fight. I let my men down when I surrendered—I let myself down. Maybe I can make up for it by getting some of us out of this place."

"You mean . . . you're not the only one who's going to do this? H-how many others?"

"Anyone who wants to take the risk with me."

I wished I had done what Mr. St. John had asked and never returned to see Robert. I couldn't possibly get involved in such a dangerous plot. I could hang for helping enemy prisoners escape. But I could also see how close to the edge of sanity Robert was, and I didn't know how to dissuade him without destroying all of his hope.

"What's wrong?" he asked when I hesitated too long.

"It's one thing for you and the other men to risk your own lives. It's another thing to ask me to risk mine. I delivered the Bible because I thought it would bring the war to an end and buy the slaves their freedom. But what you're asking now . . . for me to help you and who knows how many others to escape . . . that's an entirely different matter."

"No, it's exactly the same. You didn't let me finish telling you my plan, Caroline. Once I'm out of here, I'm going to have our under-cover people here in Richmond contact you. All the information you gather from the Confederate officials in your social circle can be passed along to them. They'll relay it to our military planners. If you help us win the war, slavery will be abolished in all the Rebel states."

"I never said I was willing to spy—"

"You've already spied," he said angrily. "Whatever your reasons were for doing it the first time, they're exactly the same reasons why you should continue to help us. In fact, this time you'll be safer. You won't even have to leave Richmond."

"I'll have to think about it."

"Fine. You think about it." His tone was bitter, his face twisted with contempt. "In the meantime, I'm going to start digging. Are you going to help me plan the tunnel's exit site, or are you too afraid to do even that?"

I hated the man Robert had become in this terrible place. After the defeat at Fredericksburg, it would be months before the Yankees could make another attempt to conquer Richmond and set him free. He would never last that long.

"What do you need to know?" I asked.

"We're only allowed to look out of the south windows. I know there's a street down below, and the canal about fifty feet away. We can't tunnel in that direction because it would probably fill with water. I need to know what's on the other three sides of this place."

I thought for a moment. "Twentieth Street runs along the western wall of the building, and Cary Street along the northern. Across the street from both of them are huge vacant lots. Nothing to hide behind in either one. You'd have to dig a very long way to be out of the guards' sight when you emerged." I paused, trying to picture the fourth side. "There's another, smaller vacant lot along the eastern wall, about fifty feet wide. There are some buildings on the other side of it—I've never looked too carefully at them, but I will if you want me to. I can let you know what I find out the next time I come." I stood, knowing that our allotted time was nearing an end.

"Measure the lot on the east side for me," Robert said.

"How on earth—"

"Pace it—like this." He stood and walked the length of the store-room, counting each step. "I'll measure your stride with my belt and use it to measure the tunnel."

When Eli and I were back out on Cary Street, I asked him if he'd heard Robert's plan. "I heard," he said quietly. "I could help him by myself, Missy Caroline, if you wanted to stay out of this."

I drew a deep breath. "No. Let's do it together. Two minds are better than one."

"All right," Eli said with a sigh. "Let's go have a look, then."

We crossed Cary Street to where the buggy was parked, and stood beside it, slowly scanning the area around the prison in all directions. What I'd remembered of the northern and western sides had been correct; the vacant lots were too wide and too desolate to serve Robert's purposes. But opposite the narrow vacant lot on the eastern side was a small, two-story brick building with a sign that said "Kerr's Warehouse." It faced Cary Street, not the prison, and behind it was a fenced yard with a small tool shed. The fence ran the length of the lot and was attached to another brick building of about the same size, facing Canal Street.

I knew Eli was thinking the same thing as me when he said, "Must be some way we can find out what's in the yard behind that fence."

"Yes. Let's drive around the block and see what that other build-ing on Canal Street is."

The sentries who patrolled the perimeter of the prison watched as we circled the building, going south on Twentieth Street to the canal instead of turning north toward home as we usually did. The December afternoon was much too damp and windy for a pleasure ride, especially along the waterfront. We rounded the corner and drove past the building that bordered the south side of the fenced yard. It housed the offices of the James River Towing Company.

"Looks to me like the best place for his tunnel to end is behind that fence," Eli said as we headed home. "Your friend only have to dig about fifty feet or so."

"I agree. Now all we need to do is find out what's on the other side of the fence."

"You always was a smart gal," Eli said. "Sure you'll think of something."

The queasy feeling returned at the thought of aiding in a prison escape. "I think I know how Rahab felt when she helped Joshua's spies escape from Jericho," I said. "I know that the Bible portrays her as a heroine, but it never occurred to me before that she had to betray her own city, her own people, in order to help her enemies escape."

"You know why she did it? Bible say it's because she believe in the power of God. She know He gonna have His way, and she determine to be His servant, no matter the cost."

"What if that cost includes Charles?" I asked quietly.

Eli sighed. "I know this ain't easy to hear, but God never take something away without giving us something even better in return— if not in this life, then in the next."

I shook my head. "If I lose Charles, I don't want anything else. And I can't imagine what God could possibly give Rahab that could replace her home or her family and friends."

Eli snapped the reins, and the mare began to a trot as she pulled the buggy up Church Hill. "Bible say Rahab's family got saved along with her. But if you want to see what else God done for Rahab, you read the first chapter of Matthew when you get home."

I turned to the passage when I was alone in my bedroom. At first I thought I must be reading the wrong passage—this was a list of

Jesus' family tree. Then my tears suddenly blurred the page. Named among our Lord's ancestors was the traitor and spy, Rahab.

I waited anxiously for Charles to answer my letter about visiting Robert in Libby Prison. When one finally arrived from him, I was afraid to read it. I knew it was the reply to my letter because he'd used the same envelope I had. A shortage of paper all over the South made it necessary to reuse every envelope by carefully opening the seams, folding it inside out, then re-gluing it. I turned the envelope over and over in my hands for the longest time before finally gathering the courage to open it and read it.

> *My dearest Caroline,*
>
> *How I long to see you. I'm looking at your picture as I write this and remembering all our wonderful times together. I even have fond memories of the arguments we used to have when we first met. You have a way of keeping me on my toes, making sure I don't take myself too seriously, and I love you for that. You look so beautiful in your picture—the most beautiful woman in the entire regiment—but I'd much rather be holding you in my arms right now than gazing at your image. When I think of how long it has been since I held you and kissed you, I sometimes feel close to despair. But I always draw hope by dreaming of our future together.*
>
> *We are wintering here outside Fredericksburg, and the weather has been freezing cold. The Yankees shelled the city before they attacked it, then looted what was left of it. Don't worry, my regiment remained safely above it on Marye's Heights. It seems that war consists of only two extremes—endless hours of tedious waiting, followed by unending moments of pure terror. We don't even have time to mourn the friends who are struck down alongside us. But I think we are winning this war. Our city—and you—are still safe, and I thank God for that.*

I must admit that I'm not happy about your visits to the prison, but not for the same reasons as my father. I fell in love with you because you are a woman of deep convictions, with the moral courage to stand up for those convictions (even when it means clubbing men on the streets of Richmond). Although I would hate to see your reputation unjustly tarnished, I love you more than ever for not allowing the fear of what other people might think to deter you from doing what God wants you to do.

No, it isn't the gossip that worries me, nor am I jealous of your cousin Robert. You will always have my complete trust. But I am very concerned for your safety. I've seen how men can sometimes turn into animals under such dire circumstances as imprisonment, and my imagination envisions a prison uprising with you being held as hostage. I know Eli would protect you at all costs, and I'm grateful that he accompanies you on your visits. But he's only one man against how many thousands of Yankees? If I can't persuade you not to go to the prison for your own safety's sake, then I beg you to please, please be careful.

It's hard to believe that I have been in the army for more than a year and a half now, and I haven't been home to see you except for that one quick visit at Rocketts Wharf. I never imagined that the war would last this long. I've been hoping to receive a furlough for Christmas to celebrate the second anniversary of our engagement, but it doesn't look as though anyone will get a furlough. The Yankees are still camped too close, across the Rappahannock River at Falmouth, and we can't risk sending anyone home. I'll think of you on that blessed day—as I do every day—and pray that this will be our last Christmas apart.

I must close before I become unbearably sad—and I make you sad along with me. This is the season of great hope, so let's draw hope for our future from the hope we have in Christ. God bless you, Caroline. I love you more than words can say.

Charles

CHAPTER 19

DECEMBER 1862

"Don't know how I'm supposed to make a decent meal when there ain't no butter," Esther grumbled as she set a bowl of yams on the table.

"Never mind you fussing," Eli said. "Just sit yourself down now so I can say the blessing."

The fragrant kitchen was a wonderful blend of smells—cinnamon and cloves, smoky bacon and ham, onions and molasses. "If it tastes half as good as it smells," I told Esther, "we'll never miss the butter."

The six servants and I had gathered around the scrubbed pine table in the kitchen for a simple Christmas Eve dinner. I hadn't been able to convince Tessie or any of the others to eat in the house at the big dining room table with me. "Just ain't right for us to eat there," Tessie insisted. "Just ain't fitting for servants to eat where the massa do." So rather than eat alone, I joined all of them at the kitchen table.

In spite of Esther's remonstrations, she had created a beautiful meal of yams, biscuits, the last slices of ham from Hilltop, her own special version of hopping John with beans and bacon, and shoofly pie for dessert. Eli bowed his head to pray.

"Don't be giving a whole sermon, now," Esther warned, "or this food gonna be stone cold." Luella and Ruby snickered.

"Massa Jesus," Eli prayed, "you been real good to us this year. We got plenty food to eat and plenty love to share round this table, and we thank you for both these things. We ask you to watch over our loved ones who're far away, and bring them back to us just as soon as you see fit. We know you always in control, because you are God Almighty. And we know you love us more than anything in the world because you sent your Son on that first Christmas night. We love you, too, Lord. And anything you want . . . well, we're here to do it for you. Thank you, Massa Jesus. Amen."

"Amen," I repeated. I started to reach for the bowl of yams, but Ruby sprang to her feet and insisted on serving me. None of the others would put a single morsel of food on their plates until I had been served and had taken my first bite.

"Mmm. This is delicious, Esther. You've prepared a feast," I said.

"My whole life I never pay more than twenty cents a pound for butter," she grumbled. "You know what they asking now, Missy Caroline? Man wanted four dollars! *Four dollars* for one pound of butter! Couldn't believe my eyes. He say, 'You gonna buy that butter or you just gonna stare at it?' I tell him, 'I'm gonna keep staring till I see what make this butter so special it cost four dollars.' Butter that expensive too valuable to eat. Even butter you get in heaven don't cost no four dollars a pound."

Luella looked up from her dinner in surprise. "You mean we be paying for things in heaven, too? I thought everything up there gonna be free."

"Don't listen to her, Luella," Eli said. "Everything free in heaven, even the butter."

"I did buy a little bacon for the hopping John," Esther said, "on account of it being Christmas. But I ain't even saying what I pay for that. Before the war, I can buy twenty pounds of bacon for the price they charging me now for one measly pound. I want to know what they feeding them pigs to make their sorry little rumps cost so much."

Eli grinned. "Maybe they feeding them some of that four-dollar butter."

The laughter and love we shared that night in the steamy kitchen brought back happy memories of my childhood. The only sorrow came with my thoughts of Grady, taken from us nearly ten years ago.

Christmas dinner at the St. Johns' the following day wasn't nearly as enjoyable as my simple meal with the servants. Mr. St. John still acted coolly toward me, and Sally's vibrancy was dimmed with worry over Jonathan. Reminders of Charles and of our engagement party two years ago magnified my loneliness. We would have been married eighteen months ago if it hadn't been for the war, enjoying our second Christmas as husband and wife. We might even have been blessed with a child by now.

The melancholy I felt was echoed all over Richmond as people gazed at the empty chairs around their tables. For many of the women from our sewing circle, mourning dress replaced their usual Christmas finery. Mrs. Goode's son was now crippled with an amputated leg, and only two of Mrs. Randolph's five sons were still fighting—one had been killed, one wounded, and one taken captive. If the war didn't end soon, I feared it was only a matter of time before something terrible happened to Charles. With all the fierce fighting he'd done, it was a miracle that he had remained uninjured for as long as he had.

Even though the St. Johns weren't in mourning, their holiday parties lacked the extravagant luxuries they'd been famous for before the war. Food shortages, inflated prices, and our depreciating currency had affected all of us, rich and poor. Sally confided that her father had invested heavily in Confederate bonds to support the war effort; that production in his flour mills had plummeted after Virginia's grain-growing regions had fallen to the enemy; and that he was now worrying about his finances for the first time in his life. Neither Sally nor I wore new dresses. They cost more than three times what they had before the war. Instead, we had carefully disassembled our worn dresses, then turned, cut, and re-sewed each piece so that frayed hems and threadbare collars wouldn't show.

In early winter, a new fear rocked the city when we were struck by an outbreak of smallpox. Doctors quarantined the victims in a hospital on the outskirts of town or in homes displaying a white flag in their windows, but no one escaped the dread of contracting the disease. Rumors raged that our enemies had purposefully sent it, but I saw it as yet another plague inflicted on us by our own hardness of heart. Hadn't we already seen plagues of darkness and famine and rivers of blood?

Illness struck the army camps as well, with dysentery, typhoid, diphtheria, and pneumonia claiming hundreds of soldiers who had successfully dodged bullets and Minie balls. *Everyone in camp is coughing,* Charles wrote. *The Yankees can probably hear us clear across the Rappahannock.*

On New Year's Day, 1863, President Lincoln's Emancipation Proclamation officially granted all of the slaves in all of the Confederate states their freedom. But across the South, nothing changed for the Negroes as the war plodded on. I decided that helping Robert escape was the least I could do to win freedom for my slaves.

On a cold January morning, Eli and I set out to explore the fenced yard east of Libby Prison, the best potential exit site for Robert's tunnel. We agreed that I would go inside Kerr's Warehouse, which faced Cary Street, while Eli snooped around in the vacant lot adjacent to it. We parked the carriage across from the prison and walked back to the warehouse so that I could pace the lot's width; I found out Robert would have to dig a tunnel thirty-three paces long.

I left Eli outside and stepped through the warehouse door into a tiny, square office. The clerk seated at a desk inside the door looked tired and ill and at least seventy-five years old. Good manners required him to stand in a woman's presence, so I scanned the small office as he struggled to his feet.

"I'd like to speak to Mr. Gallagher, please," I told him, fabricating a name.

"Who? Gallagher?" he repeated. "There's no one here by that name."

I had hoped there would be a window overlooking the backyard, but the only window faced the street. The door leading into the rest of the warehouse was closed.

"I was told Mr. Gallagher was the manager here," I said.

"You were told wrong. I'm the manager. Name's Kerr, like the sign says. Maybe I can help you."

"I don't think so. I need to see Mr. Gallagher on personal business. It concerns his sister. Is it possible that he worked here before the war? Maybe someone else might know where I can reach him." If Mr. Kerr went into the back to check, perhaps I could catch a glimpse through the open door. But he didn't move. His weary, unfriendly expression didn't change, either.

"Never has been anyone here by that name. I've worked here fifty-two years. I would know."

"Oh dear. I wonder if I have the wrong warehouse?" I tried to act flustered, digging around in my reticule as if searching for something, but I was really stalling to give Eli more time outside. "Now, where did I put that address? There isn't another Kerr's Warehouse in Richmond, is there?"

"Not that I know of."

He sounded irritated. I delayed as long as I dared, painstakingly removing my gloves, searching my coat pockets, and going through the contents of my reticule again. When Mr. Kerr looked as though he might throw me out the door, I thanked him for his trouble. "I'm very sorry to have bothered you."

Eli hurried over to the carriage to compare notes with me as soon as he saw me. "The warehouse was a dead end," I told him. "There's no view out the back. Were you able to learn anything?"

He shook his head. "Not a thing. I act like I'm bored, waiting for you. Walk all around the empty lot, looking at the ground like I expecting to find treasure. Got near the fence but it's too high to see over."

"Were the prison sentries watching?"

"You bet. One of them ask what I'm doing but I play like I just a crazy old slave looking around for pennies. They yell for me to get on out of there, so I did—taking my time, of course."

"What if they remember that we were snooping around, after the prison break?"

"Let's worry about that when it happen."

We waited a few days. Then on a snowy, overcast morning, Eli and I drove down to Canal Street and went inside the other building that shared the fenced yard—the James River Towing Company. This time the low-ceilinged office ran the width of the building, and there were indeed a pair of windows overlooking the rear yard. Unfortunately, shutters covered the lower half of the glass, blocking the view. Three desks shared space in the cramped office, but only one of them was occupied—by another very elderly man. Manners or not, he looked too frail to stand and made no attempt to do so. A wooden countertop separated his area of the office from the public.

"May I help you?" he called.

I put on my sweetest smile. "I hope so. I'd like to inquire about your towing rates. Do you haul only for commercial companies, or would you consider a small private contract?"

"You want us to haul your household goods, right?"

"Yes, how did you know? I'm concerned about protecting our family's heirlooms if the city should be torched. Do you get a lot of requests of this sort?"

Eli rocked on his tiptoes beside me as I talked, trying to peer over the shutters. We were still too far away to see out the windows. We had to get closer.

"Sure do," the man said with a sigh. "But we have more business than we can handle just hauling ore down the canal to Tredegar's. Not nearly enough labor, either, with everyone off to war. You wouldn't be interested in leasing that big Negro of yours, would you?" he asked, gesturing toward Eli.

"No, sorry. I've had a lot of offers for Eli, but I need him myself." I glanced all around the office while we talked and I spotted a yellow cat on the other side of the counter, curled up asleep on one of the desks. "What a lovely cat. May I pet her? Is she friendly?" I sidled through the opening in the counter without waiting for his reply. Eli followed as if he'd been trained to stay glued to my heels. The man didn't stop us.

"Cat's friendly enough, I suppose. I don't keep her for company. She's a pretty decent mouser."

"You don't say? We have a terrible problem with mice in our stable, don't we, Eli? They're always into the feed, and they make an awful mess. Would you consider selling her?" The cat purred as I stroked her head.

"Nope, can't sell her. I need her myself. She's always having kittens every time I turn around, though. You're welcome to the whole litter of them. I'll just have to toss them in the canal, otherwise."

I glanced over the shutters into the yard while he talked and saw why they had blocked the view. Overgrown weeds, rusted machinery, and piles of used lumber poked through the thin blanket of snow. But aside from a tool shed and all the junk, the yard was empty. I gave the cat a final scratch behind her ears and slowly retraced my steps toward the door.

"Thank you for your time," I said. "I'll stop by in the spring for a kitten, so make sure you don't drown them all."

We walked outside into the gray afternoon. Fresh snow dusted our carriage like talcum powder. "I guess we found our spot," Eli said. "Just an empty yard. Nothing in it but junk."

"You don't suppose the office hires a night watchman, do you?"

Eli shook his head. "Man said there ain't no one to hire."

The following afternoon we went to Libby Prison to tell Robert the good news. "I think Eli and I have found a good exit site for your tunnel," I said.

Robert stopped eating the cornbread I'd brought him and looked up in surprise. "How far will I have to dig?"

"Only about fifty feet—thirty-three paces, to be exact. You'll surface inside a fenced yard where the guards can't see you."

He stared into the distance for a long moment as if trying to visualize his freedom. "This couldn't come at a better time," he said. "We've loosened enough bricks to crawl inside the chimney that runs through the center of my building. We just broke through into the basement last night. The east cellar is empty. There's a kitchen and some cells for condemned prisoners in the middle one, but otherwise there's nothing much down there except rats."

Robert seemed stronger, saner, now that he was doing something to control his fate. I didn't want to remind him of the penalty if he was caught.

"Can't the guards hear you chipping into the chimney?" I asked.

"We only work in the daytime when it's noisy. Sometimes if we're afraid the guards might hear us, we get all the men to sing or start an argument or yell at the lice races to cover up the noise. But now that we've dug through the masonry, we'll be able to tunnel all night through the dirt."

"What on earth are you digging with?"

"Chunks of brick, scraps of metal, a couple of spoons—things like that. But as I said, now that we've reached the cellar we're stuck. We didn't know in which direction to dig or how far."

Eli had always stood silently beside the door without uttering a word, but he suddenly stepped forward between Robert and me. "Let me take it from here," he said. He squatted down and began drawing on the floor in the tobacco dust. "This here the northeast

310

corner of the building. This the east wall . . . Go south to the second basement window. If you start digging there . . . and go straight across beneath the empty lot for thirty-three paces . . . you come up here . . . behind a fence."

Robert was studying Eli, not the diagram. His expression was one of suspicion and disbelief. "Caroline, does he—?"

"You looking mighty amazed to see that I can talk," Eli said angrily. I'd seldom seen him this way. "Maybe you thinking there nothing up here but cotton?" he asked, tapping his head. "I always was told that Yankees see colored folk as real people. Always told that things is different up north. Guess I was told wrong."

"I'm sorry," Robert said. "Forgive me. Some of us from up north still need to change our attitudes. Please continue."

"Missy Caroline doing this for me and Tessie and the others, you know. She got a lot of love in her heart. But I don't want her getting into trouble, see? So if something go wrong and you get caught, you tell them the truth—you tell them that it was Eli who showed you where to dig and how far. Understand?"

"I would never betray either one of you."

Eli bent to return to his drawing. "Like I say, this here the northeast corner of the building. Make sure you start your tunnel here . . . by the second basement window. You be underneath a vacant lot. Go straight across it for thirty-three paces. Come up here, behind a tall fence where the guards never see you. You have to break into the south building—James River Towing Company. Then slip on out through the front door and you be on Canal Street. There still a chance the guards along the canal will see you, so you have to watch when they go around. Wait till they pass on by. You got all that?"

"Yes, thank you."

Eli swirled his hand in the dust to erase it. "Now I draw you a map so you know how to get out of the city." He showed Robert the main routes out of Richmond and explained which ones were the least traveled. "I show you again next time I come so you memorize it."

"Thank you for all your help, but that won't be necessary. I've already memorized it. From now on, we will never talk about any of this again."

"But I'd like to hear about your progress," I began, "and—"

"No!" Robert cut me off so quickly I jumped in surprise. "I'm sorry, Caroline, but I don't want you to know when I'm going to do this. That way you won't know anything about it and you can't be accused of helping. You'll just come to visit me here one day—and I'll be gone." He smiled faintly. It was the first one I remembered seeing since I'd started visiting months ago.

"I'll pray that you make it, Robert," I said.

"Amen," Eli added. "We both be praying."

On a rainy night in early March, Eli startled me out of my wits when he appeared in the darkness beside my bed and shook me awake. "Missy Caroline? Missy . . . ? Better wake up and come with me. You friend Robert is here . . . and he's hurt."

Tessie awoke, too, and quickly fetched the matches to light a lamp. Eli stopped her. "Guards gonna be all over this city when they find out there's a prison break. Better not see our lights on."

I put on my dressing gown and carefully followed Eli downstairs, the familiar furnishings looming in the eerie darkness. It was raining lightly outside, and I shivered in the cold. With no light from either moon or stars, I could barely find my way down the path to the carriage house. Robert had chosen a good night to conceal his escape.

"Why did he come here?" I whispered to Eli. "And how did he find our house?"

"Said he knew your address from writing all them letters. He thinking he just gonna hide out in the stable for while and not let us know he here. But the little mare woke me up—she don't like strangers, you know—so I go on out and see what's bothering her. There's Robert, hiding in the hay. He's bleeding, Missy Caroline. Guard shoot him in the leg."

Robert huddled in the dark in the farthest stall, looking very pale. His face, hands, and uniform were covered with dirt from the tunnel and smudged with blood. Eli had hung an old blanket over the window to mask the candlelight, and Esther and Ruby knelt beside him, doctoring his leg. The bullet had scraped across the side of his calf, taking a good-sized chunk of flesh with it. The wound was deep, but it was already starting to clot. At least there was no bullet to remove.

Robert groaned when he saw me. "I don't want to involve you, Caroline. Please, tell your servants to let me leave now."

Ruby grunted. "Humph! How far you think you gonna get, dragging this leg like a crippled grasshopper? They catch you in no time, limping along."

"I just needed to rest. I couldn't run anymore. It hurt too much, and I had to stop and wrap up my leg. Please, I can't stay here."

"Do the guards know there's been an escape?" I asked.

"They do now. A lot of us made it out, though. I volunteered to wait in the Towing Office and watch out the front window. I was timing the sentries, telling the others when it was safe to go."

"What went wrong?"

"One of the men panicked and ran out before it was safe. Three others misunderstood and ran with him. A sentry spotted them and shouted for the rest of the guards. After that, all the prisoners stampeded out. We're all in Federal uniforms, so there was no point in waiting or trying to bluff our way free. I had to run, too. One of the sentries started shooting at us with his revolver. I was lucky he only nicked me. I know he hit a couple of my friends because I saw two of them fall. Couple more jumped into the canal."

Ruby finished wrapping his leg and tied the bandage. "Don't you be moving your leg all around or it's gonna start bleeding again," she warned.

"I have no choice. Thanks for your help, but I have to go."

"They'll have roadblocks up," I said. "You'd better stay right here."

"No! I won't endanger you!"

But in the silent night we could already hear the faint sound of the alarm bell ringing downtown in Capitol Square. "Too late to worry about that," Esther said. "They ringing the alarm."

"You can't outrun the home guard," I told him. "They'll be on horseback. And they'll have torches."

"What are we going to do?" Tessie asked.

We all looked to Eli.

"Everybody go back to bed," he said. "If they come here looking for him, y'all be just waking up. I'll hide Massa Robert. That way, they ask you where he hiding, you won't have to lie because you won't know. And you won't be giving the secret away by acting nervous."

He took Robert's arm to help him up, but Esther gripped Eli's other arm to stop him. "I don't want you getting in no trouble, Eli."

"Lord can take care of me if He choose to. Now, you hurry up and go on back to bed."

I crept back into the house with Tessie and climbed into bed. I couldn't stop shivering though, nor could I go back to sleep. Downtown, the alarm bell rang and rang, probably waking all of Richmond by now. Loud shouts and the thunder of hooves drifted uphill on the wind. I thought I heard Ruby or Luella tiptoeing up the stairs and padding down the hallway, but I stayed in bed. The clock downstairs struck three.

I hadn't been this scared since the war started. I prayed and prayed until I ran out of words to say. Then, not long after three-thirty, I heard horses trotting up Grace Street, and the murmur of men's voices outside. They stopped beside my house.

"You head around back. Search the stable and all the outbuildings. We'll go around to the front." It was Major Turner from Libby Prison. I recognized his boyish voice.

Moments later, he pounded on the front door downstairs. I nearly leaped out of bed, my heart hammering along with his fist. Then I remembered that I was supposed to be asleep. It was Gilbert's job to answer the door. I waited. The pounding continued.

Finally I heard Gilbert's footsteps in the foyer. "Who's there?" he called.

"Major Thomas Turner from Libby Prison. Open up."

Tessie got up and wrapped a shawl around herself. "Keep praying, honey," she whispered as she hurried out into the stair hall. The front door squeaked slightly as Gilbert opened it.

"I need to speak to Miss Fletcher immediately," Turner said.

"She sleeping," Tessie replied. Her voice grew more distant as she hurried downstairs. "That's what everybody here trying to do. Don't you know it's the middle of the night?"

"Wake her up," Major Turner commanded. "Government orders."

"Okay . . . guess I got to do what the government says," Tessie grumbled. "But Missy need to get dressed. Gonna take few minutes."

"There's no time for that. Get her down here now."

Tessie returned to my bedroom and lit a candle. "Take you time, honey. You supposed to be asleep, remember?" She helped me into my heavy winter dressing gown. Even so I felt naked, especially in front of Turner.

"What's wrong?" I asked him as I descended the stairs. "Did something happen to Robert?"

"There's been a prison break. Your lieutenant friend is among the missing."

"Was it really necessary to scare me and my servants out of our wits just to tell us that? Couldn't it have waited until morning?"

"We need to search your house." Major Turner pushed the door to Daddy's library open and motioned for one of the two men with him to start searching it.

"Wait a minute. What do you think you're doing? May I please see your search warrant?"

"We don't need one. Our country's at war. We're under martial law."

It was useless to argue. When Eli walked into the foyer and stood behind me as if guarding me, I knew I no longer had to stall. "Gilbert, fetch us some lamps, please," I said. "Major, I will ask you and your men to kindly wipe your shoes."

They did so, grudgingly. Gilbert returned with the lamps and was sent with one of the men to search the basement. Turner and the other man searched the ground floor as Eli, Tessie, and I watched. The men were very thorough, peering into every corner, crevice, and niche. I saw Eli's wisdom in not telling us where he had hidden Robert. Like in a game of Hot and Cold, we might easily have given away his hiding place by acting nervous whenever they neared the spot.

Through the drawing room windows, I could see lights in the carriage house and in the kitchen as more soldiers searched outside. Torches bobbed in the garden like clumsy fireflies. Surely if they had found Robert outside, they would have sounded the alarm by now.

"Was my cousin the only one who escaped?" I asked as Turner peered beneath the parlor sofa.

He gave me a long, appraising look, as if trying to read my guilt or innocence. "No," he finally said. "There are more than a hundred men missing."

"How did they manage to escape?"

Turner shook one of the drapes as if Robert might flutter out of it like a moth. "I think you already know the answer to that, Miss Fletcher."

"How dare you accuse me?"

"I dare because the escape tunnel they dug was precisely placed. They obviously had outside help."

"I have never liked you, Major," I said coldly. "Tonight you have insulted me and offended me. I'm allowing this search because I have no choice. But you can be sure I'll be speaking to your superior officer tomorrow morning about the way I was treated. Instead of wasting your time here, perhaps you should find out which one of your guards is accepting bribes."

Turner closed the piano lid and stared at me darkly. "I know you helped him, Miss Fletcher."

"Is that so? Well, if you think I'm smart enough to plan a prison escape, then why would I be stupid enough to hide my cousin here?"

He didn't reply. "Upstairs," he said, motioning to his aide. The search seemed to take forever. When the guard finished down in the basement, he and Gilbert were sent up to the attic. One of the guards from outside came in to report that they hadn't found anything in the yard or outbuildings.

Finally, Turner went into my bedroom. I could see that he was growing angrier by the minute as his search proved fruitless. He poked inside my wardrobe and under the bed, then started pulling linens out of my hope chest. But when he pulled back my bed curtains to peer at my rumpled bed, I lost my temper.

"How dare you! You are a pervert, Major, and certainly not a gentleman! Are you going to paw through all my unmentionables, as well? I've had quite enough of this! Eli, go fetch Mr. St. John. We'll see what my fiancé's father has to say about the way you're treating me."

Turner saw that he had pushed me to my limit. He told Eli to wait and quickly searched the rest of my bedroom, then left without a word of apology. But before the front door closed, he made certain that I heard him say to one of his men, "Stay here day and night if you have to, but watch this house."

I shook with anger and relief. It was after six o'clock by now, but the dawning sun hid behind a gray, overcast sky. Eli and Gilbert went outside to begin their chores.

"Why don't you crawl back into bed and lie down until we get the fire going," Tessie told me. "It be a lot warmer under the covers. You shaking like a leaf." We started up the stairs together.

"Where's Robert?" I whispered, even though the major and his men were gone.

"I don't know, honey. Want me to go ask Eli?"

"No, he's right. It's probably better if we don't know. It must be a very good hiding place, though. Turner was very thorough."

"He sure was. I holding my breath till I almost forget to breathe."

I walked into my bedroom and yanked the bed curtains open, angry all over again when I recalled how the major had dared to leer inside my private sleeping place. I pulled back the covers to lie down, then let out a startled shriek.

A pair of frightened eyes looked up at me. The lump beneath the quilt at the foot of my bed was Robert. I had to grab onto the headboard to keep from falling over.

"How on earth did you get in here?"

"It was Eli's idea. He said a true Southern gentleman would never look in a lady's bed—and he said if the major turned out not to be a gentleman, you would have his hide before you would ever let him touch your bed. It turned out Eli was right."

I remembered how close Turner had come to finding Robert and I began to tremble all over again. "No, stay there," I said when Robert started to climb out. "It's the safest place."

"I'll give you fleas."

"It's a little late to worry about that now. If the fleas are smart, they've already escaped."

Giddy laughter suddenly bubbled up inside me at the absurdity of it all, a laughter born of exhaustion and fear and weary relief. Robert began laughing, too, as he lay back down on the bed again.

"Oh, Caroline . . . Oh, you have no idea how good this feels!"

"To lie in a bed?"

"No, to laugh! Turner came so close to finding me, but you were so wonderfully indignant. You called him a pervert! I wish I could have seen your face . . . and his face."

I wiped tears of joy as Robert and I laughed together. Then something in his laughter changed, and I realized that he was weeping.

"Oh, God . . ." he said, covering his face. "Oh, God, I've been locked in that place for eighteen months . . . and now . . . I can't believe it! Caroline, I'm free!"

CHAPTER

20

MARCH 1863

Tessie had just served breakfast in my room later that morning when Mr. St. John arrived at my front door. At the sound of the knock, Robert dove beneath the covers again, and I quickly composed myself and tried to walk calmly down the stairs to greet him. Mr. St. John's disheveled appearance told me that he had also been robbed of a full night's sleep. His angry face told me that he hadn't come as my protector and friend.

"Won't you come in?" I asked. "Esther just made breakfast if you would like some."

"No, thank you." He stepped inside the door so that Gilbert could close it against the March chill, but he would come no farther than the foyer. Nor would he allow Gilbert to take his coat and hat.

"I'll come right to the point," he said. "It pains me to have to ask you this, Caroline, but I must. Were you involved in last night's prison break?"

I chose my words cautiously, careful not to lie. "I was home asleep in my bed at the time. I had no idea they planned to escape last night. I admit that I continued to visit my cousin after you asked me not to, and I admit that he sometimes talked of escaping—but doesn't every prisoner?"

"Did you show him where to dig the tunnel?"

I recalled how Eli had pushed me aside so he could draw the diagram for Robert, and I thanked God for his wisdom in doing so. "No," I answered honestly. "I didn't show Robert where to dig."

"They've recaptured some twenty men—"

"Was Robert one of them?"

"No. But the major says one of those he recaptured confessed that a woman was involved."

"Major Turner is lying. If he has evidence against me, why doesn't he arrest me?"

"Because I won't allow it. Turner is convinced you were involved. Some of the sentries reported that you were snooping around the Towing Company last winter."

"I inquired about having my furniture shipped to safety. Is that against the law?"

Mr. St. John bristled at my sharp tongue and I immediately regretted my outspokenness. He raised his finger and shook it at me. "I'd be careful how I spoke if I were you, Caroline. You are in a very dangerous position right now."

"I'm sorry. Look, they searched my house thoroughly and didn't find any trace of Robert. Don't you think I've been harassed enough? If Charles knew how I was being treated, he would—"

"You wouldn't be a suspect if you had heeded my warnings and stayed away from the prison."

"I'm starting to think you believe Major Turner. You have your doubts about me and my loyalties, don't you? Would you like to search my house, too?"

"Charles has a right to know if you were involved. As his father, so do I. If you loved him and respected his family's name, you would have stayed well away from Libby."

"My love for Charles has nothing to do with this. I would be happy to let you read the letter he wrote me. He said he admired me for doing what I felt was right and visiting the prison. I mean no disrespect, Mr. St. John, but it's up to Charles, not you, to decide if I've acted appropriately. It's his place to question me and to decide my guilt or innocence when he gets home. Now, I've answered your questions, and you obviously don't believe me. I don't know what more I can do."

He studied me for a long moment, and I feared that I had made him angry again. But the expression on his face was one of confusion and bewilderment, not anger. I saw Mr. St. John for what he was—an aging, unwell man, not my enemy. He was as sick of this war and the hard choices it forced him to make as I was.

"I don't know what to believe anymore," he said. He turned and walked out the door, limping down the path to his carriage.

Robert may have been freed from Libby Prison but he was still a virtual prisoner in my house. With an intense search for the escapees going on in Richmond and the surrounding countryside, it was much too dangerous for him to risk leaving. Fearing another surprise search by Major Turner, Tessie and I decided to sleep in Mother's room for the next few days so we could continue to hide Robert in my bedroom.

After Mr. St. John left that morning, we hauled buckets of hot water upstairs, filling the copper bathtub so Robert could bathe. Luella doused his shaggy hair with turpentine and wrapped it in rags to kill the lice, then Gilbert trimmed it short after it had been scrubbed clean. Robert's long beard and mustache also had to go because of the vermin. Gilbert, who had barbered Daddy countless times, was given the job of shaving him, too.

Meanwhile, Tessie and Ruby worked to let out all the seams and hems in one of Daddy's old suits and altered one of his shirts so they would fit Robert. I burned his Federal uniform in the library's fireplace. The only things we couldn't replace were Robert's shoes—the worn-out pair the Confederate soldier had left behind when he'd stolen Robert's army boots. Daddy's shoes were too small, Eli's too large. Gilbert's shoes fit him the best, but then Gilbert would need a new pair, and shoes in Richmond cost a small fortune these days. Robert would have to go without shoes until his leg healed.

When the transformation was complete, I hardly recognized Robert. He was much thinner and lankier than he'd ever been when we lived up north, and he was very pale from the lack of sunlight for the past year and a half. But his bearing and demeanor were what had changed the most since our days in Philadelphia. There was an austere strength in his face from all that he'd endured, a rugged tilt to his jaw that made him look fierce for the first time in his life. The sadness in his gray poet's eyes was gone, replaced by a hard glint like bayonet steel. Clean-shaven and dressed in Daddy's clothes, Robert looked surprisingly handsome.

Within two weeks his leg was healing nicely—and forty-eight of the escaped prisoners had been recaptured. Two had drowned in the canal, but fifty-nine, including Robert, remained at large. "It's time for me to go," he repeated as he paced my bedroom floor to exercise his leg. I sat in a chair beside the fireplace, watching him.

"You can't just walk out the door," I told him. "For one thing, I think my house is still being watched. For another, every healthy young man your age is in the army. You'd stick out like a sore thumb. Besides, as soon as you open your mouth they'll be able to tell you're a Yankee. You need a plan."

"I'll leave at night."

I shook my head. "That's when they recaptured forty-eight of your fellow escapees. Listen, we still have Jonathan's army jacket from when he was wounded. Esther has been using it for a rag and it's in terrible shape, but we could try to patch it—"

"A Confederate uniform? I wouldn't be caught dead in one, even to escape."

I thought of how proud Charles was to wear his Confederate uniform and I lost my temper. "Don't be an idiot, Robert. You might be both—caught *and* dead."

He lifted his chin stubbornly. "Think of something else."

I drummed my fingers on the table. "They'll have all the roads blocked. And the last time I traveled outside of Richmond I needed a permit. I don't know if that's still true or not. I'd draw too much attention to myself if I started inquiring about it. Jonathan kept the permit from when we went to his brother's funeral. But I think I still have the travel permit Aunt Anne and I used when we went out to Hilltop. Maybe we could alter it or forge a new one."

"Let me see it."

I kept it in a hatbox in the bottom of my wardrobe with all of Charles' letters. Robert crossed the room to stand behind me, peering over my shoulder as I searched among the envelopes.

"Are all those letters from him?" he asked.

"He has a name," I said quietly. "It's Charles. And yes, these letters are from Charles."

"Did you save all of my letters, too?"

I hated to hurt Robert, but he needed to face the truth. I shook my head. "I'm engaged to Charles. It didn't seem right to keep letters from another man. . . . Here, I found the travel permit."

Robert took it from me and paced across the room, studying it. "This would be much too hard to forge—unless you have talents I don't know about. If we altered it, we would have to change the date and erase all the names . . . it's made out for three people."

"Three of us could use it."

"Out of the question. I won't involve you."

"You keep saying that, Robert . . . and then you keep involving me. You asked me to help you deliver the Bible, to help you escape, to try to gather information from people in my social circles. You hid in my stable and in my bed. I'm already involved." I yanked the travel permit away from him.

"I'm sorry—"

"Listen, I think I know a way we can use this with less risk. It's written for two women and their slave. If you dressed as a woman, the only thing we'd have to change is the date." I saw Robert recoil at the idea, and I lost my patience. "I suppose playing a woman is worse than wearing Rebel gray? You're running out of options, Robert. If you go waltzing out of Richmond in civilian clothes they'll assume you're a Yankee or a deserter. Either way, they'll shoot you dead. Make up your mind."

I stalked out of the room, giving him time to consider his narrowing options. In the meantime, Tessie, Ruby and I hunted down every piece of black material we could find in the house and started sewing a mourning dress big enough to fit Robert. Ruby sewed a black veil to one of Mother's old hats so his face and hair would be covered. I gave Gilbert the travel permit and he carefully sanded off the date without ripping the paper so I could write in a new one. The hardest part would be borrowing another horse to help the mare pull all three of us in the carriage. "You leave that to me," Eli said. By the time we finished, Robert had little choice but to submit to our plan.

Winter had lasted a long time that year, leaving many of the roads muddy and impassable. "All we need now is for the roads to finish drying," I told Robert on a sunny morning midway through March. "Everything else is in place."

"A diversion would help, too," Robert said. "Something to distract the Home Guards' attention for a couple of days."

A very unfortunate distraction was provided for us a day later. Robert and I were reading the morning newspaper in my room when a low, rumbling sound like a powerful explosion shook the house. It came from the direction of the river.

"What was that?" he asked, looking up in alarm. "Gun ships?"

"I don't know . . . it didn't sound like cannon. But it was very close. Too close." I ran down the hallway to Daddy's room and went out onto his balcony, which overlooked the river. A column of thick, dark smoke plumed into the sky to the west, near Shockoe Slip.

"Stay here," I told Robert. "I'll try to find out what's going on." I put on my coat and hat and headed out to the carriage house to find Eli. Gilbert stopped me along the way.

"Eli ain't home, Missy. The fish is running in the James River and he go on down to catch us some perch for dinner."

"Did you hear that explosion, Gilbert?"

"Sure did, Missy. Don't know what it's all about, though."

"Get the buggy ready, please. I think we'd better find out what's happening."

But before Gilbert had time to get the mare harnessed and ready to go, Eli came running up the hill from the river, out of breath. "Don't go down there, Missy Caroline. It's a terrible, terrible sight. That factory on Brown's Island where they make all them ammunitions just blowed up. I saw it from where I sitting along the river. The roof went straight up in the air with a *boom,* then all the walls fell in ... smoke and flames ... Oh, Lord, have mercy!"

Esther, who had hurried outside when she spotted her husband, wrapped her arms around his waist to console him as he struggled with his emotions. "They mostly all poor women and little girls who work in there," he said. "I seen them crawling out, trying to jump in the river cause they all on fire. Children ... they just little children ... I tried to go help but everybody in the city down there helping. They sent me home."

Later, the newspapers would give the details of the disaster at the Confederate States Laboratory on Brown's Island. Nearly half of the forty-five people who died were younger than sixteen years of age, the youngest little girl only nine. But for now, if what Eli said was true and everyone in Richmond had gone down to help, this could be Robert's chance to escape from the city.

"Go borrow that horse, Eli, and get the carriage ready. It's time for Robert to leave."

Gilbert bent down and removed his shoes and socks, presenting them to me like a gift. "He gonna be doing a lot of walking, he gonna need these," Gilbert said. I had tears in my eyes as he padded off to the carriage house, barefoot, to help Eli.

Ruby and Tessie dressed Robert in his disguise. We'd made the gown large enough so he could wear his shirt and trousers beneath it. With the hat and mourning veil covering his face, he looked like so many other women on the streets of Richmond, swathed in black from head to toe.

"For goodness' sake, keep your feet tucked under your skirts," Tessie warned. "Ain't no lady in the world has feet that big or shoes that ugly."

Esther packed Robert's suit coat and some food in a small satchel. We were ready to leave less than an hour later.

"I don't know how to thank all of you," Robert said as the servants came out to the carriage house to see him off.

"Go win this war," Tessie said. "That's how you can thank us. Then maybe I get my boy back."

No one said much as Eli drove the three of us north to the Mechanicsville Turnpike, each of us lost in his own private thoughts. We were stopped only once at the picket lines near the perimeter of the city, but the soldiers seemed more interested in hearing the news of the munitions explosion than in us. They never asked for our travel permit. We skirted around Hilltop, then stopped in a wooded place near a creek about a half-hour's drive beyond the plantation. It was as far as we dared travel if we hoped to make it home before dark.

Robert quickly took off the hat and skirt, and I helped him out of the bodice before we climbed down from the carriage. "Guess you on your own from here," Eli said as Robert shook hands with him. "God bless you."

"Thank you, Eli." It was all Robert could say as his voice choked with emotion.

Eli led the horses down to the creek, leaving Robert and me alone beside the road. As we studied each other, I felt my own emotions welling inside me. "I'm going to miss you," I told him. The discovery stunned me. He had been part of my life for the last ten months.

"I'll miss you, too." His eyes turned soft, the steel in them gone as the poet's sadness returned.

"Do you know which way to go from here? I never asked you about your plans."

"I'll just keep heading north, cross a couple of rivers. Once I get across the Potomac I'll be in Federal territory." He finally looked away. "Someone will contact you, Caroline. We have agents in Richmond. Any information you can give us will help—what the Rebels are thinking, what they're planning, how many troops they have, artillery, gun emplacements, troop movements. Even if it doesn't seem like much, it will help."

"I'll try, Robert. That's all I can promise." I knew that with Mr. St. John angry with me, Major Turner suspicious of me, and Helen Taylor spreading rumors about me, I wasn't likely to be invited into the Confederates' social circles.

"I'll never be able to thank you for all you've done for me," he said. Then, before I could reply, Robert suddenly pulled me into his arms. He held me tightly, yet tenderly. I could hear his heart beating, feel his breath in my hair.

"I've longed to hold you like this since the first day you walked into the prison," he whispered. "I love you, Caroline. I always will."

He bent and kissed my cheek. Then, as suddenly as he had reached for me, Robert let me go. He turned and jogged off into the woods beside the road, his footsteps muffled by the soft spring earth.

While Robert had been digging his tunnel throughout the month of February, Charles and Jonathan and one-quarter of the Army of Northern Virginia had crossed the James River with General

Longstreet and marched to the south and east of Richmond, camping near Suffolk. Part of their mission was to besiege Suffolk and discourage the Yankees from marching inland. But their greater task was to forage for food for their starving army.

Eli's son, Josiah, has been most helpful in this regard, Charles wrote in his letter later that March. *He and Jonathan have returned to the days of their boyhood, it seems—roaming the woods for game and fishing in the river. Not being much of a hunter myself, I've been detailed to gather sassafras buds and pokeweed greens, since many of the men have contracted scurvy from our meager winter diet. I'm willing to do what I can, but I'd much rather be fighting. Now that winter is over and the mud is drying, we can finally get back to the war. Let's hope we can finish it for good this year.*

My father has written to me about the prison break. I must be honest with you and admit that for your safety's sake, I'm glad you're not going to the prison anymore. I don't know what I would do if anything ever happened to you. But Father also told me that the commandant insists you were involved in the escape. I made it very clear to Father that since you deny any involvement, he must put an end to the rumors and allegations. I know you to be an honest, God-fearing woman whose word can be trusted. If you swear you were not involved, then you weren't.

I'm so sorry that you're being put through this ordeal—especially since my own father is questioning your integrity. Believe me, I'm doing everything in my power to get a furlough so I can come home and straighten things out. In the meantime, please try to be patient with him. He's under a great deal of strain right now, and he isn't well.

The realization that I hadn't been completely honest, and that Charles still upheld my integrity, devastated me. I didn't know how I would live with what I'd done, nor how I would ever face Charles when he returned. He trusted me, defended me—and I was guilty.

"What am I going to do?" I asked Eli.

We sat across from each other at the kitchen table, watching the flames dance in the fireplace. The aroma of fish, baking in a cast-iron roasting oven, filled the room.

"Sometime, probably when this war is over, you gonna have to tell Massa Charles the truth," Eli said. "Tell him what you done. And why. But it ain't fair for him or anyone else to judge the right and wrong of things until we get to the end of the matter."

"Are you saying the end justifies the means?"

"No, I'm saying right now you're trying to obey God—and God ain't finished with this whole mess yet. Maybe by the time the war is over, God gonna explain it all to Massa Charles, and he'll be able to understand the truth when you finally tell him."

A log shifted and fell in a flurry of sparks as Esther poked the fire.

"And what if Charles doesn't understand? What if he can't forgive me?"

Eli sighed. "All I know is, you can trust God. When Massa sell my son, Josiah, to Hilltop, I didn't see any good coming from that. But I know I can trust God. Even when bad things happen, He can use them for good."

On the first day of April, Gilbert opened the front door—and there was Daddy. "I'm home, Sugar," he called. As I ran into the foyer to greet him, I thanked God that Robert was already gone.

Daddy had traveled overland by train, and the wagon he'd hired at the train station was heaped with presents—crates and barrels and boxes of presents. The servants and I followed him out to the curb where the wagon was parked, and Daddy ordered Gilbert to open one of the crates and show me what was inside. There was a new bonnet from Europe, a bolt of cloth for a new dress, bags of coffee and tea—and a large sack of sugar for Esther. She cried when she saw it, then hefted it to her shoulder and carried it around back to the kitchen to start baking Daddy a pie.

"Where did all these things come from?" I asked. "I know what the prices of these goods are here in Richmond . . . all this must have cost a fortune."

"We have a fortune, Caroline. We're quite rich."

He paid the wagon driver, adding a generous tip. "Bring this box and this box into my library," he told Gilbert, pointing them out. Then he went back into the house and left Gilbert and Eli to finish unloading.

I felt uneasy as I followed my father inside. I'd heard people cursing the speculators who had gotten rich by buying goods from blockade-runners, then raising the prices to exorbitant amounts—while needy people were starving.

"What's wrong, Sugar? Why the long face?" he asked as he sank into his favorite armchair. I had followed him into the library, but I didn't sit.

"Times have been hard while you were gone, Daddy. People resent the speculators who've gotten rich—"

"I'm not a speculator," he said, frowning. "I made my money on the high seas, raiding commercial ships that were trading with our enemies. I've given my required ten percent to the Confederacy—in fact, I've given much more than that. One of the ships I stopped was carrying medicine, and I donated the entire cargo to our soldiers."

"I'm sorry. I didn't mean to accuse you. It's just that speculators aren't very popular around town."

"You needn't worry about my popularity. I have a lot of friends in top government positions now. They're well aware of the work I'm doing for the Confederacy."

A shiver went through me at his words. With my father's political connections, it might be easier than I thought to gather the kind of information Robert had asked for. But could I do it? Could I exploit my own father in order to aid his enemies?

Gilbert walked into the library just then, carrying one of my father's boxes. Sweat rolled down his forehead and formed dark crescents beneath his armpits. "Where you want this, Massa Fletcher?" he asked.

"Right over there by the bookshelf. And pry off the cover for me, would you?"

As I watched Gilbert work, I remembered why I had entangled myself in this confusing business of betrayal and deceit—it was for him and for Eli and Tessie and the millions of other slaves who had the right to be free men and women.

The crate opened with a hideous, creaking sound of bending nails and splintering wood. My father sent Gilbert back for the second box.

"Daddy . . . have you ever thought about giving Gilbert and the others their freedom?" I asked.

"Heavens, no! Why on earth would I do that?" He walked over to the open crate and began removing books from it, piling them on the floor.

"Well . . . they've worked so hard for us. They've been so faithful while you were gone . . . and so good to me."

"That's because it's expected of them. Listen, you may not like hearing this, but the truth is, they are children. They've been dependent on us all their lives. They wouldn't know how to handle their freedom if I did give it to them. Believe me, they're better off in our care."

The books appeared to be a set, bound in dark leather covers and tooled in gold. Daddy removed them one by one, scanning the titles as if searching for a particular one. When he found it, he motioned to me.

"Come over here, Sugar. I want to show you something. . . . Open it," he said. He handed me the book. It was surprisingly light.

I lifted the cover and saw that the book was hollow inside. Daddy reached into the inner pocket of his coat and removed a bulging drawstring bag. He poured the contents of it into the hollowed-out space. It was filled with gold coins.

"If anything happens to me, I want you to know where to find this money. You can live the rest of your life on this gold. And it's legal tender in any state—north or south." He removed a brass cigar box and a Chinese vase from one of the shelves and began arranging the books in their place, beginning with the phony, gold-filled one.

"I can do that for you, Massa Fletcher," Gilbert said as he returned with the second box.

"Very good. But open the box you're carrying first." Daddy dusted off his hands and returned to his chair, watching as Gilbert pried open the second box. A dozen bottles, filled with amber-colored liquid, nestled beneath layers of wood shavings. "Ah . . . I see they all made it safely," Daddy said. "Uncork one of them, Gilbert, and pour me a glass."

As I watched Gilbert scurry around the room waiting on Daddy, I realized that my father would never change. He couldn't change. His attitudes toward Negroes had been born and bred into him, hardening and solidifying year after year until they had turned to stone. He would carry them to his grave. So many of the people he lived with and worked with carried the same attitudes that no one even questioned them anymore. If the South won the war, nothing would change for the Negroes. Slavery would continue the way it had for centuries. And if Tessie and Josiah gave birth to another child, Daddy wouldn't even think twice about selling him, just as he'd sold Grady.

Many people would say I was wrong to think about deceiving my father, taking advantage of his friendship with Confederate leaders in order to help his enemies. They would say I was wrong to mislead Charles and his father about what I did at Libby Prison. But those who've been through a war will understand how right and wrong, truth and lies, can sometimes get confused in the smoke and mayhem of conflict. They certainly were no longer clear to me. What was clear, though, was that in God's eyes, my father was wrong to own people as his slaves.

"Are you home to stay this time?" I asked him.

"For a few months, anyway."

"I think we should throw a welcome-home party for you. We can invite all your friends, share some of these treats you've brought."

"That's a good idea, Sugar. I'm glad you thought of it. Thank you, Gilbert," he said as the servant finally handed him his drink. Then

Daddy happened to glance down and notice Robert's old shoes on Gilbert's feet. "Good heavens! Why are you wearing such a disgraceful pair of shoes in my house?"

"They all I got, Massa Fletcher."

"Well, what on earth have you done to wear them out that way—walk to Texas and back?"

"They were probably poorly made to begin with," I said. "I couldn't afford to buy him new ones. Shoes are very expensive these days."

My father fished another gold piece out of his pants pocket and tossed it to me. "Here . . . catch. Take him downtown tomorrow and buy him a new pair. Buy yourself a new pair, too, if you'd like."

Gilbert and I didn't notice anything unusual the next morning as we headed downtown to a store on Main Street to buy his shoes. We caused enough of a stir all by ourselves, outfitting a slave with new shoes costing twenty-five dollars a pair. Slaves usually wore their master's castoffs, whether they fit him or not.

Had we driven past the capitol, we might have noticed the huge crowd of people milling in the square, armed with knives and axes and pistols. But we drove down Main Street, not Franklin, and we had no idea of the danger we were in until the mob poured down the hill into the commercial shopping district, clamoring for food. As they streamed past the window of the store we were in, shouting for bread to feed their starving families, the alarm bell in the square started to ring. I saw that the mob was mostly women—poor and ragged, some as thin as skeletons. Many carried ragamuffin children in their arms. The woman at the head of them was as tall as a man, wearing a hat with a long white feather in it and armed with a six-shooter. The women surged into bakeries and grocery stores, grabbing food off the shelves.

"What's going on?" one of the other customers asked as we crowded near the store window to watch.

The proprietor quickly locked the door. "I think you'd better stay inside where it's safe, ladies. Those people look like rabble . . . and they're out of control."

I watched in astonishment as the crowd flooded through the shopping district, looting the stores, grabbing bread and hams, loading their arms with butter and bacon and sacks of cornmeal. More people came running from their homes to join the band of women, including dozens of men who didn't look half-starved at all. They began plundering more than food, stealing shoes and tools and bolts of cloth.

I stood frozen in front of the window, watching as the rioters rushed toward the store where Gilbert and I had taken refuge. When they discovered that the door was locked, they picked up bricks and homemade bats to smash the window. Gilbert perceived their intentions a moment before I did, and he grabbed me around the waist, whirling me away from the window, shielding me with his own body as the window shattered in a hail of shards. The proprietor was struck by a brick, several of the others cut by flying glass, but thanks to Gilbert, I was unharmed. Then he stood in front of me, brandishing a cobbler's mallet as looters poured into the store through the broken window, snatching all the merchandise they could carry.

Outside, firemen turned their hoses on the rioters, but that only seemed to make them more violent, and they turned their weapons against the volunteers. Then the Home Guard came running to the scene, alerted by the ringing alarm bell, armed with rifles and bayonets.

"Better look away, Miss Caroline, in case this get ugly," Gilbert warned. I stepped back from the window a few more paces, but I didn't want to believe that the guards would actually use their bayonets or open fire on civilian women and children.

There was a louder shout above the chaos, and the crowd parted right outside our store to let Governor Letcher pass through. "What is the governor saying?" someone asked the store owner. He had stepped cautiously toward the window to listen, holding a bloodied handkerchief to his head.

"He says he's giving them five minutes to disperse or the guard will open fire. Nobody is leaving, though. The looting has stopped, but even with bayonets pointed in their faces, no one is leaving."

The tension was as sharp and brittle as the fragments of glass beneath our feet. But before the five minutes were up and the guard would be forced to fire, President Jefferson Davis arrived. Gilbert and I edged toward the window to watch as Davis climbed onto a wagon that had been turned sideways across the street.

"Go home," he shouted to the crowd. "The Yankees are the enemy, not one another."

"We're hungry!" someone called. "We can't afford to feed ourselves or our children."

"But if you steal," the president replied, "then farmers won't bring any food at all into the city. We'll starve for certain." He reached into his pockets and pulled out all of his change, flinging money into the street. "Here . . . take it. It's all I have. I don't want anyone injured, but this lawlessness must stop. You have five minutes to disperse or you *will* be fired upon."

Davis took out his pocket watch and held it in his palm, waiting. The first three or four minutes seemed to pass very slowly as no one moved. Then the crowd gradually began to drift away, leaving only the Home Guard and a very relieved president and governor when the five minutes were up. I sagged onto the nearest chair, feeling weak.

"Those thieves didn't steal your new shoes, did they, Gilbert?" I asked shakily.

"No, Missy, they right here on my feet."

"Good." I remembered how Gilbert had pulled me away from the flying glass, how he'd protected me from the looters, and I vowed I would repay him someday. I would help win his freedom.

"I believe we've done enough shopping for one day," I told him when my strength finally returned. "Let's go home."

More than a month after I said good-bye to Robert, I sat in the drawing room one evening, reading one of my father's new books, when Gilbert tiptoed into the room and whispered in my ear.

"There's someone outside who needs to talk to you, Missy. Says he knows your friend Robert."

Daddy, who'd had more than one after-dinner drink, was snoring loudly in a chair beside me, his book falling closed on his lap. I followed Gilbert out to the backyard.

The middle-aged man waiting for me in the shadows by the carriage house was beefy and florid-faced, with reddish hair and beard. He wore suspenders and a shopkeeper's apron and smelled very strongly of fish.

"My name's Ferguson," he said, lifting his hat. "A Lieutenant Robert Hoffman sent me a message saying I should contact you."

"Where is Robert? Does this mean he made it home safely?"

"I have no idea. I never met the gentleman. And the less you and I know about each other, the better. My contact in Washington said to tell you he spoke to the lieutenant. Said maybe you'd be willing to supply us with some information that would be useful to our cause."

I suddenly felt as though a million eyes and ears were watching us, listening to us. "I don't have any information at the moment, Mr. Ferguson. But if I did . . . how would I get it to you?"

"I sell fish at a booth in the farmers' market on Eighteenth and Main. Know where that is?"

"Yes."

"Fold the information inside a bank note and hand it to me when you pay for your fish."

I glanced around nervously and saw Gilbert standing at a respectful distance, guarding me. I noticed that Ferguson had left the backyard gate open, as if prepared to flee in a hurry if he had to. I was embarking on a dangerous course.

"Is that all?" I asked.

"If either of us is caught, we're gonna swear on our grandmother's graves we never met."

He tipped his hat again and hurried off into the shadows. When the gate closed quietly behind him I knew I had just opened a door through which I could never return.

CHAPTER
21

April 1863

On the night of my father's party, our house seemed to come alive, like Rip Van Winkle waking from a long slumber. For the first time since the war began two years ago, we had people crowding into every downstairs room, food and spirits spread across our dining room table like a banquet, and brilliantly lit chandeliers filling every dark space with light and cheer. Tessie and Ruby served at the buffet table wearing starched white aprons. Gilbert padded among the men, refilling their glasses, the leather of his new shoes squeaking jauntily. Esther had outdone herself, cooking for days, refusing Daddy's offers to hire an extra cook. Now, after the spectacular meal, laughter and music spilled from the drawing room as our sated guests forgot the war and their privations for a few stolen hours.

The prominence and prestige of Daddy's friends amazed me—cabinet members, senators, army generals, city officials. The only men of importance who were missing, it seemed, were General Lee and President Davis. Of course, the St. Johns had been invited, and I was relieved to see Charles' father laughing with mine, his suspicions and accusations seemingly forgotten.

As I circulated through the drawing room, engaging my guests in conversation, accepting their compliments and congratulations, Charles' mother waved me over. With her was a group of government wives.

"This is a lovely party, Caroline," Mrs. St. John said. "You've done a wonderful job. Caroline is engaged to my son, Charles, you know," she bragged to the others. "She'll be a fine asset to him someday, don't you think?" They nodded and murmured in agreement.

One of the ladies took my hand in both of hers and pressed it warmly. "Thank you so much for a splendid evening, Miss Fletcher. My husband, Lewis, really needed this diversion. He works in the War Department, and ever since those spies were captured last week he's been under a great deal of pressure."

The very word *spies* made me shudder. I had read about their arrest in the paper.

"You mean, your husband knew that horrible Mr. Webster?" Mrs. St. John asked.

"Yes, he worked as a clerk in the War Department. We knew his wife, too. They've both been arrested. It seems they were *both* spies."

"I heard that he was a double spy," one of the ladies said. "He sold Yankee secrets to our government as well as selling ours to the Yankees."

"It will all come out in the trial, I suppose. If he's convicted of espionage he'll be condemned to hang. No telling what they'll do to his wife."

"They say there are all sorts of spies living among us," one of the generals' wives confided. "They even come to gatherings like this one. They hear every word our leaders speak in private and take it straight to the enemy. And they do it for money—can you imagine?"

"That's what upset my Lewis so much—the way those people deceived us all. Mr. Webster worked side-by-side with him. His wife even wore a secession badge. They worshipped with us at church, worked in the hospitals—and all this time they've been lying to us."

"I think they should both hang," the general's wife said. "Their treachery not only cost the lives of our men on the battlefield, but it put all of us at terrible risk. If the Yankees were to take Richmond, heaven only knows what they would do to us."

Mrs. St. John shuddered. "God will repay them for their deeds."

I stared at the floor, terrified to meet anyone's gaze, certain that these women would see me for what I was. Fear of being caught, of being hung for treason, vibrated through me. I wanted this party to end. I wanted nothing to do with passing information to Mr. Ferguson, to Robert, or to the Yankees. I couldn't remember why I had ever decided to do such a thing in the first place. I glanced up to see if anyone had noticed my anxiety, and I saw Tessie standing a few feet away. I could tell that she wanted to speak with me, but she hadn't wanted to interrupt. I thanked God for the timely escape.

"Excuse me please, ladies. I believe my servant needs me." I hoped my voice sounded normal.

I clung to Tessie's arm as we walked into the dining room. At first she didn't notice anything wrong with me or realize that I was hanging on to her for support.

"Esther's wondering when you want us to serve the coffee and dessert," she began. Then she looked at me for the first time. "What's wrong, honey? You looking like you about to faint. You need smelling salts?"

"The women were talking about those two spies who were caught . . . the Websters." My heart pounded against my corset stays. "I . . . I don't think I can do this, Tessie. What Robert asked me to do is too hard."

She rested her hands on my bare shoulders, steadying me, reassuring me. "No one saying you have to, honey. And no one blaming you if you can't. Seems like you done plenty already."

"Thanks." I saw Tessie's love for me in her warm brown eyes and felt my strength slowly returning.

All of a sudden Tessie gave a little gasp of surprise. A look crossed her face that I'd never seen before, a look of wonder and inexpressible joy.

"What is it, Tessie? Tell me."

In an instant, panic replaced her joy. When she rested her hand against her stomach protectively, I knew. Josiah had gone back to the war with Jonathan last November, five months ago.

"You're going to have a baby, aren't you?" I said.

Tessie nodded fearfully. I smiled and pulled her into my arms. "It's all right, Tessie. I'm happy for you." I felt the tension leave her as she hugged me in return.

"Let me see you," I said when we finally separated. I don't know why I hadn't noticed before. Tessie's slender, hourglass figure was fuller, the waistband of her skirt an inch higher. And a quiet joy overspread her face.

"I felt the baby move just now," she said shyly. "Ain't no feeling like that in the whole world. Ain't no way to describe what it feels like to have him kicking . . . and knowing there's a *life* inside there. He's part of me, part of Josiah, yet he his own person. You'll see for yourself, someday, with Massa Charles' baby."

Life. A new child. Life was going to go on, to triumph even in the middle of all the suffering and death. At that moment I wanted the war to end more than I ever had before. I wanted Charles to come home to me, safe and alive. I wanted to create a new life that would be his and mine and yet its own.

And I wanted Tessie's child to be born a free person, free from the fear and uncertainty his parents lived with. I remembered why I was doing this, why I was risking my life to help my nation's enemies.

"Tell Esther to serve dessert," I told Tessie.

"You ain't mad at Josiah and me?"

"No, of course I'm not mad. I'm happy for you."

But as I hugged her once more she whispered in my ear, "Please don't tell your daddy."

"I won't." I pulled myself together and walked straight into Daddy's library where the men were enjoying their cigars. I played the charming hostess again, asking if everyone was enjoying himself, if he needed anything. "We're serving dessert in a few minutes if you'd like to make your way back to the buffet table," I said. But mostly I listened to their conversations, committing every scrap of information to memory.

"The Commissary Department has their own problems," a cabinet minister was saying. "Imagine trying to come up with enough rations to feed some fifty-nine thousand men at Fredericksburg—and that's not counting the cavalry. During that blasted food riot last week, the looters took slabs of beef right out of our government warehouses."

I wandered over to another group of men who were talking with my father. "The Federals have us outnumbered two-to-one at Fredericksburg," an infantry major said. "We've got to send Lee some more troops before the Feds attack."

"I don't know where reinforcements would come from," a second officer said. "There are fewer than three thousand on active service here, guarding Richmond . . . General Wise has only about five thousand on the Peninsula . . . Imboden has maybe twenty-five hundred at Staunton. No other reinforcements can be brought to Lee in a reasonable amount of time."

"What about the men with Longstreet at Suffolk?" Daddy asked. That was where Charles and Jonathan were.

"He has three divisions. Their effective force, all told, is not even fifteen thousand men."

"I understand that D.H. Hill has been ordered up from North Carolina to reinforce Longstreet. They're saying he might take their place so Longstreet can reinforce Lee."

Daddy suddenly noticed me for the first time. "Did you need to speak with me, Caroline?"

"I only wanted to tell you gentlemen that dessert and coffee are going to be served in the dining room shortly."

"And it's real coffee, too," Daddy said, grinning. "I brought it back from South America myself."

I drifted over to another group and heard Mr. St. John say, "The defenses around Richmond are strongest at Meadow Bridge and Mechanicsville Turnpike."

"Which artillery units are manning those gun emplacements?" someone asked him.

"There are no guns in position," he said quietly. "We haven't enough to spare. The works are intended for field artillery. All we have there at the moment are Quaker guns."

Jonathan had explained to me what Quaker guns were—huge logs painted black and set up behind breastworks to look like cannon.

"Did I hear you say there was coffee, Caroline?" Mr. St. John asked.

"Yes, in the dining room with dessert," I said, smiling. "And it's the real thing."

I didn't follow them into the dining room. Instead, I hurried upstairs to my room and wrote down everything that I'd heard.

The next morning I told Esther she deserved a rest after all her hard labor, cooking for all those people. "I'll go down to the farmers' market and buy some fish for dinner," I told her. "Gilbert can drive me. Is there anything else you need while I'm downtown?" I could tell by the long, solemn look she gave me that she knew. All my servants knew what I was doing.

"No, there's nothing I need. But you be careful down there," she said. "Some rough people be shopping in that place."

"Missy knows we praying," Eli added softly. "She knows."

Ferguson's fleshy, red face was easy to spot in the farmers' market. He stood hunched over a butcher's chopping block, his apron splattered with fish scales and blood. I watched him raise his cleaver in the air and lop off the head of a large fish, then slit it down its underside with a fillet knife and scoop its entrails into a bucket. He wiped his hands on the bloody towel hanging over his shoulder before taking the customer's money, then he motioned to the next person in line. My stomach lurched, but whether it was from the stench of fish or my own unease, I couldn't say. I waited in line with the others, wondering how many of them had information wrapped inside their money.

When my turn came, I pointed to the large rockfish I'd chosen. I watched Ferguson decapitate it, gut it, wrap it, but he paid no more attention to me than he had to anyone else. He wiped his hands on the towel and held one of them out for my money. I passed it to him, my notes from last night's party folded tightly inside.

This will end it, I thought. The Rebels camped at Fredericksburg are outnumbered two-to-one. Charles is far to the south in Suffolk. He won't be involved in this impending battle. This time the war will finally end.

Ferguson stuffed my money in his apron pocket without even glancing at it, just as he'd done with all his other customers. "Who's next?" he asked.

Please, God, I silently prayed. *Please tell me I'm doing the right thing.*

The battle we had all expected finally occurred at Chancellorsville during the first few days of May. But the outcome wasn't at all what I expected. Once again, Lee's outnumbered forces silenced the Union's cries of "On to Richmond," defeating the Yankees and driving them back across the Rappahannock River. The people of Richmond rejoiced. I couldn't understand what had gone wrong.

I happened to be downtown as the Confederates paraded the captive enemy soldiers through the streets in long lines, and I heard the mocking cheers of those who had come out to watch.

"'On to Richmond,' eh, boys? . . . Guess you finally got here. . . . What took you so long? . . . Bet you never thought you'd be coming by this route. . . . Hope you enjoy your visit. . . .'"

The Confederacy had paid an enormous price, though—more than twelve thousand casualties. Once again, the hospitals filled to overflowing. Among the wounded was one of the South's bravest and most beloved generals, Stonewall Jackson, accidentally shot by friendly fire. All of Richmond waited anxiously after hearing that the surgeons had amputated his arm, praying fervently for his recovery. But on Sunday, May 10, General Jackson died.

Daddy and I, like everyone else in Richmond, were deeply grieved by the news. As we sat in the library that evening, talking about the cavalry officer's amazing career, someone knocked at our front door. I heard Gilbert answer it, heard him invite the caller to come inside, but when an unkempt, sinewy backwoodsman appeared in the library doorway, I instinctively drew back. Daddy rose to his feet, about to scold Gilbert for letting such a roughhewn stranger inside. Then the man spoke my name.

"Caroline . . ." The voice was Charles'.

I recognized him then, beneath the rugged exterior, and I leaped up and ran to him. How can I describe the miraculous feeling of Charles' arms surrounding me again, the glorious sound of his drowsy voice, deep and soothingly smooth?

"Don't cry, Caroline . . . don't cry. Listen now. You'll have us all in tears."

I would never let him go again but keep him with me always, a part of me. I ran my hands over his hair, his bearded face, his shoulders and chest, making certain he was real and alive, safe and unharmed. I alternated between holding him, looking at him, holding him—wanting to feel the strength and power of his embrace yet wanting to gaze at his beloved features.

I forgot all about my father until I heard him say quietly, "Welcome home, Charles."

"Thank you, sir." Charles kept one arm firmly around my waist as he extended his other hand to Daddy. "Please, forgive me. . . ."

"It's all right, son. I was young once. And her mother was every bit as beautiful as Caroline is." He cleared his throat, then said, "If I know Esther, she's going to want to feed you. Have you eaten?"

"No, sir. I came straight from the train station."

"Then I'll go and tell her you're here."

As soon as the door closed behind Daddy, Charles took my face in his powder-stained hands and kissed me—a year's worth of longing finally unloosed. Afterward, we clung to each other again.

"Dear God . . . how I've missed you, Caroline."

"I love you so much," I murmured. "I pray this isn't a dream . . . or if it is, that I'll never wake up."

"You scared me when you first looked at me," he said. "You didn't know me—I was a stranger to you. And I thought for one terrible moment that you no longer loved me. It was a horrible feeling."

"I truly didn't recognize you."

"Have I changed that much?"

I caressed his cheek, smiling. "Have you seen a mirror lately? No one could ever tell by looking at you that you're from one of Richmond's wealthiest families. I've taken care of soldiers from all walks of life in the hospitals, educated men and illiterate men, and there's no way you can tell the difference between most of them until they speak. They all look like you—somber faces, ragged uniforms, worn-out shoes, overgrown hair and beards."

And something more, I thought. There was a hardness in Charles' eyes and in the set of his jaw that hadn't been there before. I had seen the same deadly determination in Robert's face, and I knew what had stamped it there—hatred. How had it come to this, I wondered. How had two men who'd never even met learned to hate each other so much?

Beloved Charles. He was the same—yet he was completely changed. All the remnants of his old way of life were gone: his tailored suits, his starched shirts, his clean fingernails. He didn't seem at all aware that he smelled of woodsmoke and sweat or that he needed a bath. He had a wildness about him after more than a year of living and sleeping in the woods that made it seem as though he had never slept on linen sheets in his life or danced in formal evening attire.

"I may not always recognize you," I said, "but I'll never stop loving you."

Charles looked at me, and the hardened soldier melted away. His love for me shone in his eyes. "May I steal one more kiss from you before your father comes back?" Charles kissed me the second time as if there had never been a first.

I saw more changes in him as I sat beside him at the dining room table, watching him eat the meal Esther had laid before him. I had grown to love his relaxed, languid movements, his smooth, leisurely gestures. But now there was an alertness in his posture, a wariness about him, as if he needed to be constantly attuned to the slightest sound or movement. Even his drowsy voice seemed cold and hard at times, especially when he talked with Daddy about the war.

Charles had traveled to Richmond as an aide to General Longstreet, who had come to attend Stonewall Jackson's funeral. They would be here for only two days. But at least I could accompany Charles to the funeral.

It was very late when he finally said, "I should go. I haven't been home yet. My family doesn't even know I'm here."

I walked with him to the front door. I could tell by the way he held me, the way the muscles in his arms tensed, that he didn't want to let me go. "I should have married you before I went to war," he said hoarsely. "Then we'd be together tonight."

"I'll marry you right now, Charles," I replied. "We'll find a justice of the peace."

I saw the longing in his eyes. Then he shook his head no. "It's pure selfishness on my part," he said. "I have to think of you. General Jackson leaves behind a young widow and a baby."

I thought of Tessie, of her joy at feeling Josiah's child growing inside her. "Mrs. Jackson is probably grateful to have his child," I said. "At least she'll always have a part of him. If I were in her place, I would rather be his widow than never know what it was to be his wife. Please . . ."

Charles looked at me for a long moment, then kissed me gently, slowly. "I'll come for you in the morning," he whispered. "Good night."

When Charles came the next day, I once again recognized the man I had fallen in love with. He had bathed, trimmed his hair and beard, and scrubbed his fingernails. His servants had performed a near miracle with his uniform, cleaning it overnight somehow and mending the worst of its rips and tears and scorch marks. But I knew it would require more than one night at home to take the tension from his limbs, the coldness from his eyes. The lethal hatred I saw in them seemed to grow by the hour as we waited at the train depot for the great general's body to arrive and as Charles talked quietly about the battle at Chancellorsville.

For more than four hours, every church bell in the city slowly tolled in mourning. Then the train finally pulled into the station, and we joined the crowd that followed the hearse to the governor's mansion on Capitol Square. The mantle of grief that had fallen over the city weighed heavily on Charles, and I didn't know how to help him lift it.

Afterward, we rode to his parents' home in nearby Court End. I longed to have Charles all to myself for these two short days, but his extended family had gathered to welcome him home and I knew we must attend the dinner they gave in his honor. Throughout the long evening he talked about his experiences and the battles he'd fought; about Stonewall Jackson and General Longstreet, and the awe in which the men held General "Bobby" Lee; about the state of the Confederacy and what still had to be done to win independence. By the time he drove me home, Charles seemed to have run out of words. The dark sadness that had hung over him all day now enveloped him. I didn't beg him to talk to me but simply held him in my arms in the back of the carriage, his cheek resting against my hair.

We pulled up in front of my house, but before he kissed me good night, Charles took both of my hands in his and made me look at him, face-to-face. When he spoke, his tone was somber, resolute. "Caroline. You must prepare yourself for the fact that I might die."

"No . . . no—"

"Listen now. I've had to prepare myself . . . and you must, too." I shut my eyes, as if I could also shut out his words, but Charles squeezed my hands, forcing me to look at him again. "When it happens, I'll need you to be strong, for my parents' sake."

He helped me from the carriage and walked me to the door, kissing me gently before he left. "Good night, Caroline," he said. But it felt, for all the world, like good-bye.

The next morning I clung to Charles' arm as we attended General Jackson's funeral. I couldn't get Charles' words from last night out of my mind or stop imagining this funeral as a rehearsal of his own. That was exactly what he had intended. He'd wanted me to imagine his death, to rehearse it, so the shock of it would be less severe—so that I could survive if he didn't.

But he wasn't dead. Charles was alive, beside me. I gripped his arm so tightly that it must have been numb by the end of the day.

General Longstreet served as one of the pallbearers as they carried Stonewall's coffin, draped with the Confederate flag, out of the governor's mansion. The band began to play the "Dead March," and I thought surely the musicians must have it memorized by now, they had played it so many, many times in the past two years. Two regiments of Pickett's division led the mile-long procession through the streets, followed by soldiers from the Home Guard and Wren's battalion, along with six artillery pieces. Four white horses drew the hearse; eight generals escorted it. But I couldn't help weeping at the sight of General Jackson's riderless horse, plodding down the street with his empty cavalry boots strapped to the vacant saddle. Convalescents from the Stonewall Brigade who were well enough to leave the hospital marched bravely behind it. President Davis, Governor Letcher, and other officials brought up the rear.

When the grim procession finally returned to the capitol, the coffin was placed in the House chamber. Charles and I were among the twenty thousand mourners who filed past to pay our final respects. I saw Charles fighting his tears as he gazed at the pale, spiritless body, the vacant uniform sleeve.

"He's going to be buried in Lexington," Charles murmured as if to himself. "He taught there, at the Virginia Military Institute." When we finally stepped outside into the late afternoon sunshine again, Charles exhaled as if he'd been forced to hold his breath for a very long time. "He can't be replaced," he said. "Stonewall Jackson can never be replaced."

"Let's go home," I said, tugging on his arm. I wanted to drag him away from the depressing atmosphere of death and mourning, to help him turn away from it and welcome life and hope once more. Before sitting down beside him in my drawing room, I opened all the doors to the backyard, letting the calm May breeze drift into the room, bringing the chatter of birdsong, the faint scent of spring.

"I think this war is very close to an end," Charles said as we sipped the coffee Esther brought us. "People up north aren't going to stand for too many more losses like Fredericksburg and Chancellorsville. They're as tired of the bloodshed as we are. I have a feeling that after this latest victory, General Lee is going to take the war into Union territory again. When civilians up north suddenly see their own homes threatened, when they begin to suffer the way Virginians have suffered, they'll call an end to it."

"What about you, Charles—when it's finally over? For two years now, you've been trained to march and kill and hate. What about afterward?"

He shifted restlessly on the sofa, as if unable to relax. "It seems like the work I did in Washington, and even in my father's mills, happened a lifetime ago. I know it will be hard to adjust back to civilian life. I had a hard time adjusting to soldiering at first. But now ... Caroline, you can't imagine what an exhilarating experience it is. The camaraderie of the men ... knowing we're all in this together, working as one, fighting for our homes, our lives. There's no other feeling in the world like those final few moments before a battle."

"Are you ever afraid ... before ... ?"

"Not of the Yankees. Not even of dying, as strange as that sounds. If I'm afraid of anything, it's that I'll fail—that the Yankees will break through to Richmond, where you are. I think of what they might do, and I know that I must hold them back, keep them from ever entering this city." He shifted again and I saw the latent energy in his muscles, the warrior who couldn't relax or be still.

"But I only think those thoughts in the moments before the battle starts. Then all of a sudden the enemy is coming at me and time freezes, and all I can think about is stopping that moving wall of blue. You load, aim, fire, load again. You're aware of bullets whistling past and men falling beside you, but you don't think about it until it's over. You don't even hear their screams and moans until afterwards.

"Then you're back in camp again, and you realize that you're still alive. In fact, it feels as though life is bursting through your veins. You're exhausted, everyone is, yet the camp comes alive with music and laughter. Even the wormy food they feed us tastes wonderful because you've lived to fight another day."

"Where do you find the courage to fight again and again, to keep facing armies that are so much bigger than yours?"

"You can't muster the courage to do it when you're here, at home. It only comes when you're faced with it. And when you believe in what you're fighting for."

I nodded in understanding. "Before the war, I never would have imagined that I could work in a place like Chimborazo Hospital . . . to see such terrible, gruesome sights, to watch men suffer like that. You're right, I don't know how I do it, but I do know why."

"Ever since that first battle at Manassas, Caroline, I feel more alive than I ever have in my life. I know that sounds odd, but I think it's because there have been so many times when I might have died. I notice things now—like the way the tree branches move when I'm lying beneath them and the way the air smells before it rains. After the battle of Fredericksburg, the northern lights filled the winter sky that night. I can't even describe how beautiful it looked—as if God had lit up the heavens with His glory. I see the world differently now. And I don't think I'll ever take life for granted again."

I traced the line of his jaw with my fingers. "I know what you mean. I've seen so many lives come to an end in the hospitals where I've worked. I know how close we are to death each moment—a mere breath away—and we don't even realize it. I've also learned that the God who paints the sky with His glory is the One who holds each one of us in His hands. It's His will that's going to prevail, not ours."

Charles caught my fingers in his hand and kissed them. "The war has changed you, too, Caroline. Your faith is stronger, your compassion deeper, your love more intense than ever before. It's as if all the qualities I saw in you and fell in love with have been refined and purified. I know the war has changed me in many ways. Perhaps some of them aren't so good. I think we'll both be different people when this is over."

"I want you back, Charles. Not the soldier; the gentleman. I want the life that we had before the war."

I wanted the Charles of two years ago, handsome in his formal evening clothes, smoothly dancing me around the ballroom floor, his warm hands holding me, his sleepy voice soothing me. I wanted our life of privilege, the courtly manners, the slow pace, the laughter on a picnic blanket on a warm afternoon. It was gone, that entire way of life was gone, like the green splendor of Hilltop.

"We're never going to have it back, are we?" I murmured.

"Listen now. This war is almost over. And when it finally does end, even if we've lost some things, we'll still have each other."

Charles talked of being alive when it was over, of being with me afterwards. He was no longer anticipating his own death, and I was so relieved that I didn't wait for him to kiss me; I lifted my face to kiss him.

Daddy drove with me to the Richmond & Petersburg Railroad station the next morning to see Charles off. He and his parents were already there, and so was the train, chuffing impatiently as it built up a head of steam.

"We'll change trains at Petersburg and take the Norfolk line," I heard Charles say. "But I believe all three of our divisions will be coming back this way very soon to join up with Lee's army again."

I listened as they talked of trivial things, reluctant to begin the difficult farewells. When I had a moment, I pulled Charles aside. I had one more thing to say to him that I had forgotten to tell him in private.

"When you get back to camp, when you see Josiah, will you give him a message for me? Tell him . . . tell him he's going to be a father."

Charles stared at me as if he hadn't understood. "Is it your maid? Tessie?" he asked, frowning.

"Yes. They're married. They have been for several years." I couldn't understand why he didn't share my delight at the news. Josiah had marched and camped and gone hungry with him and Jonathan for the past two years. "What's wrong?" I asked.

"It's . . . complicated. He and Tessie belong to two separate owners, for one thing. Josiah is never going to be a father in the sense that you mean."

There was something behind Charles' words and in his attitude that I didn't want to examine too closely. Then the train whistle blew and the moment passed. The time to say good-bye had finally come. Charles drew a deep breath, as if steeling himself.

"Don't say it," I begged. "Please don't say good-bye."

He pulled me into his arms, kissed me softly on the cheek. "All right," he murmured. "I'll see you soon."

Charles marched north again with General Longstreet to rejoin Lee's army, and the news he sent was all good. General Rodes took the city of Martinsburg. General Ewell took Winchester on the same day. At the end of June they crossed the Potomac into Union territory. One year ago a huge Federal army had threatened Richmond; now Washington and Philadelphia felt threatened by the invading Confederate army. Daddy's hopes for another Rebel victory soared. Surely the North would sue for peace. It would all be over soon.

The first three days of July were the longest ones in my life as the opposing armies finally clashed in an unknown Pennsylvania town named Gettysburg. The early reports of Confederate victories raised hopes higher still. While I waited in an agony of suspense for news about Charles, a devastating blow threw the city into despair. The long siege of Vicksburg had ended in defeat. General Pemberton had surrendered the city to Federal forces on the Fourth of July. That meant the Mississippi River was in Union hands; the Confederacy was cut in half.

Then the awful truth about the battles being fought at Gettysburg slowly began to filter home. The news stunned all of us. Half of General Pickett's men had been mowed down by artillery and rifle fire in a daring but ill-fated charge up Cemetery Hill. Out of a force of two hundred fifty men in the 9th Virginia Regiment, only thirty-eight had survived. Altogether, Lee's army suffered more than twenty-eight thousand casualties—more than one-third of his men—and had gained nothing. Lee was in retreat, marching from the battlefield by night in a drenching rain.

After the way Charles had spoken about dying two months earlier, I couldn't summon the courage to go downtown and read the casualty lists from Gettysburg. *"You must prepare yourself for the fact that I might die,"* he had said. So many thousands of men had died at Gettysburg, so many more had been grievously wounded, that I lost all hope that Charles might have been spared. *"I've had to prepare myself . . . and you must, too."*

"I'll go find out for you, Caroline," Daddy said. "In the meantime, you've got to keep your hopes up." But I saw him swallow a good stiff drink to fortify himself before leaving on horseback. I waited, sick at heart, unable to hug Tessie with her enormous belly in the way. I told myself that if Daddy galloped up the hill, the news would be good; if he took his time coming home, the news was bad.

"'Yea, though I walk through the valley of the shadow of death,'" Tessie read aloud, "'I will fear no evil: for thou art with me. . . .'"

I waited. One hour slowly turned into two.

When I heard a horse trotting up the street I forced myself to walk downstairs to the foyer. Daddy burst through the door, his face flushed and dripping with sweat. "He's all right, Caroline. Charles and Jonathan both came through it safely."

I sank to the floor, weeping and thanking God.

On a hot, muggy day in August, the police arrested a Richmond woman named Mary Caroline Allan on charges of espionage. I had been making regular trips to Mr. Ferguson's booth in the farmers' market with the information I'd gleaned from social gatherings and from my father's many visitors, and the news of Mrs. Allan's arrest alarmed me, reminding me of the dangerous path I was treading.

On the very same day, Tessie went into labor. Ruby and Esther settled her into their quarters above the kitchen and forbade me to come anywhere near her. But I could hear Tessie's cries of pain through the open windows, her suffering intensified by the afternoon's sticky heat.

When Esther finally emerged with the good news that evening, she was wringing with sweat herself. "Tessie had herself a boy," she said with a weary smile. "Another beautiful little boy. And I got myself a grandchild." I was finally allowed upstairs to see them. "But just for a minute," Esther warned.

Tessie looked exhausted but radiant. Her son, whom she'd named Isaac, had Josiah's dark, scowling face. Tears filled my eyes as I thought of Grady.

"You go on out, now," Esther said, shooing me. "I gonna give Tessie a bite to eat, then she gonna have herself a rest."

Daddy had gone downtown on business, but I sat in the stair hall that sultry evening, watching out the window for his return. I barely gave him time to come through the front door before confronting him with the news. "Tessie had her baby . . . a little boy."

Daddy looked flustered. "Well. I see." Neither of us had ever said a word about her pregnancy but he certainly must have noticed it.

"I have a question," I said, following him into the library. "Does her baby belong to us or to Jonathan, since he owns the baby's father, Josiah?"

Daddy stared into space for a moment. "Josiah's the father? Are you sure?" Then he came out of his trance and glanced around the room as if he weren't sure where he was or how he got there. "Well. It doesn't really matter who sired it. The child is the property of whoever owns the mother. Negro women never tell the truth about who the sire is."

I drew a deep breath. "In that case, I would like to own the baby—as my servant. I know all the servants will be mine someday, but in the meantime I would like one of my own."

Daddy sank into his chair, his eyes never leaving mine. "Why? What are you going to do with him?"

"I don't know, but—"

"He's not a toy, Caroline, not something that you can play with like a rag doll. That's what you did with Tessie's other boy and I should have put a stop to it from the very beginning. Slaves are valuable pieces of property."

"I'd like him to be my property," I said, forcing the words from my mouth. "When he's old enough, Gilbert can teach him to drive a carriage. I'll need my own driver once Charles and I are married. Look, I'll buy the child from you if you'd like. But I really want to own him, Daddy." I gazed up at him the way I had as a little girl, begging for favors—the look he'd never been able to resist.

"If that would please you, Sugar . . . all right. But make sure you put him to work. Don't spoil him. If he grows up to be as big and strong as Josiah, he'll be worth a pretty penny."

I made Daddy draw up the ownership papers that same night, making the slave, Isaac Fletcher, my legal property. As soon as the ink dried, I went straight up to my room and transferred my deed of ownership to Isaac, writing it on the back of the same paper, using the legal terms my father had used. I hadn't even owned my slave for five minutes before granting him his freedom.

When I climbed the steep ladder that night to the stifling slaves' quarters above the kitchen, Isaac was nursing at Tessie's breast. I knelt beside them, listening to his soft, baby coos and to the gentle lullaby Tessie hummed as his tiny fingers curled around hers. I could remember her humming the same tune to me years ago.

When the baby finally slept, I gave Tessie the paper. I watched as she read it in wonder and disbelief, trying to absorb what it meant.

"Isaac is free, Tessie," I said. "That paper proves it."

"My boy . . . my son is a free man?"

"Yes. No one can ever take him from you."

Then we both wept.

22

FALL 1863

The weather stayed warm for a long time during the fall of 1863, giving us a near-perfect Indian summer. But even the finest weather couldn't dispel the twin shadows of poverty and defeat that closed in on Richmond. It became a common sight to see some of the city's wealthiest families, their clothes threadbare, trying to sell their jewelry and other valuables in order to eat. We still had some of Daddy's gold, but it did little good since so many of the stores had empty shelves. The goods that were available sold for such exorbitant prices that I watched Daddy's "fortune" rapidly dwindle.

The Confederate dollar had depreciated until it was worth only four cents. The shoes I had bought Gilbert six months ago now sold for four times as much. The four-dollar butter Esther had complained about seemed cheap with butter now selling for fifteen dollars a pound. We ate a lot of potatoes, but even they were expensive at twenty-five dollars a bushel. And flour, if you could find it, had gone from six dollars a barrel three years ago to as much as three hundred dollars a barrel. With heating fuel scarce and very costly, everyone dreaded winter.

News of the battles raging out west added to the gloom. Federal troops occupied Chattanooga, eastern Tennessee, and the Cumberland Gap. Our Rebel forces under General Bragg won an impressive victory at Chickamauga, but it cost him two-fifths of his men. The North, with its larger population, could replace their losses with fresh troops; the Confederates had no way to replace their soldiers when they fell in combat.

By November, General Ulysses Grant had taken command of the Federals. From Tennessee, they began pushing our Confederate forces back, driving them from Lookout Mountain, inching their way toward Atlanta.

Even with all this suffering, neither Daddy nor anyone else in Richmond talked of losing the war or abandoning the fight for Southern independence. Like the Old Testament pharaoh, their hearts grew harder, leaving me to wonder how many more plagues we would have to endure before the slaves finally won their freedom.

My father still entertained important guests—although on a more modest scale than before—and I continued to collect information and pass it along to Mr. Ferguson. I made it a point to learn more about military tactics so I would know which questions to ask and which facts were important. I became very skilled at acquiring information and remembering details. I not only told the Yankees what the Rebels' plans and movements were, but I told them what the Rebels already knew of the North's movements and strengths.

I no longer felt remorse at deceiving my father or using him this way. Not after eavesdropping on his conversation with Mr. St. John one afternoon. "I might be forced to sell some of my slaves this winter so we'll have fewer mouths to feed," Daddy said.

I nearly cried out. I had come into his library on the pretense of looking for a book to read, hoping to pick up some new information from the two men, but Daddy's words stunned me. I wanted to plead with him not to do this, but I was afraid that if I let him know I was listening he would stop discussing his plans. I randomly pulled

A Tale of Two Cities from the shelf and pretended to leaf through it, biting my lip as I listened.

"I didn't think you could get a decent price for slaves these days," Mr. St. John said. "I'd sell a few of mine, too, if I thought that I could get a fair price for them."

"No, no, they're not selling for anywhere near what they're worth," Daddy said. "I could use the money, but that's not why I'm thinking of selling them. Frankly, food is just too hard to come by, and I don't want the expense of feeding so many slaves this winter."

"I know what you mean," Mr. St. John said. "The way things are, it hardly seems worth feeding one just so she can polish the silver."

"Caroline and I can probably get by with two maidservants," Daddy said. "After all, there's only two of us. And I really don't need two menservants either, since we only have the one mare to care for. But it will be hard to decide whether to sell Eli or Gilbert. They're both good slaves."

I couldn't listen to any more. I closed Dickens' book and hurried from the room with it. By the time I reached the backyard where Eli was hoeing his vegetable patch, my tears were falling fast. Eli took one look at my face and dropped the hoe to run to me.

"It ain't Massa Charles, is it?" he asked, gripping my shoulders to steady me. "I seen Mr. St. John come, but I didn't think—"

"No, Charles is all right. It's . . . it's you and the others, Eli . . ." I wanted to lean against his broad chest and sob, but Eli took my arm and led me into the carriage house before trying to comfort me.

"Go ahead, Missy . . . it's all right," he soothed as he finally wrapped his arms around me. "You can tell me all about it . . . it's okay. . . ."

But it wasn't okay. I remembered the expression of joy on Gilbert's face the day Daddy returned home from blockade running, how Ruby and the others had spread a banquet in celebration, how Esther had cooked all his favorite foods. They loved Daddy, trusted him, served him faithfully—yet he planned to sell them as if they were simply useless possessions he no longer needed. I didn't want to tell Eli the terrible truth, but I knew that I had to. When I could control my tears, I raised my head to look up at him.

"My father is planning to sell three of you before winter," I said.

For a moment, Eli appeared not to believe my words. Then an expression of such intense pain filled his eyes that I had to look away. "It's okay. . . ." he murmured, "God gonna have His way . . . it's okay. . . ."

"No, it's not," I shouted. "I can't part with any of you. This is wrong, Eli. Help me think of a way to stop him."

"Can't nobody stop him, Missy. We can only pray and trust God to—"

"No! You can't let him do this. You have to escape to freedom, Eli. All of you."

"Escape?" He said it as if he'd never heard the word.

"Yes. I'll never let my father sell you. Never. I'll help all of you run away first."

I could see that Eli was deeply shaken. He had to sit down. "It ain't an easy thing to go running off, you know. Esther's ankles always swelling up . . . and Tessie has my little grandbaby to think about. Ain't such an easy thing."

"You don't have to go far. As soon as you cross over to the Yankee lines you'll be free. The Yankees are right here in Virginia. They have troops stationed at Williamsburg and Norfolk. I can draw you a map. Here . . ." I opened the book I still held in my hand and ripped out the title page. "Do you have something I can write with?"

Eli simply stared into space. The look of sorrow in his eyes was so profound it broke my heart. "Please don't give up, Eli. I'm doing everything I can to help the North win this war so you'll be free, but you've got to think of yourself and the others in the meantime. You've got to be ready to escape if my father goes through with this."

"All right," he finally said. "All right . . . There's a pencil in that box over there."

I dug through the wooden crate where Eli kept the horse brushes and some extra lengths of rope. Packed away near the bottom, wrapped in a clean rag, was his Bible—and a pencil. Using the lid of the crate for a table, I drew Eli a map of the route to Williamsburg, explaining it to him as I drew. Then I showed him another route, crossing the James River and going south to Norfolk.

"I want you to tell the others about this," I said when I finished. "They have to be ready to leave at a moment's notice. I'm quite sure that my father won't give us any warning, so make sure Gilbert pays close attention to his movements. If Daddy drives down to the slave auction on Fourteenth Street . . ."

"Okay, Missy. We all be ready," Eli said. He hadn't looked this sorrowful since the day they'd taken Grady away. "But I'm gonna be praying that God change your Daddy's mind so we don't have to go nowhere. God can do that, you know. I be praying that we never have to use this map."

My task of spying took on a new urgency. The North *had* to win— and soon. For a full week after I'd overheard my father's plans I lived with the fear that he had already sold some of our servants without my knowledge. Each time a carriage or a wagon passed the house, I worried that it had come from the slave auction, that two burly men would jump out and drag away Ruby or Luella or Gilbert the way they had dragged poor Grady. Then one night while Daddy and I were eating dinner he said, "Caroline, I've been forced to make a very difficult decision."

I stopped eating, waiting.

"I had a meeting with President Davis a few days ago," Daddy said. "He asked me to return to blockade running."

"What?" It took a moment for his words to sink in—he wasn't announcing that he had sold our servants. I closed my eyes, bowing my head in relief. Daddy mistook my reaction for grief.

"I know you're upset, Sugar, but I have to do it. The Yankees have a fleet blocking Charleston harbor, another squadron at Wilmington, North Carolina—that's why goods are so expensive. And so scarce. Our soldiers need medicine and guns. . . . The Confederacy needs my help. I'm sorry, but I'm going to do what the president asked."

"When will you leave?"

"There are a few things I need to take care of first," he said, looking away, "but as soon as I possibly can."

I knew by the way he avoided my gaze that one of those things was to sell three of our slaves. They would have to flee tonight unless I could convince my father to change his mind. Then I suddenly had another idea—but it meant taking a huge risk.

"Daddy, can I tell you something?"

"Certainly, Sugar."

"I overheard you telling Charles' father that you might sell some of the slaves."

"Now, Caroline—"

"No, listen. I admit that I was upset about it at first, but I feel differently now that I know you're leaving. It's such a huge responsibility for me to take care of this house and six servants all by myself. I'm so worried that we'll all starve this winter. I agree with you that we should sell some of them."

"It's a relief to hear you say that, Caroline. I was afraid you would fuss."

"No, this war has forced me to change. And I know they have to be sold. If you tell me who to contact, I'll take care of selling them for you. I could use a week or two to decide which ones to part with—and I know you'll want to set sail before the winter storm season begins."

"Are you certain you can do this?" he asked.

"I'm certain."

He reached for my hand. "You've grown into a strong young woman, Caroline. I'm proud of you."

My father gave me the names and addresses of two slave traders a few days before Gilbert and I drove him to the train station.

"What you gonna tell him when he come home and see you ain't sold nobody?" Gilbert asked as we waved good-bye to him.

"Hopefully the war will be over by then," I said, "and you'll all be free."

When I returned home, my servants came to me, one by one, and thanked me for what I had done for them. I didn't know how we would all get through the coming winter, but I knew that we would take care of each other and that God would provide.

My new concern was how to continue gathering military secrets without my father. I turned to Sally for help without her ever knowing it. "I'm bored and lonely now that Daddy's gone," I told her. "Will you help me plan some parties or something for entertainment?"

Sally, with her vivacious personality, eagerly embraced the idea. "I would love to. We could have musical evenings, put on plays . . . I know all sorts of parlor games. And let's have a dance, Caroline. Oh, it's been so long since I've danced. Who shall we invite?"

"I was thinking that some of our army officers and government officials and their wives could use some cheering up," I said. "Your family knows all those people don't they?"

"Oh, yes. Mother and Daddy know everyone." She gripped my arm, her eyes dancing with excitement. "I know, we could start a 'starvation club.'"

"What's that?"

"It's when everyone gets together for an evening of socializing, but the hostess doesn't serve any refreshments. In fact, she's forbidden to serve anything—mainly because no one can really afford it. But it still gives us an excuse to spend an evening in each other's company."

Food or no food, an invitation to one of the parties Sally and I hosted quickly became a coveted thing in Richmond that winter, offering welcome relief from the sadness and privation of war. Sally and I also started up the sewing circle again, gathering all the society wives together to knit socks and scarves and mittens for our soldiers. The women's conversation often proved a richer source of information than their husbands'.

It snowed just before Christmas, burying the ugliness of wartime Richmond beneath a blanket of pure white. Unbelievably, this was the third Christmas we had celebrated since the war began. The night of Charles' and my engagement seemed like a lifetime ago, instead of four years. Indeed, hadn't we both lived through a lifetime's worth of experiences since that night? The fact that no end to this war was in sight made our sorrow worse. As we gathered in church on Christmas Eve, everyone prayed that this would be the last Christmas our men would be away from us. I asked for that, too. But while the others continued to pray that the Confederate States would win their independence, I struggled to surrender to God's will, trying to pray "Thy will be done."

Christmas dinner in most Richmond homes was a somber affair. It wasn't the scarcity of food that caused the sadness but the missing faces at each meal, the ever-increasing tally of loved ones who would never return home. I shared a simple meal in the kitchen with my servants again, a quiet celebration of the fact that we were all together, that no one had been sold. The celebration was enriched by baby Isaac's robust laughter as he bounced in his grandfather's arms, pulling on his snowy beard.

I spent Christmas Day with the St. Johns again, but I eagerly looked forward to dinner with them this year because of the secret errand my cousin Jonathan had entrusted to me—delivering Sally's Christmas present on his behalf. Sally hadn't seen him in over a year, ever since he'd recovered from his injury and had returned to fight at Fredericksburg. Of course, wrapping paper and ribbons were nowhere to be found, but I managed to make the present look special by covering the little gift box with an embroidered handkerchief from my trousseau and tying it up with a ribbon cut from one of my hats. For the first time in three years, I was anticipating the holiday.

"Special delivery," I said, handing the present to Sally on Christmas Day. Her family had gathered in her little parlor that morning, huddling around a skimpy fire. "It's from someone who wishes he could have given it to you himself."

"From Jonathan? Really?" She was nearly speechless with delight.

"Go ahead, open it. There's a note from him inside, too."

Sally carefully untied the ribbon and parted the folds of the handkerchief. I saw her hands tremble as she lifted the lid off the box and pulled out a glittering topaz ring.

"Oh . . . it's beautiful!"

"It belonged to our Grandmother Fletcher. Jonathan's father made a special trip into Richmond to deliver it. Read the letter."

Sally covered her mouth with her hand in a futile attempt to hold back her tears as she read the note Jonathan had enclosed. "He's asking me to marry him," she said, looking up at her parents and me. "Daddy . . . ?"

"I know, I know. He already wrote and asked for my permission." Mr. St. John spoke gruffly, as if unwilling to reveal his emotions.

"Did you give him your blessing, Daddy?"

He nodded, frowning. "Very unusual way to court someone, if you ask me. That's the trouble with wars, they disrupt all the old traditions." Sally flew into his arms, hugging him tightly. She hugged her mother, then me.

"Now you and Jonathan are in the same boat as Charles and me," I said, "waiting for the war to end, praying that it happens soon."

"Whoever heard of an engagement by mail?" Mr. St. John mumbled, shaking his head.

Later, when Sally and I were alone in her room, I gave her a second letter from Jonathan—to be opened in private, he had said, after Sally accepted his proposal. I sat across from her on the bed, both of us wrapped in quilts to keep warm, and watched her read his letter through twice. The topaz ring sparkled on her finger.

"Jonathan doesn't want to wait until the war ends," she told me when she finished. "He's trying to get a furlough. He wants us to be married as soon as possible."

"Is that what you want, too?"

She nodded, swiping at her tears before they dripped onto the precious letter and smudged the ink. "I used to dream of a big, fancy wedding in St. Paul's with flowers and bridesmaids and hundreds of guests," she said. "I wanted to wear a beautiful gown and sail to Europe on my wedding trip . . . but now none of that seems important anymore. I only want to be Mrs. Jonathan Fletcher for as long as we both shall live. I love him, Caroline. I love him so much."

I reached for her hand. "I know. I would have gone to a justice of the peace to marry Charles the last time he was home . . . but he wouldn't do it."

"Why not? I know how much he loves you."

"This is hard to say, Sally, but he says he doesn't want to leave me . . . a widow."

The memory of Charles' terrible words sliced through my heart: *"Caroline. You must prepare yourself for the fact that I might die."*

I looked at Sally's stricken face and was sorry I had raised the specter of death on such a joyful day. "Your wedding to Jonathan might not be a lavish one," I said quickly, "but we can make sure it's a wonderful one. Let's plan it together, shall we? Then everything will be ready the moment Jonathan walks through the door. You won't have to waste a single moment of his furlough."

The idea excited her. "Which dress should I wear? My rose silk is the nicest one I have but it's old and quite frayed around the hem. Do you think I can open the seams and turn it so it looks new?"

"Let me see it." As she pulled the dress out of her wardrobe and spread it across the bed, I remembered how beautiful she had looked in it the night of her Christmas party, five years ago. She had stood in her soaring entrance hall, greeting her guests, the stairway behind her decked in candles and greenery. I had been awed by the St. Johns' wealth, their magnificent home, their countless servants. We had no way of knowing on that joyful night what the future held for all of us, that war would ravage that prosperity, that Sally would have to remake a five-year-old dress into her wedding gown. And we couldn't know what next Christmas would bring, either.

For the second time that afternoon, I recalled Charles' terrible words: *"Listen now. I've had to prepare myself . . . and you must, too."*

Quietly, tenderly, I felt the Lord's presence surrounding me, drawing me to Him, coming to dwell among us as He had that first Christmas. As the angels had sung their song of joy, no one in Bethlehem had known about the coming tragedy of the cross—or the triumph of the empty tomb. I couldn't know my future either, but I could trust the One who held it in His hand. I opened my heart and my hands to God, offering Him my dreams, trusting in His resurrection power. *Thy will be done.*

"I want you to wear my wedding dress," I told Sally.

She stared at me, openmouthed.

"I really mean it. The dress and everything else I made for my trousseau are just going to waste, moldering in a trunk at the foot of my bed. It would make me so happy to let you use my things."

"But . . . what about your own wedding?"

"Charles wants to wait until the war ends. By then we'll have boatloads of new dresses to choose from. Please, Sally, let me give it to you for a wedding present—all of it—the dress, the chemise, the petticoats and crinolines. They'll look so beautiful on you."

"I . . . I don't know what to say."

"Say *yes*. Then we can plan your reception, too. Do you suppose they have 'starvation club' receptions during wartime?"

Sally laughed and cried at the same time. "You are so dear to me, Caroline. I'll never be able to thank you. And to think I hated you the first time we met. I was so jealous of you and Jonathan."

"That was his plan that night," I said, smiling. "To storm the castle and win your heart. See how well it worked?"

In the new year, 1864, Sally and I poured our energy into planning her wedding. "You'll have the best reception 'no money' can buy," I joked. All we needed was the groom, and Jonathan wrote to say that he'd threatened to desert if his commanding officer didn't grant him a furlough soon.

While we waited, I continued to host evening get-togethers at my house and afternoon gatherings of our ladies' sewing circle. Our latest project was to stitch a new Confederate uniform jacket for Jonathan, cut from an old blanket and dyed "butternut gray" with homemade dyes. But before we had time to finish it, Sally drove up Church Hill to my house one afternoon with bad news.

"I came to tell you that there won't be any more meetings or parties," she said. "It happened again. Mrs. Fremont came home yesterday to find two of her maidservants missing. So was the emerald necklace that has been in her husband's family for eighty years."

"Oh no." I groaned as I sank into Daddy's chair. This wasn't the first time one of my guests had returned home to find that her servants had run away, taking some of the family valuables with them. "Two of them ran away?" I asked. "And it happened during sewing circle?"

Sally nodded. "That makes four times that somebody's slaves have run off while we were at your house. I'm sorry, but the ladies don't want to come to the meetings anymore. They think . . ."

"What? What do they think? That I'm involved?"

Sally shrugged. "It is an awfully big coincidence."

The thought had occurred to me that my servants might be involved in helping all these slaves run away, that they were using the map I had drawn for Eli. I would have to find out, but for now I had to allay the women's suspicions. "How could I be helping these slaves if I was here at the meeting the entire time? Did you ask them that, Sally? And don't you think it would have happened no matter where we'd met?"

"Please don't be angry with me. I never said it was your fault. I'm only saying that it's what the others think—and it's why they don't want to come here anymore. If we're meeting regularly, you see, the slaves know when to plan their escape."

"Well then," I said, trying to act unconcerned. "If the ladies don't want to come anymore it will be their loss, not mine."

I put on my cloak and gloves later that afternoon and went out to the carriage house to talk to Eli. He had the back door open so he could shovel out the manure, and the stable was freezing cold inside. I hugged myself and rubbed my arms to keep warm while I waited for him to set the shovel aside and close the door.

"If you need to talk, we can go in the kitchen where it's warm," he said.

I shook my head, trying to find a way to begin. "Eli . . . do you know anything about Mrs. Fremont's two servants running away yesterday?"

"Ivy and Lila," he said, smiling faintly. "They's mother and daughter, did you know that? Missus Fremont planning to send Lila away to North Carolina to be a nanny to her son's new baby. Lila only thirteen years old. She ain't never been away from Mama Ivy before. Don't neither one of them want to be torn apart."

His words shook me. I found it easy to see my own servants as individuals who loved and dreamed dreams, just like me. But I had looked past Mrs. Fremont's servants—and everyone else's servants— as if they weren't even there. Now I was learning that their stories were much the same. Tessie had been only fourteen when my father took her from her parents at Hilltop to be my nanny.

"I understand," I said quietly. "What about the other people who have run away?"

"Well now, let's see . . ." he said, settling down on the wooden stool. "There was the two that run off on the same day—Lizzy, the Clarks' chambermaid, and Darby, who worked for the Dunkirks. Those two young people wanting to get married real bad, but their owners wouldn't let them." I thought of Tessie and Josiah. "Mr. Clark had his eye on Lizzy . . . if you know what I mean." Eli looked away, embarrassed.

"Go on," I said after a moment.

"The Smiths' servant, Arthur, hear the massa needing some money and planning on selling him. No telling what a new massa gonna be like." Eli sighed. "I didn't think you'd mind me helping all them people, seeing as they in the same bad way we was a few months ago when your daddy gonna sell us. But I ain't never telling any of them to steal. I'm real sorry they all done that, Missy Caroline. Stealing ain't right."

Eli paused, and I heard the mare whinny softly as she stamped in her clean stall. "I sure hope you ain't mad at me, Missy."

"Not at all," I assured him. "I'm glad you helped them. I would have done the same thing."

"You ain't gonna get in trouble for what I done, are you?"

"I don't think so. It's just gossip. But everyone's afraid to go out and leave their servants alone at home. I'll have to think of another way to gather information."

"Something else you should know," Eli said as he stood and retrieved his shovel. "Two of the St. Johns' servants planning to run away next. Their massa talking about sending them out to dig trenches and build fortifications around Richmond soon as spring comes. Them army folks work the Negroes half to death. And there ain't hardly no food to feed the soldiers, let alone feeding slaves. It's a death sentence, Missy. Those two boys want their freedom, too."

"All right," I said. "Do whatever you have to do to help them, Eli. But please, ask them not to steal from Charles' family."

On a cold, clear night in March of 1864, Jonathan waltzed into my parlor. "Good evening, Cousin," he said, grinning. "Can you spare a tired soldier a bed for one night?"

I ran to hug him. "Jonathan! How did you get here?"

"Let's see, by train . . . wagon . . . horseback . . . on foot. Every means but by boat, I believe. I have a one-week furlough and I already used up a whole day of it getting here."

"How's your arm? Are you all right? Is Charles with you? How did you manage to get a furlough? Charles says they only grant them for hardship cases, and even then—"

"Whoa! One question at a time. I got a furlough by lying, of course. I told them that my—"

"Never mind, I don't think I want to know."

"You don't," he agreed, laughing. "See? That's what happens during wartime—all our fine moral principles go flying out the window and we start lying, cheating, stealing . . . whatever it takes."

I winced when I thought of all my lies and deceptions. "Is Charles with you?" I asked again.

"Sorry. He wasn't willing to risk being shot as a deserter, even to see his sister get married. I went to see Sally before I came here and she says we're getting married tomorrow. I can hardly believe it! So what are the chances of me getting a hot bath before my wedding day? I could really use one. And can your servants do anything about this sorry excuse for a uniform?"

I took a good look at Jonathan for the first time and saw a walking scarecrow. I wanted to weep. He wore a tattered slouch hat, and his coat looked shabbier than the one Eli had been too ashamed to wear in the house. His pants were not even Confederate uniform pants but were blue, like the ones Robert had worn.

"I took them off a dead Yankee," Jonathan said when he saw me eyeing them. "Borrowed his socks and boots, too. Figured he had no more need of them. A lot of our men are barefoot, Caroline. It's pitiful."

"I'm quite certain that Sally would marry you just the way you are, but don't worry, we'll get you cleaned up as good as new. Did Sally tell you? We sewed you a new uniform jacket so you'd look handsome on your wedding day. We have the entire wedding planned. Wait until you see what desperation and ingenuity can accomplish."

Jonathan pulled me into his arms again. "Sally told me everything you've done for us and how you're letting her wear your wedding gown and all. I don't know how I'll ever be able to thank you, Caroline."

"Be happy, Jonathan. That's all the thanks I want . . . just marry Sally and be happy."

I sent Jonathan up to my father's room to start cleaning up, while I ran out to the servants' quarters to tell Gilbert to prepare a bath and Esther to stoke up the fire early tomorrow morning to start baking. We had carefully hoarded flour and sugar for this occasion. But when I burst into the darkened kitchen, the only person I saw was Josiah, sitting in front of the fire with his six-month-old son asleep in his arms. He held Isaac's freedom papers in his hand. For the first time that I could ever recall, the brawny servant didn't look fierce and menacing—he was singing softly to his child.

I started to back out, not wanting to disturb them, but Josiah lifted his head. He looked up at me, and I saw tears glistening on his cheeks.

"Missy Caroline . . ." he said. "Thank you for what you done for my son."

"You're welcome," I whispered.

Jonathan and Sally's wedding day turned out to be a beautiful one. Her servants had gone all over Richmond the night before, as we'd planned, spreading the news that her wedding would be the next day at eleven o'clock at St. Paul's Church. Eli rose before dawn and used a borrowed horse and the special travel permit Mr. St. John had arranged to ride out to Hilltop to fetch Jonathan's parents and his younger brother, Thomas. They arrived just in time to clean the spring mud from their shoes and carriage wheels and race down to the church.

Guests filled the front third of St. Paul's pews; spring sunshine lit up its rainbow-hued windows. I cried as I watched Sally walk down the long aisle on her father's arm, wearing my wedding gown. She looked radiant in it. She carried a bouquet of fake flowers pilfered from all our old bonnets. I turned to glimpse Jonathan's face and saw him fighting tears as he watched Sally walk down the aisle to become his wife. He looked dashing and handsome in his new uniform jacket, even if we had made it too big, not realizing how much weight he had lost.

I thought of Charles a thousand times that day. Our wedding here in St. Paul's, planned to take place nearly three years ago, would have been much the same as this one. Three long years. I tried to picture Charles and myself in their places, tried to recite the vows in my heart along with them, promising to love Charles and cleave to him as long as we both shall live. But I knew that I was praying, *My will be done,* instead of *Thy will be done in earth, as it is in heaven.*

When Dr. Minnegerode pronounced Sally and Jonathan man and wife, I glanced across the aisle at Charles' parents. Against my will, I remembered Charles' words: *"You must prepare yourself . . . I'll need you to be strong, for my parents' sake . . ."*

There had been so few joyous moments since this terrible war began that I determined not to spoil this day with morbid thoughts. I pushed them from my mind and joined my aunt Anne and uncle William for the short carriage ride back to the St. Johns' house for the reception.

The St. Johns' vast drawing room had been opened for the first time in over a year, and every inch of it gleamed—even if there were no fires in the fireplaces and the chandeliers weren't lit. The buffet lunch of carefully hoarded foods had been stretched to the limit by Esther and the St. Johns' cook and was beautifully arrayed on polished silver platters. Daddy's wine, watered down with juice and cider, filled the punch bowl, and we raised crystal glasses to toast the new bride and groom. The only musicians we could find were the members of the Home Guard band, comprised of old men and young boys who were ineligible to fight, but we waltzed to military marches that afternoon, pretending it was Richmond's finest orchestra.

Sally and I had been unable to arrange a hotel room ahead of time. There hadn't been an empty room anywhere in town for the past three years, so Ruby, Tessie, and I prepared Mother's bedroom as a bridal suite. Sally and Jonathan retired there that evening—and didn't come out again until Jonathan's furlough was nearly over, five days later. I envied their happiness.

"Take care of her for me, Caroline," Jonathan begged when it was finally time for him to leave.

"I will. You be careful now, okay? And please, don't forget to tell Charles that I love him."

Josiah was returning to the front with Jonathan, and he could barely tear himself away from Tessie and his son. "I was afraid you and Josiah were going to run away," I told Tessie later. "I wouldn't blame you if you had."

She reached out to stroke my hair and caress my cheek. "I couldn't leave you, honey," she said. "Don't you know that you my child, too?"

23

SPRING 1864

"I understand that the roads are drying out," Mrs. St. John said with a sigh. "I suppose that means the fighting will begin again."

Sally and her mother and a mere handful of other ladies had gathered in my parlor, along with all our maidservants and Negro seamstresses, for an afternoon of sewing. We weren't sewing for the soldiers this time but for ourselves, helping each other restitch last year's faded and frayed summer clothing into something we could wear now that warmer weather had arrived in Richmond. Even if bolts of new cloth could somehow make it through the blockade and onto store shelves, none of us could afford to buy any. But Sally had the latest copy of *Godey's Lady's Book,* and we were doing our best to remake our clothes in the newest styles.

"Well, even if it does mean more fighting," one of the other ladies said, "I'm so glad another winter is finally over and done with."

"I was just thinking this morning that it's been three years since our first victory at Fort Sumter," Sally said. "Remember that night in 1861 when all of Richmond celebrated? We went together, Caroline—you and Charles, Jonathan, and me."

"Yes, I remember," I said. "In one of the speeches that night, didn't someone predict that the war would be over in sixty days or maybe even thirty days? How in the world has it stretched to three years?"

"I remember the first time we thought the Yankees were going to invade Richmond on that warship, the *Pawnee*," Mrs. St. John said, her scissors busily snipping a seam. "How foolish we were, worrying like that when there hadn't been any danger at all." She smiled at the memory.

That had been the first of many nights that I had prayed for Charles' safety. He had been in real danger many times since then, fighting in some of the bloodiest battles of the war—Manassas, Malvern Hill, Sharpsburg, Fredericksburg, Gettysburg. I had decided to trust God that first night, and so far, He had kept Charles safe.

"My husband was adding it all up the other day," Mrs. St. John said. "The Yankees have set out to make Richmond their prize six times, under six different commanding generals—McDowell, McClellan, Hooker, Burnside . . . I can't even remember all the others he named, but there were six of them. And they all failed."

"I guess that makes General Grant the seventh," Sally said, threading another needle. "I've heard he has a reputation for stubbornness, but I'm sure our men will drive him back just like they chased away all the others."

Everyone agreed with Sally except me. I silently hoped that Grant would succeed where the others had failed so that my life with Charles could finally begin. I longed for this war to end before more blood had to be shed and before the war completely ravaged the South. The longer the conflict dragged on, the greater the odds that Charles would be wounded, taken prisoner, or killed in action, like so many tens of thousands of other men. I just wanted it to end—I wanted the slaves to be freed and this terrible, bloody war to end.

"My husband said the Yankees will be coming at us from more than one direction this time," Mrs. St. John said. "Grant will go after Lee's army near Fredericksburg, and General Butler is going to come up the opposite shore of the James to try to cut us off from our southern rail lines. Some other general whose name I forget is going to move up the Shenandoah Valley to try to cut Lee off from his supply base at Lynchburg."

"Jonathan says to let them come, we'll be ready for them," Sally said. "He says our men are digging in, building a line of defense more than sixty miles long, from northeast of Richmond to south of Petersburg. When Grant attacks our fortifications he'll lose so many men that the North will finally get sick of this war."

"My husband says this is an election year up north," another woman added. "He says that Mr. Lincoln isn't very popular, so if we can just hold the Yankees off until November, maybe the new president will make peace."

"Is there any truth to the rumors that Richmond is going to be evacuated soon?" I asked, fishing for information.

But before anyone had a chance to reply, Mr. St. John suddenly arrived, storming into the parlor without waiting to be announced. He looked so badly shaken that I dropped my scissors and thimble, immediately fearing for Charles.

"My dears, you need to come home right away," he said. "Two of our servants have run off—Jeremiah and Gus."

I closed my eyes in relief. Eli had warned that the two men planned to escape rather than help dig miles and miles of fortifications for the Rebel army.

"Did they rob us? Is anything missing?" Mrs. St. John asked, hastily gathering up her sewing.

"I'm not sure. I don't know where you and Sally have hidden all your things. I think you'd better come home and help me look."

The other ladies quickly packed away their sewing, too. "Oh, I do hope nothing irreplaceable is missing," Mrs. St. John said as her servant fetched her bonnet and shawl.

"I warned you," Mr. St. John said. "I told you that I thought it unwise for you to come here together, didn't I?"

I gladly closed the front door behind him.

When I was alone, I wrapped a shawl around my shoulders against the spring chill and went out through the drawing room doors into the yard. I had watched Eli and Gilbert through the windows all afternoon as I'd sewed. They were working in our garden, planting the food we would eat in the months ahead. I silently thanked God for them—that they hadn't left me, that they knew how to keep us all from starving. The lovely mazes of flower beds and boxwood hedges were gone, but it didn't matter. With the Yankees planning to besiege Richmond, food was much more important. The last time I had looked in my father's hollow book, only four gold coins remained.

At the rear of the yard, the magnolia tree that Grady and I used to climb was getting ready to bloom. Charles had kissed me beneath that tree the night he'd left for the war. Last winter, I had told Eli he could chop it down for firewood if we needed to, but he had urged me to wait. "We can bundle up to keep warm, Missy. But a tree that fine takes too many years to grow back."

When Eli looked up and saw me he stopped digging. "Something wrong, Missy?"

I shook my head. "I just thought you'd like to know that the St. Johns' servants, Jeremiah and Gus, ran away this morning."

He leaned against his shovel. "I was expecting it any day," he said slowly. "They didn't steal nothing, did they? I made them both promise that they wouldn't."

"The St. Johns aren't sure yet. They just went home to look things over."

I stood watching the two men work for a while, their shovels and hoes churning the rich brown earth, and I was suddenly filled with an intense longing for Hilltop. I remembered the way it had looked before the war, with verdant crops growing in the fields and the smokehouse filled with hams—and Jonathan holding my hand as we walked in the fragrant woods, naming all the trees that were no longer there. I wondered if he and Charles and my father would have entered into this war so willingly if they could have seen how much they would lose. Even if the South won the war today, would it have been worth such a staggering cost?

My thoughts were interrupted when Ruby came up behind me and rested her hand on my shoulder. "Missy Caroline . . . I'm sorry, honey, but there's a man here to see you. He say he has news about your daddy."

"Oh, no . . . did he say what kind of news?"

"Tell you the truth, I was scared to ask. He waiting in the front hallway for you."

I drew a deep breath and followed Ruby inside, my heart jumping. The man waiting for me in the foyer was dressed in working clothes, like the sailors I'd seen loading my father's ships down at Rocketts Wharf. He carried a revolver stuck in his belt and looked as I imagined a pirate would, with a scarred, weather-beaten face and a mangy beard. He frightened me at first, making me wish Gilbert or Eli had come into the house with me.

"Afternoon, ma'am. My name's John Dooley." He smiled nervously, revealing a gold tooth.

"How do you do? I'm Caroline Fletcher. Would you like to step into the library?"

He shook his head, staring at his feet. I couldn't tell what was making him so uncomfortable—if it was me, our extravagant home, or the news he had brought.

"I understand you have news of my father, George Fletcher?"

"Yes, ma'am . . . that is, I wish I had news other than what I got, which is the fact that . . . well, he's missing, you see."

"Could you please explain?"

"Yes, ma'am. We was aboard a small steamship called the *Florida*, running the blockade at Wilmington. The Yanks have the main entrance to the Cape Fear River blocked, you see, but we can still use a narrow passageway around the other side because it's protected by our Confederate guns at Fort Fisher. So we did like we always done, you see, which is to chart a course along the coast, like we was planning to sail on past it. But then we turned and made a run toward shore at the last minute, trying to outrun them. This time we couldn't quite make it, ma'am. It was the coal, you see."

"The . . . coal? You mean, your cargo was too heavy?"

"No, ma'am. The coal that fires our boilers ain't worth a . . . pardon me. It's poor quality, you see, and we can't go as fast as we used to. The Yanks spotted us and came after us, firing their cannon. We took a hole in our hull on the starboard side. Captain Fletcher kept us steaming for as long as he could, trying to beach us on land, but the ship started to sink. Some of us swam to shore safely, but the Yanks sent out longboats and picked the rest of the men out of the water."

"So now they're prisoners of war?"

"That's right, ma'am. The captain was one of the last to leave, you see, making sure everybody else had a chance to get overboard. Now he's missing. Mind you, he might have been picked up by the Yanks, so you can't give up hope."

I thanked Mr. Dooley for coming and offered him payment for his trouble. He refused. "I had to come, you see, because the other fellows and me . . . well, we have the highest regard for Captain Fletcher."

I didn't break down until after Mr. Dooley left. Then I fell into Tessie's arms, praying, "Please, God . . . no. Not Daddy."

That spring, Charles and Jonathan fought in some of the fiercest battles of the entire war. The fighting that took place in the wilderness, outside Fredericksburg on May 5 and 6, was so horrific that neither Sally nor I could bear to look at the casualty lists. We waited in the carriage together, praying, while Sally's mother went to read them, then we wept and thanked God when we learned that He had spared both men.

Our grim tasks at Chimborazo Hospital began all over again, with wounded soldiers pouring in at the rate of several thousand a day. Sally and I worked for as many hours as we could bear before collapsing with exhaustion, but for all of our efforts, some days it seemed as though the angel of death laughed in our faces. I cut up the last of the linens from my hope chest to make bandages when the hospital ran out of them.

Many of the soldiers I tended wept as they described the terrible battle that had taken place in the wilderness's dense thickets and tangled woods. They told me that more than two hundred wounded men had burned to death as fires swept through the underbrush. General Longstreet, who had been Charles' commander for so long, had been severely wounded.

Our troops weren't the only ones who'd suffered. The Yankees lost so many thousands of men that everyone believed General Grant would retreat, just as all the defeated Union generals before him had. But regardless of his losses, Grant kept moving forward toward Richmond, skirting around Lee's forces to the south and east. The exhausted Rebels marched forward to meet him, battling him again at Spotsylvania on May 8. That battle surged back and forth all day, the terrible fighting continuing until after midnight. One of the thousands of wounded men I tended told me that the artillery and rifle fire had been so intense that an entire forest of trees, many more than a foot and a half thick, had been reduced to stumps by bullets and shells. In places, the dead lay piled four deep where they had fallen.

Since Charles had little time to write, his letters became more brief and, for me, more precious.

We have been fighting for six long days. When I close my eyes at night it's very difficult to erase the horrifying sights and sounds from my mind. And so I curl beneath my blanket on the hard ground and dream of the day when you will lie in my arms at night. I study your picture before every engagement so that your face is the last thing I see before the enemy charges. I carry it in my breast pocket, above my heart. . . .

In Richmond, we felt the pressure of the enemy closing in on us from several directions. While Lee's men held off the main body of Yankees, a smaller force under General Sheridan marched to the northern outskirts of the city. The Home Guard, along with every available man, young and old, scrambled to our defense. The Confederate cavalry under J.E.B. Stuart arrived in time to stop Sheridan, but Stuart himself was wounded in the fight at Yellow Tavern and later died. Meanwhile, more Yankee troops under General Butler set out from the south, making it as far as Richmond's "back door" before Rebel forces drove them away. Everyone in the city knew our armies were fighting for their very lives—and for ours.

On the first three days of June, Charles battled the Yankees again at Cold Harbor. They were now only nine miles from Richmond. We could hear the artillery and smell the gunpowder and smoke whenever the wind blew in our direction. And, of course, we tended to endless wagonloads of wounded. The Union Army had threatened Richmond before, but as Grant edged closer and closer, not giving up in spite of staggering losses, we all wondered if the city would finally fall this time.

Grant seems to have a determination that the other generals lacked. He doesn't care how many of his own men die, and has vowed to stay here all summer if he has to. Our Confederate forces were well entrenched at Cold Harbor, and we turned back fourteen separate Union assaults before the Yanks refused to obey orders to attack again. In a matter of hours, Caroline, we killed about seven thousand of their men, and I pray I never have to do anything like that again. The dead littered the ground for more than five acres. Grant may have hoped that this would be the decisive battle, but he couldn't defeat us. . . .

We all thought General Grant would move toward Richmond next, and Charles marched south again with Lee's army to meet him.

But Grant skirted around the city instead, crossing the James River on a pontoon bridge, and headed south toward Petersburg to try to choke off our main supply routes. Petersburg nearly fell on June 15, but the meager Rebel troops stationed there held off a Union force more than three times larger than their own before reinforcements arrived. Then the two armies reached a standstill.

> *This war has become a digging contest. We've attacked and killed and maimed each other for six weeks, and now both sides have dug in for a siege. I guess it will continue this way until one of us runs out of men.*
>
> *Meanwhile, we live like moles in a maze of trenches called zig-zags that are open to rain and sun, shell and mortar fire. During a battle, thousands of us are crammed in, side by side, and we can't get out, stand up, stretch our arms and legs, or even lie down to sleep, for days at a time. Something as simple as raising your head or going for a cup of water could cost you your life. At night, we can hear the enemy talking to each other in their trenches in between the shelling. We can even smell the smoke of their cigarettes.*
>
> *When the war first started, I remember how we all dove for cover whenever we heard the sound of cannon or rifle fire. But now I'm so used to the sound of bullets singing over my head and shells exploding day and night, and men dying on either side of me, that I can hardly recall any other way of life. Caroline, my love, I don't write all these alarming things to upset you, but so that you will understand the truth of my situation—and be prepared. The love we share keeps me strong. My dreams of our future together encourage me to go on.*
>
> *I love you,*
> *Charles*

"We been through a lot of hard times in this war," Esther said with a sigh, "but I do believe this summer we seen the hardest times yet. Good thing you never did eat much, Missy, cause we sure ain't having very much to eat these days."

We were all gathered in the kitchen for our supper one hot night in July. In order to conserve fuel, it was the only meal Esther cooked each day. Richmond was very close to starvation because of the siege. The food that did make it through on the remaining rail line had to be shared with the troops guarding the city. At our house we had fresh produce, thanks to Eli and Gilbert, but no meat except for the fish I brought home from my visits to Mr. Ferguson. I still brought him a few tidbits of news each week, mostly things I'd learned from the steady stream of wounded men arriving at the hospital. Sometimes I managed to glean a little more information at the countless funerals I attended.

"I'm gonna ask you something, Missy," Esther continued, fanning herself in the summer heat. "I sure hope you ain't gonna get upset with me."

"Of course not, Esther." I bent to pick up baby Isaac, who was clamoring to crawl up onto my lap. "You may ask me anything."

"Well . . . they selling meat in the market, but I ain't sure you want me to buy it. I think I can probably cook it up real nice and feed all of us a good meal for once . . . but I ain't sure if I should tell you what it is first or just serve it up. I decide I better ask you."

"What is it?" I asked quietly.

"It's rat meat." Esther must have seen by my expression that the idea revolted me. "They selling it in the butcher shop," she quickly added, "all cleaned and dressed like any other kind of meat. I talk to some folks that try it and they say it ain't no different than squirrel. Said you'd never tell the difference if you didn't know."

I looked around the table at the others. "What about all of you?" I asked. "Could the rest of you eat it?" Only Gilbert and Eli were willing to try. "Buy it and cook it for them—and for whoever else is willing," I told her. "Maybe someday I'll be hungry enough to eat rat meat, but I'm not that desperate yet."

In August we celebrated Isaac's first birthday. I had written the date in the family Bible so we would all remember. "He's a free man, not a slave," I told the others, "so it's important that he always knows when his birthday is and how old he is."

Esther baked a tiny pancake for him and drizzled it with sorghum. Tessie gave him a tallow candle to blow out, the only kind we had. I wished that I could buy dozens of presents to repay him for the joy he had brought all of us during the past year, but Isaac was content with the tiny wooden animals Gilbert had carved for him.

The city of Atlanta fell to the Yankees' General Sherman in September. They burned it to the ground. Since everyone in Richmond was already half-starved and worried about our own fate, the news was a severe blow, reminding us of what might soon happen to us. A large part of the South already lay in ruins, and Sherman had vowed to continue to battle across the state of Georgia, all the way to the Atlantic Ocean.

On the day we learned that Atlanta had fallen, my uncle William and cousin Thomas drove their wagon up to our backyard gate.

"Won't you both come in?" I invited. "I can find you something to eat and fix you some mint tea."

"Thank you, but I can't stay," Uncle William said. "I'll let your stable boy water my horses, but then I have to head home. I want to get back before dark."

"Are you staying, Thomas?" I asked. He had jumped down from the wagon, carrying a small satchel.

"I'm joining the army, Caroline," he said proudly.

"You can't be! You're only . . . how old? Sixteen?" But then I recalled how the Confederate Government, desperate for soldiers, had extended the draft to include boys aged fourteen to eighteen for the junior reserve and men aged forty-five to sixty for the senior reserve. They would be trained and kept in reserve for rear-guard duty.

"I'm finally old enough to fight, just like Jonathan," he said.

I still thought of Thomas as the six-year-old child he'd been the first time I'd visited Hilltop, even though he was several inches taller than me. But at sixteen, he was still a long way from manhood. How could any government ask its children to fight? How could they ask this family, who had already given so much to this war, for yet another one of its sons? It didn't seem fair.

"Isn't it true that if a plantation has more than twenty slaves, the owner can get an exemption from the draft?" I asked Uncle William. "Couldn't you sign over the deed to Thomas so he wouldn't have to go?"

My uncle slowly shook his head. "Caroline, there aren't that many slaves left at Hilltop."

"Besides, I want to fight," Thomas added.

"You don't mean that," I said. "Please, come to the hospital with me and talk to some of the wounded men. Let them tell you what—"

"That's enough," my uncle said quietly. "The boy has no choice. If I were one year younger, they would have drafted me, too."

"I'm sorry," I mumbled.

"May he spend the night with you, Caroline? He has to report to the armory in the morning. If you could have your driver bring him there tomorrow, I'd be obliged."

Eli had tended to the horses while we'd talked. Too soon, Uncle William was ready to make the return trip to Hilltop. I suppose it was a blessing that Thomas had no idea what he was getting into. He embraced his father with dry eyes, thinking only of the excitement that lay ahead. But my uncle's back was bowed like a very old man's as he drove away.

"May I help you?" The burly man who addressed me from behind the butcher's block in Mr. Ferguson's fish stall was a stranger. He looked straight at me, eye-to-eye, something Mr. Ferguson had never done. I couldn't reply. "Is something wrong?" he asked.

"You're not the man who usually waits on me."

"Yeah, well, he was called away unexpectedly. He has entrusted all of his business matters to me while he's away." His gaze remained locked with mine, as if he was trying to read my thoughts. "The shad is especially good today," he said.

I didn't know what to do. Should I trust him? Was he another Union agent working with Ferguson, or was this a trap? The man had phrased his explanation very oddly—*"He has entrusted all of his business matters to me."* It didn't sound like something an ordinary fish vendor would say. I carried information about possible weak spots in the Confederate defenses, but I couldn't take the risk of giving it to a stranger. What should I say to him that wouldn't arouse suspicion?

I decided to simply purchase the fish and leave. Then I remembered that I'd already wrapped up the note I was delivering inside the only currency I had. I forced myself to stay calm. If I let my panic show he would surely notice.

"How much is the shad today?" I asked.

"For a lovely lady like yourself? It's a bargain at four dollars."

"Oh. That's much more than I have," I said. "Good day." I walked back to the carriage on shaking legs and told Eli what had happened.

"Just have to wait and see," he said. "That's all we can do."

Three days later, all of Richmond had heard the news—the authorities had arrested another Yankee spy, a man by the name of Floyd Ferguson who sold fish from a stall in the farmers' market.

"That's him, ain't it?" Tessie asked, reading the paper.

"Yes," I replied. "Thank God I didn't trust the man taking his place. I think it must have been a trap."

According to the papers, Ferguson would set out on the James River in his fishing boat once a week and deliver his espionage reports to a Yankee boat sent from Fortress Monroe. Authorities suspected that several of his customers passed secret information to him as they purchased fish, since they'd discovered incriminating notes wrapped inside the money in Ferguson's apron pocket. So far, the police had not arrested anyone else.

My days of spying were over. In a way I felt enormous relief, especially since the information I'd been gathering concerned the army Charles fought with, the trenches he guarded. Yet I also felt that I had let God down.

I shared my frustration with Eli as he harvested the last of the summer vegetables from our garden. "All my hard work, all my lies and deceptions have been for nothing," I said. "They still haven't bought a Yankee victory or helped free the slaves. Why did God ask me to risk so much if it was all for nothing?"

"You don't know that it was all for nothing," Eli said, brushing dirt from the carrots he'd just pulled. "You only seeing the outside of things. Nobody except God can see what He's doing underneath. The seeds I planted last spring been growing into carrots whether we seen it or not. God gonna have His way, Missy, even when it look like His plans isn't amounting to nothing."

His answer confused me. "Then what difference does it make if I obey Him or not—whether I risk everything to spy for Him or stay at home—if He's going to do it all anyway?"

Eli pulled another clump of carrots, then slowly stood to face me. "We ain't gonna eat the tops of these carrots, are we?"

"No ... but what does that—"

"Can't you see, Missy Caroline?" he said gently. "Spying ain't the job God gave you to do in this here war. He don't need people to do stuff like that for Him. What He need is for you and me to show folks what He's like ... to love others for Him. That's the real work you done ... underneath it all."

"How? How could betraying my country possibly show God's love?"

"I tell you one way," he said, crumbling the dirt off the vegetables as he talked. "My son Josiah hate white folks. He think they all alike. He turn away from Massa Jesus because he think Jesus is the white folks' God. But Josiah seen that you different—not because you spying, but because you spying for us, so that we could be free."

I remembered the tender look I'd seen on Josiah's face as he'd held his son, the tears on his cheeks as he'd thanked me.

"I been trying to tell Josiah about God's love all his life," Eli continued, "and he ain't listening. But he seen your love, Missy Caroline, he seen how you risk everything you have for us . . . and so he finally seen God's love—in you."

My tale is nearly told now. There's only one more episode to describe, and that's the afternoon when I knew that the end had finally come for me. Charles' father arrived at my door, his face the sickly gray color of dirty water. He looked much too unwell to be out of bed, let alone out of the house.

"Are you all right? Did something happen . . . ?" He ignored my questions, pushing past me to enter my father's library. What worried me more than his obvious illness was the anger in his eyes—no, I saw hatred when he looked at me.

"I need to see one of your father's books," he said. He began perusing the shelves without waiting for my permission. I could hear his labored breathing all the way across the room, as if his lungs were a pair of worn-out bellows that could barely pump air. I was afraid he would find the hollowed-out volume, even though it now held only two or three gold pieces.

"Please, let me help you," I said. "Are you looking for a particular book?"

"Yes. This one."

He pulled *A Tale of Two Cities* from the shelf. Something about that book alarmed me but I didn't know why. Then Mr. St. John took a piece of paper from his pocket and unfolded it. It was the map I'd drawn on a page torn from that book. I watched, paralyzed, as Mr.

St. John opened the book to the beginning, to the place where the title page should be. When the map fitted perfectly into place he groaned, swaying as though he was about to collapse. I tried to help him sit down but he waved me away as if my touch would poison him.

"I knew you were involved . . . I knew it!" he said, wheezing. "They recaptured one of our escaped slaves. He had this map . . . and these false documents. . . ." I recognized the freedom papers he showed me as forgeries of the ones my father had drawn up for Isaac. The name had been changed to Jeremiah St. John.

"We got Jeremiah to confess that one of the servants from the ladies' sewing circle forged these, but he refuses to say who. Every time someone was robbed, though, the victim was here, visiting you. Now you're going to tell me which one of your slaves can read and write."

"Please . . . Mr. St. John . . ."

"If you don't tell me, then I swear I'll beat a confession out of every last one of them."

I went cold at his words. "You will not lay a hand on any of my slaves. I drew that map."

He stared at me, his eyes filled with loathing, not surprise. Perspiration dampened his hair and rolled down his flushed face.

"I drew the map for my servants when I found out that Daddy planned to sell some of them." I said. "I don't have much gold left, but I'll pay you and all the others for the slaves they lost and for the property their servants stole. It was wrong of them to steal, but I'm not sorry that any of them escaped."

He glared at me. "So you finally admit that you're a Union sympathizer?"

"I believe that slavery is morally wrong."

He set the book and the papers on Daddy's desk. "None of us ever imagined that you were deliberately deceiving us all this time, Caroline—least of all Charles. We should have guessed when you spent so much time visiting your Yankee prisoner, but we all wanted to believe that you were telling the truth, that your visits were purely humanitarian. You played us for fools. I should have listened to Major Turner. He was convinced that you were involved in that prison break. And he says you also had an improper relationship with your Yankee friend."

"That's a lie! I did no such thing!" I had listened to Mr. St. John's accusations in stunned shock, but I couldn't let the last one pass for truth.

He held up his hand to silence me. "I'm not finished. The fish vendor, Ferguson, has been suspected of spying for some time. He was watched. The police told me that you were a regular customer—which is odd since you have six slaves to do all your shopping for you. The authorities asked me if I thought you might be involved, and like a fool I defended you. Now I'm not so sure. They found incriminating notes wrapped inside the money Ferguson collected. All I need to do is compare that handwriting with your writing on this map or with some of the letters you've sent my son. What am I going to discover then, Caroline?"

I couldn't speak. I was afraid I was going to be sick.

"When I think of all the important people you've entertained in your home," he continued, "all the crucial information you might have overheard . . . That's why you continued to have social gatherings here, isn't it? Even after your father left. You deliberately deceived us! You used my son . . . my daughter . . ." He gripped his left shoulder suddenly, wincing in pain.

"Please, you need to sit down, Mr. St. John. Let me get you something—"

"No!" he shouted. "You've done enough harm as it is. And the biggest tragedy of all is that my son loves you. He loves you! I can't imagine what this news will do to him. What were you thinking, Caroline? How could you lie to Charles like this, pretending that you loved him when—"

"I wasn't pretending. I do love Charles."

"How can you possibly say you love him when you've been helping his enemies?" Mr. St. John tried to take a step, then gripped the edge of the desk to keep from falling. "I don't know what to do," he said, wheezing. "Charles must be told the truth. But if he learns it now, while lying in a filthy trench, I fear he'll be so devastated that he won't want to live. I won't let you kill my son."

His hands trembled as he refolded the map and phony documents and put them back in his coat pocket. He picked up my father's book. He stared at me, but it was as if he was looking through me. His face had been flushed with rage a moment ago, but now it was as colorless as a corpse.

"I don't know what to do about you," he said, shaking his head. "If you're guilty of half the things I think you are, then I want you arrested . . . no, I want you to hang! But if the truth about you comes out now . . . it will destroy my son. . . ."

There was nothing more I could say.

Mr. St. John managed to stagger to the door without me. I watched his servant help him into his carriage and drive away.

Two days passed, then three. Now four. I have no idea what will happen to me. All I can do is wait, wondering when my arrest will come. In the meantime, I've been unable to sleep. I decided to write this account, explaining my reasons for doing what I've done. I pray that when you read it you will understand how I became entangled in all of this. And that you will find it in your heart to forgive me.

I offer no defense except these words from the book of Proverbs: "'If thou faint in the day of adversity, thy strength is small. If thou forbear to deliver them that are drawn to death, and those that are ready to be slain; If thou sayest, Behold, we knew it not; doth not he that pondereth the heart consider it? . . . and shall not he render to every man according to his works?'"

Caroline Ruth Fletcher

September 1864

Part Two

You, O Lord, keep my lamp burning; my God turns my darkness into light. With your help I can advance against a troop; with my God I can scale a wall.

Psalm 18:28–29 NIV

CHAPTER
24

Artillery boomed in the distance, shaking the floor beneath Caroline's feet as she stood with Tessie on the balcony off her father's bedroom. "It might be coming from Drewry's Bluff," she said. "The Yankees might be trying to send warships up the river past the fort again."

"Sounds closer than that, Missy. Look there. . . ." Tessie pointed to the southeast where flashes of light illuminated the low-hanging clouds like summer lightning. "Those big guns gotta be this side of the river."

"I think you're right. Maybe it's coming from Fort Harrison."

Caroline knew from months of spying that the outer ring of Confederate defenses encircling Richmond was less than ten miles away; the inner ring, not even four. This current battle, which had begun yesterday, September 28, was one of the closest ones yet to her home. She also knew that Lee's troops, defending this sixty-five-mile-long perimeter, were spread very thinly in places.

Charles and Jonathan might be fighting out there somewhere.

In his last letter, Charles had said they were being sent up from Petersburg to counteract a rumored buildup of Yankee forces near New Market Heights. Now a horrific battle was raging out in that direction. At times, the artillery fired so rapidly that it sounded like one continuous boom.

"Here comes Eli," Tessie said, pointing down to the street below them. "Let's go see what he find out."

"Yankees started attacking the Confederate lines yesterday," Eli told them when they reached the backyard. "Rumors say they already capture Fort Harrison. Now they trying to capture Fort Gilmer."

"Get the carriage ready, Eli. I'd better go up to Chimborazo. It's the closest hospital to where they're fighting. They'll be bringing the wounded there first."

Tessie held Caroline's arm to stop her. "Honey . . . you can't," she said quietly. "Remember?"

Caroline moaned and leaned against her friend. "No . . . I completely forgot."

Two days ago, Sally Fletcher had come to her front door—a very different Sally from the friend and near-sister Caroline had known for so long. Sally had offered no word of greeting or other pleasantries, refusing to look Caroline in the eye, and would come no further than the foyer. She delivered her message in a voice that was distant and cold.

"My father told us what you've done, Caroline. I didn't want to believe it. The shock of it has made Father so ill—" she paused as her voice quavered. "So ill that he's been bedridden ever since."

"I'm so sorry."

Sally held up both hands to silence her. "Don't talk, Caroline, just listen. Father sent me in his place to tell you that until he's well enough to decide what to do with you, he wants you to remain at home. Don't go anywhere, not even to church, or he will have you arrested. Don't leave the house, and don't entertain visitors. When you write to Charles, you can't tell him anything about this."

"Sally, please listen. You're my dearest friend, and nothing I've done will ever change that."

"You're wrong. I feel so betrayed by you, Caroline. I trusted you . . . loved you. I can't even imagine what this news will do to Charles, but I agree with my father—Charles must not be told about you while he's still fighting. If he found out right now that he's in love with a traitor, it would kill him. But as soon as Charles is safe, Father is going to tell him everything."

Even now as Caroline stood in her backyard, the memory of Sally's words sent a shiver through her. Her dearest friend wouldn't even try to understand or forgive her. She was not trusted to care for wounded soldiers at Chimborazo.

The sounds of battle continued all day. Artillery still echoed sporadically off Richmond's hills later that night as Caroline sat in the kitchen with her servants, talking quietly after their evening meal. The only light came from the fireplace, now dying into embers. Outside, clouds shrouded the moon and stars while cannon fire flickered on the horizon.

A sound outside made Caroline look up. Her heart pounded with dread when she saw Josiah standing in the open doorway.

He wore no shirt, only ragged trousers. Dried blood smeared his broad chest and hands. Caroline took one look at his dark, somber face and scrambled to her feet, terrified of what he might say.

"Make her sit down," Josiah said, pointing to her.

"No . . . Oh, God, no . . . not Jonathan . . ." she cried out. Eli pulled Caroline into his arms and held her tightly. She felt as if she stood onboard a ship in a storm and was about to be blown overboard.

"It ain't Jonathan," Josiah said. "It's Massa Charles."

"No!" Pain tore through Caroline, as sharp and real as any gunshot.

"He's hurt real bad," Josiah continued. "They bring him to that big hospital up on the hill, just now."

"Oh, God, please don't let him die," Caroline wept. "Please . . . please . . ."

"I'll get the carriage ready," Gilbert said. Josiah stepped aside as the servant hurried out the door.

"What happened, son?" Eli asked.

"They been fighting hard all day. I went looking for Massa Jonathan when he ain't coming back with some of the others. Couldn't find him. I look everywhere . . . lots of dead and wounded . . . but I ain't seeing him. I only find Massa Charles, lying there in that hole."

"Sweet Massa Jesus . . ." Tessie prayed as she rocked Isaac, who was sleeping on her lap. "Help him, Massa Jesus . . ."

"Ain't gonna lie to you and pretend it ain't bad," Josiah said. "The men who picking up the wounded walk right on past him, thinking he good as dead with two big holes in him and bleeding so bad. But I tore up my shirt and stuffed the hole in his chest like I seen the doctors do, and I wrap one of the shirtsleeves around his leg. His head bleeding bad, too. Then I carry him to the forward aid station, but they keep walking past him, saying there ain't much hope. So I carry him to the field hospital, about half-mile back, and put him on the first ambulance I see, not waiting for nobody's permission. Ambulance just now bring him to that big place up on the hill."

Esther handed Josiah his father's coat to put on. "Does his family know about Massa Charles?"

Josiah shook his head. "I came here first."

"Guess someone better go on down and tell them," Eli said. "But first we got to get Missy up to the hospital."

Gilbert returned to the kitchen just then. "Carriage ready," he said.

Caroline tried to walk but her legs wouldn't hold her. Eli lifted her into his arms. "Oh, God, please don't take Charles," she pleaded as he carried her outside into the dark autumn night. "Please don't take him!"

They crossed the backyard toward the open gate, and a memory came to Caroline, sharp and clear. Eli had carried Tessie in his arms the same way while Tessie had pleaded, *"Don't take him . . . please don't take him!"* But the men had dragged Grady through the open gate in spite of Tessie's pleas.

A terrible fear suddenly gripped Caroline. Charles was going to die in payment for that sin.

It seemed to Caroline that hours passed before she found out where they'd taken Charles in the sprawling hospital complex. In spite of Josiah's warning, she wasn't prepared for the sight of him—his uniform drenched in his own blood, his face as pale as death. Huge, raw wounds punctured his right shoulder and thigh and creased the side of his head. She lifted his hand and found a faint heartbeat, touched her lips to his and felt the warmth of his breath.

"Please, God . . ."

It took longer still for Caroline to find a doctor who would agree to waste time on such a seemingly hopeless case. He finally consented only because he recognized Caroline and remembered her tireless work at the hospital. Charles' family arrived, and they waited in icy silence for the doctor to finish the surgery. He came out to speak with them when he was done.

"He's still alive . . . but barely. I'm sorry I can't offer you a great deal of hope."

"We're taking him home," Charles' father announced.

"If you move him now you'll kill him," the doctor said. "He's too weak. Wait a few days, until he recovers from the surgery. Miss Fletcher knows how to administer the very finest care. She has done excellent work here."

The St. Johns stayed for several hours, hoping in vain that Charles would regain consciousness. But Mr. St. John was still quite ill himself, and Sally was distraught over the news that Jonathan was missing. They decided to return home for the night. Before leaving, Charles' father stunned Caroline with an announcement. "Your cousin's servant, Josiah, will remain with us. Since Sally is Jonathan's wife, the Negro now belongs to her."

"No, wait. . . ." Caroline begged. "Josiah's wife and child live with me. At least let them be together—"

"Why? So you can help him escape like you helped all the others? You must take me for a fool."

"But Josiah saved Charles' life. Your son would be lying dead in a trench out there if Josiah hadn't brought him here. You have to—"

"Don't you dare tell me what I have to do with my slaves." Mr. St. John limped to the door, then turned to look at his son again before leaving. His eyes filled with tears. "I'll let you take care of him for now because I want him to live. But as soon as he's well enough, I'm going to tell him the truth about you." He left without another word.

As Caroline waited by Charles' bedside that long night, some of the other men in the room began to moan. One of them wept softly. Without even thinking, Caroline went to them, one by one, and tended to their needs—giving one a drink of water, quietly praying with another. She closed the staring eyes of one young man who had died and gently pulled the sheet over his face. When she returned to Charles' cot, she noticed Eli still sitting on the floor beside him.

"You may as well go home, too, Eli. I don't intend to leave Charles' side."

"Me either," he said, shaking his head. "I staying here to pray for him. And for you."

"Thank you," she whispered. Caroline sank down on her knees beside Charles' cot and took his limp hand in her own. He was barely alive. The slender thread had never seemed more ragged and frail. Caroline's tears began to fall again as she silently prayed.

"Please, Lord. All I ask of you is that you allow Charles to live. In return . . . in return . . . I . . ."

She paused, unsure of what she could offer God in return for so great a gift as Charles' life. The debt she already owed God for all the injustices done to Grady, to Tessie and Josiah, to the slaves her family had kept at Hilltop, was much too great an account to ever repay. She had no close family members now that her mother was dead, her father and Jonathan missing. Her servants were her family, but their lives weren't hers to barter. All she had was herself.

"In return for Charles' life, I offer you my own. I offer you the life Charles and I would have had together as husband and wife, the son we might have had if we'd married. It doesn't matter what you do with me, Lord. It doesn't matter if Charles ever forgives me . . . or if I go to prison . . . or if I hang for my crimes. Whatever you ask of me, Lord, I'll do. I'll obey you as your servant. I only ask that you let Charles live. Please . . . let him live. . . ."

Caroline stayed by his bedside day and night for the next week, afraid to leave. Her servants brought her meals. The first time Charles regained consciousness and saw her sitting beside him he smiled, then closed his eyes again. Even before he'd been wounded, Charles had lost so much weight after weeks of dysentery and near-starvation that at first he didn't seem to have the strength to get well. Caroline fed him the vegetable broth Esther had cooked; she made sure he drank water; she changed the dressings on his wounds herself to keep them clean; she bathed him with cool water when he grew feverish. All the while she never stopped praying, offering her future as Charles' wife in return for his life.

Charles' family came to the hospital every day, too, spending hours by his bedside. When Charles was conscious, Caroline thought he would surely notice the looks of hatred his father gave her, or the way his mother glared at Caroline every time she touched him, or the fact that Sally never spoke a single word to her. But Charles was much too sick to be aware of what went on around him. Sally had decided to wait until he was out of danger to tell him that Jonathan was missing. No one knew if Jonathan had been taken prisoner or if he had been blown to pieces in an explosion. It seemed to Caroline that Sally was on the verge of a breakdown as she waited for news of her husband.

Gradually, the color seeped back into Charles' face. Strength returned to his body, and he was able to weather an attack of pneumonia. His wounds slowly began to heal with no signs of infection. But throughout the long months that she nursed him, Caroline was aware of what would happen once it became certain that he would live. Charles' father would tell him the truth.

She saw that day inching closer when the doctors allowed Charles to leave the hospital and recuperate at home in Court End. His servants carried him inside and laid him in the bed they'd prepared in the small parlor, near the fireplace. His father still allowed Caroline to come and see him for a few hours each day, but Mr. St. John never left them alone in the room, watching her closely, listening to every word she said.

"I want to marry you," Charles murmured to her one day, more than two months after he'd been wounded.

"I know. You already asked me." She slipped her hand into his so he could feel the engagement ring on her finger.

"No . . . I mean now . . . before the war ends. Like Sally and Jonathan."

Caroline felt Mr. St. John's eyes on her, boring into her. She glanced up at him, then quickly looked away. But she'd seen the unspoken threat in his eyes as he silently shook his head. *No.*

Caroline gently squeezed Charles' hand, willing herself not to cry. "You've been away so long you hardly know me anymore. I've changed since the war began. Maybe you should get to know me all over again before you decide if you still want to marry me."

"I know all that I need to," Charles said. "I know that you have a tender, loving heart . . . that injustice makes you angry . . . that you want to make the world right more than you want pretty dresses. Those are all the reasons why I fell in love with you. Have any of those things changed?"

She lost the battle with her tears.

"Listen now. Don't cry. Maybe it's not fair to ask you to marry me when I'm ... like this. ..."

"Oh, Charles, it's not because you're wounded. You're the only man I will ever love or ever want to marry."

Mr. St. John slowly rose from his chair at her words. He planted his hands on his hips. Charles didn't notice, but Caroline did.

"There are some other things about me ... that you don't know," she told Charles.

"Then tell me."

"I can't. There isn't enough time today. I have to go home now so you can rest. We'll talk tomorrow."

She stood to leave, but Charles clung to her hand for a long moment, refusing to let go. "I should have listened to you, Caroline," he said softly. "I should have married you the last time I came home."

Yes, she thought. *Yes, if only you had.*

A light blanket of snow covered the ground the next morning when Caroline awoke. It dusted the tree branches and squeaked beneath the carriage wheels as she and Gilbert drove down the hill to Charles' house. Richmond looked almost beautiful again, its war-torn shabbiness hidden by the sparkling whiteness. Even the city's usual noises seemed muffled and still, the streets nearly deserted as few people ventured outside into the cold.

"Everything looks so pretty, doesn't it?" she asked Gilbert.

"Yes, Missy, it sure do."

But when the St. Johns' butler opened the door for her, the mansion seemed ominously silent, as if the cold air that had breathed across the city had seeped inside, turning its inhabitants to ice. Caroline walked into the parlor and noticed right away that Charles was alone. His father's chair stood empty.

Charles stared at her from across the room, his face white with pain, his eyes red with grief.

"What's wrong?" she cried out. She started toward him.

"Wait." He held up his hand.

"Is it your father . . . ?"

He shook his head. "I had a long talk with my father last night after you left. We talked some more this morning."

Caroline grew very still. The moment she'd dreaded had finally come.

"He accused you of some terrible things. Things I didn't want to believe. He said he had proof. He showed me the book from your father's library, the map he says you drew. I still don't want to believe him. . . ." Charles could barely speak. "Listen now. If I ask you . . . will you tell me the truth?"

Caroline knew by the anguish on his face, the coldness in his voice, that if she told Charles the truth she would lose him. But she also knew that she could never hold on to his love or build a life with him based on a foundation of lies. She closed her eyes.

God, help me. Help me tell him the truth in a way that he'll understand.

Then she looked at him. "I love you, Charles. I swear that I will never lie to you."

He drew a ragged breath. "Father showed me the map Jeremiah used to escape. He showed me how it matched your book. . . ."

"I drew that map for my own servants. My father was planning to sell them, and I couldn't let that happen. I drew it to help them escape . . . but that shouldn't shock you, Charles. From the very first day we met you knew how much I hated slavery. And you also knew how much Eli and the others meant to me."

"Five families were robbed of their slaves and their valuables while being entertained in your home—including my own family." The anger in his voice was slowly rising. "Yes, I knew you believed in abolition, but I didn't think you would encourage slaves to steal or to break the law by running away from their lawful owners."

"I didn't do any of those things. The map and the papers were intended for my own servants. I didn't know that they would . . ."

Caroline stopped, unwilling to incriminate Tessie or Eli with her words. "I don't condone what they chose to do with the map. But I do understand why they did it. When freedom is just a few short miles away—"

"If your slaves were responsible, then they must be punished. Have you disciplined them for what they've done?"

"No. And I'm not going to. I'll take the blame for their actions myself before I'll ever allow them to be punished."

His eyes flashed with anger. "Do you hear what you're saying? Your slaves are involved in criminal activities, and you're not going to stop them?"

"All of the servants who escaped were about to be separated from their loved ones or have their lives turned upside down—including your own slaves. We helped them escape because the greater wrong would have been to stand by and watch them suffer. No one was hurt in the escapes or the robberies. I'm sorry about the thefts, I don't condone them, but . . ."

She stopped. Charles was shaking his head. Caroline knew he wasn't hearing her, wasn't understanding what she was trying to say. The silence that followed was terrible. She was afraid she might be sick.

When he spoke again, his voice was quiet, cold. "What about the prison break at Libby? Were you involved in *any* way?"

She had to force the words out of her mouth. "Yes. I was."

"So, you lied to my father? And then you let me play the fool, defending your integrity?"

"It wasn't like that, Charles—"

"What was it like, Caroline? You tell me. You lied when you told Father you had nothing to do with it, didn't you? Did you lie about your relationship with that prisoner, too?"

"No." Tears rolled silently down her face at the resentment in his voice, the distrust in his eyes where love had always been. "Robert has never been anything more to me than a friend."

"Oh, really," he said, scornfully. "Is he in love with you?"

Caroline hesitated, knowing what the truth would sound like. Charles saw her hesitation and said, "You promised you would tell me the truth, Caroline."

"Robert says that he loves me. But I always made it very clear to him that I loved you, that we were engaged and—"

"Did you hide him from the authorities?"

She could only nod.

"Where? My father said they searched your house."

Caroline saw his love slipping away like a ship sailing down-river, getting smaller and less distinct as it faded into the distance. There was nothing she could do to stop it. She told him the truth. "While the guards were searching downstairs, Eli hid Robert in my bed."

"Dear God . . . Caroline . . ."

"Please believe me . . . I did nothing improper. If I had, would I have told you the truth about his hiding place?"

"I don't know. I don't know what to believe anymore." Pain had replaced the anger in his eyes. His chest rose and fell as he struggled with his emotions.

Caroline knew he would ask her about Ferguson soon, and she dreaded telling him. At the same time, she wanted this terrible inquisition to end. If she couldn't make him understand why she had helped the slaves or why she'd helped Robert, she knew he would never understand why she had passed information to his enemies— much less forgive her for it.

"I don't want to believe any of this," Charles said. "Especially the accusations that you were involved with this spy, Ferguson—that you passed secret information to him. I told my father that it couldn't possibly be true, that you would never do such a thing. But he believes you went out of your way to cultivate friendships with army officials and cabinet members, hosting parties for them—then you shared all their confidences with our enemies. He says we could compare your handwriting and learn the truth . . . but I told him I wanted to ask you myself."

She could no longer face Charles. The grief and betrayal in his eyes were too painful to see. Caroline covered her own face and wept.

"If I've just accused you falsely," he said in a trembling voice, "tell me and I'll apologize. Tell me that my father is wrong, and I'll defend you before the highest court."

"No ..." she said. "No. It's true."

"Oh, God ..." Charles moaned in pain. Then he began to shout, as if the only way he could keep from weeping was to smother his grief with rage. "I was lying out there in a trench, in danger, and you betrayed me to the enemy? I was being shot at and shelled day after day and you told them where to aim? I risked my life for you. For *you*, Caroline! I could have died a hundred times because of the information you gave them, and you expect me to believe that you love me?"

"I begged you not to fight. I never believed in your cause. And I never understood why you did. You said you loved me, yet you left me here, all alone, to cope with my fear and hunger and loss—you and my father and Jonathan, you all left me! The only people who stayed and prayed with me and helped me find enough food to stay alive and enough fuel to stay warm were my slaves. You fought in a war you admitted we could never win. You did what you wanted to do, regardless of how I felt, regardless of whether I agreed with you or not. You were fighting against everything I believed in, Charles. Can't you see that you did the same thing you accuse me of doing? Does that mean you never loved me?"

"I never lied to you about what I believed or which side I was fighting for."

"And I never lied to you about slavery. That's why I passed information to Mr. Ferguson. If the South wins, slavery wins. I did it because slavery is wrong, not because I didn't love you. I prayed that God would spare you, and He has."

"And did you think I could still love you when I found out what you've been doing all this time?"

"I prayed that you would understand."

"Well, I don't. A lot of good, brave men have been butchered by your Yankee friends . . . including your own cousins and maybe your father. Now I'm lying here, a pathetic invalid . . . I don't know how you can expect me to forgive you."

Caroline covered her face. The price she had offered God—her future with Charles—would now be paid in full. But at least he was alive. At least the man she loved would live.

"Listen now," Charles said coldly. "I told my father that if it were true, that if you were guilty . . . I didn't want you arrested here in Richmond. I don't need to see you publicly condemned or locked away in Castle Thunder. I hate what you've done, but seeking revenge won't change anything. When Timothy Webster and his wife were caught spying they hanged him, but they sent Mrs. Webster across enemy lines into exile. That's not a possibility right now, since we're under siege, but when the time comes, when there's another prisoner exchange . . ." Charles' voice trembled. "You'll be sent away. In the meantime, as long as you remain at home . . ." He couldn't finish.

Caroline didn't think it was possible to hurt as much as she did and still live. She slowly pulled the ring from her finger and laid it on the sheet in front of him. She longed to caress his face, to feel the touch of his hands on hers one last time. But he turned his face away from her. She saw tears in Charles' eyes before he closed them. She looked at the man she loved for the last time, then hurried away.

For the first time in Caroline's life, neither Tessie nor Eli was able to comfort her.

CHAPTER 25

December 1864

"Can this really be the fourth Christmas that we've been at war?" Caroline wondered aloud. She'd awakened to the sound of bells ringing on Christmas morning at nearby St. John's Church.

"Yes, Missy. I been counting them, too," Ruby replied. "And I been asking Massa Jesus to please let this one be the last." She rose from her pallet in Caroline's room where she slept. Ever since Isaac was born, Ruby had taken Tessie's place as Caroline's chambermaid. Now she hurried over to the fireplace and began poking the embers back to life.

"Let the fire go out, Ruby. Let's not waste the wood."

"But it's too cold in here for you to be getting dressed. You'll catch your death."

"I'll dress quickly. I don't need all my hoops and petticoats and things. It'll be nice and warm when we get down to the kitchen."

Caroline couldn't help shivering, though, as she stood on the icy floor and waited for Ruby to tie her corset laces and help fasten her bodice. She put on both pairs of her stockings to warm her feet, even

410

though they made her shoes feel too tight. Ruby quickly brushed her hair and pinned it up.

The church bells sounded louder as Caroline hurried outside to the kitchen. The carillon of St. Paul's Church downtown, and dozens of others across the city, had joined in with St. John's Church, each chiming different tones. She wished they would stop. They reminded her that it was Christmas, and Christmas reminded her of Charles and of their engagement five years ago. Sally would be remembering her engagement to Jonathan this morning, too, and praying that she wasn't a widow.

In the darkness last night, Caroline had silently wept into her pillow, longing to be in beautiful St. Paul's for the midnight Christmas Eve service. Confined to her home, she hadn't been able to attend church in weeks. She wondered if Charles had gone, if he was well enough now to leave his bed and his house.

As soon as Caroline entered the kitchen, little Isaac gently nudged her sorrow aside, running to her with arms outstretched, as overjoyed to see her today as he was every day. She lifted him in her arms to kiss his soft cheeks, accepting his own wet kiss in return. He was a beautiful child, with Tessie's almond-shaped eyes, Josiah's ebony skin, and Eli's broad smile.

"Merry Christmas, Isaac," Caroline said, caressing his dark, woolly head. "You don't even know what that means, do you?"

"Oh yes, he does," Tessie said. "Don't you know his granddaddy been telling him all about baby Jesus in the manger, and the angels singing, and the shepherds coming? That boy gonna have the whole Bible memorized before he has a mouthful of teeth."

"It might be Christmas," Esther said with a sigh, "but we sure ain't having much of a Christmas dinner this year. We eating the same old thing we eat every day—dried peas, salt pork, and these here potatoes."

Eli walked into the kitchen with a few sticks of firewood just then and heard Esther's complaint. "You know what the Bible says about eating poor?" he asked. "Says it's better to eat a stale old piece of bread in a kitchen full of love than a great big feast in a mansion where everybody arguing all the time."

"Well, we certainly got plenty of love around here," Esther said, "but that's about all we got."

"Something smells good," Caroline said, sniffing the air. "What's baking in the cast-iron oven?"

"Oh, that's just some sweet potatoes I'm fixing with sorghum and spices and such. Thought it might taste a little bit like sweet potato pie . . . without the crust, since there ain't much flour."

Against her will, Caroline thought of Charles and his family again. Their flour mills had been at a near standstill ever since the wheat harvests in the Shenandoah Valley had been lost to the enemy. Tessie heard through the slave grapevine that Mr. St. John had hired Josiah out to labor in the mines somewhere to earn extra money. Tessie hadn't seen her husband since the night he'd brought Charles to the hospital. Yet in all the years that Tessie had spent apart from Josiah, Caroline had never heard her complain or seen her shed tears. She longed to ask Tessie what the secret was to forgetting. How much time had to pass before she would stop thinking of the man she loved every hour of every day, wondering where he was, what he was doing?

When their simple meal was on the table, ready to eat, Eli climbed up to the loft to wake Gilbert, who had been allowed to sleep late. The two men took turns staying awake all night, guarding Caroline's property—and especially their meager supplies of food and firewood. Starving souls roamed the besieged city at night, stealing from anyone who had a little more than they did.

When everyone was seated around the table, Eli spoke the blessing. "Lord, I thank you for this food, and I ask you to bless those sorry folks who don't even have this much. I thank you that Massa Lincoln won the election up north, cause he promise to set all us colored folks free. I thank you for sending your Son on this happy day and for loving us so much you adopt us into your family. Thank you, Massa Jesus. Amen."

Caroline looked around at her servants and silently thanked God that they had adopted her into their family. Her own mother and father may have both chosen to leave her, but Tessie and Eli had stayed, even when it meant giving up their chance at freedom. She remembered her conversation with Eli a long time ago about Rahab the spy, who had betrayed her city, but who later became part of Christ's family. Maybe Eli was right; maybe God did give something in return for what was lost.

"I'm thinking this war is just about over," Eli said as they ate. "Ain't that right, Missy?"

"Yes," she replied, "anyone who's realistic and has read about all the defeats we've suffered lately knows that it's nearly over. And that the South has lost."

According to the papers, General Sherman had just made good on his promise to deliver the city of Savannah to President Lincoln for a Christmas gift. But news of the desolation Sherman had left in his wake made Caroline disgusted with the Yankees. As much as she longed to see the slaves emancipated, she hated that it had cost such a staggering price.

"Now that our freedom is almost here," Eli continued, "we have to start thinking about the future—what we all gonna do once we free. And most important, what job God asking us to do for Him. I think we should go round the table and let each person say what they dreaming about. Then we know how to pray for each other in the New Year."

Heads nodded in agreement as Eli looked around the table at everyone. Caroline had never told any of her servants that her punishment for spying was going to be exile. If the war didn't end before spring, before the next prisoner exchange, she would very likely be banished from her home in Richmond and sent north. But as she listened to her servants' dreams for the future, she decided not to spoil the day by telling them what awaited her.

"All right then," Eli said. "Guess I'll go first . . . When I'm a free man I want to start a church where I can preach about the love of Massa Jesus. I believe He wants me to help all the colored folk learn how to serve their new Massa." He turned to Esther, seated beside him.

"Now, Eli," she said with a frown. "You know the Lord ain't giving me no fancy plans like yours."

"That don't matter," he said. "God needs people to do all kind of things, big and small. Just tell us what's on your heart."

"Well . . . I want to be able to cook again, to have me some food in this kitchen so I can feed the people I love. I want to have my son, Josiah, home. And I want to watch this little grandbaby of mine grow up into a man. That's all."

"Those are fine things to wish for," Eli said. "How about you, Gilbert?"

He stared down at his plate for so long that Caroline didn't think this normally quiet man was going to share his thoughts with the others. When he finally did, he surprised her.

"I'm praying that your daddy comes back, Missy Caroline. And that when he does . . . well, I'd like to get a job working on one of his ships. I ain't never seen the ocean before. I'd like to sail down to one of them islands where the sugarcane grows. I hear they got some pretty colored women living down there, and I'd like to find me a wife."

Luella was next. She spoke without ever looking up at anyone, blushing the entire time. "I promised Gus that I would marry him when we free. Gus use to drive for Missy Sally before he run off. He gonna find us a place to live and come back for me."

Caroline winced at this reminder of Sally and Charles—and at her own ignorance of her servants' lives. During all those years that the St. Johns had visited her home, Caroline had never guessed that their driver and Luella were falling in love.

"Gus a good man," Eli said. "He'll keep his word. . . . Tell us what you wishing for, Ruby."

She shook her head. "Can't recall ever wishing for anything, Eli. I took care of your mama, Missy Caroline, now I taking care you. I'd like to take care your babies and grandbabies if you let me."

Caroline fought back tears. "I'd like that, too, Ruby," she said. But she had no hope of ever loving another man besides Charles. Nor could she envision a future with children of her own for Ruby to care for.

Tessie spoke next. "I'm praying that my boy Grady come home," she began.

"How old that boy be now?" Esther asked.

"Almost twenty. I still think of him as my boy, but he a man already. And, of course, I want Josiah to come home, too. I just want us all to live together for once in our lives—me and Josiah and Grady and Isaac. And to never have to be apart again. Missy Caroline, you my child, too, so I hoping Ruby will let me share some of your babies and grandbabies."

"Sure can," Ruby said. "Every child in the world need two grand-mas."

Caroline smiled, even though she didn't dare to share her servants' dreams. She remembered a night in Philadelphia, long ago, when her cousin Julia had hugged her pillow in the dark, pretending it was her husband. Caroline had tried it but found that the pillow had no face, that there was no one she could imagine marrying. Years later, that was still true. When she tried to picture Charles' face, she saw it as she'd seen it last, his eyes filled with anger and the pain of her betrayal.

After a moment, Caroline noticed that the kitchen had gone quiet. She looked up. "How about you, honey?" Tessie asked her.

"I wish that the war would end," Caroline said, her voice hoarse.

"Amen. But how about after that?" Eli asked gently.

Caroline brushed away a tear. She had prayed that Charles would live, and God had answered. In her deepest heart, all she wanted was for Charles to forgive her, to love her as he once had. But that wasn't going to happen. A year ago she had begun to let go of that dream when she gave her wedding dress to Sally. No other dream had taken its place.

"I pray that my father comes home safely," she finally said. "And my cousin Jonathan, too . . . I really haven't thought much beyond that."

"All right," Eli said. "Let's all pray . . . Massa Jesus, you see our dreams and know our hearts. You hold our futures in your hand. We can pray 'Thy will be done' with joy in our hearts because there's hope in that prayer—hope that because you love us, your will is the very best thing for us. Take our dreams and your dreams for us, Lord, and make them one and the same. In Massa Jesus' name, amen."

As Eli prayed, Caroline felt God drawing near to her, just as He had a year ago in Sally's bedroom. She realized that she still clung to Charles in her heart, hoping that he'd take her back—just as she'd clung to her wedding dress and trousseau long after the planned date had come and gone. Once again, Caroline opened her heart and her hands to God, surrendering her love for Charles to His will. By the time Eli said "amen," Caroline felt at peace—even though the terrible pain of losing Charles still filled her heart.

"And now we got a little surprise for you, honey," Tessie said.

Caroline opened her eyes and looked up. All of her servants were watching her. Tessie handed the baby to Eli and went over to the fireplace to fetch his Bible from the mantel. "We all been working on this surprise for a long time," she said, searching for a bookmark as she talked, "but we saved it for a special day, like Christmas. We got something we want to show you." She handed the open Bible to Ruby.

"'O give thanks unto the Lord, for he is good: for his mercy endureth for ever,'" Ruby read, pronouncing each word slowly, carefully. "'Let the redeemed of the Lord say so, whom he hath redeemed from the hand of enemy; And gathered them out of the lands, from the east, and from the west, from the north, and from the south.'"

Ruby passed the book to Luella, and she began to read: "'They wandered in the wilderness in a solitary way; they found no city to dwell in. Hungry and thirsty, their soul fainted in them.'"

Gilbert took the Bible next. "'Then they cried unto the Lord in their trouble,'" he read, "'and he delivered them out of their distresses. And he led them forth by the right way, that they might go to a city of habitation.'"

Gilbert gave the book to Esther. "'Oh that men would praise the Lord for his goodness, and for his wonderful works to the children of men! For he satisfieth the longing soul, and filleth the hungry soul with goodness.'"

Caroline could barely speak. Her servants could read! "How . . . ?"

"You such a good teacher," Tessie said, "all I did was tell them everything you tell me. You the one who really taught them."

"She's right," Eli said. "You planted the seeds and God been making them grow, even if you ain't seeing it."

"You should be a teacher after the war," Tessie said. "Lot of colored folks gonna need one."

"You like your surprise, Missy Caroline?" Gilbert asked shyly.

"Yes," she said through her tears. "It's the most wonderful gift anyone ever gave me."

"Oh no, honey," Tessie said, hugging her. "You're the one who gave the gift to us."

Spring 1865

Caroline closed the newspaper and folded it carefully, resisting the urge to crumple it up and toss it into the kitchen fireplace. The paper on which it was printed was of such poor quality that if she didn't handle it carefully there would be nothing left of it for the others to read. But Tessie, sensitive to her moods, noticed her frustration.

"Guess it ain't good news you're reading this morning?"

"No. It's the worst. The peace negotiations at Fortress Monroe have ended in failure. President Lincoln demanded unconditional surrender, and of course, the Confederates refused. They're still insisting on 'the preservation of their institutions'—meaning slavery."

"Lord have mercy!" Esther said. "Don't them Rebels know it ain't doing them no good to fight for slavery if all us slaves starve to death first?"

"The other big news," Caroline continued, "is that the Confederate Congress is considering a law to conscript slaves."

"You mean, make them fight in the army? For the South?" Tessie asked in amazement.

"Yes. The paper says that General Lee has been begging for such a law for a long time because he needs men so badly. Thousands of his troops have gone home on furlough and have never come back. He can't possibly defeat General Grant this spring unless he gets more men."

Tessie shook her head in amazement. "So they gonna put slaves in uniforms and give them guns? Ain't they afraid we gonna turn the guns around on them?"

"I guess not. It shows how determined the South is to keep fighting—and how desperate they are." Caroline remembered how shocked and outraged the South had been when they'd first encountered Negro soldiers who were fighting for the Federals. Now that they'd seen how well the Negroes could fight, they were about to draft them into the Confederate army, too.

"They ain't gonna take Eli and Gilbert, are they?" Ruby asked.

Caroline shook her head. "They can't draft anyone without his owner's consent. And I'll certainly never give it."

"Maybe they both be better off in the army," Esther muttered as she mixed up a skimpy batch of corn bread. "Maybe they finally get a decent meal if they soldiers."

"No, I don't think the soldiers are eating any better than we are," Caroline said. "One entire page of the newspaper was a notice from the Commissary General along with a plea from General Lee, begging people to turn over any extra food supplies they have to the army so they can feed the starving soldiers."

Esther huffed. "Like we got anything extra to hand over!"

When it was time for the noon meal, Eli arrived home. Caroline had sent him downtown that morning, and she was eager to hear any scraps of news he had picked up through the servants' grapevine. Since she had been confined to her home all these months, the grapevine had become her only source of news about Charles and his family.

"I saw a whole bunch of Rebel troops passing through the city this morning," Eli said after he'd blessed the food. "They heading south. I tell you, if it wasn't for all them white faces, I'd swear I'm seeing a gang of slaves going by on the way to the cotton fields. They so sorry-looking, all in rags, shoes falling off their feet, heads hanging down . . . and the horses nothing but skin and bones."

"Did you talk to any of the St. Johns' servants?" Caroline asked.

Eli lowered his head, concentrating on his plate of food as if he hadn't heard. That could only mean one thing—he had bad news that he was unwilling to share. Caroline laid down her fork.

"Tell me, Eli. Please. Don't you understand that not knowing is worse torture for me than hearing the truth?"

When he still didn't reply, Esther said, "Tell her. That gal ain't gonna eat a bite of food unless you do."

Eli sighed. "Massa Charles has gone on back in the army to fight."

Caroline closed her eyes. For a moment the room went utterly still. Even little Isaac seemed to sense everyone's shock and didn't make a sound.

"Has Charles fully recovered from his wounds, then?" Caroline asked when she finally opened her eyes. She had to stare at Eli for a long time before he replied.

"His shoulder still stiff, and he limping some, but he determine to fight. He arguing with his daddy 'cause his daddy want Massa

Charles to stay home—but Mr. St. John too sick to stop him. That's all I know, Missy. That's the truth."

Caroline excused herself and fled to her room. *It was all for nothing,* she thought. In a few weeks it would be spring, and the war would resume, and this time she had nothing left to offer God in return for Charles' life. She had bargained away her future with him so that Charles would live. But now he was going back to the trenches outside Petersburg again, where he might very well be killed. The Rebels would surely lose this war, and then her sacrifice—and Charles' life—would both have been spent in vain.

She stood gazing out of her bedroom window, shivering in her unheated room, when she heard a voice behind her. "Missy Caroline . . ." She turned, astonished to see Eli standing in her doorway. Except for the night Robert had escaped, he had never dared to come into the big house unbidden, much less come upstairs to her room. It showed Caroline, more dramatically than anything else could, just how much her world had changed.

"Missy, I know you ain't gonna like hearing this . . . but you got to put Massa Charles in God's hands and trust Him, no matter what."

"Why did he have to go back to fight?" she cried. "I gave God the only thing I had left—my future with Charles—so that He would allow him to live. But my sacrifice will all be for nothing if Charles goes back there again and gets killed."

Eli frowned as he took a few hesitant steps into the room. "You telling me you try and make some kinda bargain with God?"

"Yes. That's why He answered my prayers and allowed Charles to live."

"No, Missy . . . no," he said, shaking his head. "That ain't the way God does things. You can't barter and haggle with Him like He's a vendor down in the farmers' market. He let Massa Charles live 'cause He have a purpose in him living, not 'cause you give Him something for it. You really want a God like that? Someone you can control and order all around—whoever gives God the most gets what they want? That the way you want Him to run the world?"

She thought of all the people, North and South, kneeling in their churches, praying for two opposing favors from God. "No . . ."

"Then let Him run things the way He knows best, according to His will. Trust Him, Missy. Trust that everything you done for Him and everything you gave up for Him has a purpose. God will give it all meaning in the end. When this war is finally over, things are gonna be the way He wants them to be—in Massa Charles' life, in my life, and in your life, too."

The fighting began in earnest at the end of March. Word quickly spread all over town that a battle was raging at Fort Stedman, outside of Petersburg. For the first time since the war began, Caroline couldn't go to the *Enquirer* office to listen for news or to look for Charles' name on the casualty lists. All of her slaves could read, but she didn't dare send any of them to read the lists and risk discovery. She could only live in an agony of uncertainty, praying for Charles' safety, waiting for the lists to be printed in the newspapers.

There was another battle at Five Forks on April 1. The Yankees drove the Confederates from their defenses southwest of Petersburg, taking the Southside Railroad, strangling Richmond's last remaining supply line.

"No one talking about licking the Yankees anymore," Eli reported from his trip downtown that afternoon. "They talking about leaving town any way they can."

"It's almost over," Caroline murmured. "Seems like we've waited so long for this day to come, and now that it's finally here . . . I'm scared, Eli. What on earth is going to happen to us? People have always predicted that the Yankees would run wild through the city once they captured it, raping and murdering . . ."

"Now, you know Gilbert and me ain't gonna let no Yankees come near this house. We got your daddy's pistols, and we certainly ain't afraid to use them if we have to." But Caroline was finding it harder and harder to sleep at night.

On the following morning, Sunday, April 2, the sun dawned so warm and bright that Caroline could almost believe that the Yankees were camped nine hundred miles from Richmond instead of a mere nine. Nothing disturbed the Sunday calm except the tolling of church bells as Eli went downtown to try to find out the latest news. When he finally returned home, a little before two o'clock, he made everyone gather around the table in the kitchen, even though dinner wasn't quite ready.

"Word's all over town that Lee's army is in trouble. The Yankees broke through our defenses in three places and things are falling apart fast 'cause he ain't got enough men to fight the Yankees off. General Lee send a message to President Davis while he sitting in church this morning, saying that he and everybody else better get on out of Richmond."

"Are you certain that it isn't just a rumor?" Caroline asked. "Because they've said the city was in trouble before, and the warnings were always false alarms."

"No, this time I think the Yankees really are coming. Ain't nothing to stop them if Lee retreats with his men. And that's what he's fixing to do."

"What should we do?" she asked the people she loved, gathered all around her.

"Best thing is to pray," Eli said, "and ask God what He thinks."

But even after they'd prayed and had eaten the small meal Esther had prepared, Caroline still wasn't certain whether they should remain in Richmond or try to flee to a safer place. "Will you take me downtown, Eli?" she finally asked. "Maybe if I see for myself what's going on, I'll have a better idea what we should do."

"Ain't you supposed to stay at home?"

"If all the rumors are true, no one will really care where I go anymore."

Eli got the buggy ready, and they drove down the hill through the crowded streets. Most people were headed west or southwest, the only directions that weren't blocked by thousands of Yankee troops. Caroline wondered how she and Eli would ever be able to move against the tide and get back up the hill again to their home.

As they passed Capitol Square, she saw people frantically packing government documents and hurrying them out of the building. In the business district, all the banks were open, even though it was Sunday, and people had lined up for blocks to withdraw their money. Wagons and carts of all sizes and descriptions filled the roads and bridges, loaded with trunks and boxes and household goods. Hundreds of people were fleeing on foot, walking the canal towpath out of town toward Lynchburg, carrying bundles on their backs. Ashen-faced soldiers with missing limbs hobbled by on crutches or were carried along on makeshift stretchers. Caroline saw one desperate mother loading her three small children into a goat cart. Every means of transportation imaginable was being used to leave Richmond.

Confusion and panic reigned over the entire city, growing and spreading like an epidemic. Seeing the terror on every face, Caroline remembered the story Eli had once told her of men running in fear from the giant, Goliath. Only little David had faith in God's deliverance. She made up her mind. "I don't think God wants us to run away in fear like this, do you, Eli?" she asked.

"No, Missy. Ain't nothing wrong with being afraid—that's only human. But we need to give our fear to Massa Jesus instead of letting our imaginations run off with it."

"Let's go home." But even after making her decision, Caroline had to pray away her own panic as they headed back up the hill again.

It proved even more difficult than she had guessed to wade through the moving stream of people and vehicles, all headed in the opposite direction. Eli had to walk beside the panicked mare, leading her by the halter, to get her to move at all. At least a dozen people stopped them, begging Caroline to sell them her horse so they could transport a family member who was old or ailing. She turned away offers of Confederate dollars, U.S. greenbacks, and even gold pieces worth as much as a thousand dollars. She began to worry that someone would simply steal the horse, and she wished that Eli had brought one of her father's pistols along.

When they reached the top of the hill, they saw a column of Confederate soldiers marching toward them, double quick. "We have to get off the main road," Caroline cried. "Hurry. We can't let them see our horse or they'll take her."

But instead of speeding up, Eli halted the carriage. "Jump down, Missy, and grab hold of these reins. She'll go faster without the buggy." As quickly as he could, he unhitched the horse as the sound of tramping feet drew closer. "Run with her, Missy. Run down that side street. Get her home, quick."

All her life, Caroline had been afraid of horses, but she wasn't about to lose the last one she owned to the Confederates. She grabbed the halter next to the horse's muzzle and began to run. Five minutes later she stumbled into the carriage house, her heart pounding. She was breathless with exhaustion, but at least the mare was safe. When she could breathe again, she sent Gilbert back to help Eli pull the buggy home.

"We're staying," Caroline told her servants when they were all together again. "We'll try to guard the house and the mare as best we can, but they're not the most important things. What's important is each other. Nothing else matters as long as we all come through this safely."

For Caroline, waiting proved the hardest part—as it always had. She stood on her father's balcony and watched the refugees stream across Mayo's Bridge toward Manchester until it grew too dark to see. After nightfall, she could hear the chaos and tumult down in the city streets—shouts and cries and the sounds of breaking glass as mobs looted stores and some of the homes that had been evacuated downtown. She later learned that all the guards at the city prisons had fled, allowing convicts to escape and join the pillaging.

Caroline made her servants bring blankets and pillows into the drawing room where they would sleep that night, dressed in their street clothes and shoes. They tethered the mare right outside the doors to the backyard. She armed Eli and Gilbert with her father's pistols. Even so, no one slept much, except for the baby.

Close to midnight, Caroline heard the cry of a train whistle as President Davis and the last of the Confederate government officials left town on the Danville Railroad. She lay awake in the darkness, praying for Charles and for all the people she loved, huddled in the drawing room beside her.

A long time after that, she finally managed to drift off into a very light sleep.

26

April 1865

The sky was barely turning light the next morning when a monumental explosion jolted Caroline right off of the sofa and onto her feet. It was as though a hundred cannon had fired at the same time. Moments later there was a second blast, every bit as powerful as the first. Then a third. The concussions seemed to shake the house to its foundations. Caroline cowered in terror as windows on the south side of her house shattered from the force of the explosions.

For a moment, she felt dazed, then panic-stricken. She was afraid that the house would collapse on all of them. Isaac was screaming in fear, Luella and Ruby were crying, Gilbert was holding his head and moaning. Her own head ached from the detonation. She wanted to run but didn't know in which direction to flee.

"It's okay. We're all okay," Eli said, holding Esther in his arms. Then he saw the terrified mare, straining at her rope as a shower of splinters and glass rained down on her, and he hurried outside to soothe her.

When Caroline had calmed down enough to think, she decided

to run upstairs to her father's balcony and try to see what had happened. She had to step carefully over the broken glass that littered the floor. Three Confederate warships had long been anchored in the James River below, ready to defend the city in case the Union fleet made it past Drewry's Bluff. Now they were gone. The retreating Rebels had blown them to pieces rather than allow the Yankees to retrieve their cannon and stores of ammunition. Dense smoke, filled with thousands of fiery fragments, billowed into the sky where the ships had been anchored.

"Oh, God, help us," she murmured. Those ships probably weren't the only things the fleeing Confederates would destroy. In the past, each time Richmond had been threatened, city officials had talked of torching the town rather than leaving anything for the Yankees to gloat over.

She hurried downstairs to tell the others. "I think that was just the beginning," she said. "The Rebels will probably blow up everything they don't want the Yankees to get. There will be more blasts when the arsenal goes up. I'm afraid they're going to set the entire city on fire."

It took everyone a moment to digest the news. "I think we'll be all right, up here on the hill," Eli finally said.

"Probably," Caroline agreed, "but each of us had better pack some belongings, just in case. We can watch from the balcony, and if the fire starts spreading this way, we'll be ready to run."

She climbed the stairs again with Gilbert, and they watched in horrified fascination as all the ships docked at the wharf caught fire. A row of tobacco warehouses near her father's went up next, flames licking through the windows and roofs. As time passed, fire and smoke began to curl into the sky from several more locations in the lower city, and Caroline could hear the hungry crackle and roar of the growing inferno, even at this distance.

"Look . . . Confederate soldiers," Gilbert said, pointing. A long gray column of men snaked across the James River on Mayo's Bridge, heading south. That probably meant that the northeastern approaches to the city had been left unguarded.

"They've set the railroad bridges on fire," Gilbert said. Caroline watched the flames inch across the slender wooden structures like a creeping predator until the bridges began to collapse, dropping into the river in a cloud of steam. When nearly all of the soldiers had reached the other side of the James, they torched Mayo's Bridge, as well. The river reflected the glowing flames as if it, too, were on fire.

Tears fell silently down Caroline's cheeks as she stood on the balcony for nearly two hours, watching Richmond burn. She felt utterly helpless as flames consumed more and more of the business district, spreading at last to the flour mill that Charles' family had owned for several generations. How would he and his family survive if their livelihood went up in smoke?

"At least the fire ain't spreading up this way," Gilbert said when he noticed her tears. But then Caroline realized in which direction the conflagration was spreading—to the west and north, inching up from the river toward Capitol Square and nearby Court End. Toward Charles' home.

"I wonder if Sally and her parents fled the city last night?" she asked aloud. But Charles' father had been ill for months, too weak to travel very far. If they were home, Sally would be terrified, with no safe place to go. "I promised Jonathan I would look after her," she murmured.

Gilbert looked at her. "Who, Missy?"

"His wife, Sally. Would you be willing to drive me downtown to her house?" she asked. "I won't make you do it unless you want to, Gilbert. The Yankees will be here any minute, and you'll be a free man. You're not obliged to follow my orders anymore."

"Ain't safe for either one of us to go down there."

"Maybe not. But Sally's servants won't stay with her and help her like you're all helping me. She and her parents won't have any way to hitch up the carriage or get out of Court End if the fire spreads in that direction. I need to bring them up here, where it's safe."

"I can go get them for you, Missy. Ain't no need for you to risk your life."

His courage brought tears to her eyes, but she shook her head. "I need to go," she said quietly. "I need to make it up to them for using them the way I did. Please, if you'll just get the buggy ready, I can probably drive it myself."

Gilbert gripped her shoulders, something he had never done before in his life. His gaze met hers. "I promise your daddy I gonna look after you. I ain't letting you go down there alone."

"Then we'll both go. Come on."

Eli tried in vain to stop them. "Just pray for us," she told him. "This is something I have to do."

Gilbert whipped the horse into a near gallop once they were on Main Street, and headed down Church Hill. When they reached the bottom they could hear the crackling flames, roaring and hissing like a living creature. Mixed in were shouts and cries as looters wove among the burning buildings like ghosts, keeping ahead of the flames. Dense black smoke billowed into the sky, showering Caroline and Gilbert with ash and soot until they could scarcely breathe. She could feel the heated air with each breath she took. Flaming bits of debris showered down around them. Surely this was like the earth's final end, when fire would engulf the planet and the firmament itself would melt with a fervent heat.

The entire lower city, all the way to the river, was in flames. Caroline saw great sheets of fire leaping from window to window, building to building, like children skipping across a stream from stone to stone. Several downtown banks were on fire. Flames soared through the roof of the *Enquirer* building. Two of the city's biggest hotels, the American and the Columbian, were enveloped. She heard a low rumble and saw one wall of the post office building collapse. The flames moved on to devour the state courthouse and all the public records stored there. People were running up to the square from the lower city to escape the fire, women and children, old and young, weeping, screaming. Thankfully, the fire hadn't reached Capitol Square yet, or St. Paul's Church.

But adding to the horror of the destruction was the fact that no one was rushing to put out the fire. Caroline didn't see a single fire wagon in the streets or even hear a clanging alarm bell. The people she saw were either fleeing, looting, or watching in mute horror as the city burned.

Gilbert had just turned north off Main Street when the inferno reached the Confederate arsenal. The explosions that followed were so horrific, Caroline thought the earth would rock off its axis. The mare reared in terror, tipping the buggy and throwing Gilbert to the ground as the reverberations went on and on. Caroline grabbed onto the seat in time and managed to hold on until the buggy righted itself, but her screams were lost in the endless rumble of sound as several hundred railcars full of ammunition continued to detonate. Then, still dazed, she saw that Gilbert was about to be trampled by the panicked horse. Caroline leaped down and grabbed the mare's bridle, stopping her just in time. It took every ounce of strength she had to hang on as the horse reared and bucked in terror.

"Gilbert!" she screamed above the unceasing roar of exploding shells. "Gilbert!" *Please, God . . . let him be all right!* She watched as he slowly rolled over, then sat up, looking stunned but unhurt. When he saw her clinging to the frightened horse, he scrambled to his feet to help her.

"Gilbert, thank God. I'm so sorry I got you into this," she said. But Caroline could barely hear her own voice and knew he couldn't possibly hear her above the sound of the blasts. They walked for the next few blocks to the St. Johns' house, holding the horse tightly between them. When they finally arrived, Gilbert led the mare into the carriage house to calm her down and try to get her out of the smoke, while Caroline walked up to the door of the mansion alone.

After pounding for several minutes, it occurred to her that no one inside could possibly hear her above the fusillade from the arsenal, so she simply opened the door herself and went inside. As she had guessed, all of the St. Johns' servants had fled. She found Sally and her mother alone in the house, huddled beneath the dining room table, nearly insane with terror. They clung to her when they saw her, as if she was the last person alive on the earth.

"It's all right," she soothed. "Everything is going to be all right. You're okay. You're both safe." Eventually the sound of her voice calmed them, and they were able to bring their tears under control.

"Where's your father?" Caroline asked Sally.

"H-his flour mill. He t-took the horse," she stammered.

Caroline knew that his mill had been on fire for some time. She feared for his safety, but she kept her thoughts to herself. "I've come to take you home with me. It's safer up on Church Hill. The fires aren't spreading that way."

"But we can't go out there," Mrs. St. John wept. "The Yankees are bombarding us."

"No, they're not," she said gently, rubbing the older woman's shoulder. "Those explosions are from the Confederates. They're burning their own arsenals and ammunition dumps. Come with me, please. I'll take you to where it's safe."

"W-what about my father?" Sally asked.

He never should have left you here all alone, she wanted to say. But she didn't. "We can leave him a note and tell him where you are. If he has a horse, he'll find us."

She finally convinced them to leave, each bringing a bundle of valuables with them. Caroline scavenged in the kitchen while they packed, finding a small bag of flour and a little bacon. Then she soaked four towels in water so they could cover their mouths, and led the two frightened women out to the carriage house where Gilbert was waiting. She was eager to leave before they changed their minds.

Caroline felt more accustomed to the roar of the flames and the sound of bursting shells her second time out, but the other two women cowered on the carriage seat and whimpered in terror. The buggy would only hold the three women, so Gilbert walked beside the horse, leading her by the bridle. As they slowly made their way back toward Capitol Square, a new sight made Caroline suddenly go cold with fear, even though the air around her felt nearly as hot as a furnace.

Yankees.

The United States Cavalry had already arrived in the square, followed by long, unending lines of blue-coated soldiers, tramping down the hill into the city. Hundreds of those soldiers were Negroes. The Stars and Stripes already flew from the roof of the capitol building again, and a band had begun to play the "Star Spangled Banner." Crowds of Richmond's former slaves lined the streets to cheer the conquerors. It was like a scene from a nightmare, Caroline thought, to hear gaiety and celebration in the midst of burning and horror.

Gilbert deftly avoided the marching soldiers and spreading fire, weaving his way down side streets until they were climbing Church Hill once again. An hour later they were home, safely inside, away from the smoke and the fear and the roar of the flames.

Caroline continued to console the two women, holding them in her arms, talking with them, praying with them. Esther brought them a little warm soup to eat. Late that afternoon, when Sally and her mother were fed and comforted, Caroline put them to bed in her mother's room.

As evening fell, a pall of black smoke hid the setting sun. In the distance, shells continued to explode at the arsenal and at the Trede-gar Iron Works, now in flames as well. But the Yankees had worked hard all afternoon, putting out most of the fires. They had stopped it from spreading to the rest of the city. Eli locked and bolted the doors as Caroline and her servants prepared to spend another night in the drawing room.

It was only then, after the day's harrowing events were far behind her, that Caroline fully realized what she had seen that morning. She leaped up from the sofa, startling all of her servants. "The Yankees are here!" she said. "They were flying the American flag."

"Yes, Missy," Eli said. "We know. Gilbert told us."

"But that means you're all free. Finally! You aren't slaves anymore. You're free men and women—all of you."

Eli broke into a wide grin. "We know that, too, Missy. We knowing it all day, now."

"Well, for goodness' sakes, why aren't you celebrating?" Caroline began grabbing them, one after the other, and hugging them—even Gilbert.

Eli squeezed her hard in return. "Didn't seem right for us to celebrate, seeing as you and the other women losing so much."

"You don't have to feel that way," Caroline said. "Come on, let's dance . . . laugh . . . sing! This is the most wonderful day of your life! You're free!"

She tried to pull Gilbert to his feet, but he shook his head, smiling shyly. "If you don't mind, Missy, I think we all like to celebrate by getting a good night's sleep."

"Amen," Esther said. "Besides, it don't feel any different being free than it did when I ain't free."

"That's because you always love us, Missy," Tessie said. "We ain't never been slaves in your eyes."

"Or in God's eyes, either," Eli said. "Best way to celebrate is to thank Massa Jesus for what He done." Caroline heard the powerful emotions in his voice. "It was the Lord's mighty hand that delivered us out of slavery," he said, "with Missy Caroline helping Him. Don't any of you ever forget that. Make sure you tell little Isaac and all our other children and grandchildren. Pass it down through all generations. It was the Lord God who hear our groaning. He's the One who set us free. And the Bible says that if the Son make us free, we be free indeed. And I say, Thank you, Massa Jesus! Amen!"

For the second morning in a row, Caroline was jolted awake at dawn, this time by someone pounding on her front door. Gilbert ran to open it. A moment later she heard Mr. St. John shouting, "Where are they? What have you done with my wife and daughter?"

Caroline hurried into the foyer. Soot smudged Mr. St. John's face and hands. His charred clothes reeked of smoke. He was coughing, wheezing, but when he saw her, he began shouting louder still. "What kind of chicanery are you trying to pull, stealing my family away from me this way? Your little deceptions won't work anymore. We know what you are—"

"Daddy, stop," Sally cried out from the top of the stairs. "Caroline hasn't done anything wrong. She helped Mother and me."

"Helped you! Get down here. Both of you. I'm taking you home."

"We were terrified yesterday, Daddy," Sally said as she helped her mother down the stairs. "You left us, and the servants all ran off, and we thought we were going to die. If Caroline hadn't come and brought us here where it was safe, I don't know what we would have done."

"Get in the carriage," he said coldly. Mr. St. John opened the front door himself and pointed toward the street. Caroline saw his carriage parked at the curb, but it was without a driver.

"Did you even hear a word that Sally just said?" Mrs. St. John asked him.

He glared at her. "Our mill burned to the ground yesterday. You can thank Caroline and her Yankee friends for that. Now get in the carriage."

They started to leave, but before she reached the door, Sally turned and ran back to take Caroline in her arms. "Thank you," she whispered as she held her tightly. "I'll never forget what you did for us yesterday."

Morning revealed that most of the fires were out. Caroline and Gilbert drove downtown to see what was left of Richmond.

Fifty-four city blocks lay in charred ruins. Nearly the entire business district was gone. More than nine hundred homes and businesses. Nothing remained except skeletal brick walls, or maybe a blackened fireplace and chimney rising from the smoking debris. In some places, the rubble of fallen bricks was piled so high it blocked the streets. The town didn't even look like Richmond.

The enemy's occupying forces had moved into President Davis' Confederate White House. Everywhere that Caroline and Gilbert looked, on every street corner and city block, she saw armed soldiers dressed in blue standing guard. They drove past Capitol Square, where hundreds of Yankee horses grazed, and Caroline remembered sitting on a bench in that square beside Charles the night Virginia had seceded. Four years ago this month, the city had celebrated the birth of the Confederacy. But Charles had looked at her that night, his eyes filled with sorrow, and said, *"You deserve to know the truth . . . I don't think we can possibly win this war."*

If Charles had known just how much he would lose—not only the war itself, but his city, his livelihood, thousands of his fellow soldiers, and worst of all, their love, their future—would he still have fought? If she had known that fighting to abolish slavery would have cost her Charles' love, would she still have done it?

Her questions had no answers. It was useless to ask them, as useless as trying to pick up the fallen bricks from among the rubble to put the city back together again. It couldn't be done. *"Trust that everything you done for God and everything you gave up for Him has a purpose,"* Eli had said. *"God will give it all meaning in the end."* Caroline could only pray that it would be so.

When she could no longer stand the sight of her beloved city, she asked Gilbert to take her home.

That day, April 4, President Lincoln arrived to tour the vanquished city. Eli and Gilbert took all of the other servants down to Capitol Square to cheer for the president who had purchased their freedom. Even baby Isaac got a glimpse of the man the Negroes hailed as their Moses.

Not quite a week after Richmond fell, General Lee and his exhausted troops surrendered to General Grant at Appomattox Court House. Charles laid down his rifle for the last time in bitter defeat. He and the friends he had fought and starved beside for four long years would finally go home. But when Charles arrived in Richmond, it was to a house of mourning. His father had died on April 9, the day Lee surrendered.

One week after the surrender at Appomattox, Josiah walked through the kitchen door as Caroline and the others were eating their dinner. Between the three of them, Tessie, Eli, and Esther, they hugged Josiah so hard they nearly knocked him to the ground.

"Ain't no one ever gonna make us be apart again," Tessie cried. "We're free!"

But their joyful reunion was tempered with sorrow as Eli told his son the news: "President Lincoln, the man who set us free, died today from an assassin's bullet."

"Dear Lord have mercy!" Esther cried, running from the house to the backyard. "Would y'all come inside and look who's here!"

Caroline was in the backyard with the others that warm May evening, watching Eli, Josiah, and Gilbert dig up another section of the yard to plant vegetables. The air was ripe with the scent of spring and with the horse manure the men were spading into the soil. Esther had heard the front door chimes and offered to see who it was. Now she was dancing from one foot to the other in excitement.

"Come on, y'all! Hurry up!"

Caroline ran inside ahead of the others, then stopped in amazement when she reached the foyer. The two thin, bedraggled-looking men standing in her doorway were her father and her cousin Jonathan. She didn't know which one to hug first.

"Thank God, thank God," she wept as she hugged them both

again and again. "Where have you been all this time? I thought you were dead."

"I thought I was, too, Sugar. More than once," her father said.

"We ran into each other at Fort Delaware—the prisoner of war camp," Jonathan explained. "Uncle George kept me alive. I thought the least I could do was bring him home."

"Kept you alive?"

"He used some of the gold he had with him to bribe the guards, buying us extra rations and a warm blanket. I owe him my life."

"I still can't believe you're both here . . . that you're alive!" she repeated.

"Didn't I promise that I would be back to dance with you?" Jonathan grinned and pulled her into his arms to waltz her around the foyer. He wore the same lively, impish grin she had loved since the day they'd first met. She was so glad that at least one thing hadn't changed. "I'll be back to collect a second dance another day," he said. "I want to see Sally. I want to go home to my wife."

"She'll be the happiest woman in the world when she sees you."

Jonathan's smile faded for a moment. "Where's Charles?" he asked. "Why isn't he here with you? Please tell me that he made it through the war all right."

Pain knifed through Caroline at the mention of his name. Jonathan would learn the truth soon enough. She decided not to spoil his joyful homecoming. "Charles made it through, safe and sound," she said, smiling bravely.

"You mean I made it home in time for your wedding?"

"Go now. Hurry!" she said as tears filled her eyes. "Sally's waiting."

Suddenly Josiah spoke up from behind her. "I be glad to drive you down there, Jonathan," he said. "It's awful far to walk."

Jonathan looked stunned. "Thanks, Josiah," he finally said. "I'd appreciate a ride."

Caroline drew her cousin into her arms again, hugging him close for what she knew would be the last time. Sally and Charles would tell him what she had done. Like the others, Jonathan would neither understand nor forgive her. His brother Will was dead, his home at Hilltop ruined. And she had helped his enemies.

"Good-bye," she whispered. "Thanks for bringing Daddy home."

When they were gone, Caroline became aware, for the first time, of all the servants, standing in the hallway behind her, staring at her father as if they were seeing a ghost. She wasn't entirely sure that they weren't.

"Sure is good to see you, Massa Fletcher," Gilbert said.

"Well, now. It's good to see all of you, too. I thought for sure y'all would have run off by now, like every other servant in the state of Virginia."

"No, Daddy. They all stayed here with me. They saved my life. I would have starved to death if it weren't for them."

He looked at them for a long moment. "I'm grateful to you," he said quietly. "Now then, I don't suppose a man could get something to drink around here?"

"Sorry, sir," Gilbert said. "Drink's been long gone."

"I ran out of gold a long time ago, Daddy. It went fast, with flour costing five hundred dollars a barrel."

"Well, here. Maybe this will help." He removed his jacket and handed it to Caroline.

"This jacket weighs a ton."

"I know. It's a wonder I didn't sink to the bottom of the harbor when those blasted Yankees sank my boat. I sewed my gold inside the seams so it would be safe. For goodness' sake, rip it out and buy me something to eat. I'm starved."

"That's music to my ears," Esther said.

"You mean . . . we're not broke?" Caroline asked.

"Heavens, no. I told you I made a fortune as a privateer. I just wasn't able to get it all home safely during the war. We have plenty of gold and even some U.S. Treasury notes hidden away down in the islands. I plan to go collect it all, first chance I get. I could use someone to go with me, but I don't suppose Jonathan or Charles will want to leave home anytime soon."

Caroline couldn't stop the smile from spreading across her face. "I know someone who would love to go with you, Daddy."

"Who?"

"Gilbert."

Her father looked at Caroline, then at Gilbert, as if they were both out of their minds. "Go ahead, Daddy," she said. "Ask him."

"I'd be mighty pleased to go with you, Massa Fletcher," Gilbert said before her father could open his mouth. "I been hoping you'd ask me someday."

"Well, I'll be darned," he said. He looked around at all of them in amazement, then noticed the walls of the foyer for the first time. "Good heavens!" he cried as he stared at the ragged patches of bare plaster where the wallpaper had been. "What on earth have you done to my house?"

CHAPTER

27

JUNE 1865

"Some of these books are going to be easier for my students to read than others," Caroline told Ruby as she handed her another pile.

"Easy or hard, they could all use a good dusting," Ruby grumbled.

Caroline had attended worship services with Eli at his African Baptist Church, where he'd announced to his congregation that she was willing to teach classes to anyone who wanted to learn to read and write. Hundreds of former slaves had hurried forward to sign up. Now she was working in her father's library, putting his books in order and making a list of the titles she could use with her students.

When the front door chimes suddenly rang, Ruby set her armload of books on the desk. "Who's pestering us now?"

"If it's someone who wants to sign up for classes, send him in," she called after Ruby. Then she realized that all of her potential students were former slaves who would never dream of coming to her front door. She listened for a moment to see if she could recognize the person's voice. Instead, she heard Ruby shouting in anger.

440

"You get on out of here! Ain't no Yankees welcome in this house! Go away!"

Caroline jumped down from the chair she was standing on and ran to the foyer. Ruby was trying to close the door on a man in a Federal uniform. The officer had his foot wedged inside, preventing it from shutting.

"Wait a minute, please," the Yankee begged. "It's me, Robert Hoffman."

Caroline froze in shock at the name, then stared in disbelief. She recognized him now. Robert had gained back the weight he'd lost in Libby Prison, and he looked surprisingly handsome in his navy blue uniform, his black hair and mustache neatly groomed, his brass buttons and belt buckle shiny, his boots polished. She couldn't believe her eyes. For the first time in his life, Robert looked every inch the army officer he'd always longed to be.

"Go away!" Ruby said, pushing hard against the door. "You gonna get Miss Caroline and the rest of us in trouble waltzing up to the front door in that uniform. You the enemy! Get on out of here!"

"Caroline, it's me," Robert shouted when he saw her. "What's wrong with Ruby? She's acting like I'm a stranger. Please, tell her to let me in."

"No. She's right, Robert. You have to go away. You're putting me in danger."

"What are you talking about? I would never—"

"There are rumors all over town that I betrayed the Confederacy. I'm hated enough as it is. Please leave."

Robert looked at her for a long moment in sorrow and disbelief. Then he pulled his foot out of the way and left. Ruby slammed the door behind him.

"I'm awful sorry for turning Massa Robert away like that. But everybody in the whole neighborhood looking out their windows and watching that Yankee man sashay up to your door, tying his fat Yankee horse to our post. We let him inside, they be hating you for certain."

"Thank you, Ruby," she said. "You did the right thing."

But later that night, when it was dark, Robert returned. He came to the back door this time, tying his fat Yankee horse to her back gate where fewer people would see it. He was dressed in civilian clothes instead of his uniform. Even so, Caroline didn't invite him into the house but stood outside the open drawing room doors to talk to him. The June evening was clear and warm, the sky sprinkled with stars.

"I'm sorry for coming to the front door this morning," he said. "I never meant to get you into trouble. I didn't know . . ."

"That I'd been caught spying?"

"There wasn't any record of your arrest . . . I checked."

"That's because Richmond fell and the war ended before they had a chance to punish me for my crimes."

"I'm sorry. I only wanted to make sure that you were all right and to see if there was anything you needed. I'm stationed here in Richmond for the time being. I can make sure that you receive food rations, that you're protected. The army wants to show you their appreciation for all your help . . . and so do I."

Caroline folded her arms across her chest, hugging herself. "The best way to help me is to stay far away and leave me alone. If you hang around here, bringing me food and doing special favors for me, it will only make things worse."

"You sound so bitter, Caroline. I thought you wanted to see the Union restored and the slaves freed."

"I did."

"Then why . . . ?" He stopped himself. Gently, carefully, he unfolded her arms and took her left hand in his. He rubbed the empty place on her finger where the ruby ring had once been.

"What happened, Caroline?"

She bit her lip, unable to answer.

"Forgive me for hurting you, but I need to know. Your fiancé . . . ?"

442

"Charles survived the war," she finally managed to say. "But he can't forgive me for helping you."

"How did he find out?"

"I told him."

"I'm sorry . . . I'm so sorry. I wouldn't blame you if you hated me, since I was the one who got you involved—"

"I don't blame you or hate you," she said wearily. "I could have refused to help you. I knew what I was getting into. And deep down I guess I always knew I was risking my future with Charles."

They stood in silence for a long moment as crickets chirped and a carriage rattled past on the street out front. Caroline wanted Robert to leave, and yet she didn't. His voice was warm, his presence comforting somehow. He was the first visitor she had talked to since her father had left on his voyage three weeks ago. And she was so very tired of being alone.

"I know my timing is probably all wrong," Robert said quietly, "and that I'm being very insensitive, but I have to say this. I love you, Caroline. I never stopped loving you from the time we first danced together in Philadelphia. My love grew even stronger when you visited me in prison for all those months. And when you helped me escape."

"Robert . . . please, don't . . ."

"I would take good care of you, Caroline. We could move away from here if you wanted to, and go home to Philadelphia. Or we could start all over again someplace new, wherever you choose. I know you don't love me yet, but maybe in time . . . they say love can sometimes grow from fondness and friendship if you give it a chance."

Sweet, gentle Robert. He was offering to rescue her, willing to play the role he had played in Philadelphia and be her island of safety, her refuge. But was it fair to use him this way? He had always been her dear friend. Might love grow from that friendship?

She was about to answer, to tell him that it was still too soon to make such an important decision about her future, when Robert spoke first.

"I don't need an answer now. I'll wait, Caroline. I'll wait forever if I have to. In the meantime, may I visit you again?"

She felt the ache of loneliness and nodded.

"Thank you." He lifted her hand and kissed it tenderly. He rested his cheek against it for a moment, then kissed it again. She remembered Charles once kissing her hand the same way. She watched Robert walk through the gate, mount his horse, and ride away.

She was still standing outside the drawing room doors, gazing at the star-filled sky through her tears, when Tessie walked quietly across the yard to stand by her side.

"Is Isaac asleep already?" Caroline asked her.

"No, but his daddy's gonna put him to bed tonight," she said, smiling slightly. "He in there telling him stories."

For some reason, Caroline remembered the morning in the train station when she had asked Charles to tell Josiah that he was going to be a father. *"Josiah is never going to be a father in the sense that you mean,"* Charles had said. But now he was. She wished that Charles could see how happy Josiah was for the first time in his life. She wondered what Charles would say if he could see him rocking his son to sleep.

All of her servants were happy. Six months ago, on Christmas Day, they had shared their dreams for the future, dreams that were being wonderfully fulfilled. Josiah was back home. Eli had his church. Esther had food to cook again. Luella had married her sweetheart, Gus. And as improbable as Gilbert's dream had seemed, he was now on his way to Bermuda with Daddy and might even find himself a wife. Caroline's own wish that her father and her cousin Jonathan would return home safely had been miraculously fulfilled. And Caroline loved her work as a teacher. Why, then, did she still feel so restless and unhappy?

"You all right, honey?" Tessie asked.

"Robert was just here."

"I know. . . . You all right?"

"He told me that he loves me. He asked me to marry him. He

said he would take me away from Richmond if I wanted to go. We could live in Philadelphia . . . anywhere, he said."

"That what you wanting to do?" Tessie asked. "Get away from here and all the memories?"

"I don't know, Tessie. I don't know what I want. I hoped that by now my love for Charles would start to fade. That I would be able to stop thinking about him, stop hoping that he would come back someday. I'm so tired of hurting, so tired of living without him."

"Do you think Robert could ever take Massa Charles' place in your heart?"

"When I saw him standing out here in the darkness tonight, his face was in the shadows . . . and for one terrible, wonderful moment I thought he was Charles." She paused, biting her lip.

"If it had been him," Tessie asked, "would you still marry him?"

"Yes—a thousand times, yes. But it will never happen." A single tear rolled down her cheek. "You told me that love only comes around once in most people's lives . . . that we don't get a second chance. Remember, Tessie?"

"Seem like a long time ago, honey. Back when you still writing all those letters to Massa Robert at West Point."

"Tonight, after I'd talked to Robert for a while, I really didn't want him to leave. It was so nice to have him here. So nice to have . . . a friend to talk to. I'm fond of Robert. He says our friendship could grow into love if I gave it a chance. Do you think he's right, Tessie? Do you think if we moved away from Richmond and started all over again someplace else that I would learn to love him someday? I know he would be good to me. . . ."

Tessie's brow furrowed with concern. "Do you have to decide right away?"

"No. Robert said he would wait. I told him he could come back and visit me again."

"Please, take your time, Missy. It's too soon for you to decide to stay or go. Give your heart a chance to heal."

Caroline looked up at the stars again. They looked blurry through her tears. "I honestly don't think it ever will heal," she murmured.

Tessie climbed the ladder to the loft above the kitchen where she and Josiah slept. Moonlight, filtering through the leaves outside, made the room dim, but she could see her husband leaning with his back against the wall, holding their sleeping son in his arms.

"You can go on and lay him down now," she said. "He's asleep."

"I know. I like holding him."

Tessie's heart swelled with love as she looked at Josiah. She cupped his face in both her hands to kiss him and felt the hard muscles in his jaw, the stubble of beard on his cheeks. She had waited for so many years for them to be together this way, and now they finally were. But when she thought of the emptiness in Missy Caroline's heart, tears came to her eyes.

"What's wrong, Tessie?" Josiah asked. "You thinking about Grady again?"

"No, my Grady coming home someday. I know he is." She sat down on the floor beside Josiah, leaning against his muscled shoulder. "I keep thinking about Missy Caroline. She always looking out for you and me, all these years . . . always fighting so we can be together. Now we are—and she lost the man she love because she helping us. That ain't right, Jo."

"I know. But there ain't nothing we can do."

"She talking tonight about going off with Massa Robert. She ask me what I think. I think it's a mistake because she don't love him. But it breaks my heart to see her so lonely. Ain't no other man in Richmond gonna marry her after what she done."

"There ain't enough men left in Richmond to marry all the girls who still alone. I watched them all die, Tessie, one right after the other."

"When you was away at war with Massa Charles . . . he ever talk about Missy?"

"All the time. Seem like he loved Missy more than anything else in the world."

"Do you think he still does?"

"I don't know. I ain't seen him since the night I carried him to the hospital."

Tessie lifted Isaac from Josiah's arms and laid him on the bed, patting his bottom for a moment until he fell back asleep. Then she took his place in Josiah's arms. "Will you take me to see Massa Charles tomorrow?" she asked.

"Why? What good that gonna do?"

"I don't know. I just want to talk to him, ask him if he still loves her. I got to try, Jo . . . for Missy's sake. She fought for us, now I got to try and fight for her."

"That make you happy, Tessie?"

"Yes," she nodded. "Yes, it will."

"Then I'll go," Josiah said. "I'll talk to him."

Charles stood among the ashes of his burned-out mill and swallowed the bile that had risen in his throat. All that remained of the huge brick building was a blackened shell. Gaping holes, like empty eye sockets, showed where the windows had once been. He kicked uselessly at the rubble beneath his feet. The loss of the flour mill had killed Charles' father. And deep in his heart, Charles wished that the skeletal walls would fall in on him, burying him among the ruins.

He had come down this morning to see if maybe the gears that turned the mill wheels were still good, to see if there was any hope of salvaging something, of rebuilding. But it took hope to rebuild, and Charles' hope had died with the Confederacy.

An enormous ceiling beam lay across the floor, blocking his path. He bent to lift the charred wood, but he still hadn't recovered the full use of his arm and shoulder. The beam wouldn't budge. He kicked at it in frustration.

"Need help with that?"

Charles whirled around. Jonathan's former slave, Josiah, stood a few feet away. Charles' first reaction was to refuse his help. He felt bitter toward the burly Negro without knowing exactly why. But Josiah was already bending to grip the beam. Charles grabbed the other end. Josiah moved it as though it weighed nothing.

"Thanks," Charles said. There was an awkward silence. "What are you doing down here?"

Josiah's expression stiffened. "I'm a free man. Guess I can go wherever I want, talk to whoever I want." Then he seemed to catch himself, and his features softened. "It's time we had a talk about the night you was shot."

Charles ran his hand over his face. He hated being indebted to any man—especially this one, the son of Caroline's beloved servant. He didn't want to be reminded of her. He wanted to forget.

"I'm glad you came," he finally said. "Listen now. I never had a chance to thank you for taking me to the hospital. I didn't remember how I got there at first. And by the time my memories of that night started to come back, you were gone."

Charles hated remembering that day, how the Yankees had streamed over the embankment, punching a hole through the Rebel lines, moving relentlessly forward, shouting in victory. He had lain on the bottom of the filthy trench between two dead men, unable to move, feeling the warmth of his own blood pumping from his wounds and soaking his clothes, shocked that death had come for him at last. His last thoughts were of Caroline. He'd wanted to take her picture out of his pocket, look at it one last time before he died. . . .

"I don't want your thanks," Josiah said. "I didn't do it for your sake, or for Jonathan's."

"May I ask why, then?"

"I did it for Missy Caroline."

Charles' stomach clenched at her name. He bent and began picking up fallen bricks, moving them uselessly from the ruined floor and tossing them aside.

"Before we was free," Josiah said, "when things was against Tessie and me, Missy Caroline always make sure we can be together. When my son was born, she ask her daddy to give him to her for her slave. Then she set him free . . . she give my son his freedom."

Charles looked up at Josiah as he suddenly realized something. "You could have been free the day I was wounded. The Yankees were right there. You would have been free if you had just kept walking. But you carried me to the field hospital."

"When I went to war with Massa Jonathan, my pa made me promise I would look out for you, make sure nothing bad happens to you, because Missy can't live without you. That gal loves you. So I kept my promise."

"I'm grateful."

"Then why you breaking her heart, leaving her like you done?"

Charles felt a sudden rush of anger at this man for poking at a wound that hadn't healed. "That's really none of your business."

"If I give up my freedom to save your life, it's my business. I'll tell you something else. I almost left you there to die, not because I want to run to the Yankees, but because there was so much hatred in my heart. I hate Missy Caroline all my life because I hate her father. George Fletcher use my Tessie. He make her pregnant with his son, Grady, then sell that boy to the auction. Sell me, too, so he could have Tessie all to himself, even though he already have a wife."

Charles saw the fury on Josiah's face, the clenched muscles in his arms and fists. He knew the other man's pain was at least as deep as his own.

"My pa say I can't punish Missy Caroline for the sins of her father," Josiah said. "He say I have to forgive. But when I seen you laying there I knew I could get even. Let all you white folks see what it feels like to lose someone you love for once." He paused, shaking his head. "But I can't do it. What Missy done during the war she done for us, out of love, so we could be free. That's why she was fighting—to help people be free. Why were you fighting?"

Charles answered automatically, angrily. "I was fighting because states should have the right—"

"That's all I hear you white boys saying—'states' rights, states' rights.' But you name me one other right you wanting besides the right to keep me your slave?"

Charles couldn't reply. The South had lost, his city was in ruins. What difference did it make, anymore, why he had fought?

"You were fighting to have your own way," Josiah said. "To keep us your slaves. Missy did the unselfish thing, like the Bible say to do, not for herself. If anyone gonna say they sorry for what they done during the war it should be you, not Missy Caroline."

Charles looked away, unable to face Josiah. But everywhere he looked, in every direction, he saw nothing but rubble.

"God use that war to show you white boys what it's like to be a slave," Josiah continued. "For four years, you sleeping on the ground instead of in your fine houses. You eating food that no one would feed a dog. You wearing rags and going barefoot and marching all day beneath a hot sun until you so weary you want to die. You ain't allowed to see your family or the woman you love. Your life ain't even your own anymore, with someone telling you what to do and when to get up and when you can go to bed. How you like it, Massa Charles? How you like trading places with me?"

"Get out of here," Charles said in a shaking voice.

"This is what Missy Caroline done for me. I'm a free man. I got a wife and a son. That's more than you got. You got no family, no money, no future . . . you just like a slave. Except no one took all those things from you—you threw them away. We changed places, Massa Charles. You want to know whose side God's on? Look at what you got left and tell me if you think God believes in states' rights. Missy Caroline done right. You the one who's wrong. You ought to be asking her to forgive you."

"Get out of here and leave me alone!" Charles shouted. He didn't think he could bear to hear her name one more time.

"No sir, I ain't leaving yet. I come here to give you this." He removed the burlap bag that was slung over his shoulder and pulled out a ragged stack of paper, tied together with string. "Tessie say for you to read this. Missy Caroline don't know I'm giving it to you."

Charles stared at the bundle of paper Josiah had shoved into his shaking hands. It looked like ragged sheets of wallpaper from Caroline's foyer. It was covered with her beautiful handwriting. He recognized it from all the letters she had faithfully written to him, and he felt a pain greater than any of his other wounds.

"Tessie say Missy still loves you. You didn't lose everything. She still loves you. You sent her away because you won't try to understand the reason why she helped us or forgive her for it. Now her Yankee friend Robert's coming around, offering her his love. Says he'll give her a new start in a new town. She don't love him, but she awful lonely. This your last chance . . . you gonna throw it away?"

"I listened to you because you saved my life," Charles said in a trembling voice. "I owed you that much. But what goes on between Caroline and me is none of your business." The anger and rage that gnawed at him swelled from a dull ache to an agonizing pain. All he could do was lash out. "The Yankees are here and you have your freedom, Josiah. Go flaunt it someplace else."

"I won my freedom long before the Yankees came," Josiah said quietly. "I was free the moment I picked you up and decided to forgive Missy Caroline and her daddy. You can start living as a free man, too, once you forgive. Maybe then God will start giving back all the things you threw away."

Josiah turned then, and walked away. When he was gone, Charles sank down onto the charred beam and buried his face in his hands. Pain and anger filled every inch of him, until he thought it would consume him. But even in the blind heat of his rage, he knew two things: that Josiah had spoken the truth and that the reason he so deeply resented facing that truth was because the man who had spoken it was a Negro.

Against his will, Charles remembered his first few encounters with Caroline, how her outspokenness had angered him. He knew, now, that it was because she had shone a beam of light on the darkness that was inside him, exposing the racism that he'd never wanted to admit was there. He'd seen a little Negro boy as a thief, not a hungry child. He'd seen a Negro carriage driver as a convenience, not a man.

But hadn't that also been what had drawn him to Caroline from the very beginning—the deep compassion she had for all people? The light that had shone so brightly from her?

Charles looked down at her handwriting on the ragged pile of paper on his lap. Then the words slowly slid into focus. He began to read:

As I write this by candlelight, Union troops have my beloved city of Richmond under siege. The hall clock tells me that it is well past midnight, but I am unable to sleep. I no longer know what tomorrow will bring, nor do I know when my arrest will come—but I'm now quite certain that it will come . . . I'm not sure anyone will ever understand why I've acted the way I have. I can only pray that they will try . . .

Twenty little Negro children sat in a circle at Caroline's feet in her drawing room, listening in wide-eyed wonder as she read Longfellow's poem, *The Song of Hiawatha,* to them. When she first began teaching these young students, it had brought back memories of Hilltop and of her afternoons beneath the pear tree with the little slave children gathered around her. Caroline enjoyed teaching her adult students very much, but these little ones had become as dear to her as her very own children.

She finished the poem and looked up at them. One small boy raised his hand. "Yes, Jesse? What is it?"

"Someone here to see you." He pointed behind her. Caroline turned around.

Charles stood in the doorway.

Her heart felt as though it was being squeezed so tightly she wasn't sure she could bear the pain. His eyes—so wide and expressive, so deeply blue—gazed down at her with a softness she thought she'd never see in them again.

"I can come back at a better time," he said.

"No . . . give me a minute." Her voice shook as she quietly told her class to take out their slates and practice writing their names. The slates had been a present from Robert. He had used his army connections to help stock her school with supplies. "Please work quietly until I come back," she said.

Charles followed her through the drawing room doors into the backyard. The June day was warm and very humid, a foretaste of the summer that fast approached.

"You're a wonderful teacher," he said. "I was watching you."

Caroline couldn't answer, couldn't speak past the knot of emotion in her throat. She didn't know why Charles had come, but she knew now that she would have to tell Robert that she could never marry him. It wouldn't be fair to spend her life with one man when she still loved another so deeply. Even after all this time, all the sorrow and pain.

"I came to give this back to you," he said. He took his battered army haversack off his shoulder and pulled out a ragged pile of papers—her papers, the story she had written on torn sheets of wallpaper.

"How did you get that?"

"Josiah gave it to me."

He looked away from her, gazing into the distance at things she couldn't see. Caroline was afraid to hope that he had come back into her life to stay. She silently prayed the only words that mattered anymore—*Thy will be done*—trusting in God's love, knowing that His will was the very best thing for her life.

453

"After reading this," Charles said, "I realized how different we are. Those differences should have been obvious from the first day we met. Even now, I look at that roomful of Negro children in there, and I know I don't see them the way you do."

He paused, then turned to face her again. "I wish I could see them your way. I've lost everything but my blindness, it seems—I've lost the war, my father, most of my friends, my wealth. The mill is gone and I have no money to rebuild it, no future. But Josiah said I hadn't lost you. He said you still love me. And I don't think it would hurt to see you as much as it does unless I still loved you, too.

"Listen now," he said softly. "Am I too late, Caroline? Could you ever forgive me and start all over again?"

She moved into his arms as if she and Charles had never argued or parted. He clung to her, holding her tightly in return. "I love you, Charles," she told him.

Behind Caroline was her schoolroom full of bright, eager students. God had given them to her as a gift, to show her that the sacrifices she'd made did have meaning. His purposes for her life would be partly fulfilled in them, and in those children's futures. And now He was giving her still another gift, giving Charles back to her.

"Thank you, Lord," she whispered as she held him in her arms. "Thank you."

LYNN AUSTIN has sold more than one million copies of her books worldwide. She is an eight-time Christy Award winner and an inaugural inductee into the Christy Award Hall of Fame, as well as a popular speaker at retreats, conventions, women's groups, and book clubs. She lives with her husband in Michigan.

More From Lynn Austin

To learn more about Lynn and her books, visit lynnaustin.org.

Bringing to life the biblical books of Ezra and Nehemiah, *Return to Me* is the compelling story of Babylonian exiles Iddo and Zechariah, the women who love them, and the faithful followers who struggle to rebuild their lives in obedience to the God who beckons them home.

Return to Me
THE RESTORATION CHRONICLES #1

For the first time, beloved author Lynn Austin offers a glimpse into her private life as she shares the inspiring, deeply personal story of her search for spiritual renewal in the Holy Land. With gripping honesty, Lynn seamlessly weaves personal events with insights from Scripture as she finds hope, renewed faith, and a new sense of direction in her journey throughout Israel.

Pilgrimage

BETHANYHOUSE

Stay up-to-date on your favorite books and authors with our free e-newsletters. Sign up today at bethanyhouse.com.

Find us on Facebook. facebook.com/bethanyhousepublishers

Free exclusive resources for your book group! bethanyhouse.com/anopenbook

You May Also Enjoy…

After a devastating fire destroys her city, Mollie Knox struggles to rebuild her business while two men vie for her affections. Can Mollie rise from the ashes with both her company and her heart intact?

Into the Whirlwind by Elizabeth Camden
elizabethcamden.com

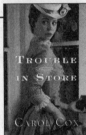

Melanie and Caleb thought their mutual claims to the mercantile were a problem, but there's deeper trouble in store when a body is discovered on their doorstep.

Trouble in Store by Carol Cox
authorcarolcox.com

When an abandoned child brings Nick Lovelace and Anne Tillerton together, is Nick prepared to risk his future plans for an unexpected chance at love?

Caught in the Middle by Regina Jennings
reginajennings.com

◈BETHANYHOUSE

 Stay up-to-date on your favorite books and authors with our free e-newsletters. Sign up today at bethanyhouse.com.

 Find us on Facebook. facebook.com/bethanyhousepublishers

 Free exclusive resources for your book group! bethanyhouse.com/anopenbook